NO PLACE TO HIDE

REBECCA GRIFFITHS

For Steven, with love.
Without you there would be nothing.

Cry Baby Bunting
Daddy's gone a-hunting
Gone to fetch a rabbit skin
To wrap poor Baby Bunting in.

— TRADITIONAL NURSERY RHYME

EIGHT YEARS BEFORE

I climb the stairs. Hatred building with each creaking tread. I'm in the mood for trouble. She's had it coming for years. Going about like a tart in her short skirts and make-up, rubbing my nose in it… Yeah, she's had it coming all right.

I open the door without bothering to knock and see the window's been flung wide open to receive the dying day. She's sitting with her back to me, dolling herself up in the mirror. When she twists around, I see her red painted mouth.

'What d'you want? You're not supposed to be in here.' She doesn't look as bothered to see me as she should.

I watch her take a last leisurely pull on her fag, squash it flat in an ashtray, and fumble for the table edge. I can tell she's been drinking. That she needs its support to get to her feet. Good, it'll make what I've got to do easier. She stands where the last slant of daylight partitions the room and I close the door behind me, shutting us in. There's no one else around. There's no one to see what I'm going to do. We are alone. I wonder if she knows this, knows how much danger she is in?

She gives me the "just you try it" look, so I think I might as well, and inch towards her. Close enough to smell the booze on her breath. Sickly sweet like rotting fruit. Disgusted, I turn my head away for a second or two. Think: she's on the brink of doing this anyway, so there's no need to feel bad, I'm only doing what she's too gutless to do. Yes, of course, this is what she wants, and if not, who cares? I'm a saviour, I should be rewarded for helping her out – rewarded for saving her from the life that's killing her.

'I asked you what you want?' She thinks she's being assertive, her fists on her hips. 'I know you think you can stop me from going out, but you can't.' Her eyes are dark and feisty, and I know I will have to box clever. Not that I'm overly concerned, I worked it all out before getting here. I won't fail. I can't fail. There's too much at stake. 'Just get out. I don't want you in here. I don't want you anywhere near me.'

'Since when have you been fussy about anyone coming near you? You've always been happy to spread your legs for anyone. And that's been the problem, hasn't it? That's why I'm here now.'

Why am I bothering to retaliate when it's all too late for arguing? I must stay focused. I can't let myself be diverted. I've only got one shot at this.

'Get out! I want you to get out!' she shrieks, all indignant. It makes me want to smash her face in.

'I don't think you're in any position to tell me what to do.'

I must communicate something in my expression because she responds by tottering backwards to press her spine to the frame of the open window in an attempt to distance herself.

It gives me another idea. A better idea than the one I came in here with.

'I wouldn't stand there if I were you,' I tell her and feel myself smile. I've never felt so powerful, so in control.

'Get away from me. Go on, get out!'

I'm not going anywhere. I am wise. I take my time.

Outside, the sun is setting over the sea. Salmon pink and curd yellow as night folds itself into the darkening blue. We stand for what seems an age, neither saying a word. I can tell that me watching her like this is making her nervous. Her hands keep fidgeting with her hair and tugging down her miniskirt. She wants to tell me to stop looking but knows this is a waste of breath, that nothing she says will help her, that she isn't getting out of here.

'What d'you want?' she asks again.

Then, as if reading my mind, her eyes widen in fear as I take another step closer. It pleases me to see her flinch… terror taking shape behind her eyes.

It wouldn't take much to push her. To make it look as if she jumped.

Most of the town knows she's a drunk, they would think it was an accident. Or that she took her own life. Who cares what the gossips think? As long as no one links it back to me. That's all that matters.

What's left of the daylight is shining pink on her cheeks and I hear her suck back her breath.

'There's no point screaming,' I tell her. 'No one's going to hear you.'

She wipes her mouth on an agitated fist. Lipstick leaving a blood-red smear behind on her hand. She inadvertently tips back her head to the ceiling, exposes the white curve of her throat. Then, sensing her own defencelessness, she drops her head.

'Please go away. Leave me alone,' she pleads.

'Leave you? Yeah, I'll leave you,' I tell her, feeling no pity. 'I'll leave you after I've killed you.'

CHAPTER ONE

PRESENT DAY

Melanie struggles to hear what her husband is telling her above the din of the call centre.

'You what, Gareth? I missed that.'

'I said we've got it.'

'What? We've got the pub?'

'Sale went through five minutes ago. It's all ours, Mel.'

'Brilliant.' Her whoops for joy rise above the clamour of buzzing telephones.

'Go and tell your boss today's your last day.'

'I can't just drop them in it. I'll have to give notice.'

'Why? You don't need a reference. You'll be working for yourself from now on.' His voice is as measured and forthright as always.

Melanie ends their call and intends to do as he suggests, just as soon as she's worked out what to say. Head in hands, her mind drifts. The stiffened sails of her memory pulled wide by her demons, as it so often is when she's sitting here, watching the clock above her manager's door, counting the hours before logging off and going home. On her desk is a framed photograph of her and Gareth on their honeymoon. She searches their faces for any sign of what had been marching towards them on life's horizon and is thankful to find nothing of the horror that was to come. Her gaze then shifts to a snapshot of their twin daughters: Georgie and Sophie, then aged four. Her chest tightens, her breathing audible. This is possibly the last picture ever taken of them together.

Her boss doesn't ask Melanie to sit. She doesn't congratulate or wish her luck with her exciting new venture either.

'A gastropub in Wales?' The tone is derisive and critical. 'Who d'you think you are – someone off *Escape to the Country?*'

'Spiteful cow,' Melanie mumbles on the walk back to her desk to collect her stuff. Which aside from the pair of photographs, a tube of hand cream and a plastic Shaun the Sheep toy from last year's Secret Santa, amounts to little.

'Watch out,' she warns those she is leaving behind. Not that anyone looks up from their monitors. 'Go and do something worthwhile. Otherwise, this will be all you have to show for your life.' She shakes her carrier bag and exits the building.

CHAPTER TWO

A shock. The sea. Melanie, waking stale and stiff in the passenger seat of their Mazda is stunned by the drama of it. The monotony of the motorway has been swapped for a tunnel of hedgerows, and when Gareth turns off, it is to swing down onto a track that travels out on a finger of rock pointing into the sea.

'See that island—' His finger guides her gaze beyond the sheep-scattered slopes, to a rocky outcrop girdled by a glittering belt of blue. 'That's an ancient site of Celtic spirituality.'

His voice is proud. As if there marks the very stepping stone to heaven and she stares obediently out through the window at the fields under the lean acres of sky.

The route into this small Pembrokeshire town is only just wide enough for the car, and shrubbery scrapes against its sides as if meaning to hold them back. Tangled and high, the thorny hedges are thick with blackberries. Melanie makes a mental note to take Georgie out to gather them in before the birds claim them.

'You've made brilliant time.' She yawns and studies his profile. The dark stubble on his jaw she swears has grown in the hours she's been sleeping. 'Sorry for nodding off.'

'That's all right. But you've been grinding your teeth. You're not anxious? Regretting this move?'

'No, I'm excited.' She turns to their seven-year-old daughter on the back seat. 'Are you all right, Georgie? Did you get any shut-eye?'

'Yes, Mummy. But Bumble's tired.' Her daughter pushes her soft pink teddy forwards for her to see.

'Get some air in here. Liven us up.'

Melanie drops the window and inhales the sea and something of her childhood. Not the vinegar-laden chip shop smell sampled on summers in Hunstanton on her grandmother's farm, but something of the wild, the essential. Aside from when they came to view the pub, it must have been eight years since Gareth first brought her to Wales. The week of his father's funeral, when she was introduced to her mother-in-law for the first time.

The road dips and as the Mazda begins its slow pull out onto the main road through the town, Gareth puts his foot down. Takes the half-moon bridge over the river too fast. The car bounces and Melanie clutches her stomach.

'Sorry.' He chuckles. 'I used to do that with my sister when I first passed my test.'

'Bet Bethan didn't like it either.' Melanie grimaces. '*Pen-car-raw.*' She reads the name of the town on a sign.

'Pencarew,' Gareth corrects her, sounding more Welsh than ever. 'We're home. Are you happy?'

'I'm happy.' She smiles. And for the first time in three years, this isn't a lie.

The road dips again, down between a row of tall, pastel-coloured B&Bs advertising en-suite rooms and Wi-Fi. Their gardens, sheltered by the hills rising steeply behind, show off blue hydrangeas, large as heads clad in 1940s swimming caps. They pass gift shops and tearooms with tables set out on the pavement in the late-August sunshine. A classy-looking homeware store. Jimmy's Fish Bar. Its sign like a sail and flapping in the soft Welsh breeze. And the Peppermint Post Espresso Bar, where she and Gareth enjoyed a celebratory breakfast after viewing the Monkstone Arms on that lovely spring day.

'I wasn't expecting it to be as busy this late in the season.'

'Bank holiday weekend. Sun's out.' Gareth twiddles the dark chest hair that peeps over the collar of his rugby shirt. 'This place is a little goldmine.'

'Look, there's the pub.' Melanie jabs an excited finger to where the Monkstone Arms nestles high above the bay. It commands a striking position, with the plunge of the sea at the bottom of its garden. 'I can't believe it's ours. Well, partly ours, I know the bank owns most of it. But it's got Mr and Mrs Sayer on the deeds.'

She slides a hand onto his thigh and continues to pick out interesting landmarks for their daughter, who is eager to be liberated from the confines of the car seat she is almost too big for.

'There's your new school.' She swivels to Georgie again. Sees her gummy smile, the bounce of sunshine on her light-brown plaits... The glaringly unoccupied space beside her on the back seat. A space that has been empty for three whole years.

Melanie's stomach lurches again. But it has nothing to do with the road this time.

CHAPTER THREE

The flat above the pub, where they are to live, is surprisingly habitable. Now the removals firm has been and gone, Melanie, Gareth and Georgie pace the accommodation piled with plywood crates, sofas and bookcases, familiarising themselves with its layout.

'Look, Mummy. The sea.' Georgie reaches up on tiptoes. 'This is going to be my bedroom.'

'Is it now?' Melanie gathers her in a ball of giggles.

'How's about we leave the unpacking till later?' Gareth suggests as he tugs on a crew-neck sweater. 'Explore the beach.'

'Could fetch fish and chips on the way back.'

They make this arrangement standing opposite each other. Holding hands as if caught in a still moment in a dance.

Downstairs, in what they hope will be the bar and restaurant in precisely four months, they swap their smart urban shoes for the rubber boots they bought for this new rural life.

'Can Bumble and me go outside?' Georgie asks.

'No, darling. Best wait for us.'

'It's all right, Mel. She can't come to harm here.'

Looking out on what will be the beer garden once they've

exchanged the giant plastic dinosaur and rusty climbing frame for a set of wooden benches and tables, they watch Georgie skipping over the grass, chatting to Bumble as she gives him a guided tour of their new playground. Then, with a quick exchange of smiles, they refocus on the pub's potential. Keen to reaffirm why they risked selling their three-bed semi on a pleasant estate in Bromley for a venture with no guaranteed returns and something their less-encouraging friends call hare-brained. Shadowy and cool, the pub smells of stale beer as they move around the low-beamed spaces, touching the giant inglenook fireplaces the sales particulars boasted date back to the Middle Ages. They see the abandoned goggles and gloves, the numerous brown-ringed coffee mugs, a lone broom propped against a far wall. Evidence the workmen – employed by their brother-in-law, Bryn, and off enjoying a well-earned bank holiday weekend – will be back on Tuesday.

Kicking through debris, trying not to inhale plaster dust from the rough floor, they absorb the rambling beauty of this extraordinary setting. Sensing the ghostly presence of generations past, Melanie pats the peeling wallpaper and imagines the souls of their predecessors pressed between the centuries-old colours and patterns. Thinks the chipped gloss on skirting boards and doors, showing layers of yellow, turquoise, then finally brown, mark the passing of years like the rings on a tree.

'Bryn's lot haven't wasted time. They're an improvement.' She points at the new patio doors.

'Still needs a load of work, but yeah, it's coming on.' Gareth puts an arm around her.

'And I'll be pitching in when Georgie's back at school.'

'D'you reckon it'll be ready by Christmas?'

'No problem.' She nuzzles close to his ear. His dark, day-old stubble is rough against her lips. 'But I'm going to miss you.' She breathes in his aftershave, storing it away for when he's back in London and she and Georgie are on their own.

'I'll be here weekends. The weeks will fly by. I'll try and get home Thursdays when I can. The internet signal's strong enough to work from here.' He checks his mobile to verify his claim. 'And it's an extra short week this week. I don't have to go back till Wednesday.'

'Hardly worth going back at all.' She twists away, reluctant to show she's teary.

'Better show my face, Mel. You know what they're like.' He rolls his eyes. 'But when this place is up and running, it'll be goodbye job, goodbye London, and we three can be together all the time.'

Down on the beach, the lowering sun is surprisingly hot. They take off their boots, tuck their socks inside and roll up the bottoms of their jeans. Holding hands, three in a row, they race to the shore and wade in up to their knees. A dog, ownerless and self-governing, stops to sniff their bare ankles, making them giggle before it trots off like a little pony to cock its leg against a chunk of driftwood. When Georgie breaks away to splash through the shallows, plaits swinging and gabbling to Bumble, Melanie removes her sweater, knots it around her middle and sits down beside Gareth on the sand.

She trails the progress of a silver cloud and lets her gaze travel the necklace of cottages that line the curved throat of the bay. The broken spine of Pencarew Castle, romantic and melancholy, perched on its rocky promontory. During the break in their conversation, Gareth stares off into the distance, watching their child. He is smiling and looks the most contented she's seen him in ages. Without shifting his gaze, he places his hand on hers; a hand that is brown to the wrist, like a yachtsman's hand. How handsome he is, she smiles to herself, falling in love with him all over again.

Closing her eyes, the sun strong on her face, Melanie's mind loops back to those dreadful days that spanned into months after Sophie died. When she didn't dare open the curtains, didn't dare feel the sun on her face, refusing the reality. A buzzing from above has them stretching their necks to watch a white-winged Cessna make its airy flight over the bay and head inland. Melanie knows Gareth will be remembering his father: a local businessman wealthy enough to keep up his private pilot's licence and his flying hours right until the end. An end that came just before the twins were born.

'When are we seeing your mum?' Her question betrays her. He'll know she's been thinking of Rhodri – the father-in-law she never met.

'She'll be at the party. Bethan's invited the whole town.'

'You're going to have a great time.'

'Aren't you?'

'You know me and parties.' She notices their lengthening shadows. 'Shall we go and get fish and chips?'

Gareth grins and calls for Georgie. They regroup in a dip in the dunes to brush damp feet free of sand and put on their socks and wellingtons.

A woman, striking because of her diminutive frame and long black hair, scurries past. She turns her head as she walks, nervously tugging the cuffs of her outsized jumper over her red knuckles. Melanie smiles. A programmed response that is not reciprocated. The woman isn't looking at her. She's too busy staring at Gareth. And the eyes beneath their thick straight brows are as dark and sour as apple seeds.

CHAPTER FOUR

Night has somehow become dawn, and Melanie, cold beneath her dressing gown, rotates in her kitchen chair to receive it. Her face, as grey as the tide, is reflected in the glass panel of the back door. She went to bed, but as soon as her head hit the pillow, it was all colour charts and kitchen tiles. With Gareth and Georgie asleep in upstairs rooms, she steps out onto the dewy lawn, thankful the wind has eased. All night long, the south-westerly squall has been throwing its weight against the high walls of the pub. It makes her worry what winter will be like.

Following the path to the boundary fence, she senses, rather than sees, the sway of the sea, and a movement from below has her peering down to where the tide has been and gone. The sand is hard and rippled, and the pattern reminds her of the candlewick bedspread in a room on her grandmother's Norfolk farm. A room she could call her own for a few short weeks each year that, away from the hearth, was as cold as a morgue but still more welcoming than anything she was to experience after her grandmother died and the farm was sold.

She scans the shoreline and blows on her hands to warm them up. There is a sudden sound of scrabbling and whimpering coming from beyond the fishing net graveyard and creel pots. She tightens the belt of her dressing gown and dives through the gateway, the crunch of sand beneath her slippers as she rushes down the steep path to the beach. *A child?* She hopes not. The whimpering is louder now, and she breaks into a run. Whipping off her slippers when she hits the fudge-soft sand. She sees it just as it sees her. Yelping, cartwheeling, pulled up onto hind legs by a chain – it must be the skinniest dog she has ever seen. Inching forwards, more accustomed to cats, Melanie is unsure what to do.

'Are you a nice doggy?' She hopes the animal is more enthusiastic than wrathful. 'Who's tied you up and left you like this?' Crouching, palms extended, the dog calms and pushes its snout into her hand in some form of greeting.

Nearly light. The beach is deserted. Only a stir of indistinguishable seabirds disturbs the spill of rocks. Unhooking the dog, Melanie carries it and her slippers barefoot up the precipitous track back to the pub. Once inside the kitchen, she runs the dog a bowl of water and wipes her feet free of sand.

'I won't be long.' She responds to the dog's sorrowful stare. 'Don't look at me like that, I'm going to try and snatch forty winks.'

Willing it to understand, she shuts the door on the dog and the soft thrum of the few household appliances the previous owners left for them to use until their new ones arrive. She hovers in the bar, waiting for the dog to make a noise. When it doesn't, she heads upstairs to join her husband.

CHAPTER FIVE

A shriek from below. Georgie has found the dog. Melanie, still wet from the shower, goes downstairs with a Buzz Lightyear towel wrapped around her.

'I found the poor thing chained to a boat.' Water from her hair drips down between her shoulder blades. 'But we can't keep him, sweetheart.'

'Why not?' Gareth is behind her. His toothpaste breath fresh on her neck. 'God, he's thin.' He moves past Melanie and bends to stroke the dog's ears and knotted black coat. 'We'll nip him to the vets. Get him checked over.'

'We don't know the first thing about keeping a dog.'

'It's not difficult.' He laughs when it licks his hand. 'All he needs is a warm place to kip, some decent food and regular walks.'

'But we don't want some crackpot accusing us of stealing him. He wasn't a stray; he obviously belongs to someone.'

'Someone who doesn't deserve him.' Gareth in a shirt as blue as his eyes.

'Please, Mummy. Please.' Georgie is kneeling amid bricks and rubble, cuddling the dog.

'Okay.' Melanie adjusts her towel. 'But we'd better feed him. Try soaking some Shreddies, Georgie. I bet he'd like them.' She points to the now motionless tail, worn out from wagging. 'Looks like he's about to keel over.'

'D'you think Aunty Bethan's invited some children for me to play with?' Georgie, sitting up at the kitchen table, scrapes out her cereal bowl.

'I'm sure she has.' Gareth is rummaging through bags of groceries. There is nowhere to unpack.

'Bumble's excited about it.' The faded blue beany toy Georgie's had since her cradle is made to dance in her lap.

Melanie pours out tea. Passes Gareth a mug as Georgie jumps down from her chair to put her bowl in the rusted metal sink. Tries to turn the tap and fails.

'Don't worry, sweetheart.' She reaches over to help. 'This—' she forces the hot tap open and rust comes off on her hand, 'is all going to be replaced soon.'

Georgie strokes the dog and looks pleased to see he's eaten every scrap of his breakfast just as she's done. 'I've called him Slinky Dog.'

'That was a quick decision.' Melanie blows on her tea, swaps secret smiles with her husband.

When she shifts her attention to the bottom of the pine table, she finds the ghost of her dead daughter. Melanie was concerned that Sophie would be left behind in their old home and wouldn't know how to follow them to Wales. But there she was. Smiling, forever trapped in childhood.

'Do you want some breakfast, Gareth?' Snapping back to the now, her hand hovers over the sliced wholemeal.

'No, I'll get some at the golf club.'

'Bet you'll have a fry-up.' Georgie giggles. 'Can we trust him, Mummy?' She has found the notches chiselled into the door frame that, rising higher and higher, probably charted the previous owners' children as they grew up.

'I'm down another four pounds this week.'

'If you say so.' Georgie pokes a finger at his stomach.

'Go on, you don't want to keep Bryn waiting.' Melanie replenishes what's been relegated to a dog's bowl with another serving of Shreddies. 'Shall we meet you there?'

'Good idea.' Gareth drains the last of his tea. 'Have you seen my jacket?' He taps the pockets of his jeans for the car keys.

She points to the back of a chair and watches him throw his blazer over his shoulders. Not once has she seen him rush. Every gesture he makes is considered and, enriched by his striking good looks, means you have no choice but to look at him. Not that Gareth is the kind of bloke you would want to turn your back on – or so Melanie, eavesdropping on conversations, has heard. His colleagues say that it is impossible to predict his moves because he gives nothing away. They say he revels in risk-taking, that the bigger the gamble, the better, and admit he has a rare gift for reading the financial markets in ways others don't. She supposes it must be true. Unlike many of his contemporaries, her husband has remained relatively unscathed by the economic instability of recent times.

Gareth is kissing her goodbye when his mobile beeps in his pocket. He takes it out, scans the screen.

'Who's that?' Melanie enquires.

He doesn't respond.

'I hope that's not work pestering you on a Sunday?'

'What?' He looks up. Does she glimpse a look of fear on his face? 'Oh, it's no one.' He puts his phone away. 'No one you need to worry about. Catch you later, yeah?'

And with a quick inspection of his blazer, a hand to his hair in the mirror by the door, he's gone.

CHAPTER SIX

Melanie and Georgie walk along Castle Row, looking for the footpath Bethan told them to take. Passing well-to-do villas that hang well back from the cliff edge and the sheltered shore below, they eventually find the sign beneath its hood of ivy. The path spirals upwards between a high rocky outcrop where wood sage and greater celandine cling to crevices in the slabs of blue slate.

'This is steeper than I thought.' Melanie, panting, looks down at the rocky shore below and envisages calamitous shipwrecks and pirates.

The track continues to climb, providing ever more spectacular views of the coastline, until they reach an elevated grassy knoll and a battered kissing gate with a sign saying: TO THE BEACH. They lean over it and gasp, thrilled by its terrifying steepness.

'There's the golf club.' Georgie points to where the path dips and widens out between a bank of gorse.

'Not so far. And thankfully all downhill.' Melanie considers the building nosing out across the low dunes towards Ireland.

'Hot, isn't it?' She tugs the neck of her dress and blows down inside. 'I'd have been better in jeans. Do I look too dressed up?'

'No, Mummy. You look pretty. You always look pretty.' Georgie grins her gap-toothed grin.

Melanie cuddles her child. 'You are the loveliest girl to your silly old mum.'

'You're not silly, Mummy. And you're not old.' Georgie: a swish of her plaits, a flash of her father's blue eyes.

'Shall we get this over with?' She checks her face in her vanity mirror and applies fresh lipstick.

'Don't you want to go?' Perceptive as always, Georgie purses her mouth and points a finger, indicating she too would like a touch of Firefly.

'Yes.' Melanie obliges and dabs on lipstick. 'This is a chance to make new friends.' She snaps shut the mirror just as a bay mare gallops along the fence beside them.

Georgie squeals excitedly at the sight of her.

'D'you want me to see if there's a riding stables nearby?'

Georgie nods.

'I might have some lessons myself. I used to love riding when I was a kid.'

'I didn't know you could ride.'

'Cousin Cassie had a pony. Just as sweet as this little one.' Melanie pats the mare that stops to say hello and guides Georgie's hand to stroke her muzzle. 'When I stayed with my gran, which I did every school holiday until I was nine, Cassie would let me ride him on the beach.'

'I bet that was brilliant.' Georgie giggles, pulling her hand away when the horse snorts. 'I'd love to do that.'

'There you go.' Melanie's brother-in-law passes her a glass of white wine. 'I thought you could do with another.'

'Thanks, Bryn.'

'Enjoying yourself?' He drinks from his pint.

'Yeah, it's great.' She takes a sip and wipes lipstick off the rim. Bryn's caught the sun, the brick-red band across his forehead looks sore.

'Why are you over here on your own then?'

'Just taking a breather.' She watches sunlight through the trees throw a stirring pattern across the ceiling.

'You settling in okay?'

'Yes, everything's fine.' She fiddles with the beads on her necklace.

'Why don't I believe you?' He winks, boyish, cheeky. 'Has Bronwyn been having a go?'

Melanie drinks more wine. Feels it spread through her like sunshine. 'No, the silent treatment seems to be sufficient for this evening.'

'She's not forgiven you for marrying her precious boy, that's her trouble.' Bryn drinks his beer and she watches the bob of his Adam's apple.

'I think it's got more to do with me not being Elizabeth.'

'*Ugh*, she'll get over it.'

'When? We've been married years.'

'My mam's the same with Bethan. No one's good enough for her little boy.'

'But Bethan's lovely.'

'And so are you.' Another wink to put her at ease.

They stare out at the impressive sea views through a set of sliding doors that open onto the smooth fairway of the eighteenth hole. The smart decking area with benches and parasols gives Melanie ideas for the pub.

'Fab weather.'

'Better make the most of it. You city slickers aren't gonna know what's hit you when winter comes.'

'I think I will. I grew up in rural Norfolk.' She shivers into her memories of the flint-sharp easterly wind of her childhood.

'Oh, I didn't know that. You still got family there?'

'Only Mum. I never knew my dad.'

'Brothers or sisters?'

'No. Mum had enough trouble bringing me up.' A tight laugh she knows doesn't reach her eyes.

'D'you get home much?'

'Not if I can help it. Sad times. Bad memories. Best to keep away.'

'That's a shame.'

'I suppose.' A stiff smile. 'But I've Gareth and Georgie now, they're my family. And you guys.' Emotion quivering means she's unable to share how blessed she feels nowadays. As a youngster, when things were only her and her mother (and not always her mother), she had watched families together, jealous of their closeness, believing it was something for others and never for her. 'Did you and Gareth enjoy your game of golf?' She steers their conversation to safer waters.

'It was okay.' Bryn rubs a hand over his goatee and Melanie sees a tattooed B and F on the inside of his wrist. 'Better when I could get him to put his blasted phone away.'

'It's his job,' Melanie says as if this explains everything. 'They never give him a moment's peace.'

Bryn shrugs and takes another pull on his pint.

The air is warm with the spent breath of conversations, and sweat breaks out along her hairline, between her shoulder blades. She wonders how she might appear in her beautifully tailored dress. Her matching red lipstick and silver dragonfly earrings. *Husband Stealer... Home Wrecker...* the ugly phrases she imagines people call her are never far away. Do people know how she and Gareth got together? Only if Bronwyn's filled them in. Melanie tries to accept it could be her paranoia misinterpreting the looks and uncertain smiles from these strangers but, believing herself to be at fault and deserving of criticism, it's difficult to take their friendliness at face value.

Her self-recriminations are severed by the sudden appearance of her daughter leading a gaggle of children in a conga through the chattering grown-ups.

'She's got them all licked into shape.' Her sister-in-law emerges too, in emerald green. The dribbling infant Ffion in her arms.

'Bethan!' Melanie, careful not to spill her wine, greets them with a hug. 'Wow! You look gorgeous.' And she does, the pink glow of evening is reflected in Bethan's chestnut waves. 'It's so good of you to organise this. Quite a gathering. I had no idea Gareth had so many friends.'

'Any excuse for a knees-up.' Bethan, a twinkle in her eye. 'Nice Bryn's been looking after you.' She kisses her husband, who in turn kisses the baby. 'That brother of mine's hopeless. Fancy leaving you on your own.'

'He's allowed to enjoy himself. He's not seen some of these people for years.' She flaps a hand in the general direction of her husband.

'Not sure I'd be so understanding. Elizabeth certainly wasn't.'

'He knows I don't like the limelight. But look at him, he's a natural. That's why we're going to be such a great team. Him doing front-of-house, me in charge of the kitchen.'

Melanie, Bethan and Bryn watch Gareth work the room, pressing the flesh.

'You'd think he was running for president. Reckons he's a right player.'

'Anyone would think you didn't like your brother.'

'Course I like him, I'm just not blind to his ways like you... cos you're in *lurve*.'

'Take no notice of her, Mel,' Bryn chips in. 'Your dad was the same,' he reminds his wife. 'A real schmoozer was Rhodri. This lot are probably picking Gareth's brains for advice on where to invest their cash. Or whatever it is he does. It's way over my head.'

'D'you really think he'll give it all up when the pub opens?' Bethan eyes her.

'It's what he says.'

'But what about his whopping salary? The bonuses? He'll miss the money, won't he? Not to mention the highlife.'

'He's not making that much. Not compared to some.' Melanie wants to play it down. 'And we'll be earning a good living from the pub if all goes to plan.'

Bethan and Bryn swap looks.

'Oh, there's Tom and Sian.' Bryn drains the last of his pint. 'Mind if I leave you ladies to it? It's about the sink unit we ordered,' he says to Melanie. 'I want to know if Tom managed to get hold of the supplier.'

'Bet you've not eaten yet, have you?' Bethan jiggles Ffion to stave off grizzling.

Melanie shakes her head.

'No wonder you stay so lovely and slim.' Her sister-in-law prods her own midriff. 'You're like a model. You make it look easy but I bet you work out all the time.'

'I don't. Apart from walking, I don't do anything.'

'Just lucky then?' Bethan swaps her baby to the opposite hip.

'Just lucky.' The words stick in Melanie's throat.

'That's why I'm surprised Gareth doesn't want to show you off.'

'I can survive on my own.'

'Good job when he's going to be away in London all week. Hey – that's probably why... He doesn't want to draw attention to his lovely wife when she's going to be on her own.'

'What's that?' Gareth is suddenly beside them. He kisses the nape of Melanie's neck and triggers a shiver that travels her spine. 'What don't I want to draw attention to?' He's caught the sun as Bryn has done but, with his olive complexion, he hasn't gone red.

'Your sister reckons I'm going to be inundated with unwanted attention as soon as your back's turned.' She strokes his hand, loving the weight of him against her, the warmth of his body through his clothes. But the pleasure is accompanied by a stab of unhappiness to think that the day after tomorrow, he'll be miles away.

A laugh they all recognise splinters the general hum. They turn in unison to Bronwyn – Gareth and Bethan's mother – as she cruises into the room accompanied by several of her Women's Institute cronies. A hand is raised in their general direction, but she doesn't come over.

'I'd best go and say hello.' Gareth ducks away. 'I'll nip to the bar on the way back. Can you have a glass of wine if you're breastfeeding?' he checks with his sister.

Bethan's eyes travel over Ffion. 'Oh, go on then. A small one won't do much harm.'

'Get you another, Mel?'

'Yes, please.' She watches Gareth stride away. Hears the exaggerated shriek Bronwyn gives when she sees him.

'Best thing he did, marrying you.' Bethan gives Melanie an affectionate squeeze.

'Shame your mum doesn't think so.'

'She's pleased you persuaded Gareth to come back here, and told me to invite you to her Macmillan coffee morning next week.'

A gulp of wine. Then another to finish it. 'Will you be there?'

'Probably.' Bethan sniffs Ffion's nappy. 'Better change her. Won't be a minute.'

Melanie watches Gareth saunter to the bar. Handsome bugger, she smiles at how relaxed and happy he looks. But seconds later, exchanging words with the woman who serves him, his cheeriness mutates to a glower. She may be too far away to hear their exchange, but she can tell it's more complex than ordering and paying for drinks. She recognises the woman as the one who walked past them on the beach yesterday. The one who couldn't take her eyes off Gareth. She is even tinier than Melanie remembers, but curiously striking, despite her dowdy dress sense. It's her hair, Melanie decides: a mane of liquorice-black, twitching like a feral creature about her shoulders. She watches the woman scribble something down on a cardboard beer mat and force it into Gareth's reluctant hand.

'Do you know the woman working the bar?' she asks when Bethan comes back.

'Yes, that's Delyth Powell. She and Gareth used to be in the same class at school.' A glance at the now sleeping Ffion. 'Delyth had a massive crush on him.' A laugh. 'Well, most of the girls did.'

'Flattering she still remembers him.' Melanie refuses to be jealous of her husband's popularity in the way she knows his first wife was.

Bethan giggles. 'He doesn't look very happy to see her.'

Melanie laughs too. 'Is Delyth married?'

'No. As far as I know, she's never been in a steady relationship with anyone.'

'Does she live in Pencarew?' She takes care to pronounce the name of the town the way Gareth taught her.

'Six, seven miles away. On the coast road. Fab spot. Her parents' farm. Gweld Y Môr.' Bethan slips easily into Welsh.

'Sounds pretty. What does it mean?'

'See the sea. Well, that's a rough translation. The place was legendary for its Welsh black cattle when her father was alive. He died just before Gareth went to uni.'

'So Delyth would've only been eighteen... That's sad.' Melanie darts another look at the raven-haired woman.

'Yes, poor Delyth's had a tough time of things, all in all.'

Melanie watches Gareth pay for their drinks and pocket the change. But curiously, before he picks them up to carry them over, he rips the beer mat in half, then half again. And with a furtive look around, drops it on a nearby table.

CHAPTER SEVEN

'If you drive me to the station in the morning, you can have the car.' Gareth flicks the indicator and takes a sharp right turn. 'They're giving me a company car next week. I don't know what, but it's bound to be decent. I'll drive back here in it Friday.'

'Friday?' Melanie strokes the dog who sits between her knees in the footwell. 'I thought you were coming home Thursday?'

'Hardly worth going back for one day.'

'I suppose.' She abandons her appeal before it has the chance to sprout wings and stares out through the car window. Sees the perfect bow of a rainbow spearing the humpbacked bruise of cloud.

They have been to the vets in Pwllglas. A woman – after taking their details to pass to the police and giving Slinky Dog a thorough going over – quelled their concerns by affirming how, after twenty-eight days, if no one claimed him, the dog was legally theirs. Slinky hasn't been badly treated. The fact he's thin is probably due to the owners needing to choose between feeding him or feeding themselves, and it won't take long to bring him up to peak condition.

'What? No way!' Gareth yelps when he steers the Mazda between the high stone pillars marking the entrance to the Monkstone Arms. 'What the fuck does she want?'

Melanie is about to tell him not to swear in front of Georgie, then remembers Georgie isn't with them. Invited to her new friend Nia's house for tea, she won't be back for hours.

'Not her. Please, not her.' Gareth parks up beside a muddy blue Defender and cuts the engine. 'I'll deal with this,' he says, his mouth pulled into a hard, straight line. 'You stay here.'

He unclips his seatbelt and pitches from the car, slamming the door behind him. Melanie watches him stomp away under a hood of squabbling seabirds. His operatic hand gestures are almost comical. She recognises that thing he does with his neck and knows he's projecting his voice ahead of him. But shut inside the car, she can't hear what he's saying and can't see the person he's shouting at either. Not until she unwraps her long legs from around the dog and squeezes herself over the gear stick into the driving seat.

The woman standing on the pub's doorstep is someone Melanie is coming to recognise as Delyth Powell. Drowned in a pair of monster boots and a jumper the colours of Neapolitan ice cream, she looks like a child who has raided a dressing-up box. How dejected and sad she looks. Melanie feels instantly sorry for her. She turns the ignition and lowers the window, hoping to catch something of their exchange. But she is too far away. But not too far away to see the woman offer Gareth an envelope and a jar of something that he refuses to take. Whatever he says makes Delyth flinch, and she sets down the things she brought with her on the front step and walks away.

Melanie is cross with Gareth for ordering her to stay in the car, but crosser with herself for doing as she was told. She blushes when the woman returns to her bashed-up Defender, passing close enough to the Mazda's open window for Melanie to hear her muttering some misplaced apology. And keen to offset her husband's hostility, she raises a hand to wave hello. But Gareth is beside her, his bulk blocking her view, and the shock when he smacks her arm down makes her gasp.

'Ouch, that hurt.' Melanie brings her hand back inside the car. 'What the hell's got into you? That was really rude. She was only being kind. What have you got against her?'

He refuses to answer and, to communicate her annoyance, she slips free of the car and ignores him. Trailing the dog behind her, she bends to retrieve the jar of jam and envelope with its greasy thumbprint and steps into the gloomy bar without once looking back.

CHAPTER EIGHT

Minutes later, in the hollowed-out shell of the pub kitchen, Melanie sets about making tea. The only sound is of water rising to the boil. She slices open a new packet of biscuits, watches Gareth snatch one, two, then three, munching them in quick succession. Melanie takes one for herself. Feeds half to the dog. Now the workmen have gone home for the day, the place is eerily quiet. With nowhere to sit, they stand amid dust sheets and scaffolding, the work-in-progress.

Gareth licks his fingers, opens the flap of the envelope and pulls out a crudely-made card. The capital letters spelling: HAPPY NEW HOME in glitter and felt-tip pen.

'You should've at least said thank you. She must've made that especially,' Melanie says, in case the thought has escaped him. 'It was kind of her to go to such trouble.' A gentle nudge, wanting to rally him, wanting him to snap out of whatever's got into him. 'The jam looks nice. It's home-made. Strawberry. You love strawberry.' A flash of the woman's pitiful eyes, her restless hands. 'What did you say to her?' she quizzes. 'She looked very upset.'

Gareth, holding the card at arm's length as if he's afraid it might contaminate him, persists in his silence.

'Talk to me. What did you say to her?'

He jerks his head as if he's only just hearing. '*I said*' – a weighted pause – 'that I didn't want her bothering us. *I said* I was going to be away all week and you had your hands full getting this place up and running.' He leans back against the pockmarked work surface, folds his arms. '*I said* I didn't want her pestering you.'

'Well, I certainly think she got the message.' Melanie, sarcastic, weighs up whether to make him his tea. Thinking he doesn't deserve it but pours it anyway. 'I don't see why you had to speak on my behalf.' She passes him his mug, pours one for herself. 'I can make my own decisions. I am a big girl.'

'I know that, but I needed to nip whatever agenda she has in the bud.'

'Agenda?' Melanie mocks his choice of word. 'She was only being friendly.'

Gareth gives no indication he's listening. In the same way, he makes no apology for his behaviour, it seems as though everything, now the woman has gone, is business as usual. Melanie sips her tea and watches the curl of his lip when he reads whatever's been written inside the card, before screwing it up and dropping it into the bin. He squints at the jam and is about to fling that too when she stops him; a hand on his arm, lifting it from his grasp.

'I never liked her at school.' Lost in private thought, he replenishes the dog's water bowl. 'She was always a pain in the neck,' he adds, over sounds of Slinky's lapping.

'I saw her talking to you at the golf club yesterday. Bethan told me about her. Sounds like she's had a difficult time. I feel sorry for her.'

'Well, don't.' Gareth looks the angriest she's ever seen him. 'She's a malicious, moaning cow.'

'Gareth!' Melanie is startled by his outburst. 'What's got into you, why are you being so horrible?'

He presses his palms to the cracked wall tiles, opens his mouth as if to say something, then changes his mind.

'I was really embarrassed about the way you behaved just now. We should have invited her in, it's the least we could have done. I would have.'

'That's because you're a soft touch,' he snaps, relinquishing the wall.

'Better to be a soft touch than a rude bastard.' She stands her ground. Wonders if this is the ruthless side she's heard others speak of and, if it is, why she hasn't seen it before? 'That was shameful, whatever would your mother say?'

'Leave my mother out of this,' he shouts, then takes another biscuit.

Whoever that woman is: a wisp of air, as soft as breath, a fleeting, floating shadow; she's certainly made her presence felt and has undoubtedly altered the dynamics between her and her husband. Yes, Melanie thinks, small and insignificant Delyth may be, but she's certainly rattled Gareth's cage.

'What's the matter with us?' she probes through his crunching sounds. 'We never argue.'

'I know, we don't.' He swallows, gives her cheek a brusque kiss. 'This is what she wants. That woman would love nothing more than for us to be at loggerheads.'

'She seemed harmless enough to me.'

'You wouldn't say that if you knew her,' he says darkly. 'She's so fucking needy.'

'And we all know how much you hate that.'

'Yes, I do. And I make no apology for it.' He raises his hands, but this is no surrender. 'That woman's a parasite, Mel. She feeds off the kindness of others. Kind people like you. I've seen the way she operates and I want you to promise me you'll stay away from her.'

'For God's sake, have you heard yourself? And anyway, since when did you get to tell me who I can and cannot spend time with?'

'You're right. I'm sorry.' Contrite, he drinks his tea. 'But you're too soft by half, you are.'

'So you keep saying.'

'It's why I love you.' His cheek is hot when he presses it to hers. Her kind and gentle husband back again. 'I'm just trying to protect you, that's all,' he says, turning to leave.

'Protect me from what?' she blurts. 'Anyone can see that woman couldn't hurt a fly.'

But Gareth has gone, and the room turns and settles around her. The minutes pass, then she remembers the home-made card and fishes it from the bin. Finding it and removing an old teabag it's stuck itself to, she smooths it out and reads the message written inside:

Welcome back, Gareth... it says, in a slanting hand... *I'm sure you and your family will be very happy here. And don't worry, you know how good I am at keeping secrets.*

CHAPTER NINE

Brambled and fruit-stained, Melanie and Georgie, their harvest of blackberries in plastic bags swinging in time with their marching, head home for a cup of tea and an iced bun bought from the Co-op. With Slinky Dog working as a chaperon, his leash looped over Melanie's arm, their chatter is easy.

'You must be looking forward to starting school tomorrow?'

Georgie gives an enthusiastic nod. 'Nia said she's going to show me round.'

'You've made a real friend there.' Warm from her uphill climb from the coastal path, Melanie unzips her parka.

'I'm going to be learning Welsh.'

'You'll be able to teach me.'

'Did Daddy go to my new school?'

'He did.'

'Was Daddy born in Pencarew?'

'Yes. Nanna Bronwyn had Daddy and Aunty Bethan at home. Lord knows where the nearest hospital is.'

'There's one in Pwllglas.'

'Get you, Little Miss Information.'

The September evening, gathering clouds to the west, turns from gas-blue to yellow to blood-red.

'Are we going to bake a pie?' Georgie digs her purple-stained fingers into the bag and plucks out a blackberry. Inspects it for the spiders she's been warned about before popping it in her mouth.

'Not until Uncle Bryn's fitted the stove. We'll have to freeze them for now.'

'I'm fed up with them microwave dinners.'

'*Those* microwave dinners,' Melanie corrects. 'Me too, sweetheart.'

'Look, Mummy.' Georgie dives to retrieve a large wing feather from the tarmac. Passes it to Melanie.

'Wow, that belongs to a big bird. I wonder what? Your daddy would know.'

She thinks of Gareth as she tests the sharpness of its point against her palm. Thinks how handsome he looked in his burgundy tie and dark suit when she dropped him off at Pwllglas station. A shave and a shower, and he'd transformed himself into the City Boy once more. She thinks of the text she sent him: words of love she'd whispered as they'd kissed goodbye that she wanted to reiterate. Not that she's heard anything back. But she mustn't mind. He will be home soon and it isn't as if she hasn't got her daughter and the dog for company. She won't leave him more messages, hating him to think she was needy. That was a label he stuck on his first wife – a label he stuck on that Delyth woman too.

'People used to write with these,' she tells her only child. 'They'd dip them in ink and do the most beautiful handwriting.'

'But not now?'

'No, we all use biros now.'

'Miss Patel said I've got lovely handwriting.' Georgie gives her a look. 'But I won't be seeing her again, will I?'

'Probably not.' Melanie lay the feather on the verge. 'But you're going to have lots of nice teachers at your new school.'

'What are you doing with that feather, Mummy?'

'I'm leaving it here in case the bird who lost it comes back for it.' They look up to where a red kite floats in a placid arc above them. 'Like you do when you find someone's glove.'

'Could it belong to him?' Georgie, eyes shining, points upwards at the large bird of prey.

'Maybe.' She ruffles her daughter's hair, that for once isn't constrained by plaits. 'And if it does, he can have it back, can't he?'

They are still giggling when a man in shabby clothes limps past them, downhill, towards the church and the sea. He is big and dark like a bear. Not that Melanie's been close to a bear, but it's what he makes her think of with his heavy growth of beard, his thick head of hair. As untidy as the hedgerows they've spent the afternoon foraging, the sight of him strangles the laughter in their throats.

Quickly evaluating his raggedness, his lameness, Melanie decides this is someone who's seen a battle or two. He reminds her of the homeless people who would congregate around Charing Cross station in the years she worked as a pastry chef at the Savoy. The army of dispossessed men, women, sometimes teenagers, she would give the perfectly edible cakes and pastries the hotel would otherwise have slung out.

Georgie, stretching the length of her arm, is transfixed by the man. Melanie does her best to pull her back but her daughter is oddly persistent. The dog is curious about the stranger too: straining on his lead and wagging. He won't be drawn back either.

'Don't stare, Georgie. I've told you, it's rude to stare.'

'But it's that man, Mummy. He's staring at us,' Georgie protests. 'And he looks really, really cross.'

CHAPTER TEN

Out under a patchwork blue and white sky, Melanie, towed along by Slinky Dog, is high on the headland. Rain is forecast for later, but for now, conditions are clear enough to enjoy uninterrupted views across the sea. As she walks, Melanie thinks about how she fell in love with the Monkstone Arms even before she and Gareth stepped over the threshold. On a day when April was blossoming in the town, once inside the building, with the potential its beamed rooms were showing them, it took root in her soul. After a childhood spent in and out of care, followed by years of renting shabby digs in London, then the soulless suburban semi where Gareth lived with his first wife – a house that never felt like Melanie's – the pub showed her the possibilities of a home. A vision of stability, peace and comfort, the decision to buy was instantaneous on her part. A place with boundless opportunities is how she relayed it to Georgie when they returned to Bromley: 'It'll be a new beginning for the three of us.'

Unclipping the dog's lead and turning to look back on how far she's climbed, she sees the pub garden sloping down to the crumbling shoreline. Up this high, she gets a bird's-eye view. What a fine building it is. She sighs into the plump thermals rolling in off the sea. The most impressive building for miles, with its steep, stucco-clad sides that bravely brace whatever the Irish Sea hurls at it. How proud it makes her. But as quickly as her pride balloons, it is punctured by the familiar stab of fear, and she enters the same silent plea. Praying to the rocks and the wind for nothing else to go wrong in their lives. For them to be allowed to keep this happiness, now they've found it.

When it starts to spit, Melanie tugs the hood of her parka over her head and calls for the dog. Searches her coat for his tennis ball. Her fingers rasp against the sediment of sand she carries around with her. Always filling her pockets with shells from the beach, she pulls one out to look at its sculptured form. Strokes the indentations on its surface. The pink insides remind her of how perfect the skin of her newborn twins had been, and her eyes prick with tears. She puts the shell away and throws the ball for the dog under the wall-eyed gaze of cows. Keeps on until her arm aches more than her memories. A check of her watch tells her she should start heading back if she's to collect Georgie from school on time.

Hang on... Who the hell's that?

She squints through a shaft of unexpected sunlight. Someone's in the pub garden. Melanie bristles with irritation. She knows she'll have to get used to strangers enjoying her home, but not yet, not until they open for business.

Whoever they are, their movements are slow and furtive and suspicion tightens its grip. She narrows her eyes. Despite the plastic dinosaur and rotting climbing frame having been cleared away, she can't get a clear view of who it is.

Odd, she thinks. It could be Bryn or one of his men but, starting before seven each morning, they're usually gone by now. *Odd,* she thinks again, breaking into a run with the dog bounding along beside her, now he's back on his lead. Whoever they are, they should not be there.

CHAPTER ELEVEN

Rain pushes its way along the cliffs. A grey curtain sweeping indiscriminately eastwards over the town. It crackles against the material of her hood and cold droplets slide down inside her collar. But she doesn't stop, she keeps on running, the dog pulling her along. Down from the headland to the beach, then over the dunes, her needless detour via the pub has made her late. Very late. And it was a waste of time. When she got back to the Monkstone Arms, whoever had been snooping around was gone.

Pounding tarmac, splashing uphill through puddles, her feet inside their thin socks chafe the frayed lining of her boots. Why didn't she take the car? It would have been quicker to drive. Rain slaps her face like a wet flannel as she passes the little park with its assortment of swings and roundabouts. A brief thought of the sunny afternoon when she took pictures of Gareth pushing Georgie high into the blue sky. Pictures she posted on Facebook to show friends back in Kent just how wonderful their new lives were.

Her skeleton jars against the road, making her jaw ache, but she won't slow down. Gareth would be impressed with her surge of speed, her endurance; he's the runner, not her. Except impressed is the last thing he'd be. Late to collect their daughter from school – how irresponsible is that? What kind of a mother is she? One with a bad track record. She visualises the black blot on her copybook she can never erase. It will be all right... she tries to convince herself, running, running. Half an hour won't hurt. It doesn't mean she's a bad mother. It doesn't mean she doesn't deserve to have children.

The main road at last. She gasps. Tastes wood smoke from the tall chimneys of the town's elegant houses. Suddenly too hot for her hood, she pushes it off and presses a hand to the burning sensation in her chest. A coach sends up a spray of rainwater and a flurry of dead leaves as it pulls into the kerb, drenching her already sopping jeans. The hiss of brakes, and she is forced to slow to a walk as it decants the day-trippers who have come to wander the castle, take in the views.

'Excuse me. Excuse me,' she calls through the knot of tourists. Oblivious to anything but themselves, they are barely on the tarmac before snapping out selfies.

Weaving through them, the dog's lean, black shape out in front, Melanie finally sees the school. Squat and white, a magnolia tree propped like a drunkard against the railings. She charges down the slope of playground marked out for hopscotch and netball, tethers the dog to a section of drainpipe and dives into the porch.

'Hello? Is anyone there?' Dripping rainwater onto the brush mat, she propels her voice down the empty hallway and the vacated classrooms beyond. She hears voices and the closing of a door, but unfamiliar with the layout, she can't place where they are coming from.

She takes a tentative step inside, her wellingtons sliding on the mopped linoleum, the tang of disinfectant in her nostrils.

'Georgie. Hello?' Her voice is absorbed by a corridor

decorated with A3 sheets of collage. Flakes cut from magazines to form monstrous peaks, their thick silhouettes jutting against a bilious sky. Strange the way little minds work. She shivers, zipping her damp coat to her chin. 'Is anyone there?' she tries again.

Bolder, the need to find her child spurring her on, Melanie tiptoes over the wet floor. Mindful of her sandy soles, she peeps into empty classrooms before opening the door on the cloakroom. Scans the wooden benches, the pegs labelled with children's names. Then she spots the back of her daughter's head, her narrow child's body. And along with the huge relief the sight of her gives, comes an unexplained tightening in her chest.

'Georgie!' she cries and charges over. 'I'm so sorry I'm late, sweetheart. Have you been okay?' She flicks her wet fringe from her eyes. 'Your mummy's such a twit.'

'There's nothing to fret about,' a woman in a checked overall answers. Her face is obscured by a forgotten coat hanging in front of her. 'I've been taking care of Georgie. We've been getting to know one another.'

'Aren't there any teachers here?'

'They're having a meeting in the staff room.' When the woman steps forwards, Melanie sees who it is.

'I was walking the dog and I saw someone in the pub garden, so I nipped back to check. I thought I'd had time.'

'There's nothing to worry about, I'm always here.' The woman picks up her mop and bucket, then sets it down again.

'I thought it was after-school club tonight?' Melanie sees the puddle of rainwater she's made.

'That's Tuesdays and Wednesdays.'

'Oh, dear. I can't seem to get my head around the school timetable.'

'It's easy to get confused when everything's new.'

'Thanks so much for looking after Georgie.' Melanie helps her daughter on with her coat. 'It's Delyth, isn't it?' She remembers the name Bethan gave her. The one written on the greetings card Gareth threw away. 'I hear you were at school with my husband.'

'It's still raining. You can't possibly walk in that. Give me five minutes to finish up here, and I'll give you a lift,' Delyth offers.

'But I'm soaking. I'll make your seats wet.'

'Does your mammy always fuss like this?' Delyth makes Georgie laugh.

'And I've got the dog.' She remembers Slinky out in the rain.

'You can't have seen the state of my car. A wet dog won't make much difference.'

Delyth slips out of her overall and tidies her cleaning things away in a cupboard. Melanie notices that although Delyth's hair has no style to speak of, it's well cared for. Not a knot, or a tangle, it looks as shiny and heavy as glass. How does she keep it so immaculate? A hand to her own short, shaggy cut, doubting she could be bothered.

'Come on.' Delyth winks at Georgie. 'Let's get you two home.'

Melanie unties the dog from the drainpipe and they all dash through the rain to the car park at the rear of the school.

'Slinky Dog!' Georgie, ruffling his fur, makes her usual fuss of him.

'You and Bumble get in the back,' she tells Georgie. 'Slinky can sit with me.' And steering the tail of her daughter's coat away from the Defender's muddy sides, Melanie helps her inside and fastens the seatbelt. The interior of the car is surprisingly clean. From Delyth's warning, she was imagining all sorts.

Melanie feels enormous beside Delyth. Her knees butting up against the glove box, there's barely room for the dog.

'Push the seat back if you want.' Perched on a fat foam cushion so she can see over the steering wheel, Delyth's gaze travels the length of Melanie's thighs in their wet jeans.

Releasing the bar beneath the seat, she stretches her legs. 'That's better.'

'I've seen that dog around, haven't I?' Delyth brushes the back of an arm across the steamy windscreen.

'I don't know, have you?' She jerks upright, feels rainwater track over her scalp, tickling like ants.

'I'm sure I have. Where did you find him?'

'Chained up on the beach.' Melanie scratches her head.

'He belongs to someone then?' Delyth's hair swings forwards when she digs a spectacles case from the side pocket of the door. When she puts them on, Melanie sees they are black-framed things that look as if they belong to a man. 'For driving,' the explanation, almost an apology.

'If he did, they didn't look after him very well,' Georgie pipes up from the back. 'Slinky was starving when Mummy brought him home. And his coat was all knotty and dirty. The vet says he belongs to us now.'

'Not quite, sweetheart,' Melanie is quick to correct. '*If,*' she reminds her daughter, 'after twenty-eight days the police still haven't found his owners, then he's ours.'

'I'm glad you reported him to the police.' Delyth sounds relieved.

'We filled out a form at the vets.'

Delyth starts the engine, turns up the Defender's demisters. With feet just about reaching the pedals, she miraculously reverses out into the road. Melanie, the rasp of her wet clothes above the thump, thump of windscreen wipers, strokes the dog's damp head and whispers nonsense things, like whether he'd prefer a tin of chicken or beef dog food when they get home.

'He's certainly taken to you.' Delyth pushes the spectacles up her nose. But too big, they instantly slip down again.

'He's part of the family now. We'd be heartbroken if it turns out we can't keep him.'

'It's nearly dark already.' Delyth switches on the sidelights. 'Winter's really drawing in.'

They drive through a swirl of leaves the inadequate wipers struggle to clear. Melanie stares out through the smeary glass at the steady rain and the wet town beyond.

'How long have you worked at the school?'

'Since leaving sixth form.' Delyth shifts the car up into third. Melanie notices again how coarse and red the woman's hands are. Working hands, she considers, before averting her gaze.

'My mum used to be a cleaner,' Melanie volunteers. Omitting the times she was sober enough to hold down a job. 'Hard, isn't it?'

'Needs must. It's not so bad.'

'Are we nearly home? I'm really hungry,' Georgie interrupts.

'Yes, darling. Nearly there,' Melanie quickly answers her, before continuing her conversation with Delyth. 'You work at the golf club too. I saw you there the other night.'

'Only when there's a function. I wish I could get more hours there; the pay's loads better. I work at the Co-op as well.'

'Do you? I've never seen you.'

'I've seen you.' Delyth turns the dark of her eye on Melanie for the briefest moment. 'I was going to say hello.'

'You should have.'

'I will next time.'

'Didn't you want to go to college... University?'

'Couldn't. Not after my father died. Sudden, it was. An accident on the farm. He got trapped in the bailer.' Melanie listens to the sadness in Delyth's voice. 'I came home after sitting my last exam to find the ambulance taking him away.'

'Oh, that's dreadful.' She remembers Bethan telling her something about this. 'It must have been terrible for you and your family.'

'I was all set to go to college. I had good enough A levels, but,' Delyth swings her gaze to Melanie again, then transfers it back to the road, 'there was the farm to run. I couldn't let it go to ruin. And I had Mam to look after. She suffers terrible with depression. Never got over the shock. Drinks, see.'

Melanie nods. She does see. Clearly. Growing up with a mother battling alcohol addiction meant a disrupted childhood spent in and out of care. She understands the implications all too well.

'Mam never leaves the farm now.'

'That's a shame.'

'She used to work for Gareth's father, back in the day. She was one of his top employees. Cut quite a dash, did Mam.' A thin laugh. 'She was a good-looking woman. Good-looking like you.' Another sideways glance at Melanie. 'But she fell to pieces after Daddy died. She gave up on life, I suppose. It's been up to me to put bread on the table ever since. And there's plenty of work round here if you don't mind what you do.' A hand to the shiny gold crucifix on a chain around her neck. 'And with Andrew to look after, I'll do anything if it means he gets the chances I didn't.'

'Andrew? Is he your boy?'

'My boy. He's in his first year of A levels. His teachers say he's going to do ever so well.'

'I'm sure he is. All credit to you. It's tough bringing up kids on your own.' Another transient thought of her own troubled upbringing.

Melanie studies Delyth through the rhythmic thud of wipers. Decides she is a woman who has little or no self-image in her frumpy, mismatched clothes. Poor thing, she thinks, reading the premature lines around her mouth, the set of her wide, brown eyes, the little turned-up nose. She could be really attractive if she got a decent haircut, spent some money on herself. But everything, from the sound of it, is for her son.

'I do admire you,' she says, to be kind. 'It's amazing the way you've coped. Most people would have gone to pieces.'

'There we go.' Delyth turns into the Monkstone Arms and brings the Defender to a standstill.

'Thanks for the lift.' She repositions her hood that, with wet hair, is a waste of time. 'Would you like a cup of tea? The kitchen's still mostly rubble but we've a kettle, teabags.'

'Best not.' Delyth lifts the handbrake. 'I should get back for Mam.'

'Another time then?' Melanie undoes her seatbelt, hooks the lead on the dog.

'That'd be nice.' Delyth smiles for the first time. It instantly softens her features. 'D'you want to swap numbers?'

'Good idea.' Melanie searches her pockets for her smartphone, then reels off her number. 'Cor, that takes me back,' she jokes as Delyth presses the digits into an old Nokia, immediately wishing she hadn't, the woman probably can't afford an upgrade.

'It's Andrew who's got all the latest gizmos. What do I need with that world-wide-web stuff?' Delyth tucks the Nokia away again.

'Thank you for your card and jam, by the way,' she remembers to say. 'I'm sorry if Gareth was short with you.'

'Not for you to be sorry.'

'No, I suppose not.' Melanie feels a blush travel up from her neck. 'He's been under a lot of pressure lately, what with the move and everything.'

'You don't have to make excuses for him. He doesn't like me. He never did.'

'I'm sure that's not true.'

Delyth turns her head. Slowly, deliberately, levelling Melanie with her stare.

'What did you mean in your card?' She opens the car door and encourages the dog out into the rain. 'When you said you're good at keeping secrets? What secrets?'

'I think that's a conversation you should be having with your husband. It's not for me to say.'

'I have, but he says he doesn't know.' Melanie thinks about the grilling she gave Gareth while she helps Georgie out.

'Then he's a bigger liar than I thought he was.'

Swathed in the eerie hush of morning, Melanie is mindful her breathing keeps strange rhythm with the suck and sigh of the waves. Smart in black jeans and jacket, she walks briskly, following her tall shadow past a string of cottages facing the shore and the churchyard with its NO DOGS sign. The glare off the water means she can't see beyond the fishing boats straining on their moorings and is unaware of the large, shadowy figure of a man loitering among the jumble of tombstones watching her.

She is on her way to her mother-in-law's house. She is going to show willing, to please Gareth, because these kinds of social gatherings are not her thing. Plas Newydd is one of Pencarew's finer residences. A detached red-brick of Victorian origin set well back from the road on an elevated slope. With high chimneys scuffing the Welsh sky, the porthole-like apertures on its upper floors blink blindly onto the unsuspecting town, while the ground floor windows are besieged by prissy nets and floral curtains.

What a place to grow up. She sighs as she progresses up the driveway. No wonder Gareth can't understand what it was like for her in institutionalised care.

Above the crunch of gravel, the harsh chuckle of a magpie drops down into the treetops. *One for sorrow...* The opening line of the superstitious rhyme learnt long ago curls back to her. Was it really eight years ago when she was last here? It hardly seems possible. Apart from the heavy fatigue that came with being seven months pregnant and the community of gnomes positioned around the carp pond – that to her amusement are still there – she remembers little of that fraught day of Rhodri Sayer's funeral.

The front door, flung wide open in anticipation of guests, lets in the withering smells of autumn and the eternal chatter of seabirds. Stepping into the passageway, with no sign of Bronwyn, Melanie follows the sound of a television and finds her sister-in-law, bleary-eyed and trying to placate the grizzling Ffion.

'Teething,' Bethan says as a form of greeting, switching the television off. 'None of us are getting any sleep.'

'You poor buggers. Let me take Ffion. You go and have a lie-down.' She prises the cherry-cheeked baby from her sister-in-law's arms.

'You're a lifesaver.' Bethan flops down on a chintzy sofa. 'Fancy an éclair?' Her eyes are dull beneath pale lashes.

'No, you have them. Your need is greater than mine.'

'They're all through there.' Bethan jabs what's left of her cake in the direction of the hall, licks cream from her fingers. 'Go on, you go. I'm not really up to it.'

'Shall I take Ffion with me? Give you a chance to have a

rest.' She jiggles the baby up and down, pleased she has, at last, stopped crying.

'You've the magic touch. Try putting her in her cot.' Bethan smiles her appreciation. 'She might settle, with any luck.'

Melanie does, and to her astonishment, Ffion's eyelids flutter and close.

'Mam's been telling everyone you're coming. She can't wait to introduce you.'

'She's changed her tune.' Melanie looks around at the various photographs of Gareth and Bethan when they were little. Ones of Rhodri dressed as Biggles. Until her eyes land on a picture of Gareth's first wife. Her pretty face held in a silver frame.

Bethan sees what she's looking at. 'Mam had another card from her this morning.'

'Oh, right.' Melanie tries to sound indifferent.

'Starting some new research post at the university. She still works there. And she's still single.' Bethan screws up her mouth. 'For the record, I don't know why Mam bothers with her.'

'Probably to spite me.'

They swap mirthful looks.

'You're good not to mind. I'd have to say something if Bryn's mother behaved like that with me.'

'None of my business.'

'Of course it's your business... Your mother-in-law fraternising with the enemy.'

'Elizabeth's not the enemy, Bethan. I was the one in the wrong.'

'Rubbish. Gareth was doing the cheating. Anyway, I can't believe it's even still an issue. It was a lifetime ago.'

'I agree. But your parents adored Elizabeth and they're difficult shoes to fill. Maybe if she'd found someone else.'

'Someone else?' Bethan laughs and lifts another éclair to her lips. 'She was lucky to have Gareth for as long as she did. Calling her difficult would be an understatement. No wonder my brother fell in love with you.'

Melanie smiles. Not in the business of scoring points off her husband's ex, she lets it go. 'Want me to bring you a coffee?'

'No, thanks. Sleep, I want. Not climbing the walls.'

'I'll leave you to it.' Melanie leans over the soundly sleeping Ffion, admiring the delicacy of her shell-pink eyelids. 'Hopefully this little flamer will give you the chance to chill a while.'

A kiss goodbye to Bethan, and Melanie is out in the passageway, walking in the direction she believes Bronwyn's front room to be when her mobile rings in her bag.

Gareth.

'Hi, Mel. What you up to?' Voices in the background: not working voices, it sounds as if he's in a bar.

'I'm at your mum's. Coffee morning. I've just got here, not seen her yet.'

'She'll be pleased you made the effort.' Melanie hears him swap the phone to his other ear. 'She didn't expect you to do any baking, I did say our kitchen's out of action?'

'No. According to Bethan, she just wants to introduce me to some people. Which is nice of her.' The words stick in her throat.

'You what?' A shout goes up behind him. 'What d'you say?'

'Where are you?' She can't bring herself to deliver the generosity a second time.

'Client meeting... Lunch, you know. Off Leicester Square. Nice place, you'd like it.'

She looks at her watch. It isn't even eleven. 'If it's any good, get a photo of the menu for me? Useful for the pub.'

'Will do.'

'Did you ring for something specific? Only I'd best go and show my face.'

'*Erm.*' His voice tightens and she knows he's got bad news. 'Thing is, Mel... And I'm sorry about this—'

'What?' She braces herself.

'I'm not going to be able to get back this weekend. I'm snowed under with paperwork. You know how it is.'

'Okay,' she croaks, it's all she can manage.

'You're not too disappointed, are you?'

'No, course not. You do what you need to do. But won't Julie and Mike mind you staying? You were supposed to be out of their hair at weekends.'

'They're cool. Julie's taking the kids to see her parents, so it'll just be me and Mike.'

'Boys alone,' she says crisply, she can't help it. 'Takeaways and rugby on the TV.'

'I won't have time for that, Mel.' He sounds as upset as she is. 'It's only a small sacrifice until we get things up and running.'

She gulps back tears.

'Mel? You still there?'

'Still here.' She sniffs.

'Aw, don't be sad.' Gareth is firm. 'I'll be missing you and Georgie like mad, but I need to keep earning. We need the money. At least for the time being.'

'I know. And I'm grateful to you for sticking with it.' Suddenly, Delyth's voice is in her head, taunting: *Then he's a bigger liar than I thought he was.*

'Melanie!' Bronwyn is there, clogging the hallway with her permed hair and bolster bosom.

'Your mum's seen me, I'd better go,' she whispers to Gareth as she waves at her mother-in-law. 'Speak later?'

'I love you. Say hello to Mam for me.'

'I will,' she says and ends the call.

'Was that my boy?' Bronwyn deposits a kiss on her cheek she isn't ready for. 'How is he, the darling? Not working too hard, I hope.'

'He's on a jolly.' Melanie dabs away her tears and any smudged mascara. 'A client lunch in some swanky joint, by the sounds of it.' She trails behind along the passageway made unnecessarily dark by the mock-Regency wallpaper.

'Good.' Bronwyn drops the word over her shoulder as she sways ahead. 'He deserves some fun. Not that I could ever get my Rhodri to take a day off work... Right then, everyone!' A theatrical clap. Bronwyn stops conversations and causes heads to turn. 'This is Gareth's new wife, Melanie.'

'*New?* We've been married years,' she mumbles as Bronwyn prods her in the small of her back. Urging her forwards to shake the hands that are being held out to her.

Bronwyn's decision to host a Macmillan coffee morning is little more than an opportunity to show off and, once the introductions are over, Melanie sidesteps those who are being ushered through to admire the new conservatory and takes herself off for a nose around instead. Wandering the remaining downstairs rooms, their carpets the colour of treacle sponge, she looks at a collection of majolica earthenware. Touches the spine of a lumpy glazed monkey straddling a yellow teapot. Everything is fuss and clobber, the choice of décor overdone. Nothing, not even the walls, has escaped Bronwyn's amplified attention. This is a mid-nineteenth-century house, featuring its original coving and fireplaces. Such genuine features are rare and should be harnessed, not smothered. It's what they're trying to do with the Monkstone Arms. The fireplace is a beauty, though, and Melanie takes a closer look. Examines the whimsical William De Morgan blue-green peacocks and dragons on its tiled surround, before turning to the picture windows to lift the frilly nets obscuring fine sea views.

'Do help yourselves, ladies.' Bronwyn's voice rises above the thrum of conversation Melanie isn't included in. 'It's all home-made.' The announcement is given to the room: to the chapel-going brigade Bronwyn counts among her buddies. 'I don't want any leftovers.'

Pouring a coffee, Melanie sees there isn't a variant of cake that hasn't been made for this morning's event and can't help but admire Bronwyn's skill. She cuts a slice of chocolate cake. Its ganache topping is shiny enough to see her face in. With the sweetness dissolving on her tongue, she thinks of Gareth. Wonders about his client meeting. She regrets showing any weakness when he told her he wasn't coming home tomorrow because at least he is coming home, and she and Georgie aren't on their own. Her thoughts swing to Delyth, and she sees her frailty, the bird-like fluttering of her nervous hands. Cruel for a woman like that to be left to bring up a child alone and needing to work every hour to make ends meet. She will offer her the hand of friendship and invite her over. Try to make up for Gareth's rudeness the other day. Try, if she can, to get her to elaborate on what she meant in her card and why she called him a liar. Georgie likes her and, with Gareth away all week, Melanie can spend time with whomever she likes, can't she?

CHAPTER FOURTEEN

Melanie sleeps. An arm flung out to the side. The room is hot. The radiators no one seems to have the power to turn off are raging. Her lips move. What is she saying?

'Sophie, Sophie, Sophie.'

She opens her eyes onto the ceiling. Her dream took her back to their old street in Bromley. To a time almost four years ago where Sophie appears as alive and real as the day leaching in through the bedroom curtains. It is a dream she often has. A trauma in her past she doubts she will ever recover from.

Muffled thuds and hammering from the workmen downstairs. The lavatory flushes. Then sounds of Georgie padding along the landing. Was she woken by bad dreams too? Melanie washes and dresses and looks out over the grey swill of sea moving below the window, while her mind – a butterfly – flits from thing to thing. A flash of the junior doctor who came to find them in the waiting room. How he pressed his soft hands together when he told them there was nothing they could do.

Snapping back to the present, she goes to check on her daughter.

'Oh, I see.' She smiles when she sees Slinky curled up on

the bed. 'That's where he's sleeping, is it?' The dog yawns and flaps his ears.

'We can't leave him in the kitchen, Mummy.' Georgie hands her the brush. 'Not with all the workmen.'

Melanie brushes out her daughter's light-brown hair. Twisting it into the plaits Georgie insists on. They don't exchange more than a couple of words during this daily ritual. Choosing, as they often do, to communicate in looks and gestures, such is their closeness, their deep connection.

'Ready.' She secures the final band.

Standing at the landing window, they stop to assess the quality of the morning. Look out on the shifting silhouettes of trees against a pale sky. Then they proceed downstairs, hand in hand, the dog between them. Into the bright kitchen where Melanie opens the fridge and invents breakfast from its meagre contents.

'I really must go shopping,' she says to no one, sniffing leftover smells of takeaway bacon rolls along with the vinegary smell of grout and silicone as the last of the floor tiles are laid.

She can't be heard above the din of hammers and drills and Radio Two, and needs to tiptoe around Bryn's men. Some are standing, some are sitting. Legs splayed, their head and shoulders lost inside the skeletons of new kitchen cupboards, the gaps in the masonry. Dusty-skinned men who help themselves to the biscuits, teabags and coffee she leaves out for them.

'That sink you ordered has finally arrived.' Bryn, a mug of milky coffee in hand, is suddenly beside her. 'Should be able to fit it today.'

'Brilliant.' Melanie claps her hands. 'And the floor's looking amazing.'

'Everything's taking shape now.'

'Can't believe how quickly it's coming together. Those units look fab.' She points at the marble worktops.

'Still no news on the stove. We'll get onto them again. The new fridge and chest freezers too.' Bryn rinses his empty mug, shakes out the water droplets. 'How are you enjoying your new school, Georgie?'

'I love it.' She grins up at her uncle, twirls a hand over her heavy plaits.

'You making lots of new friends?'

Georgie nods, then lists them for him.

Breakfast over and Georgie's backpack sorted, Melanie slings it over her shoulder and hooks the wagging Slinky on his lead. They stroll up through town under the usual clatter of herring gulls.

'You do know you must never talk to strangers, don't you, Georgie?' Melanie's voice surprises her. Walking for fifteen minutes, they have almost reached the school without exchanging a word. 'I've been worrying about it.' She squeezes her daughter's hand to accentuate the point. 'I meant to say, but with everything else going on.'

'But I don't talk to strangers,' Georgie protests.

'Delyth was a stranger. I know she was at school with Daddy, but you didn't know anything about her before last week. And just because this is Wales and we're living in the country, it doesn't mean you don't have to be just as careful.'

'But how can Delyth be a stranger when she knew all about Sophie?' Georgie stops to pull up her socks. 'Strangers don't know about what happened to Sophie.'

Melanie yanks back her hand. The casual way her child

drops the name of her dead twin sister into their conversation startles her.

'She knows all about me too,' Georgie adds, borderline gleeful. 'And about you and Daddy.'

'About me and Daddy?' Melanie listens to the tremor in her voice. 'What did she say?'

Her daughter swings Bumble round in a circle and seems to change her mind. 'I don't know. I can't remember.'

'Then tell me what you do remember.' Sterner than she means to be.

'She said Sophie was happy and you didn't need to blame yourself anymore.'

'What? What does that mean?' The pain of grief that is never far away, tightens its hold and tears sting her eyes.

'Delyth says that even though Sophie's leg got crushed up by her trike, it was all better now. And that bang she had on her head when the car hit her, she says that's gone away too.'

'How can she know about that?'

'I don't know.' Georgie looks up at her, wide-eyed and innocent. 'But she said Sophie was as good as new. It's what she told me, Mummy.'

'What else did Delyth tell you?' Melanie sees the school railings up ahead and intensifies her grip on Slinky's lead.

'That she's gone to a lovely place where Jesus is looking after her. So we don't have to be sad anymore.'

As if they have summoned her, Delyth Powell rattles past in her car. Heading down in the direction of the harbour, Melanie lifts an arm to wave: robotic, programmed. Is faintly aggrieved when it isn't returned.

'What a strange woman you are... Talking about such things with my seven-year-old. How come you know so much about our lives?' she mumbles as she watches the Defender's downward progress. Delyth's small, dark head, barely visible through the vehicle's smeary rear window.

CHAPTER FIFTEEN

Along the seafront, past smells from a mobile burger van, the road tilts steeply down to Pencarew Quay. Metal rigging from the moored fishing boats clink against their masts in the wind, and a dog barks at the door of the site office to be let inside. Without Slinky for a change, Melanie follows it. Buoyed along by the improvements the workmen have made to the pub, she must start sourcing local suppliers in readiness of opening.

Sniffing the wet fish smell of the docks, she bangs on the office door. Waiting long after the dog gets fed up and creeps away. She scans around. Sees weather-beaten men in oilskins milling about the netting and concrete made slippery with the spent casings of prawns.

'Can we help you?'

Melanie turns. The door she knocked on remains firmly shut and the question comes from a pair of men. One tall and thin, one short and round. Both clad in stereotypical fishermen's jumpers, flat caps and waders.

'Hello. Yes. I'm here to enquire about—' She falters, the grinning pair put her off her stride. 'About buying from you direct.'

'Aren't you Gareth Sayer's new missus?' the short one asks.

'Hardly new.' *What is it with people around here?*

'I heard he'd bought the Monkstone.'

'That's right, we have.'

'Bit of a state,' the taller one chips in.

'Well, yes, it needs some work.' Melanie smiles, she knows she has to be friendly. 'Erm... Is there someone I can talk to about the business side of things?' She hasn't got time for idle chit-chat.

'Come with us.' The men in harmony. 'You'll want Boss.'

'Great.' Melanie follows them inside the site office.

'Boss?' one of them says. 'Someone here to see you.'

'How interesting.' Boss is a man who looks like Santa Claus.

'What's your name?' the short one whispers to her.

'Melanie.'

'Melanie here,' he shouts as if Boss might be hard of hearing, 'has come to buy fish.'

Boss rises from his desk and goes to the window. Stares out on the industry he's responsible for, before stepping back into the room and pushing a poker deep into the fire. Flames lick. Yellow and orange ribbons, until it's ablaze.

'I know you.' Close to Melanie, his breath smells of lemon drops. 'You're married to Rhodri Sayer's boy. What's his name again?'

'Gareth.'

'Aye, Gareth. Lovely boy.' Boss, who doesn't introduce himself, sits down again and slides a photocopied form over the desk to her. 'Just sign the top and give us your phone number. Then tick what you want from the list.' He passes Melanie a pen. 'How will you be paying?'

'Oh, I'm not ready to start ordering just yet.'

'No?' The white eyebrows bob like rabbit tails.

'As I was explaining to—' She turns, but Little and Large

have gone. 'We've bought the Monkstone Arms and we're hoping to open mid-December.'

'I see.' The broad, ruddy face widens into a grin. 'No problem. You hold on to the form. You can see what we sell. Some things are seasonal, but it's all self-explanatory. Will there be anything else?'

'No, that's great.' Melanie flaps the sheet of paper between them. 'I'll be in touch nearer the time.'

When she turns to go, she collides with a titan of a man whose head scrapes the ceiling of the hut. Craggy and broad like a fallen bough left out in all seasons, this is the man she and Georgie saw the day they went blackberry picking. It's a shock to find him blocking the only exit.

'Excuse me.' Melanie, intimidated by the intensity of his gaze, is keen to distance herself. But he doesn't move and, with no choice other than to push against him, she's met by a solid wall of muscle beneath the ripped donkey jacket.

Stalemate. The situation is faintly ridiculous and she could laugh if it wasn't for his unforgiving stare. Self-conscious under the uninvited scrutiny, she sees sand on his elbows, in the oily deepness of his beard, and up close the smells of wet wool and seaweed, along with something else, harshly antiseptic. Something belonging to her childhood, but slippery, elusive, she can't bring it to mind.

'Excuse me,' she tries again, dropping her hands to her sides.

The man eventually shifts sideways and she hears the unmistakeable drag of his left leg. Not once does he avert his gaze. Dark and accusing from beneath his brows, she carries his look as she descends the metal steps of the site hut. It's the same look he gave her with Georgie. She expects him to speak, but he doesn't utter a word. And striding away, Melanie throws her gaze as high as she can, wanting to fling off the sense of unease this stranger gives her. Then she identifies the smell. Carbolic soap. And her sense of unease intensifies.

CHAPTER SIXTEEN

Heading home after walking along the headland, Melanie calls by the deli for a takeaway flat white. Unsure where to drink it, she carries it downhill, beneath the glamorous spread of chestnut trees, marvelling at the flame-coloured leaves. Passing the black-belled church and feeling rebellious, she ignores the NO DOGS sign and opens the timber lychgate that's been worn smooth by the hands of parishioners. She pulls Slinky in after her. The dog seems to know where he's going. Wagging and eager, he tows her in the direction of the church porch, where there are several empty lager cans tidied into a pile on the chipped flagstones. The dog sniffs through them, licks up the pools of spilt beer. Hunting for what? She doesn't know, but she fears the hollow metal clattering may summon unwanted attention, and so urges him away.

She finds a bench and sits down. Peels back the plastic lid on her coffee and brings it to her lips. Too hot, she puts it down and looks about while she waits for it to cool. She loves graveyards, especially ones as full as this. Friends, as well as Gareth, think she's macabre, but she finds the calming quality of these settings comforting. The spaces between the headstones are bolstered by sprays of bright flowers and the odd bobbing crow. And when a robust sun shows itself through a tear in the cloud, its hot eye strikes the top of her head. With Slinky panting against her ankles, she listens to the song of a robin and sips her coffee.

Finished, she squashes the empty carton into a pocket and removes her parka. Weaves among the listing tombstones with it tied around her middle, she reads the inscriptions chiselled into the Welsh stone made black with rain. Melanie doesn't mind when the dead have lived long lives; it's the children's graves that bother her. Tears come when she sees the sad inscription for little Philip, claiming his all-important eight and a half hours on earth. And her thoughts swerve to Sophie's grave – something that is the furthest away it has ever been.

Pulling Slinky away before he has the chance to cock his leg against a headstone, she sees a rather grand memorial of speckled marble standing proud among its slanting neighbours.

ERIN POWELL OF GWELD Y MÔR.

ASLEEP WITH THE ANGELS.

1994 – 2017

'Gweld Y Môr.' Melanie gathers up the Welsh words she remembers Bethan giving her, as she kicks through the drifts of confetti that have gathered here and there. 'That's the name of Delyth's farm,' she confirms to the wind that combs the bare boughs of trees. 'Who was Erin? A sister, maybe?'

Melanie does the sums and realises that whoever she was, she would have been four years younger than either her or Gareth, four years younger than Delyth.

'The poor thing was only twenty-three when she died.' Cuddling Slinky, her eyes travel the spines of other gravestones, as she thinks about how small life is, how cruel. 'I wonder what happened to her.'

A bird flies up.

Startled by something in the unruly undergrowth at the rear of the cemetery, Slinky barks. Melanie sees what's set him off. A man: big and dark and loitering in the shadows cast by the crippled boughs of apple trees.

It's him again. Mr Grizzly.

She gave him this name after the unsettling experience down at the harbour. Is he following her? The idea is alarming. But there isn't time to think about it. With the dog barking and wagging, more insistent than ever, he is almost too strong for her to hold on to. The man turns in their direction and steps into the illuminating sunshine, and she notices that, as well as a limp, his left arm hangs uselessly by his side.

'He's seen us now.' She blames the dog. 'All that racket you're making.'

'You're not supposed to bring him in here,' the man booms, his left leg dragging like the tide.

Increasingly flustered, Melanie tugs on Slinky's lead. But the dog thumps his fox-brush tail against her shins and refuses to budge. With his four paws planted squarely on the ground, he's wagging enthusiastically, extra friendly. There is no choice but to pick him up. A dead weight in her arms as she staggers towards the lychgate. She is squeezing through it when her fleece snags on a straggle of thorns.

'All right, I'm going.' She raises a hand; she wants no trouble. But realising the man is gaining on her, she rips her sleeve in her dash to escape.

'Hey! Wait!' he roars after her.

But Melanie doesn't want to wait. She wants to put as much distance between her and this man as possible. *But look how bedraggled he is. How sad.* She is as sorry for him as she is afraid.

She pushes out through the lychgate and listens to it bang behind her as she sets the dog on the ground. She charges away, Slinky still trailing behind on his lead, she doesn't dare stop to inspect the damage to her top. Desperate to get away from this man, she runs up the slight incline that leads to the Monkstone Arms. Repeatedly checking over her shoulder, she is relieved to find he isn't following.

She rounds the stone pillars that pinpoint the entrance to the pub. The reassuring crunch of gravel under her boots. Exhaling her relief, she listens to the usual rattle of rooks and briefly contemplates the dark shapes of their wings against the sky. Then, dropping her gaze, she sees something on the doorstep. Something that shouldn't be there.

'What's that?'

Inching towards it, trepidation banging beneath her collarbone, she scans around for the person who left it. But the place is empty. Even the builders' van has gone for the day. There is only the Mazda, parked in its usual space between the spreading rose bush and the crumbling stone wall. Nothing else. Nothing human. Just the merest hiss of a breeze scouring the branches of nearby trees.

When she reaches the main door, she sees what's been left for her. A large, square Tupperware container. She bends to retrieve it. Peers through the plastic lid at a pile of flat scone-like cakes. There's a message taped to the lid, and she reads the familiar sloping scrawl.

Sorry. From Delyth.

'Sorry for what? For not waving to me? For feeding Georgie a load of nonsense about her dead sister?'

Melanie shivers as a creeping sense of unease crawls over her skin. And without quite knowing why, she feels more exposed than she has since she arrived.

CHAPTER SEVENTEEN

'Sorry, sweetheart, but he's not here.' Melanie puts a consoling arm around her daughter. 'D'you think you could have dropped him on the way home?'

'I don't know.' Georgie begins to cry. 'Can you check again?'

Melanie does. Unpacking and repacking her daughter's backpack for the third time. She rinses out her lunchbox, turns it upside down to dry on the newly-fitted double drainer. Takes a break from the drama to stroke the handsome tiled surround, the curve of the stainless-steel taps and the Belfast sink of sparkling-white porcelain. Her mind wanders further, despite Georgie's mounting distress, and she appraises the beautiful floor Bryn's men finished laying the previous day.

'I'm sorry, my darling.' A sigh. 'But Bumble isn't here.'

'But he must be.' Georgie is distraught. 'Poor Bumble, it's going to be dark soon... We can't leave him out in the dark on his own.'

Melanie looks out through the kitchen window. Her child is right. On this downward push into autumn, the evenings are drawing in a little more each day. 'He can't have gone far. Let's put our coats back on and go and find him.'

Before they have the chance, there is a sharp rapping at the pub's front door. A sound that vibrates through the empty bar. The dog barks his warning and trots away to see whoever it is off the premises.

'I'll get it.' Georgie, brightening. 'It might be Bumble. He might have found his own way home.'

Melanie, close on her daughter's heels, glances out through the patio windows at a sky that is like a crumpled piece of silk being dragged towards the horizon.

'Delyth. Hi.' She opens the door, lets in the bite of cold. 'Come in. Come in,' she beckons, not that the woman moves. Nervy and breathless, her red hands feverishly pushing the dog's snout away. 'Thanks for the cakes you left the other day.' Melanie's pleased with herself for remembering. 'It was very kind of you.'

'It's all right.' Her small voice is clipped. 'I made them for Georgie really.' The dog, still taking an embarrassing amount of interest in the woman, sniffs the greasy hem of her waxed coat. 'She told me you still didn't have your oven.' Delyth, now shoving Slinky's snout away with her rough hands, seems unwilling to step inside. 'But it would have been nice,' she adds, hanging her head, 'if you'd taken the time to text me a thank you.' Melanie, slightly taken aback, hears something of the self-pitying trait Gareth complained of. But there isn't time to respond. 'I found this little chap in the school cloakroom.' Delyth addresses Georgie. She need only bend slightly; Melanie's child is already up to her shoulder. 'He is yours, isn't he?'

'Bumble! Bumble!' Georgie squeals her delight and, taking her toy, presses its soft blue head to her lips.

'What do we say?' Melanie prompts her, fearing Delyth will if she doesn't.

'Thank you. Thank you,' Georgie gushes.

'So, he's called Bumble, is he?'

'Yes, he is.' Georgie, gleeful, spins on her heels and charges up to the flat. 'Me and Bumble are going to watch CBeebies.'

'Take Slinky with you,' Melanie calls after her, dragging the dog away from Delyth by his collar. 'I'll bring you up a sandwich. It'll put you on till dinnertime and Daddy's home... Thanks so much for bringing him over,' she returns to Delyth. 'Please, come in?' she encourages, opening the door as wide as it will go. 'I'll show you around if you like?' A small nod from her visitor. 'And I'm sure I could stretch to a cup of tea. Have one of your cakes to go with it.' She throws out a laugh that bounces around the hollow bar. A laugh Delyth does not throw back.

'Oh, no,' Delyth says, finally stepping over the threshold. 'You've ripped everything out.' The tone conveys a disappointment Melanie immediately counters.

'Sorry if it's a shock. But we wanted a clean sweep. We want —' she pauses, wary of offending, 'to attract a different kind of clientele. And you have to admit the place was stuck in the seventies.'

'I liked how it was.' The disappointment continues. 'And I should think there's lots of others round here that liked how it was too.'

She guides Delyth through the downstairs rooms. Over rubble, naked wires and stepladders leaning against stripped-down walls. The usual evidence of workmen who've gone home for the weekend. Dispensing periodic warnings of: 'Don't trip over that,' and 'Watch your step,' as she identifies to a now staunchly silent Delyth what will go where and building a picture of how it's going to look when everything's finished.

'There used to be a pool table. In that corner.' The woman stabs the air with a chapped finger. 'Us sixth formers would end up in here at lunchtimes. Or when we were mitching.'

Melanie doesn't understand.

'Bunking off school.'

'Oh, I see.' Her face relaxes into a smile. 'I did a fair amount of that myself, as I remember.'

They go into the kitchen and Melanie explains that aside from the stove, it's near completion.

'It must be costing you a fortune.' Delyth, eyes restless from beneath their hard line of eyebrow. Melanie sees her attention flit across the floor to the smart new sink and double drainer. 'But I suppose Gareth can afford it.'

'I admit it's a massive outlay, but you've got to speculate to accumulate.' She supposes it must be difficult for Delyth to see such apparent carefree spending when she struggles to keep the wolf from the door.

'It's funny, but I didn't think for a million years he'd come back to this place.' Delyth fixes Melanie with her gaze. 'Always thought he was too good for round here.'

Your opinion, or what you think Gareth thinks of himself? Melanie doesn't ask.

'He can't have been home more than a handful of times in all the years he's been away. He's seen next to nothing of his mother, or sister?'

'Bronwyn and Bethan used to come and stay with us in Kent.' Melanie sets her straight. 'It's quite a hike from Bromley, and Gareth could never get enough time off work.'

'But he must have had holidays?'

'Barely. A fortnight a year, tops. Plus a few extra days at Christmas.' *Not that it's any business of yours,* her thoughts while maintaining a polite smile. 'If he did, by some miracle, manage a whole week off, he always liked to take us away somewhere hot.'

'Aren't you the lucky one.' Delyth sniffs and undoes her outsized coat.

'Shall I take that for you?' Melanie says tersely. She's had enough of this, and regrets inviting her in. What right has this woman got to question their lives?

'No, I'll keep it on for now.' The coat is pulled tight around her. 'You're so lucky. The pair of you.' Delyth; pale, elfin, peeps out from her screen of hair. Her fretful hands set Melanie on edge. 'I wish I'd been able to get away from this town and make something of myself like Gareth has.'

'It's not too late.' Melanie is keen to lighten things between them. 'Andrew's growing up fast. It won't be long before he's off doing his own thing.'

'Oh, no, I don't want him leaving home.' Delyth is horrified. 'I don't want him leaving me. I'll have no one if he leaves me.'

God, what is it about mothers and sons? Melanie's thoughts drift to Bronwyn, to what Bryn said his mother was like with Bethan. 'Well, yes, it'll be strange to start with, but you said yourself he's a clever boy, he's going to want to spread his wings.'

'But Andrew is my rock. He knows I can't do without him.' Delyth stares at her feet, all sorrowful.

'I can appreciate it must be hard when your babies leave home.' She studies Delyth: half woman, half child. She can't imagine her all round like a peach with a baby inside. Where did she put it? There's nothing of her. 'But I can't imagine standing in Georgie's way. You've got to let them do what they want.' She stops short of calling Delyth selfish. 'We all want our kids to grow up and be independent of us. Dear me, the alternative is unimaginable. And just think,' she adds, as upbeat as she can be, 'you'll be free to do your own thing then. You could go to college. Train for something you want to do.'

'Don't be ridiculous, I'm thirty-five.' Delyth gives her a filthy look. 'My life's over.'

'Over?' Melanie laughs without meaning to. 'Ta very much. I'm the same age as you and I don't consider my life to be over.'

'But it's different for you.'

'Is it? How so?'

'You've got Gareth. You've got this place. You're so lucky. Far luckier than me.' Delyth has tears in her eyes.

'Things haven't always been this good.' Melanie is feeling pressurised to justify her good fortune. 'I've had bad stuff happen too. Things were tough for me as a kid, but I got out of that as soon as I could. And yes, you're right, I have got Gareth.' She lowers her voice. 'And he's totally changed my life.'

'He was married before you. Some girl he met at university.' Delyth rubs her arms through her man-sized coat. 'I heard the two of you had an affair.' The tone, now disapproving, is accompanied by a little tap of her gold crucifix. 'That he got you pregnant, and that's why he left her.'

Melanie is gobsmacked by this woman's bluntness. 'How d'you know about that?'

'I know lots about your husband he'd rather I didn't.' Her eyes narrow into slits. 'And this is a small town, don't forget. Word gets around.' Delyth picks the skin around her thumbs and Melanie resists the urge to smack her hands still. 'Must have taken some doing.'

'What did?' She shrinks from the question.

'Gareth. Living a double life. Cheating.' The woman holds Melanie's gaze. 'They say a leopard never changes its spots. Don't you worry he'll do the same to you?'

'Goodness, what a thing to say. No, I don't.' Melanie is resolute. 'His first wife didn't make him happy.'

'And you do?'

'Yes, I do. He's the happiest he's ever been. And so am I.' Sensing she is under attack, she is on the verge of asking Delyth to leave, when the woman swings their conversation in another direction.

'I used to work here. For the old owners. Cleaning. Working the bar. That kind of thing. I know every inch of this place,'

Delyth shares in her girly voice. 'I also know it split them up. I hope the stress of it doesn't split you and Gareth up.'

Melanie isn't sure how to answer, so she doesn't.

'Going to be quite a job.' Delyth looks around. 'And I hope you don't mind me saying, but I think you might have underestimated it. D'you know what it takes to run a catering establishment like this?'

'I've some experience.'

Delyth nods. 'You got someone to run the kitchen? You'll need a proper chef if you want to open a restaurant.'

'I'm running the kitchen. I was a chef before I had Georgie.' It feels good to inform her. 'So, we know what we've taken on.'

'I can't imagine you as a chef.' Delyth bestows a watery smile. 'I've seen them programmes on the telly. *MasterChef*, that Gordon Ramsay. It's heavy work. And I don't mean to sound rude, but look at you, you don't look robust enough.'

'Don't I?' She straightens her spine; already head and shoulders above Delyth, she makes herself as tall as she can.

'Yes, I know you're tall, but you're not tough, you're too refined.'

'That's a new one for me. I've never been called that before.'

'Well, you are,' Delyth insists. 'And those environments, they're all swearing and aggressive.' A shudder. 'Oh, no, I can't imagine you doing that.'

'Hah! I learnt to swear along with the best of them.'

'You did?' The look is of disgust and comes with another touch of the gold crucifix. 'Have you worked anywhere I've heard of?'

'The Savoy.'

Delyth, her mouth widening into an admiring O. 'I've heard of that.'

'I thought you might.' Melanie, happy to have trumped her. 'I headed up the pastry section but I had to give it up when the

—' She tweaks what she's about to say. 'When Georgie was born. The shifts and the commute from Bromley... It all got too difficult.'

'You worked anywhere since?'

'Not cheffing, no. What with one thing and another, I ended up at a call centre. It was all I could really do after—' Melanie closes her mouth, she doesn't want this woman knowing everything. Although, from the things Georgie said she was saying, Delyth already knows about Sophie and the part Melanie played that meant she never made it to her fifth birthday. 'But anything was better than moping around the house.'

'I'd best stop baking you cakes.' A chuckle. 'You're bound to be better than me.'

The questions Melanie has about how Delyth knows so much about her dead child must wait for another time. 'I don't know anything about traditional Welsh recipes,' she says instead. 'You're going to have to teach me.' She laughs too, but listening to herself, she's ashamed how false she sounds. 'And anyway, you can't stop. Georgie loves your cakes. Oh, is that the time.' A check of her watch. 'I promised her something to eat. She's always hungry after a day at school.'

Delyth stands beside her as she sets about preparing her daughter's drink and customary banana sandwiches. Measuring herself against Delyth's mousiness, Melanie feels her personality is too big and her mannerisms too dramatic in the presence of this diminutive woman.

'Would you like a job, when we open for business?' She makes the offer as she cuts the sandwiches into quarters. 'I'd like it if you did. What with your experience, and the fact you know this place inside out.' She realises she should run this idea past Gareth first, but because it lifts the mood, she's pleased she suggested it.

'Really?'

'Yes, you'd be a huge asset.'

'Thanks.' Delyth looks delighted. 'I think I'd like that very much.'

'Good.' Melanie rubs breadcrumbs off her hands. 'Oops, hang on. Best not forget to give Georgie one of your cakes.' She puts one on the side plate. 'D'you want to come up to the flat?' she says, licking sugar from her fingers.

They find Georgie, TV on, happily playing with Bumble and Slinky in the living room. Legs up on the dimpled sofa lost in her own little world. *Just like your father* – Melanie's realisation, no matter how often it occurs, is always potent.

'Here you go, sweetheart.' She sits beside her, strokes Georgie's and Slinky's heads in turn. She doesn't notice Delyth has taken herself off for a wander, so when she eventually joins her, it's a surprise to find her rooting through the last of the crates still left to unpack.

'My final year at school. I'm here somewhere.' Delyth eagerly unfurls a two-foot colour photograph. 'Look, that's me. And there's Gareth... and Bethan.'

This is the most animated Melanie's seen her and, moving closer, she looks over Delyth's shoulder at the rows of fresh-faced youngsters.

'Gareth keeps threatening to frame it and stick it on the wall,' she says, as Delyth continues to identify various children, their names meaning nothing. Until:

'Erin,' Delyth says and swallows: a dry, wretched sound that is strangled at the back of her throat.

Erin was your sister, wasn't she? Your sister who lies in Pencarew's churchyard. Melanie's thoughts tumble over themselves as she scrutinises the pretty girl in the second row. A girl who was already womanlier than her big sister two rows back. In fact, she's womanlier than her sister is today. Melanie would love to ask Delyth to explain what happened to Erin, but in the same way she can't talk about Sophie, she doesn't know how to broach such a delicate subject. Decides, if Delyth wants to talk about her sister she will, it's not for her to go wading in with her size sevens.

'Oh, he was popular with the girls, was Gareth. A real heartthrob,' Delyth says, returning from wherever her memories took her. 'We all loved him you know. Even the teachers. He was Head Boy and a real star on the rugby field. He's not changed a bit.'

'Neither have you,' Melanie says because it's true – the woman looks as small and childlike as she did then.

'You wouldn't believe how many women would swap places with you right now.' Delyth heaves a sigh into the lopsided compliment. 'But it must be a worry, what with him being away in London and you stuck here. Bet he gets up to all sorts.' A sly smile that makes Melanie wonder if the woman wants to deliberately provoke her.

She snatches the photograph. Rolls it up and slides it down inside the crate. 'I just need the bathroom.' Fearful of what she might say, she wants to put some distance between them. 'I'll see you back downstairs. I'll make us some tea.'

Hiding behind the bathroom door, Melanie waits until the coast is clear, before edging out onto the landing to check on her daughter.

'Are we having fish and chips when Daddy comes home?' Georgie asks, her plate nearly empty.

'Yes, sweetheart.' Smiling broadly at her child's hearty appetite that is not unlike her own.

'Is Delyth staying?'

'Would you like her to?'

Georgie nods. 'She's kind. Kind to Bumble too.'

'She is kind, yes. It was very sweet of her to bring Bumble

home safe.' Melanie is determined to quash the misgivings she has about the woman. 'I'd best get back downstairs. Will you be all right up here?'

'Don't worry about me.' Georgie, finishing the last quarter of her sandwich, is offering the crust to Slinky.

'You're a good girl.' Melanie kisses the top of her head. 'You know where I am if you need me.'

CHAPTER EIGHTEEN

'Right then,' Melanie says as she breezes into the kitchen. 'How's about a nice cup of tea?'

She is mid-reach for the kettle before she notices Delyth has removed her coat and is crying. Her thin shoulders shaking beneath her flimsy dress.

'Shit!' Melanie drops the kettle she had been about to fill down on the counter. 'What the hell are you doing?'

A tap to the elbow and she knocks the carving knife from Delyth's hand. It clatters noisily into the sink. Bright-red blood on the white ceramic. Melanie could cry herself. The unit, with its state-of-the-art taps, cost over four hundred quid and, installed only that morning, she's barely had the chance to use it.

Melanie takes a few short breaths and smooths the legs of her jeans. She is scared to touch her and watches blood drip onto the floor. Scarlet coins against the new anti-slip porcelain tiles. She hopes they can be cleaned, in the way the sink can be cleaned, and the floor won't be spoilt before they've even opened for business.

Staring at the dark-blue veins on the insides of Delyth's arms,

Melanie realises she has intervened in the nick of time. Any later and this would have been a very different story. She assesses the damage. The neat slices, clean and straight. Makes a noise as if she too has been wounded. All fingers and thumbs, she sluices, then binds Delyth's arms with the only thing to hand: one of the posh new towels purchased for the bed-and-breakfast guests who've already paid deposits on reservations that steadily fill the diary. Offering hot, sweet tea, Melanie listens to her own voice, but not to what she is saying, as fresh blood seeps through the christening-white fabric.

'I've-got-nothing-everything-ruined,' Delyth babbles, incoherent, in her little-girl voice. 'Took my-life-too.'

Melanie bites her lip and guides her silently to a chair. Seated, Delyth peers out through her black swathe of waist-length hair that opens like a pair of curtains. Her eyes, beneath wet lashes, dart around as if she is surprised to find herself here.

With no idea how to respond, Melanie stares at the woman's severe centre parting, at the line of gleaming white scalp and her rough, trembling hands.

'His fault. Took-my-dreams-from-me,' Delyth rattles on, hiccupping through tears. 'I-was-the-one-made-sacrifices-look-at-me.'

And Melanie does. She regards the thin gold chain weighted with its crucifix lying heavy on her skin. The spray of freckles travelling over her neck and down inside the ill-fitting dress that has slipped over a shoulder.

'I'm-a-wreck-left-to-rot-in-this-dump-I-could-have-been-someone-too.' A deathly-pale Delyth raises her eyes. A slow movement that gives the impression her hair is too heavy for her neck. 'Help me,' she pleads in the same small voice, but with the added tremor of a punished little girl. 'Please, help me.'

Ticky-ticky-ticky sounds behind them.

'Georgie!' Melanie spins around, expecting to see her child.

Is relieved the only other witness to this horror is the dog who, sniffing out the coins of blood at their feet, licks them clean. 'Slinky, no!' she shouts and shoves him away with her foot. 'No! Slinky, stop it.'

Appalled by the amount of blood, Melanie blots it with another towel to staunch the flow. Such large, coarse hands for such a tiny woman – a passing thought as she presses a thumb to the crude tourniquet. Shocked by very little nowadays, she doesn't ask for clarification, instead, she is patient and kind, reassuring with the same catalogue of platitudes she dishes out to Georgie when applying plasters to her playground scrapes. It isn't that she doesn't have questions – questions as to why this woman believed it acceptable to violently self-harm while her young child was in an upstairs room – she simply keeps them to herself.

'Stay still for me,' her calm demand and Delyth closes her eyes, then opens one to see what it is Melanie's doing. There is less blood then, the cuts bleed more slowly, contained by the towels. 'You hold it here.' She shows her, then dips away. 'Good boy,' she tells Slinky, relieved to see him now lying on his bed. She crouches to hunt the skeletons of kitchen units awaiting their doors. 'Bandages, we need bandages... where the bloody hell?' She waves her arms around inside the gritty, empty innards. 'I'd swear I put them here, for emergencies... and this is a bloody emergency.' Melanie, upright, presses a frantic hand to her brow.

'In the bar.' Delyth, head bowed, face hidden. 'The first aid box always used to be in the bar.'

'I'll go and look. Don't move.' *Don't drip any more of your blood in my kitchen...* Her thoughts trailing behind her as she runs up the stone steps.

She finds a rusted red tin with a cross painted on in Tippex.

Inside, dressings, a sterile bandage still in its wrapper, a tube of antiseptic. Not her first aid box, but it will do.

Back in the kitchen, a rapid wash of hands, then she sits beside Delyth and gingerly unwraps the towels. Nasty and raw, the cuts are dreadful, but she gives nothing away as she smears on antiseptic cream, her movements small and gentle, mindful of the woman's winces, her hissing noises.

'We should get you to hospital. Get you checked out.' Melanie applies the squares of dressing, secures them with strips of bandage.

'I've-got-nothing-ruined-I'm-ruined.' Delyth sobs through words Melanie can't sew into any kind of meaning. 'My life,' she says, tears wetting her cheeks. 'Life-over-took-my-dreams.'

She stops what she's doing to look at the moving mouth and reminds herself this woman was once a child, that she wouldn't have always been this way. Life, with its cruel twists, is what's brought her here. Delyth would have been happy once, there would have been moments, as Melanie herself had moments, when she would have laughed a carefree laugh. But in the same way it's hard to look out on a winter landscape and imagine the flowers of summer, so it is with Delyth Powell.

'I learnt this at Girl Guides.' Her turn to prattle, but only because she can't make sense of what Delyth's saying. 'Never needed it until now, but there's a first time for everything.'

Close enough to see the striations on Delyth's forehead, the light from the single ceiling bulb reflected in the curve of her eye, Melanie proceeds to bind the wounds with the length of bandage. Delyth has stopped her gabbling and is now regarding her with the quick, dark eyes of a scolded child.

Finished, she gets up and steps aside. Wanting the woman to settle, she sets about making tea but gets no further than filling the kettle. It's difficult to focus, the questions she wants answers to buzz like flies. Why did she do this to herself? How come she knows so much about Sophie? And if that is her sister's grave in the churchyard, then what happened to her? But now isn't the time, so it's without speaking that Melanie retrieves a bucket from the bar, fills it with hot, soapy water and gets down on her hands and knees to clean Delyth's blood from the floor.

'I've got to take you to A&E.' She straightens up and drags the back of an arm over her perspiring forehead. 'We should let a professional take a look at you.'

'I don't want to go to hospital.' The small voice is surprisingly assertive. 'I'm so embarrassed.' Delyth is crying again. Melanie drops her cloth into the cloudy pink water and goes and puts an arm around her.

'There, there,' she comforts. 'It's all right.'

Delyth tilts forwards. 'I'm sorry, I shouldn't have done that here. In your home. Can you ever forgive me?'

'It's okay. There, there,' Melanie repeats. What else is there to say? All words are inadequate. 'You're in a very bad place.'

'I am, but I shouldn't have put you in this position.'

'Would you like a shot of something? How about a whisky? I could certainly do with one,' she says, emptying the bloody water away and washing her hands.

'No, I never drink. Not alcohol.'

'I'll make us a pot of tea?' She fits the lid of the electric kettle back on and notices the tremor in her hands – she could think Delyth is more in control than she is.

Melanie's mobile rings from the back pocket of her jeans. She tugs it out, looks at the screen. 'It's Gareth,' she says out loud.

'Don't tell him I'm here.' Delyth presses her lips together when more tears sprout. 'And please, please, don't tell him what I've done,' she implores. 'You won't, will you? Promise me.'

Melanie promises and passes her a box of tissues before activating the call.

'Gareth.' She exhales and watches Delyth blow her nose, dab the skin under her eyes. Her face is red and blotchy from crying. 'Hi, love. Are you far away?' She returns the tissues to the side. 'That soon? Wow, you've made great time.' She looks at Delyth. 'Yes, okay, I'll nip out for them. Same as usual? Great, see you in a while. Drive carefully.' And she hangs up. 'That was Gareth,' she says as if Delyth didn't know. 'He's on his way home.'

At this, Delyth springs upright. Wobbly on her feet, she reaches for the tabletop to steady herself.

'Whoa!' Melanie leaps forwards. 'You're not going anywhere. Sit. Sit down.' And she guides her back to the chair.

'But I've got to get home.' Delyth crumples the soggy tissue in her fist.

'No, you don't. I'm sure your mum and Andrew can survive without you for an hour or two. Just stay there.'

'No, it isn't that.' Delyth frowns. 'I don't think it's a good idea if I'm here when Gareth gets home.'

'But you're in no fit state to drive.' Melanie switches the kettle on. 'At least stay for a cup of something, get your strength back. One of us can run you home later.'

'No, no, no.' Delyth looks frightened. 'You don't understand. I don't want to see him. I only came because I knew he wasn't here.'

'Oh, dear, please don't stress yourself.' Melanie is fearful of upsetting the woman further. 'But honestly, you can't leave yet. Not after... after that.' She waves at Delyth's bandaged arms. All the things she wants to say, like, *You might try it again, and I'd never forgive myself if you didn't make it home in one piece,* dissolve in her mouth. 'Please, stay. Just for a while,' she urges, more for herself. 'I'm sure Gareth won't mind you being here.'

And Delyth feeds her a look that says they both know this isn't true.

CHAPTER NINETEEN

'Let's go, Georgie.' Melanie grabs her parka and handbag from the peg on the door. 'Daddy will be here soon. We'd better go and fetch our fish and chips.'

'I can look after her.' Tears dry, her deathly pallor less so, Delyth is sitting up at the kitchen table with Georgie. They are doing a jigsaw together.

'You don't mind?' Melanie isn't sure, but she can't say she doesn't trust her.

'Not at all.' Delyth, quite bold, appears to have recovered from the trauma. If it wasn't for the bandages, Melanie could pretend nothing had gone on here.

'I'll be about twenty minutes.' She looks at her watch, then at Delyth and Georgie. How well these two get on.

'Are you sure you want fish and chips?' Delyth slides another piece of the background into place.

'Beg your pardon?'

'I know you don't need to watch your figure; it's not that. You've a shape like a proper woman, not like me.' A timid laugh. 'I've never had the shape men like. Never had much that men like, truth be told.' She senses Delyth's gaze travel the length of her. 'But fish and chips? Surely you've got something better to eat.'

Melanie is stumped. 'I don't know. I suppose there's things in the freezer. Bits and bobs in the fridge—'

'It's not good for this little one,' Delyth interrupts and takes a sidelong look at Georgie. 'Living on takeaways and ready meals all the time.'

'You are right.' She scans the half-finished kitchen. 'Ordinarily, I'd cook myself. This takeaway thing's only for the short-term.'

'Oh, don't take any notice of me, Georgie's your daughter.' Delyth wrinkles her nose. 'You do what you think best.'

'Thing is, we're running low on everything. We're going to do a proper shop tomorrow.' She riffles the scanty contents in the fridge. 'I suppose I could rustle up a salad. I've a bag of lettuce leaves and some tomatoes. Half a red pepper. Oh, and here's a couple of onions.'

'There you go then.' Delyth looks satisfied.

'But it isn't enough.' Melanie holds out her hands to show the meagre offerings. 'We'll need something hot.' She taps a finger against her mouth, thinking. 'Hang on. I've got a lasagne in the freezer. How about that?'

'Shop bought?'

'From the supermarket. I only got it in for emergencies.'

Delyth lifts then drops her thin shoulders.

'Might it be healthier than fish and chips?'

'I suppose.' It seems this is all her dinner guest is prepared to say, before refocusing on the cartwheel Georgie's completed at the bottom of the jigsaw. 'Clever girl,' Delyth congratulates. 'You can fit the horse together now.'

'Lasagne it is then.' Melanie slips out of her coat, returns it and her handbag to the peg behind the door. 'Won't be a tick.'

'If you want,' Delyth starts, an engine warming up, 'I could make you something next week. Do you like casseroles?' She directs her question to Georgie, who blithely grins her reply; the idea of something home-cooked obviously appealing. 'I thought you would. What would you like – chicken, some beef?'

'Oh, now,' Melanie steps in. 'That's very kind of you, Delyth, but you can't afford to feed us as well.'

'It's no problem. While I'm doing for us, I can do extra for you. Casseroles are mostly vegetables and I grow them in the garden. How about it, Georgie?' Delyth claps her hands, then winces, forgetting for a moment how sore her arms are.

'Yes, please.' Georgie grins.

'It's not that I'm—' Whatever Melanie had been about to say, evaporates before it forms.

'No need for you to feel bad.' Delyth reads her mind. 'You do your best, but a microwave is next to useless. Look at it as me helping you out.' Another smile for Georgie, who is now holding Delyth's hand. 'Because it's important this little one gets proper, home-cooked food.'

Melanie grabs the bloodied towels and leaves Delyth and Georgie to it. Flicking the light switch, she descends the stone steps into the basement to where the new chest freezers and catering-sized cooler are. Cold down here, she shivers, despite her numerous layers. She catches a slice of her reflection in the side of the cooler and decides she should go and tidy herself up for Gareth. At least put some lippy on and pull a brush through her hair. Especially now it's not as styled as it once was.

Thinking of three nights and two whole days with him lifts her heart. But when she remembers the woman who is sitting in her kitchen and the terrible thing she tried to do, her mood takes a dive. Melanie drops the towels into the stainless-steel sink, runs the hot tap and sprinkles on washing powder. She knows this is futile, that the white fabric is ruined. Experience tells her no matter how many times she might scrub them she won't be able to wash away the stains. They will forever haunt the weft and warp like rose-coloured phantoms. They will bloom and swell with each fresh soaking. Poor Delyth, she must be dreadfully unhappy to have done that to herself and in such a small window of time. She can't have been on her own for more than ten minutes. As someone whose own life has brought her down low, so low there was a time she believed it wasn't worth living either, Melanie forgives Delyth's prickliness, her resentfulness, and wonders if there's anything she can do to help her. Letting Delyth cook them a meal might be a start. Maybe this is her way of apologising. Because what she did, with Georgie dangerously close by, was a desperate act by anyone's standards.

Yes, Melanie decides, *what harm could it do?*

She leaves the towels to soak and, drying her hands on her jeans, lifts the lid of the freezer to hunt its frosty innards. Moving the bags of blackberries she and Georgie picked on that sunny afternoon, she finds what she's looking for. Light off, she hurries up the steps, the family-size lasagne cold between fingers and thumb. She hears Georgie's excited squeals as she approaches the kitchen.

'Gareth! Oh, it's so good to see you.' Melanie puts down the frozen ready meal and throws her arms around him. But wooden beneath her embrace, she can tell he isn't happy.

'Daddy's home! Daddy's home!' Georgie, joyful, has abandoned her jigsaw to dance about the kitchen. Pausing to include the dog who, wagging and excited, looks as pleased with Gareth being home as she is.

'What's going on here then?' He passes Melanie a bunch of roses and cocks his head in Delyth's direction. 'You didn't say we had visitors.' And leaning in, as if to kiss Melanie, he whispers through gritted teeth, 'What the fuck is she doing here?'

'Daddy. Daddy.' Georgie hurtles towards him and Melanie stands aside; watches Gareth lift his daughter up by her middle.

'How's my best, best girl then?' He kisses her, then sets her down.

'I'll tell you later,' Melanie says, noticing the muscles tighten in his jaw.

'Flowers, eh?' Delyth remarks when Melanie brushes past to place them in the sink. 'He either really loves you, or he's guilty of something.'

'I'm sorry, what did you say?' She half-turns, unsure if she heard correctly. 'The roses are beautiful, thanks, love,' she calls to her husband and, stroking the vermilion-red petals, tries not to think of Delyth's blood.

'I see they've finished the floor.' Gareth shrugs out of his suit jacket, folds it over the back of a chair. 'Looks fab.' He removes his tie and undoes his top button, completely blanking Delyth.

'The Belfast sink's in. Look.' Melanie runs the cold tap, hunts for scissors in the rack on the drainer. 'And you want to have a look at the restaurant. They've put the panels in and plastered the alcove.'

'It's coming on great.' He rubs a hand over the stubble she knows he would have shaved clean that morning. Inspects his palm as if its inky blackness has been transferred there.

'I've made a start on the website too.' Melanie unwraps the roses, lifts one to her nose to inhale the perfume that isn't there. 'Loaded up those brilliant views we took the day we arrived.'

'The website? Well done.'

'Everything's progressing nicely. Shame about the stove. We could cancel if we hadn't paid a walloping deposit.'

'I don't know what you expect me to do about it?' Gareth,

unusually offhand. She can tell it's because of what he's come home to. 'I've got my work in London.'

'I know that. I was only giving you an update.' Self-conscious in front of their unexpected guest, she glances at Delyth who is doing a noble job of pretending the jigsaw is more entertaining than the conversation she and Gareth are having. 'These roses are gorgeous.' She returns to her stem-trimming. 'I'll get a vase.' And jogging away, Gareth is swift on her heels.

'What the fuck's she doing here?' he hisses, angry in the unlit bar. 'It's just supposed to be me, you and Georgie. Christ, Mel.' He grits his teeth. 'What the hell did you invite her for? I've not seen you for ages.'

Melanie puts an arm around his waist, feels him stiffen and pull away. 'I didn't invite her.' She lets go of him to tug open the swollen cupboard door, wrinkles her nose at the musty smell. 'She called round with Bumble. Georgie had left him at school.' She finds a vase. 'I was so grateful, I invited her in for a look around, said she could stay for dinner.' Melanie leaves it there, remembering the promise she made to Delyth.

Gareth grunts. 'I'll fetch us a bottle of wine from the basement. What d'you want?'

'Whatever you like. I don't mind.' Melanie heads back to her roses. Placing them in the centre of the table once they've been arranged. 'You'll need to clear that away before we eat,' she explains to Georgie who is fitting together the horse's rump.

'I don't want to.' Her daughter spreads her little hands in a brave attempt to protect the half-finished jigsaw.

'You have to, we need the table, sweetheart.'

'Why are there two of our new guest towels soaking in the sink downstairs?' Gareth, back from the cellar, a bottle of Shiraz in his hand.

'There was a little accident.' Melanie and Delyth swap glances.

'Looks like blood. Did one of Bryn's men injure themselves?'

'Georgie, can you please do as you're told and tidy that away.' Melanie, fiercer than she means to be. She had forgotten about the towels.

'Mel? What's gone on?'

'It's nothing. I'll tell you later.'

'And where's our fish and chips? I'm starving after that drive. I had bugger all for lunch, deliberately.'

Melanie, peeling the first of two onions, blinks through wet lashes. 'I thought we should try to eat a little healthier, so we're having lasagne tonight.' She lifts her hand, shiny with onion juice, jabs the sharpened stump of her paring knife at the microwave. 'I'm making a salad to go with it. We had loads to use up in the fridge, it'll only go to waste.'

'What? I thought we agreed.' Gareth drags his mouth south and wanders over to peer through the steamed-up glass at their cellophane-wrapped dinner. 'There's no way that's going to stretch to four. Let me fetch some chips to go with it, yeah?' His face brightening. 'Chips will do it.'

'Gareth?' Melanie wipes her eyes on a cloth, looks at Delyth again. 'We're not having chips, okay?' The bowl of salad finished, she puts it, and the cruet, on the table. 'Georgie?'

'Yes, Mummy.'

'Stop that now and put it away, please. I've asked you twice.'

'Bread, then. A basket of bread?' Gareth suggests. 'Want me to cut some?'

'Sorry, bit stale. What's left is only good for toast. No, come on, there'll be plenty.'

'You are kind, but I'm just in the way.' Delyth thrusts herself back from the table and makes to go. 'I don't have to stay.'

'No, you don't—' Gareth does nothing to hide his contempt.

'Yes, you do. Sit,' Melanie insists, cutting him off. 'Now,

who's for wine?' She ignores the black look Gareth is giving her. 'I know I could do with some.'

Delyth seals a hand over the top of the glass Melanie sets before her. 'Just water, please. I never touch the stuff. You wouldn't either if you'd seen what it's done to my mam.'

'Christ, woman, it's only a glassful. We're not asking you to drink the whole bloody bottle.'

Melanie sees Delyth touch the crucifix at her neck. 'Gareth? Not in front of Georgie.' The excuse of protecting her daughter's sensitivities allows her to shield Delyth's too. But looking around, Georgie isn't here. She's packed away the jigsaw and is returning it to her room.

'Oops, *sor-ry*.' Gareth, mocking, focuses on Delyth for the first time. 'What've you been doing to yourself?' He waves the corkscrew at her arms. 'You're bleeding.'

Melanie, up behind him with cutlery and placemats, sees that blood has seeped through the bandages.

Delyth lowers her eyes.

'What's up? Cat got your tongue,' Gareth persists.

'Leave it, love,' Melanie warns and leads him away once she's set the table. 'Delyth's fine now.' The last thing she wants is him upsetting her, the woman's fragile enough as it is.

Gareth rolls his shirtsleeves to the elbow and pours wine into two glasses. He holds one to the light and turns away from Delyth to take a mouthful. 'Bloody nutcase,' he mutters, swirling a finger at his temple.

'Oh, Georgie, there you are,' Melanie calls exaggeratedly to drown out her husband. 'Good girl for putting your jigsaw away. You sit up next to Delyth. Dinner won't be long.'

At the ping of the microwave, Melanie retrieves their meal. It doesn't look very appetising and, tearing off the cellophane lid, she finds it smells little better. Why was she swayed by Delyth, why didn't she just stick to the plan and get them a takeaway? They eat in awkward silence. Melanie listens to the scraping of knives and forks against the cold plates that, without a stove, she couldn't even set to warm before serving.

'Remind me again why we're not having fish and chips?' Gareth drains his glass, pours another. 'Because I don't know about you guys, but this tastes revolting.' He lifts the sodden layers of pasta with his fork, rakes through the unappetising filling, then pushes his plate away. Melanie, watching, wishes he wouldn't, Georgie copies all his bad habits.

'Delyth was saying, and I agree with her.' She notices her daughter has left most of hers too. 'Living off takeaways isn't good for us, never mind Georgie.'

'What! So, we're eating this rubbish because of her?' Looking outraged, he treats Delyth to a good hard stare.

Melanie puts down her knife and lays a restraining hand on Gareth's hairy forearm. 'We'll have fish and chips tomorrow. Now can we please talk about something else?'

But there doesn't appear to be anything else to talk about, so no one does, for quite some time.

'Who's for ice cream?' Melanie asks while she clears the table. Is surprised that even her daughter declines. 'What's the matter, sweetheart? It's not like you to turn down pudding.'

'I'm all right,' Georgie says, but she doesn't sound sure.

'I'll feed this to the dog, shall I?' Melanie nudges Gareth.

'If you think he'll eat it.' He curls his lip.

'Can I get down now?' Georgie asks. 'I want to go to bed.'

'Are you tired?' Melanie kisses her child's soft little brow. 'Do you want Daddy to come and read you a story?'

Georgie nods and slips from her chair. A stroke of the dog to let him know she's going upstairs, and he slinks away after her.

'Mind if I use your bathroom?' Delyth rises to her feet.

'Course not. You know where it is.' Melanie smiles.

'Are you going to tell me what's been going on?' Gareth

demands as soon as Delyth is out of earshot. 'What are those bandages on her arms for?'

'I don't know.' The lie is hard in her mouth; treacherous, the ultimate betrayal. She doesn't understand why she should feel protective towards Delyth. Yes, she promised not to tell, but she's made bigger promises to Gareth. Melanie gulps a mouthful of wine and sneaks a look at the eight-piece knife set in their stunning acacia block and swallows. 'I think she hurt herself at work.'

'I still don't know why you had to ask her to stay for dinner, or how you let her persuade you against getting a takeaway.' Gareth puts an arm around her. 'That was one of the worst meals I've ever had.'

'I'm sorry.'

He hugs her tighter, whispers into her ear, 'As long as you make sure it doesn't happen again.'

'What – giving you a horrible meal?' she teases.

'No. Inviting her round here.'

'Oh, Gareth, she's all right.' Melanie thinks of the offer of a job she gave Delyth earlier and pulls away.

'Why does she keep calling round, what does she want? Creepy cow.'

'*Shh.*' A finger to her lips. 'Keep your voice down.'

'God, I hate that look she gives. I always did.' He ignores Melanie's warning. 'All woe-with-me. I don't buy any of it.' Gareth makes a fist, punches his other palm. Melanie finds it alarming. 'And neither should you. You don't know her like I do.'

'Tell me what happened with her then. It's not my fault if you won't talk to me about it.'

'Why isn't it enough for you to do as I say about this? I've asked you to stay away from her, why d'you have to keep on with your bloody questions? She's off her head, Mel; you only have to look at her to know that.' His tone isn't one she has ever heard him use before and she doesn't much like it.

'Gareth, for pity's sake.' She flicks her eyes to the doorway, is relieved to find it empty. 'She's had a rough time and she's got three different jobs and an elderly mother to look after. Who, for the record, sounds a bit of a nightmare. And she's her boy to bring up, don't forget.'

'That's another thing I can't get my head around. That kid of hers, he's going on seventeen, yeah? Well, that would've made her eighteen and still at school when she got pregnant. And I don't know anyone who'd have been desperate enough to shag her.'

'God, you're vile. Why can't you just be nice? She's not had any of the chances you've had.'

A rustling behind them.

'*Shh*, she's coming,' Melanie warns.

'I'd better get going.' Delyth, uncertain from the threshold. 'Thanks for the lovely dinner.' She addresses Melanie while stealing a look at Gareth.

'Hardly lovely.' A forced laugh. 'When we've got something to cook on, you'll have to come over for a proper meal.' She sees Gareth open his mouth, about to speak. A touch of his shoulder stops him.

'Well, thanks anyway.' With timid little movements, Delyth retrieves her coat from where she left it and slips it on.

She looks pathetic, her arms aren't even long enough for the sleeves and, with a rush of pity, Melanie dives forwards to give her a hug. But the disconcerting frailty of bones beneath the waxy material has her pulling back, fearful of crushing her.

'Let me come and see you out.'

'No need.' Delyth lifts a hand. 'I know my way.'

CHAPTER TWENTY

Minutes later, Melanie, elbow-deep in suds, is passing Gareth the plates for him to dry and put away.

'You don't like Delyth at all, do you?' Her question bounces against the kitchen walls.

'No, I bloody don't. And I don't want her having anything to do with our daughter either.'

'Why not? What's she ever done to you?' She runs the cold tap and the spray soaks her cuffs. 'It's not like you to take against someone like this.'

'I don't trust her.'

'On what grounds?' Melanie passes him a fork.

Gareth wipes it, puts it away. 'Because she's creepy. Go on, admit it.'

'I think she's unhappy.'

'Huh.' He sneers. 'She's a moaner. Always was. D'you know what we used to call her at school?'

Melanie shakes her head, of course she doesn't.

'Cry baby. Cry baby bunting, daddy's gone a-hunting...' He trails the nursery rhyme he used to sing to the twins when they were babies, to the bin and back. It has a sinister ring now and tarnishes her cherished memory. 'Suits her, don't you think?'

'Maybe she had something to cry about.' Melanie thinks of what Delyth told her about her home life, her mother's dependency, her financial worries. The feeling life has passed her by. Circumstances, she believes, that led her to do what she did in their kitchen sink.

'Been feeding you some sob story, has she?'

'She mentioned some stuff.'

'Don't get sucked in, Mel. Please.' Gareth kisses her. 'You're not her bloody social worker.'

'I don't encourage her. I was only being nice. I can't help it if I find it hard to say no to her, I feel sorry for her.'

'She's like a stone in your shoe,' he snaps. 'Yes, she's small and doesn't take up much space, but she's bloody irritating and there's no ignoring her.'

'You did a pretty good impression of ignoring her.' Melanie rinses out the washing-up bowl.

'Why are you defending her?' He reaches for his wine glass. 'Taking her side over mine?'

'I'm not. I just don't think she's done anything wrong.' Melanie dries her hands.

'You're too trusting, that's your trouble. Always seeing the good in people.'

'Yes, until I'm shown otherwise.' She stands her ground. 'Delyth's been kind to me and Georgie, baking us cakes and stuff—'

'That woman bakes you cakes?' Gareth cuts in.

'Yeah, I told you on the phone. She brought some round the other day. Georgie loves her cooking.'

'You let Georgie eat them! I don't want her eating anything that woman's touched. And anyway.' Gareth pauses, something occurring to him. 'Why's she doing that, what does she want?

She's not the type to do anyone a favour and not expect something in return.'

'She doesn't want anything.' Melanie glares at him. 'She's just being neighbourly. She knows we've only got a microwave —' She closes her mouth, reluctant to rake through the reasons again. Instead, she attempts to shift their discussion in a more positive direction. 'Isn't the kitchen looking great? I'm glad you love the floor.' A blaze of Delyth's blood. 'And this sink and drainer are the business.' Another image of the bright-red streaks against the white ceramic.

Gareth dries a spoon, holds it up to his face and scowls at his distorted reflection. He puts the spoon away. 'I still don't know why she had to stay for dinner. You knew how much I was looking forward to coming home. I've missed you and Georgie so much. And I end up having to sit there with that thing, dictating what we eat, the cheeky cow. She hardly said a word and I don't see why I should have to make the effort after the week I've had. Certainly not with her. Christ, Mel, talk about awkward. You could've cut the atmosphere with a knife.'

'All right, I've said I'm sorry.' Melanie winces at his choice of words.

'Just for the record—'

'A broken record,' she butts in.

'Just for the record, that was a shit evening, so please don't invite her again. Okay?'

Melanie makes a sound, audible enough to communicate without words how unreasonable she thinks he is being.

'Look,' he drops the tea towel on the side, puts his hands around her waist, 'I'm sorry if I sound unfeeling.' He pulls her towards him. 'But I just don't like her, I never did. Can't you see it? She's a bloody weirdo.' He strokes her cheek; tender, loving. 'She'll only drag you down and you've been doing so well these past months, weaning yourself off the tablets. You get involved with her and I'm frightened you'll spiral down again. She's bad news, Mel, trust me. And this is supposed to be a new start for us.'

But I'm already involved, she thinks, looking over his shoulder, wondering again why Delyth chose their kitchen to do what she did, and what Gareth would do if he knew.

'Oh, come on. I think you're painting an overly black picture here,' she says. 'She's nice. Bit lonely maybe, poor thing. Why have you got such a problem with her? She went out of her way to bring Bumble back. She didn't have to bother.'

'Greeks bearing gifts.'

Melanie rolls her eyes. 'Talking of gifts, are you going to tell me what she meant in her card? I know I've asked you before, but I want to know.'

'I told you, I haven't the foggiest.'

'I don't believe you. Tell me. What did she mean she was good at keeping secrets – what secrets?'

'I've said, I don't know. How can I? I've not seen her for years.'

Melanie gives him a look that says she's not going to let him get away that lightly.

'I don't know,' he says, still holding her tight. 'I might have been smoking at school, or she saw me mitching and covered for me. Something childish like that. So what? She's still living in the past; a past she wants to relive now I've come back.' He tugs her closer, gives her the trust-me blue of his eyes.

'There must be more to it than that.' Melanie removes his hands from her hips and steps away. 'She wouldn't still be going on about not telling the teacher on you.'

'Not if it's still a big issue in her mind,' he argues. 'It's obvious she's never grown up, never moved on. She's still living with her mother. She's just a silly little village girl who'd rather wallow in self-pity than sort her life out. I'm sorry, but—' He must clock the look Melanie gives and so softens what he was about to say. 'She's her own worst enemy. It's why people round here don't bother with her anymore. They're all sick of her moaning.'

'How would you know what people round here think? You've not lived here for years.'

Gareth doesn't answer.

'And anyway, that's not what I heard,' she informs him. 'So far as I can tell, you're the only one who's got a problem with Delyth. Others I've spoken to think she's nice.'

'Yeah, what others? Who've you been talking to?' He sounds alarmed.

'Why are you so bothered?'

'Who've you been talking to?'

'Your sister.'

'Huh, like she'd know.' Gareth looks relieved. 'Butter wouldn't melt. Lovely little Delyth. She's hoodwinked the pair of you.'

'Okay.' Melanie sighs. 'Then it's everyone else against you, Gareth, is it? Except it's the majority that wins, I'd say.'

'Look, I don't give a damn about anyone else, I don't like her. And I don't want her coming here pestering you.' That tone again, the one she doesn't like. 'And I don't want her anywhere near our daughter either. She's not all there.' He taps his temple.

'Ooh, you're an obstinate sod, Gareth Sayer.' Melanie, aware that the precious hours they have together are ticking away. 'For what it's worth, I reckon Delyth Powell's still got a crush on you.'

'You what?'

'Yes.' She grins. 'I have got eyes in my head. I saw the way she was looking at you.'

'What are you on about? She didn't look at me, that was the problem. It's why our evening was so bloody excruciating.'

'Exactly. That's how I know. She couldn't look you in the eye. Bethan said she used to follow you around at school.' Melanie kisses him. 'Is that the Big Secret? Are you afraid to admit it because you think I'm going to be jealous?'

'And would you be?'

'Maybe,' she says, playful.

'Mm, you smell good.' His lips against her ear, the brush of stubble on her cheek. 'Have I told you how gorgeous you're looking? I'd have told you earlier had we not been entertaining the Grim Reaper. Anyway, never mind about her.' She feels the weight of his gaze. 'You're looking the best I've seen you since—' He pulls up, skims around the elephant in the room, the unspoken loss they share their lives with.

And it is her turn to look at him. To wonder why, when their lives and experiences are as entwined as the roots of a tree, there should be this glaring no-go area in their marriage? The one thing she can never bring up for fear of distressing him, even though there are times, like now, when she wishes they could talk. Of her. Their dead daughter. But Gareth asked her, didn't he? He asked her to leave Sophie alone, to stop mentioning her, to lay her to rest. Saying this was the only chance they had of living what remained of their lives. For Georgie's sake, he said. These are her thoughts, and his too, she guesses. And so much of her wants to tell him it's wrong to box Sophie away. But then his sorrow is different to hers. He's not looking for forgiveness for the part he played. Unlike Melanie, Gareth isn't beleaguered by self-hatred and remorse, or the stomach-churning memory of that moment she let go of Sophie's hand.

'It's because I'm happy,' she tells him. What else can she say? He's only home for a little while and she, like him, is reluctant to talk of sad things. 'I've been feeling loads better.'

'It shows.'

'It's being out in the fresh air. All the walking I'm doing, I love it. My therapist said that being close to nature was one of the best things for depression. And I do feel brighter, out with Slinky, the scenery is breathtaking. I know it's been a long, slow road for me and how patient you've been.' She wraps her arms about him again. 'Coming here's the best decision we've ever made.'

'Mummy. Mummy.' Georgie, barefoot in pyjamas and holding Bumble, looks up at them through sleepy eyes.

'Darling. What's up?' Melanie releases Gareth and bends to cuddle their child. 'Did you have one of your bad dreams?' She tests Georgie's temperature with the back of her hand.

'I've got a bad tummy.'

'Oh, sweetheart. Show me where it hurts.'

Georgie presses her abdomen. 'I feel sick.'

'Oh, sweetheart. You do look a little peaky. You've probably picked up a bug at school.' Melanie scoops her in her arms and darts a look of concern to Gareth. 'Daddy make you some cocoa? Settle your tummy.' A puff of her daughter's breath, sweet as a lamb's, against her neck.

Gareth nods and reaches for a mug, then inside the fridge for the milk.

'Come on, little one. Let's get you tucked up in the warm. Dear me, your feet are freezing.' She folds her palm over her daughter's little foot. 'Get you nice and cosy and read you a story, shall we?' She feels her daughter's nod, the weight of her skull against her collarbone. 'Thanks, love.' She turns to Gareth. 'Are you happy to close up down here, bring Georgie's cocoa and my wine upstairs?'

'No probs. Where's the Calpol?' He drapes the damp tea towel over the sparkling chrome taps to dry.

'In the bathroom. Can you dig it out?'

With Georgie in her arms, Melanie swaps the brightness of the kitchen for the dark bar. Empty but for its moon-washed walls, the ochre light leaking from the flat upstairs is enough to go by. A scuttling sound and a rasp of rubble against the concrete floor. She spins around. Alarmed. At first, she thinks it is Sophie's ghost she sees – so small, so pale, the way she often glimpses her. But this isn't Sophie. This is Delyth. Her crucifix glinting through the indeterminate light.

She's heard it all... Every single word.

Melanie's realisation is not a comfortable one. In the tightening seconds she scrabbles over the contents of her and Gareth's conversation. Feeling queasy and holding on to Georgie who grows heavier by the second, she flicks the light switch to extinguish the gloom.

But Delyth has gone. And rushing after her, desperate to put things right, by the time she reaches the door, all that remains of Delyth is the sting of her Defender's exhaust polluting the night-time air.

CHAPTER TWENTY-ONE

'Mummy, look!' Georgie, up at her bedroom window, gazes out on the garden. The sea they both know is out there has been lost to a ribbon of mist. 'It's like a fairyland.'

Half-term has crept up on them already and they wake to their first hard, blue frost.

'Oh, it's beautiful.' Melanie, halfway through making her daughter's bed, looks up. 'We're going to need our hats and gloves.' She strokes the dog's velvety ears, then tucks the duvet in at the bottom. 'I'll dig them out.' She relinquishes Slinky to test the radiator, that for once doesn't scorch her hand.

Minutes later, sitting side by side at the pine kitchen table, sharing a breakfast of mashed banana on toast with the dog, they map out their day.

'How's about this for an idea?' Melanie projects her voice over the clatter and banging of workmen as she cuts the toast into triangles. 'What if I come and collect you from Nia's at two.' She puts the plate in front of her daughter and licks her fingers. 'We could drive to Pwllglas?' Georgie gathers a few dead rose petals that have dropped to the table. 'Go to Franco's for a pizza.'

The kettle comes to the boil.

'That's what I call perfect timing.' Bryn stands in the doorway, his hair white with plaster dust.

'How's it going?' Melanie pours a little water into the teapot, swills it round.

'Great.' He is looking far from great himself: his red-rimmed eyes and unkempt beard tell her he isn't getting much sleep.

'Ffion still teething?' She reaches for another mug.

'How can you tell?' He yawns.

'It does get better.' Melanie glances at Georgie.

'Tom's fixed the central heating, so you won't be needing a new boiler.'

'Gareth will be pleased.' They trade smiles and she hands him a mug of tea.

'Ta.' Bryn blows on it, takes a sip. 'Oh, and I think you've got a mouse problem. Not surprising, but you'll need to sort it before you open.'

'Mice?'

'Yep.' He drinks more of his tea. 'Anyway,' he jabs a thumb at the bar, 'best get back to it.'

Melanie watches him go, the turn-ups on his overalls dragging through the rubble.

'Right, little one.' She pours herself a mug of tea and sits back down. 'Where were we?'

'You said we could go to Pwllglas.' Georgie plays with her food.

'That's right.' Melanie worries her daughter might be suffering from another tummy ache. 'We could see what's on at the cinema too.' Georgie pushes her half-finished breakfast away. 'Come on, eat up.' She slides the plate back again and brushes crumbs from Georgie's top. 'You'll never have curls like your daddy if you don't eat your crusts.'

'But I don't want curls.' Her daughter twirls her heavy plaits over her hand.

'I was desperate for curly hair when I was little.' Melanie bites off a corner of toast, chews it slowly. 'Why don't you want your breakfast? Are you feeling bloated again?'

'No, I'm much better.'

'Okay. Well, see if Slinky wants that. As he's rather partial to bananas.'

The dog responds by thumping his tail against the floor, and Georgie passes him her unfinished toast. 'Can I have one of those cakes Delyth made me?'

'The raspberry muffins?'

Georgie nods.

'I suppose so, if it means you eat something.' Melanie finishes her breakfast while Georgie retrieves the Tupperware box. 'You do love her baking. It was ever so kind of her to bring them to school. You did remember to thank her?'

'Yes, Mummy.' Georgie prises the lid off and lifts one out. 'She said if I give her the box back when I've finished, she'll make me some more.'

'That's sweet of her. Did she happen to say why she didn't bring them here herself?'

'No.' Her daughter, eating with gusto.

'I think I've a fair idea,' Melanie says to herself, as she makes a start on the washing-up.

Melanie waves a gloved hand to Nia's mother as the door of number seven Castle Row closes and heads down to the beach. The tide is out, and she lets the dog off his lead as soon as they hit the dunes. She loves the way he bounds alongside; his eagerness and zest for life are cheering. Then her thoughts curl back to Delyth Powell and blacken at their edges. She still hasn't recovered from the shock of what she did in their kitchen, but as Delyth is clearly avoiding the pub – and who can blame her – she thinks she should be the one to extend the hand of friendship. A text to thank her for the muffins would be a good way to start. Gareth doesn't need to know.

With barely a stir of wind, the freeze of morning catches her lungs. This is her favourite kind of weather. The only sound is the sea, and, with purposeful strides, holding the faux fur collar of her hood to her jaw, she makes light work of the stretch of shoreline. She lifts her gaze to the wildness of the headland. Sees the Monkstone Arms rising against its patchwork of hedged fields on the fringes of town. Its high slate roof, beaten back by the weather, has taken on the shapes of the waves and looks frozen solid on such a cold day. Can she and Georgie actually rattle around alone in such a huge place after dark? It hardly seems possible, and she pushes away the uncomfortable feelings its isolated setting brings whenever she thinks about it. She needs to start back soon. Even if she didn't have to get ready to take Georgie out later, the sun at this time of year barely shifts beyond the rim of the horizon and sets so suddenly, the temperature dips to below zero in seconds. She calls for Slinky. Sees her breath steaming before her. It's amazing how quickly he's learnt his name, and it makes her smile to see him hurtle back to her. His lead secured to his collar again, they walk back the way they came, passing the bleached bellies of upturned fishing boats pulled onto the dunes and safe from the tide.

'Oi! You!' a loud cry goes up behind her. Powerful, commanding; it's lifted high as the wheeling seabirds above. 'Wait!'

She does as she's told and turns. Sees the man who chased her out of the churchyard. The man she's been calling Mr Grizzly. Big and dark, the sight of him in his donkey jacket frightens her, and her initial impulse is to flee. But something in his look won't let her. This is not someone she can ignore. And the way he drags his left leg to walk, it would be cruel to run away just because she can.

'That's my dog!' he shouts when he eventually joins her on the dunes. 'You've got my dog.'

Close enough to see the accusation burning in his eyes beneath his dense facial hair, her mouth falls open. She has nothing to say.

'It was you.' He points with his good arm. 'You took my dog. I watched you doing it, so don't bother denying it.'

CHAPTER TWENTY-TWO

A loud crash from downstairs. Melanie turns off the shower. Waits in the drip, drip, dripping for whatever it was to sound again. When it does, she grabs a towel and wraps it around her. Out on the landing, the moon through the skylight is bright enough to go by, and she stops at Georgie's half-open door to lean inside. She is met by a little draught of her daughter's sleepy smells and the slow turn of the night light sprinkling soft pink stars over the ceiling and walls. A favourite of Sophie's, come bedtime, that since her twin died, Georgie always asks for. Everything is as it should be. Her child is sleeping. Except where's Slinky? And as if on cue, he barks from somewhere downstairs.

Barefoot, with wet hair trickling into her eyes, she tiptoes down through her shadow to stand among the rubble in the moon-spilt bar. This place is spooky after dark, and her imagination is in danger of running wild. Shivering beneath her damp towel, she hunts the dimness. But there's nothing. And no sign of the dog either. Eerily quiet. Only the odd scratching sound of the mice Bryn warned her about. She makes a mental note to ask Gareth about getting a cat, as she breathes in the raw wood and fresh plaster smells. Prickling with goosebumps, Melanie will never admit to Gareth how vulnerable this place makes her feel when she and Georgie are here alone. And that the weekends, when he's home, can't come quick enough.

The dog is suddenly by her side. His wet snout seeking out her hand. He lifts his head and gives her a quizzical look. The whites of his eyes caught in the moonlight.

'What are you doing down here on your own? Let's get you back up to Georgie.' She strokes Slinky's bony head, feels her heartbeat slow to normal. 'It was probably only the wind. This is an old place, there's bound to be noises.'

A sudden clattering from outside. Slinky barks and she jumps. But neither move. Melanie crushes the edge of her towel into a tight ball and holds her breath. When she hears it sound again, the two of them bolt for the kitchen.

'Who's there?'

Looking around, she traces the familiar shapes of electric appliances, the new floor-to-ceiling units streaked in moonlight. Then she identifies the smell of cigarette smoke. None of the builders would smoke inside, and anyway, they left hours ago. This is fresh. She sees the vase of wizened roses from Gareth that she couldn't bring herself to throw away. It lies smashed on the floor. That must have been what the crashing was.

'You did that, didn't you?' Melanie blames the dog – it's easier to blame the dog. She bends to pick up the broken pieces and is putting them in the bin, when she spots that the back door has been left slightly ajar.

Weird.

She is always so careful and swears she locked it before going to bed.

Something crunches underfoot. Melanie yelps in pain and lifts her foot to inspect the damage, but, reluctant to put a light on, fearing there may be eyes looking in from outside, she can't see much. A flash of white against the blackened windowpane. Torchlight. It strikes the glass, then bounces away.

'What the hell?' Ignoring the pain of her injured foot, she flings the door wide to the night.

Nothing.

Slinky tears away down the side of the pub and the car park beyond, and dead leaves skid in across the floor tiles. Her mother was someone who believed the wind carrying dead leaves into a house brings bad luck and unhappiness. But that was her mother. Full of stupid superstitions that, despite Melanie's best efforts, continue to jingle in her head like loose change at the bottom of her handbag. She inhales the briny breath of the sea and looks up at the big Welsh sky salted with stars. The cold wind against her skin is almost human, and she listens to it nudge through the dry-stalked honeysuckle. She shivers. Could it have been that man from earlier? The one who shouted at her on the beach. Accusing her of taking his dog. Melanie hopes not. She shivers again. She wouldn't stand a chance against him.

An owl answers the moon. Into the spookiness, Melanie tries to persuade herself that there is nothing to fear. That she and Georgie are perfectly safe here alone. But only when the dog returns, reassuring and wagging, his bright eyes telling her all is as it should be, does she let herself believe it.

'Good boy.' She smiles, grateful for his company.

Only when the back door has been firmly locked and the new window blinds pulled down does she feel safe enough to flick on the light switch. But what the string of halogen ceiling bulbs illuminate makes her suck back her breath in horror.

A trail of bloody footprints.

Red and wrong against her gleaming floor.

She screams.

CHAPTER TWENTY-THREE

A day or so later, home from dropping Georgie at school and a quick walk along the headland with the dog, Melanie, in an old rugby jersey of Gareth's, is on her hands and knees amid smells of paint stripper, wood dust and varnish. She is glossing the skirting boards and dado rails in the area that will be the public bar.

'Hey, Mel.' One of Bryn's men with a mop of ginger hair. 'You heard the news? Tom and Sian are gonna tie the knot.'

'Oh, that's wonderful. Congratulations, Tom.'

'She's finally ground you down, ain't she, mate?' another joins in.

'When's the big day?' she asks.

'Depends when we finish.' Tom, a drill bit between his lips. 'Sian wants the reception here.' He secures another wooden panel to the opposite wall.

'Then you'd better pull your bloody fingers out and get it finished.' Bryn breezes in, winks at Melanie. Smart in suit and tie, she wonders where he's been. 'That's right, isn't it, Mel?'

She dips her brush into the pot of plum-coloured paint. 'D'you want me to pencil something in the diary?'

'Nah, Sian will sort the dates. She's the one in charge.'

A cheer goes up from his workmates.

'You're learning, boyo.' The redhead again.

Melanie doesn't rise to it, she wants to finish this job today and, half-listening to their banter, humming along to Radio Two, before she knows it, she's completed an entire length of skirting and finished all four dado rails.

'Are you okay?' Bryn asks, returning to her after a quick inspection of the progress.

'Okay? Yeah, I'm fine.'

'Only Bethan said you phoned the other night in a state.'

'Oh, I'm sorry. I didn't mean to scare you.' She gets up off her knees. 'I thought I heard something, but it was probably just the wind. The back door was open and I was sure I'd locked it, and there was all this blood on the floor. I just freaked.'

'Blood?'

'My foot,' she explains. 'I cut my foot. It frightened the life out of me.'

'Not surprised. Is it okay now?'

'Bit sore. Serves me right for going around with bare feet.'

Bryn loosens his tie. 'D'you think someone could've broken in?'

'No... Well, I hope not.' She pulls a face. 'But the previous owners, maybe someone who used to work here – could they still have a key?'

'It's possible.' Bryn loosens his tie. 'Perhaps it would be safer to get the locks changed. I'll sort it for you.'

Finished, Melanie cleans the excess paint from the brush and reseals the lid. Heads to the kitchen to wipe her hands with the turps and paper towels she left on the side. A glance at the clock. Almost midday. Coffee-time. She is mid-reach for the kettle when something shifts beyond the window.

Slinky barks and she jerks her head to it. Sees a face at the glass.

'Delyth.' Melanie opens the window. 'How are you? Not seen you in ages. D'you want to come in? I was about to make coffee.'

The question goes unanswered. Delyth thrusts forwards a spindly forearm instead. And with the cuff of her coat pulled back, Melanie sees the dressings and bandages have gone and only plasters remain.

'You can cut us a slice of this to go with it if you want?'

'Oh, you've been baking again.' She accepts the cling-film-wrapped offering. 'Goodness, it's heavy. Looks delicious. Smells delicious.' She unwraps it, sniffs its knobbly, glossy top. 'D'you want to come in?' Melanie repeats.

A timid shake of the head. 'I'd rather stay out here if it's okay?'

'Isn't it too cold?' A glance at the bright, blue day going on outside.

'Not with a coat on.'

'All right. I'll join you in a minute. You go round the side, there's benches and tables... lovely view, now we've cleared that eyesore of a dinosaur...' she chatters, preparing a tray. 'Hopefully the seats aren't wet...' When she looks up, Delyth has gone.

'You're right, it is warm in the sunshine.' Melanie, carrying the tray and zipped into her perky red parka, joins Delyth on a bench positioned against the rear wall of the pub. 'Bit of a sun-trap.'

'We've got to make the most of it. Days like this are rare now the clocks have gone back.'

Melanie passes Delyth a mug of coffee and a generous slice of her fruit loaf. 'Help yourself to milk and sugar. Mm, terrific cake.' She bites off a corner.

'It's *Bara brith*.' Her visitor spoons two heaped sugars into her mug and stirs noisily. 'Speckled bread. It's Welsh. You soak the fruit in tea.'

'Delicious. You should go on *The Great British Bake Off*.'

'Don't be silly.' Delyth chuckles but Melanie can tell she's flattered.

'I'm serious.' She takes another mouthful and looks at the dog who's followed her outside. 'Sorry, boy.' She strokes his head. 'I'm not sure this is good for you.' She turns to Delyth. 'Honestly, that dog's a walking bin.'

'You spoil him.' The opinion is non-negotiable.

'I can't help it. Who could resist those eyes?'

'You found out who he belongs to yet?' With an irritated shove, Delyth pushes the dog's snout away.

'No.' Melanie chews through her lie; loath to share her strange exchange with Mr Grizzly. 'Did you get my text to thank you for the muffins?'

Delyth nods and rummages through her bag. 'I bought you this.'

'Welsh recipes.' Melanie takes the slim volume that is handed to her and flicks through the illustrated pages. 'Oh, how thoughtful. Thanks. Not that I can compete with you.'

'Nonsense. You're the qualified chef, I'm just an amateur.'

'Hardly. It's a job to get Georgie to eat anything else now she's sampled your baking.'

'She's such a sweet little girl.' Delyth drinks her coffee and Melanie follows her gaze as it travels the beer garden, away to the blue band of sea beyond the boundary fence. 'I said I was going to make you a casserole, didn't I? I'm sorry.'

'Sorry?' Melanie polishes off her cake. 'With the goodies you've been sending Georgie home with?' She dabs up the last of the crumbs. 'I don't want you going to any more trouble, you've been way too generous already.' *Far more than we deserve, considering the awful things you must have heard Gareth calling you.*

'It's no trouble. I like cooking.' Delyth rifles the pockets of her coat and pulls out a battered packet of cigarettes. 'You don't mind, do you?'

'Course not.' Melanie smiles. It's a relief to see the woman has some vices.

'I've managed to cut down to a couple a day.' Delyth lights up, shakes out the match. 'But I can't totally give them up.'

'One or two won't do much harm.' Melanie sniffs the chemical smell; it doesn't conjure happy memories. 'My mum's a chain-smoker. Everything to excess, my mother. It'll kill her in the end.' It is with a little shudder she suddenly remembers when she last smelt cigarette smoke... In the kitchen in the middle of the night when the door she knew she locked was open.

'How's Georgie?' Delyth takes a deep drag, flicks ash on the grass.

'She's actually been feeling off these past few weeks.'

'Oh dear.' Delyth exhales a snake of smoke.

Melanie watches it disperse into the crisp clear air and drinks her coffee. 'Complaining of stomach cramps and gripes. I don't think it's anything serious. It's just a bit uncomfortable now and again.'

'Peppermint's good for things like that. I grow it on the farm. You can make tea with the leaves.' Finished with her cigarette, Delyth leans down to screw it out on the leg of the bench.

'I suppose it's worth a try.' Melanie frowns. She hopes it doesn't damage the wood. This new garden furniture cost a fortune. 'I think I should take her to see a doctor. I've been meaning to register at the surgery.'

'Ask for Dr Cassidy when you do.' Delyth traces the rambling rose pattern on her mug with a forefinger, spots a tiny beetle on her hand and swats it. 'He's a good man.'

'I will, thanks for the advice.'

'Surprisingly toasty in the sun.' Delyth smiles.

'Gorgeous.' Melanie closes her eyes and tilts her face to breathe in the last of summer. 'How's Andrew doing? Your mum?'

'They're fine,' is all Delyth gives. Cleaning her nails on the corner of the cigarette box, the grubby crescent moons float to the ground.

She studies Delyth. Thinks she can see beneath her skin, down to the truth of this unhappy, haunted, half-lost soul. Is this why she feels strangely connected to her? Because Delyth Powell isn't the kind of person she'd usually associate with.

'I am sorry about what Gareth said the other night.' Melanie breathes against the steam rising from her mug. 'It must've hurt to hear him say such horrible things.'

'No matter.' Delyth shifts in her seat.

'It's no excuse, but he didn't know you were there. We thought you'd gone home.'

'Look, Melanie,' Delyth holds her gaze. 'I've said before that you don't have to apologise for him. You're not accountable for his actions.'

'I know that.' She sets the recipe book down on the tray. 'But I am sorry if he upset you.'

'He didn't.' Delyth turns away.

'Okay, but just to say, it's not like him. Not like him at all.'

'You're sure about that?' The voice is hard.

'Yes, I am. And I know, deep down, that he's sorry.'

'Sorry I overheard him, or sorry he thinks like that about me?'

They slip into an awkward silence and listen to the creep of the tide.

Melanie breaks it. 'Look, it would help if I knew what had gone on between the two of you. I'm stuck in the middle here.'

Delyth, fidgety, reaches up and under the cuff of her coat. Picks at the edge of a plaster. It sets Melanie's teeth on edge. 'Are your arms still sore?' She surprises herself for bringing up the subject, even if it is obliquely.

'No, they've healed up good.' To Melanie's relief, Delyth drops her hands into her lap. 'I'm sorry about what I did that day. It was wrong of me to involve you.'

So softly spoken, Melanie must lean forwards to hear her. Delyth's is a voice that would be lost among others and she half-wonders if it could be deliberate on Delyth's part. A clever ploy if it is. Forcing you to listen. Forcing you to give more attention than you would ordinarily do. But that would make the woman calculating, cunning even, and she's sure this isn't the case. Melanie has always been good at reading people. A useful skill, and one she honed during her childhood. Shunted from care home to foster home and back to her mother, she needed to differentiate between the liars and the genuine. And Delyth Powell is definitely the latter. Such a gentle, vulnerable person. A truly troubled soul. It's why she can't understand why Gareth is so mean about her.

'It was shameful of me. So weak and shameful.' Delyth continues to harangue herself in her quietly-spoken way. 'I'm so embarrassed.' Her hair, black as the last of the sloes in the surrounding hedgerows, is blown open by a sudden gust of wind. It reveals her woebegone face. 'You won't tell anyone what I did? You haven't said anything to Gareth, have you?'

'I've not breathed a word. It can be our secret.'

'Thank you.' Delyth wrings her hands. 'What must you think of me?'

'I don't think anything of you,' Melanie promises. 'Only that you're obviously very sad about something, about life.' She hesitates, unsure whether to share what's on her mind. 'Have you ever thought about talking to somebody?'

'What d'you mean?'

'A professional. A counsellor.'

'Oh, no. I don't need anyone like that, I've got God.' Her fingers fly to her neck and forage under her layers to touch the crucifix.

'It's great you've such strong beliefs, but—' She is about to say, *Where was God when you decided to slice into your arms in my kitchen? He didn't do anything to talk you out of that. It's help from the corporeal world you need.* 'There's no shame in it. I saw a counsellor for a while. She was the loveliest woman. She helped straighten me out. I was a complete wreck after—' She hesitates.

'After Sophie died?'

'Y-yes... after Sophie.' Melanie swallows. 'I've been meaning to ask how you know so much about her?'

'It's not a secret. I'm sorry if you thought it was. Most of the town knows.'

'That's as maybe, but don't you think it was irresponsible to —' She breaks off, approaches it in another angle. 'I mean, what was that nonsense you were telling Georgie?'

'It wasn't nonsense.' Another touch of the crucifix. 'I see things.'

'You see things?' Melanie splutters. 'I don't understand.' And she doesn't. How would this kind of thinking fit with the woman's obvious strict Catholic faith?

'I see things. Things beyond this world.' Enigmatic and

dark, Delyth gives Melanie a look she can't push past. 'I know you blame yourself. I know you're ashamed and think it was your carelessness that caused it. That if you hadn't been so selfish, Sophie might still be alive today. If you hadn't stopped to chat with your neighbour. If you hadn't let go of the trike...'

'What? What did you say?' Horrified, Melanie gawps at her. *How does she know? How does she know?* She stares in disbelief at this relative stranger who, in turn, is staring fixedly out to sea. 'What are you talking about? You don't know the first thing about me.'

'It's why you came to Wales. This is your chance for a fresh start. To wean yourself off the antidepressants, to give up your crummy job. The only job you could hold down after Sophie's accident.' The words are delivered slowly and Melanie wants to grab hold of her, make her look her in the eye. But she doesn't. Too stunned to move, she lets Delyth talk. 'I know what it feels like,' the voice continues, speaking thoughts Melanie believed had been buried deep. But here they are, tumbling out of this other woman. This puzzlingly perceptive woman. 'You can't believe the sun keeps setting and the dawn keeps rising. That days roll over into months, so before you know it, another year's gone by. And people are so selfish, aren't they?' Delyth doesn't wait for an answer, answers aren't required. 'They're oblivious to your suffering because they're too wrapped up in their own problems. It doesn't matter how shocked and saddened they were at the time – it doesn't take them long to forget your dead child. For her to slip from view. We both know the world doesn't stop turning just because you're suffering.'

'I do blame myself,' Melanie admits, refusing to cry. 'But how d'you know?' A floating image of Erin Powell's gravestone.

'Because it's what I think about myself and the people I've loved and lost. If only I'd done that, if only I'd done this.'

'In the weeks following Sophie's death,' she continues, 'I

could tell Gareth looked at me differently. Or I imagined he did, believing I deserved it. I'd failed as a mother, you see, so he's bound to love me less. I love myself less.'

'Have you talked to him about it?'

'I want to, but I'm frightened it will widen his pain, and mine, beyond all measure.'

'Speaking of a death doesn't worsen it. Your daughter can't suffer again.'

'You're right but I can't remember the last time we spoke about her.'

'You must. Your girl is gone, but by speaking of her you give her a second life. A life she can live alongside yours and Georgie's.'

'D'you think?' Melanie blinks through the surprising sunshine, her chest heaving beneath her winter clothes. How perceptive this woman is. What sense she talks. She keeps reassessing her take on her. What she does and doesn't know. Her opinions of Delyth Powell are in a constant state of flux.

'Be gentle with yourself, Melanie. Don't try to understand God's mystery or wisdom, none of us can know that. Think of the child you've got, the curiosity that is Georgie. Thank the Lord daily for her little life. The Lord's unfailing love and mercy will still continue if you go to Him and ask for His forgiveness for whatever badness you do, as sure as the sun sets each evening.'

Melanie bristles a little at this. She can't help it. It's how she feels whenever someone pushes their religious beliefs onto her. She wants to believe this woman. She wants to trust her. But she can't help thinking that what Delyth says doesn't quite come from the heart. That the phrases are second-hand and learnt from the reading of religious texts. That they sound rehearsed.

'But you say you see things beyond this world – and I'm not disputing that. But how does it fit with the church?'

There isn't time for Delyth to answer.

'Mel!' The redhead in Bryn's team opens the patio doors. 'I thought you'd want to know... Your mobile's been ringing and ringing.'

'Oh, bugger.' She gets up and, with Delyth and the dog following, goes inside.

On their approach to the kitchen, her mobile rings again. Vociferous and demanding, she dashes away to answer it.

It's Gareth. A nervous smile at Delyth who is close on her heels.

'Hey, Mel. Where've you been? I've been calling and calling.' The voice she loves sounds far away.

'Sorry, Gareth. I've been in the garden.'

'God, I've missed you.' She hears him sigh. 'It's been a hell of a slog so far this week, I can't wait till I'm home,' he whispers. 'Tell me what you're wearing?' His question, the way he delivers it, she can tell he wants to talk sexy. 'What underwear have you got on? Mel... tell me, tell me. I need you to give me a picture, I miss you so much... so much.' It reminds her of when they were first together: the text messages, lustful, exciting. Except now there's no Elizabeth to worry about. But she can't engage in this with him now, not with Delyth listening. 'Two more days, Mel. Only two more days... and I've been thinking,' she hears him grinning, 'are you gonna let me do whatever I want with you when I get home?' A gravelly chuckle. 'I can't wait to get my hands on you. I can't wait to—' He pulls up short, sensing her reluctance, her muted response. 'You're not on your own, are you?'

'No.' Melanie shoots a look at Delyth.

'Who's there?'

'*Erm.*'

'Mel?'

'Delyth,' she says nonchalantly. 'Delyth's here.'

'What? Now?'

'Yes. That's right. She called round with a beautiful cake.' Melanie hears Gareth's irritation rasp against her ear and, conscious Delyth is staring at her, she does her best not to reflect it in her expression.

'I don't believe it. After everything we agreed.' He is angry. Horribly angry.

'Yes, she just called over,' Melanie continues calmly for Delyth's benefit. 'We're just having a coffee in the garden. It's glorious here, I don't know what it's like—'

'Get rid of her!' Gareth bellows, cutting her off. 'Get fucking rid of her. Now!'

CHAPTER TWENTY-FOUR

The mountain of a man Melanie has been calling Mr Grizzly, invites her and Slinky into a cave-like room tacked onto the rear of the church. Swapping the bright day for the gloomy interior with its carbolic soap and damp root smell, she realises, not only is it little larger than her larder, but it's barely high enough for either of them to stand up in.

'Thanks for bringing him to see me.' The man who asks to be called John motions to the armchair. 'Sit. Please, sit.'

She does and, gripping her knees, tries to make as little contact with the moth-eaten material as possible. What's she doing here? She must be crazy. He could be anyone. He could be some knife-wielding madman. She shouldn't have come. It was stupid to let him persuade her. No one knows she's here. Nervously watching him play with the dog, Melanie sees him dig through the flabby-mouthed pocket of his jacket for the scraps he says he's been holding on to in the hope she would keep her promise.

'Paw.' He booms in the same voice that stopped her in her tracks on the beach.

Slinky needs prompting, needs a little tap against his front leg, but when, at last, he obliges, she can't help but smile.

'He remembers.' That deep baritone again. It fills the limited space much as he does. John raises his eyes in time to catch her smile and returns it. 'Putting on weight, I see.' He strokes the dog's well-covered ribs.

'It hasn't taken much. He was pretty thin.'

Melanie absorbs her surroundings. The condensation-wet walls that were she to spread wide her arms she could probably touch both sides at the same time. A shredded rug under her boots. A narrow camp bed with a mattress no thicker than a slice of bread, its sheets and blankets folded into a regimented square at one end. No ornaments, no photographs. His only luxuries, from the looks of things, is a single bookcase stuffed with old paperbacks. How does he manage? With no television, radio, internet, or any other of the twenty-first century trappings the likes of her and Gareth couldn't do without. *You can't live here, surely? Not with your bad arm and stiff leg. What's brought you down so low?* She longs to ask but curbs her curiosity and considers him instead. Sees that although his clothes are shabby, he is clean. His hair and beard both washed and brushed. His scant quarters orderly.

John reaches over to the rickety sideboard. The rasp of a match and he lights an outdated gas lamp. It instantly throws his giant shadow against the lumpy whitewashed walls. He transports the lit match to his makeshift kitchen, lights the camping stove, then blows it out, distributing its sulphur smell. His troublesome leg collides with a tin bucket that's been positioned in the centre of the room. Its clattering makes her jump.

'There's no need to be scared of me. I'm not angry with you.'

'No?' She looks up at a crack in the ceiling. At the yellow stain on the plaster where rainwater leaks in.

'No, I'm happy he's got a good home. As you can probably guess, I've barely enough to feed myself.' He wipes out two enamel mugs with the stiffened tail of his jacket. 'I was ashamed how thin he'd got.' John stoops to give the wagging Slinky the attention he craves.

'He's a great dog. My daughter's besotted with him. But,' she trails her gaze along a line of lager cans cooling on the only windowsill, 'I suppose you'll be wanting him back now.'

'And break your little girl's heart?' John gives her a lopsided smile. 'Nah, he's better off with you.' He fills a kettle from an old copper tap fixed to the wall. 'You'll have tea?'

She nods, watches him place the dumpy kettle on the blackened camping stove and adjust the flames.

'What have you called him?'

'Slinky. My daughter's choice. It's a character from *Toy Story*.' His look is blank. 'A Disney film, computer-animated?' A quick laugh, Melanie's anxieties ebbing. 'If it wasn't for her, I wouldn't know about it either.'

'I like it.' Kneeling, his good leg taking the strain, John strokes the dog. 'Slinky suits you, doesn't it, mate?'

'Why did you keep him chained up on the beach?' Melanie's bluntness seems to startle him, and he doesn't immediately answer.

'You've seen the sign on the gate?' he says, at last. 'They allow me to live here, just, but not with a dog. They wouldn't stretch to a dog.'

'Why didn't you just take him to the RSPCA?'

'Because...' John struggles to his feet. 'B-because h-he was all I had in the world.' He bursts into tears. The water in the kettle bubbling beyond his shoulder, filling the tiny space with steam.

Melanie doesn't move, at a loss to know what to do. Instinct tells her to comfort him, console him, but it also tells her to keep her distance.

'But it's worked out okay, hasn't it?' He rights himself, sniffs against a fraying cuff. 'You're only at the pub.' He tips back his head, narrowly misses the ceiling. 'It's not like he's gone miles away.'

'You know we're at the pub?' Melanie is surprised.

'You've bought the Monkstone. I followed you. After I saw you take—' He hesitates, rubs a hand over his beard. 'Slinky,' he says, testing the dog's new name. 'Then there was another day. I came to see you, but you weren't in. I had a good look round your garden, but I couldn't find him.'

'That was you, was it? I was up on the headland, I saw you.'

'Guilty as charged.' His eyes, dark beneath their dense brows. 'You're Gareth Sayer's missus.'

'That's right.' She twirls her wedding ring around her finger and realises she hasn't told John her name. 'I'm Melanie.' She taps the front of her parka.

'Melanie,' he repeats.

'So—' She clears her throat. 'How d'you know Gareth?'

'I was in his class at school.'

'Oh, right.' Melanie smiles but her smile is not returned this time.

'He definitely hit the jackpot with you.' John, awkward, looks away. 'But then he always was a jammy bugger.'

Lost in his thoughts, he appears to have forgotten the kettle and is oblivious to its high-pitched screaming. Melanie goes to lift it from the heat.

'Careful.' He steps up behind her. 'Hope you don't mind it black. I haven't any milk.'

'Fine by me.' She returns to the armchair. 'You work down the docks, don't you?'

'When my leg's not playing up.'

'What happened to you, if you don't mind me asking?' She

takes the mug he passes, noticing again his left arm hanging limp and useless by his side.

'Afghanistan. I served two terms.'

'Right. I see.' Except she doesn't see. How could she possibly understand the horrors he's lived through. 'Is that how you hurt your arm?'

'My arm and my leg. An exploding bomb. Well, they're the injuries you can see.'

Melanie nods, sympathetic to the subtext. 'You must've been terribly traumatised.'

'I was. *Am.* They debrief you, but it's not enough. You can't be unprogrammed. It's why I live here. It's too hard in a normal house, in a normal street. I'm like a coiled spring and I'm fearful I could blow at any moment. I tried, but I just don't fit in anymore. I lived with my sister, Nerys, when I first came back from Afghanistan. She means well but she doesn't understand and I didn't trust myself, not after what I saw, what I did... What I'm trained to do.'

'Oh.' Melanie stares at her tea, at a bubble travelling over the surface. What else can she say?

'It's not my sister's fault,' John is quick to explain. 'I was impossible. I couldn't stand the kids, all that noise and screaming. She couldn't cope with me, which is hardly surprising, I can hardly cope with myself.' He lifts then drops his good arm. 'But don't feel sorry for me, this is my choice. Being too close to people and their pity – I can't stand it.'

'I can sort of understand that.' She takes a tentative sip of tea.

'I can sort of tell.' His tea untouched on the sideboard.

'How did you end up here?'

'The vicar. Have you met him?'

Melanie shakes her head.

'Him and his wife, they're the kindest people. They let me

stay here for free. No questions asked, no pressure. It's a bit primitive, but they let me use the washroom in the vestry. And Mrs Evans—'

'The vicar's wife?'

He nods. 'She brings me meals. The odd box of teabags.'

'Lager too?' Melanie eyes the windowsill.

'Now and again.' He lowers his gaze. 'I need it sometimes. It helps me sleep.'

'They sound lovely people.' She purses her lips. She's sorry she mentioned the cans, it's none of her business. Always moved by the generosity of others, she wishes she thought to bring him the rest of Delyth's *Bara brith*. 'You make a nice cuppa,' she says to be kind.

'Good. Does that mean you and Slinky will come and see me again?'

'If you like?'

'I would. Very much.' His eyes are sad again.

'It's funny,' Melanie begins, 'but you frightened me to start with. Shouting like that in the graveyard, then again on the beach. You're pretty formidable.'

'That's my army training.' He laughs, for real this time. 'But you're not frightened of me anymore?'

No time to answer. Her mobile rings from inside her coat pocket.

'It's my daughter's school.' Melanie frowns before answering. 'Mrs Jenkins? Hello... Oh dear.' Her hand flies to her mouth. 'Oh dear. Oh no.' She pushes her alarm through her fingers. 'Yes, yes. I'll come right away.'

CHAPTER TWENTY-FIVE

'Slinky! Stop it.' The dog is about to cock his leg against one of her mother-in-law's garden gnomes.

'It's all right.' A laughing Bethan in the doorway of Plas Newydd is jigging Ffion in her arms. 'Mam's away.'

Melanie, breathing hard after her climb from the beach. 'I know, but she might still have her spies out.'

'How's Georgie? Did Hopalong say what it was?'

'Hop Along?' Melanie's turn to laugh. 'D'you mean Doctor Cassidy?'

Bethan nods. 'It's what Mam calls him – *Hopalong Cassidy* was some old TV programme... Some cowboy thing.'

'He reckons it was gastric flu. Said it's doing the rounds. He told me to keep her home.'

'But she's not with you?' Bethan kisses her baby's head.

'No. I kept her home Wednesday and yesterday, but she got up this morning, full of beans, saying she felt better and didn't want to miss more school.' She joins her sister-in-law on the step. 'I've just dropped her off.'

'Bit late. It's almost half ten.' Bethan steps aside to let Melanie into the hall.

'I've been walking the dog,' she explains as she bends to check Slinky's paws, decides he's clean enough for Bronwyn's fussy hall carpet.

'I thought you might've gone to see John Hughes again.'

'John Hughes?' Melanie removes her parka and pegs it up.

'Ex-squaddie. Lives in the churchyard.'

Melanie senses the weight of Bethan's gaze as it searches her face. 'Oh, him.' She unravels her scarf. 'How d'you know about him?'

'Saw you coming out of there the other day.'

'Wow. I didn't know I was under surveillance.'

'I just happened to be passing.' A flash of her sister-in-law's occasional sharpness.

Melanie shakes off her wellingtons, leaves them in the porch. 'No, I haven't seen him today.' She straightens her socks and pulls off her bobble hat. 'But Slinky used to belong to him, so I'll be taking him to see him now and again. Not that it's anyone's business.'

'I'm just saying to take care.' A little wriggle of the hips as Bethan repositions Ffion. 'This is a small town. People gossip.'

'Obviously.' On her walk along the beach, Melanie had been wondering about asking Bethan if Bryn would mind doing some maintenance on John's roof but changes her mind. 'You got the kettle on? I'm gasping,' she says with a forced cheeriness to hide her irritation.

'I like your hair. Are you letting it grow?'

'Not deliberately.' She runs her fingers through it. 'Just not got around to getting it cut.'

'Well, leave it. It suits you.' Bethan, poised to turn. 'Sian's here. She managed to get the morning off work to talk weddings.'

'Great, I hope she's got some dates in mind.' Melanie returns to her coat, pulls out a notebook. 'The diary's looking quite full.'

'You must be getting fit, all this walking you're doing.' Bethan leads the way along the hall, her blue slippers clashing with the mocha-swirl of carpet.

'It's the dog. He won't take no for an answer.' She unfastens Slinky's lead and they watch him trot daintily off to the kitchen.

'Hi, Mel.' The scrape of stool against the floor, and Sian rises to her feet. The movement threatens to topple a vase of tiger lilies over the sea of wedding magazines spread over the table. 'You look all rosy and fresh. Have you been walking?'

'She does look lovely, doesn't she?' Bethan, generous as always. It's difficult for Melanie to stay irked with her for long. 'She doesn't need make-up like the rest of us. She's one of those naturally beautiful people.'

'Get away, you two. You're making me blush.' She gives Bethan a jokey shove. 'Hi, Sian. Yes, a good yomp to wear him out. Nice day, windy but nice. How are you?'

'Excited.' Sian giggles.

'I bet. Many congratulations by the way. It's fab news about you and Tom.'

'Thanks, Mel.'

'Oh, I love this room.' She sighs and looks about her at the rustic wooden island, the matching units, the handsome Aga. The polka dot cotton curtains hanging above windowsills busy with robust houseplants. No fuss, no frills, just homely and welcoming. 'I told Bryn this is how I want our kitchen to look.'

'You stand more of a chance than me. You're paying him. I want him to give ours an overhaul, but he says he's too busy.' Bethan lays Ffion in her carrycot.

'D'you mind if I wash my hands?' Melanie steps up to the sink, peeks in on her baby niece. At her fluttering eyelids, the webbing of delicate blue veins. *Gorgeous,* she thinks, turning the tap.

'That's another thing I love about her,' Bethan whispers to Sian. 'She's so polite.'

'Lovely dog.' Sian, perched on board her stool again, reaches over her comfortable middle to stroke Slinky's black head. 'Bethan says you found him.'

'Did she?' Melanie turns the tap off and looks at her sister-in-law.

'Turns out he belongs to John Hughes.' Bethan avoids her gaze.

'Who's he?' Sian asks.

'He's a tramp. Lives in the churchyard.'

'He's not a tramp,' Melanie sets them straight. 'He lives at the back of the vestry.'

'He is a tramp, Mel.' Bethan, emphatic. 'With good reason, I know. Poor man.'

'Why poor man?' Sian is all ears.

'Ex-army. Injured out. Suffering from PTSD most probably. Screwed his mind up, I think, poor thing.'

'Why's he living at the back of the church?' Sian wants to know.

'It's a long story.' Melanie dries her hands.

'I bet it is.' Bethan says.

'And what? This John's cool with you taking his dog?'

Melanie pulls up a stool and sits down. 'He says he's grateful to us for giving him a home.'

'Huh,' Bethan grunts and pours a kettle-full of boiled water into the cafetière.

'You don't have to go to all that trouble for me, I'd be just as happy with instant.' Melanie ignores whatever the *huh* means.

'Yes, I do. I'm living the highlife with Mam away. Got some nice biscuits to go with it. I'm enjoying myself. Being here's way better than home.'

'Your place is lovely. What are you going on about?' Sian enthuses. 'Wish me and Tom could afford our own home.'

'Something will turn up.' Bethan sweeps aside the magazines and sets three dainty cups with matching saucers down on the table with a clatter. 'There's talk of extending the estate we're on. A percentage given over to affordable housing.'

'Yeah?'

'Bryn went to a council meeting the other day. Put a bid in for some of the work. But you better get your name down quick. If they do build, they're gonna go like hot cakes.'

'House prices have gone mental the past few years,' Melanie joins in. 'We wouldn't have been able to afford the pub had it not needed a complete overhaul.'

'Come off it. You and Gareth are loaded.'

The state of their finances is no one's business, and Melanie changes the subject. 'Thanks for choosing us to host your special day.' She turns to the bride-to-be. 'We'll make sure you have a wonderful day and not bankrupt you at the same time.' She takes a biscuit from the plate being offered to her. 'You'll be our first.'

'Guinea pigs then?' Sian laughs.

'Erm, I don't think so,' Bethan nips in. 'You're looking at a top-notch chef here. Mel was head pastry chef at the Savoy.' She pours the coffee with one eye on her baby.

'Sweet of you to brag me up.' She bites her biscuit in two.

'Wow. The Savoy. That's really something. Would you be able to make our cake?'

'Sure, I can.'

'Oh, that's brilliant.'

Melanie casts a look at her baby niece. 'It'll be your turn next.'

'I hope.' Sian is smiling broadly.

'Are you and Gareth going to have any more?' Bethan asks. 'Gareth said he wants to.'

'He said that?' Melanie nearly chokes on the last of her biscuit. 'He's said nothing to me.'

'No?'

'No.'

'You don't sound keen.' Bethan rakes a freckly hand through her auburn waves.

'That's because I'm not. How can we have a baby now? We've got a business to get off the ground.'

'People manage.'

'But I don't want to just *manage*.'

'I'm only telling you what Gareth said.'

'No, Bethan. Our priority has to be Georgie. She's been through enough upheaval already.'

'That's why a little brother or sister would be good for her.'

'Why do I feel like I'm under attack?' Melanie blinks back sudden tears. 'You're a bloody terrier, Bethan. When you get on the scent of something—' She stops, mid-flow, conscious of Sian shifting uncomfortably beside her. 'You want the truth? I'll give you the truth. I'm afraid to have more children. I can't trust myself. How can I trust myself?'

The awfulness of her question and all it implies spins through the disturbed silence.

'Don't get upset.' Sian puts a comforting arm around her.

'You're right, it's none of my business.' Bethan, flushing bright red, slips from the table under the pretext of checking on Ffion. 'I'm sorry, Mel. Me and my big mouth. I didn't mean to upset you.'

Melanie is unsure how much Sian knows of her history, so in the hope of easing the awkwardness, she changes the subject again. 'Have you a date in mind for your wedding?'

'Between Christmas and New Year?' Sian pulls back her arm.

'Great. I love winter weddings. The pub will be looking extra pretty too, with all the Christmas decorations.' Melanie sneezes.

'Oh, dear.' Bethan passes her a box of tissues. 'Hope you're not coming down with the dreaded lurgy?'

'No, it's not that.' She takes one, points to the spray of lilies. 'I'm allergic to those beauties.'

'I forgot to ask. How's little Georgie?' Sian says as Bethan moves the vase to the furthest window ledge.

Melanie blows her nose. 'She's much better, thanks. It was a hell of a shock when the school phoned me.'

'I can imagine.'

'Thing is, she's been feeling off-colour for a while. Complaining of tummy aches, off her food.'

'She probably takes after Gareth.' Bethan, seated again, takes a biscuit, then another. *You take after Gareth too*, Melanie thinks with a smile. 'He was always a picky eater. It used to drive our mam up the wall.'

'Georgie never used to be fussy. It could be a protest thing because we've only got a microwave to cook in.'

'But you said Hopalong didn't seem bothered?' Bethan, crunching.

'No. He said schools are incubators for all sorts. But I have to say, if it weren't for Delyth's baking, I don't know what she'd be living off. It's all she seems to want to eat.'

'Delyth? Delyth Powell. She bakes things for you?'

Melanie nods.

'You are honoured.'

'Am I?'

'Yeah. She keeps herself very much to herself. Definitely not one for mixing, let alone making cakes for people.'

'Really? Well, she often pops over. Is always bringing me and Georgie goodies.'

'Seriously, Mel, she doesn't bother with anyone. Does she, Sian?'

Sian shakes her head.

'Well, well.' Bethan eyes her. 'Fancy Delyth taking a shine to you. I'd take that as a big compliment. From what I can tell, she never lets anyone close, so it's nice she's found a friend in you. Life's not been much fun for her, poor thing.'

'Delyth's talked about things. Talked about her mother too.'

'Norah? Aye.' Bethan gives her a look. 'I've heard she's a worry. And that farm of theirs. I don't know how they've managed to keep it going. Place is crumbling to bits. Better for them if they moved into town.'

'Fetch a tidy sum,' Sian adds when Bethan is alerted to the grizzling Ffion. 'Amazing position, overlooking the sea like that.'

'Perhaps they like living there,' Melanie suggests. 'Maybe it suits them being out of it.' *Away from the gossips,* she thinks, but keeps this to herself.

'I suppose.' Ffion settled, Bethan rinses out the cafetière, spoons in more of Bronwyn's best coffee. 'It doesn't suit everyone, being in the thick of things.'

The thick of things – Pencarew? Melanie stifles a giggle. 'They'll probably sell up after Andrew's left home.'

'Andrew, leaving home? I can't imagine Delyth agreeing to that,' Sian interjects. 'She dotes on that boy something terrible.'

'I told her it would be a perfect time to go to college. To do something she wants to do.'

'Good for you. Coming up with something positive for her future. No wonder she likes you.'

'Gareth told me off. He says I'm too soft. According to him, Delyth isn't someone who wants help, she likes moaning and I'm to stay away from her.'

'He said that? Take no notice. He can be a funny bugger, my brother. It's Mam's fault, she spoilt him rotten.'

Sian laughs.

'I'm serious. He used to be a right arrogant sod when he was younger. All the girls fancying him, the boys in awe of him. I suppose it would go to your head.' Bethan refills the kettle, sets it to boil. 'Delyth spoils Andrew too. But he's such a nice kid. She's done a great job bringing him up.'

'It's no joke being a single mother.'

'Mother?' Bethan blurts. 'Oh, no, Andrew's not hers. He's not Delyth's.'

'Not Delyth's? I thought he was her son?'

'Whatever gave you that idea?'

'I thought she did. But I must've got the wrong end of the stick. Whose boy is he then?'

'He was Erin's.'

A flash of the marble headstone. 'She was Delyth's sister?'

A nod. 'She got herself pregnant when she was fourteen. Really shocking at the time.' Bethan transports the coffee to the table. 'The shame of it, you know, what with her being so young.'

'Must've been worse again with them being such a religious bunch?' An image of Delyth's gold crucifix comes to mind.

'I didn't know that.'

'Staunch Catholics.'

'News to me.' Bethan pushes the heel of her hand to the plunger and refills their cups.

'Erin died, didn't she?' Melanie asks.

'Yes. It was so sad. She was only twenty-three.'

'What happened to her?'

'It was a terrible accident. She fell out of an attic window up at the farm.'

'God, that's awful.'

'She had a bad drink problem, apparently. There were a lot of rumours doing the rounds at the time. But the goings-on up at Gweld Y Môr...' Bethan takes a breath. 'Well, it's always been a closed shop.'

'Did you know Erin? What was she like?'

'Nothing like Delyth, that's for sure.' A sharp laugh. 'She was super popular at school. Great fun, you know? And so pretty, the boys all loved her. No wonder Delyth was jealous.'

'She was jealous?'

'God, yeah. Delyth was such a plain little thing. She still is, really.' Bethan says this in a way that suggests the thought has just occurred to her. 'Even I was jealous of Erin.'

'Was she in your class?' Melanie can't remember the dates on the tombstone.

'Two years above. I looked up to her, she was so special. It's all so sad. She never came back to school. Didn't sit her GCSEs or anything. I heard she struggled terribly with the baby. Was depressed and unhappy about being stuck up at the farm. It's why she drank, I suppose.' Bethan gets up to check on Ffion again and smiles when she sees she is sound asleep. 'Erin tried to run away a couple of times. One time she ended up in a squat in Swansea. Doing drugs, people said. Police found her. Brought her back with her tail between her legs.'

'Please tell me she didn't take the baby there?'

'Well, Andrew wasn't a baby by then. But, no, she left him at the farm with her mam and Delyth.'

A whimper from beneath the table and three pairs of eyes go to Slinky who is lying stretched out under their feet. They watch him for a moment, see he's dreaming, his back legs moving.

'Look, he's riding a bicycle.' Sian chuckles.

'Did you never visit her after Andrew was born?' Melanie is keen to return to the topic of Delyth's sister.

'I tried, but I never got very far. Was never invited further than the front step. You'd know what I mean if you went there. It's a weird set-up.' Bethan shrugs and sips her coffee. 'It was like Erin suddenly changed from this fun-loving, popular kid, to someone who hid herself away.'

'Or *they* hid her away?' Sian drops the sinister suggestion into their conversation.

'Maybe.' Bethan considers the idea. 'There's a lot of Welsh families like that. Batten down the hatches when stuff happens. Specially them in the rural farming community.'

'And Delyth – what? She just stepped in to look after Andrew after Erin died?'

'Yes, she did.'

'That was good of her. I can't imagine many who'd put their lives on hold to bring up someone else's kid.'

'Hardly someone else's, Mel. Andrew is her nephew.'

'Even so.'

'Didn't the boy's father want to get involved?' Sian asks.

'Erin never let on who he was,' Bethan tells them. 'Doubt he even knew he was a dad.'

'Then it's doubly admirable of Delyth.'

'Some reckon she tried to legally adopt Andrew when Erin was still alive. Apparently, she got social services round. Claimed her sister wasn't a fit parent.'

'Bit mean.' Sian pulls a face.

'But didn't you say Erin abandoned him, and buggered off to Swansea to live in some squat?' Melanie reminds them. 'Well, I'd say Delyth was putting Andrew first – wouldn't you?'

'Yeah, she's always put that boy's needs above her own. She's a really good person.' Bethan, thoughtful. 'That's why it's odd about Gareth telling you to stay away from her.'

'Do either of you know what went on between the two of

them? And I'm not talking about some silly teenage crush because I know it's way more than that.'

'Why would you think anything went on?' Bethan, in a chair pulled up to the window, is unbuttoning her top to give Ffion a feed.

'Because of the way Gareth speaks to her... About her. I've never heard him be that nasty about anyone.'

'I can't imagine your Gareth being nasty.' Sian folds back the cuffs of a raspberry-pink jumper that clashes with her home-dyed hair.

'He is to Delyth.'

Neither Bethan nor Sian reply. Melanie looks past them. Out through the picture windows at a blustery day by the sea. Imagines what these two women would say if they knew what Delyth did in the pub kitchen.

'I know she used to wind him up at school.' Bethan, from her window seat.

'But that was seventeen years ago. Why would he still have a problem with her?'

'Have you asked him?' Bethan – the personification of motherhood – is haloed by the pale light dripping in through the window.

'I've asked them both, but they won't tell me,' Melanie explains. 'I forgot to tell you something – that first weekend we arrived, Delyth called round with a pot of jam and a home-made card.'

'Aw, that's nice of her.'

'It was. But what she wrote in it was strange.'

'Go on,' Bethan and Sian chorus.

'Something about her being good at keeping secrets.'

'Weird.'

'It is, isn't it?'

'She used to have the hots for Gareth at school, I told you

that. He used to think she was a pest. Well, you've only got to look at yourself to know the sort of girl he goes for, Mel. He's a good-looking guy, and little mousy Delyth, well, she wouldn't be his type at all.'

'But all that was when they were kids,' Melanie reasons. 'He should have more understanding now. She's not a love-struck teenager anymore.'

'You are quite a bit younger than Gareth and Delyth though, Bethan,' Sian chips in. 'You might not have been all that clued-up on the ins and outs of it. And if they were in the sixth form when you were just starting secondary school, they'd have seemed miles away.'

'I suppose.' Bethan rebuttons her top and settles Ffion in her carrycot again. 'But I saw the way she used to trail around after him. I wasn't too young to know that.' She reaches for one of Bronwyn's majolica earthenware bowls from a shelf and fills it with water for the dog. 'But it is strange for him to still be holding it against her now.' Sounds of Slinky's lapping. 'Maybe Gareth's just got a lot on his mind. Maybe he's just being protective of you.'

'What?' Melanie is bewildered. 'Why would I need protecting from Delyth? What harm could she possibly do?'

CHAPTER TWENTY-SIX

Barefoot and in her pyjamas, Melanie is brushing her teeth over the bathroom basin. She turns off the tap to listen to the weather throw its weight against the pub's exterior walls. The ferocity of the rain and wind is alarming. The pub feels like a ship out on a sea, churning like a washing machine. All day, the Met Office has been warning of gale-force winds and flash flooding along this stretch of Welsh coast. It's why Gareth isn't here. He's holed up in a hotel somewhere beyond Pwllglas and, with the local radio talking of roads into Pencarew still being impassable come morning, she's worried he may not make it home at all this weekend.

She rinses her mouth and stares at her reflection in the mirror. Her face – naked now she's removed the make-up she applied in readiness for Gareth's homecoming – looks sallow in this yellowy light. And refusing to be spooked by the fact she and Georgie are cut off and totally alone, she applies her night-time moisturiser in firm, determined circles. She is about to go to bed when the electricity fails. The bathroom light snaps off, and she is cast into a blackness so solid she could push her fingers into it. Lightning. A stark sheet of lilac falling between breaths illuminates the bathroom for a heartbeat. It is quickly followed by a violent crack of thunder that clatters against the roof, making her jump. She gropes forwards and stumbles onto the landing where the amplified rush of rain against the skylight makes her stomach bubble with apprehension.

Everything is pitch black, inside and out. She isn't sure what to do. Then the ring of her mobile summons her to the bedroom. She follows the sound and pushes on the open door, is guided through the dark to the bedside cabinet by its winking blue screen.

'Gareth.' She dives on it when she sees his name flag up. 'Oh, God, it's so good to hear your voice.' She slumps down on the bed. 'The power's just gone out here.'

'Are you okay? Is Georgie all right?' He sounds a long way away.

Another flash of lightning and Melanie sees the dog and that he's cowering. The startled whites of his eyes seized in the split-second brightness. She taps her leg to beckon him over but he refuses to move.

'Slinky is terrified. I haven't had the chance to check on Georgie.'

'Do it,' Gareth urges. 'Take me with you.'

'I can't see anything. Where did I put the torch?'

'Try the bedside cabinet. My side.'

She stretches over the duvet. Tugs open the drawer and fumbles its contents. 'Brilliant. Got it.' She switches it on and shadows bloom and swell against the walls. 'Let's go and check on Georgie,' she tells the dog and Gareth.

Within a few short steps, she reaches the door to her daughter's bedroom. A tentative shine of the torch shows Georgie is asleep with Bumble on her pillow. She is making little whimpering noises as if she might be chasing a rabbit across the illustrated pages of her Beatrix Potter book.

'She's fine,' Melanie whispers and transports her husband, via the phone, back to their bedroom. 'Out for the count, thank God.' She plonks down on the bed and pats the space beside her for the dog. But he still can't be persuaded. 'I miss you,' she tells Gareth.

'I miss you too.'

She hears him swap his phone to his other ear. The clunk of the handset against his wedding ring. 'What's your room like?'

'Lonely.' The word hovers between them. She hears him take a mouthful of something and swallow. 'Got a bottle of the house red to keep me company.'

A fierce beeping from her mobile. 'Oh, no.' She activates the dozing screen and stares at it. 'Battery's nearly out.'

'And nothing to recharge it with,' Gareth finishes. 'You'd better save whatever juice you've got left, Mel. For emergencies.'

'You're right.' She sighs. 'Oh, great, now the torch is dying on me.' Melanie bangs it up and down on her thigh. Watches it bounce into life, then fade.

'Switch that off too,' Gareth advises. 'You might need it.'

She does as he says and smiles through the dark. At what she carries of him in her heart. 'I'm going to need candles. Do you remember where we put them?'

'In the kitchen. Cupboard under the sink.' She hears him take another mouthful of wine. 'I put a box of them there. I think we've got another torch in there too.'

'Great. Okay. Look,' she assesses the battery indicator on her phone – twelve per cent, 'I'd better go. Love you.' Melanie hangs up and sits in the darkness. The dog is cringing at her calves. 'Are you frightened, boy?' She strokes his ears to the accompanying drumroll of thunder. 'We'll be all right.'

She yawns and drops down on the pillows, pulls the duvet over her. She should go and find the candles but, suddenly overwhelmed by tiredness, she closes her eyes and listens to the bang and clatter of the storm instead. This old building is a sounding box. Even on quieter nights, its rickety windows are no deterrent to the wind that pesters to be let inside. Often, lying in bed, unable to sleep, is when the night-time motorbike riders come. Their headlamps scribbling dazzling patterns across the ceiling. Young men in black leather, clanking with buckles. Their hair flying out behind like party streamers. They remind her of Dave. Her long-ago boyfriend. These lads from nearby towns come to race along the shoreline. She likes listening to the thrum of their engines, their shouts floating up from the shore. Feels less lonely to think of them scoring figures of eight in the sand just as she did astride Cassie's pony on Hunstanton beach before her grandmother died and her mother drank herself into oblivion. A nightmare that forced concerned neighbours to call social services, who had no choice other than to take Melanie into care.

There are no motorbike riders tonight. And tonight, she feels lonelier than ever. Another flash of lightning that is quickly replaced by an inscrutable blackness. A blackness she doubts she will ever adjust to. It presses its face to the window along with the pulsating rain as the cold moves in between the bedcovers and her nightclothes, extinguishing all sense of tiredness. Melanie holds her breath for the next clap of thunder that, when it comes, is the most violent yet. She sits up and reaches down to comfort the dog. Wide awake again, she puts her slippers on and ventures downstairs for a glass of wine in the hope it will settle her nerves. She switches on the torch. Barely there. She thumps it against her thigh again, and it bounces into life. It might last long enough to get her to the kitchen and find the candles if she makes a dash for it.

She is at the top of the stairs, about to descend, when a loud, rapid pounding on the front door reverberates up through the floorboards. Trepidation thumps in her throat. It is accompanied by a stark memory of the police officers who called to take statements after Sophie died. Wanting to hear her side of things. Wanting to know if she blamed the driver of the car, and if so, why wasn't she interested in pressing charges?

More knocking. Insistent, pervasive.

'Gareth?'

A spark of hope through her quivering unease. Has he made it home after all? The possibility is enough to galvanise her into action.

'I'm coming,' she hisses, fearful of waking Georgie. 'But he'd never have made it through this weather, he's miles away... Never mind the wine he's drunk,' she mumbles to herself, groping for the banisters, her pulse banging in her wrists. 'And if he did, he'd have used his key to get in... Not if I put the bolts on.'

Speaking in disjointed sentences, she trails her fear, along with the dog and the waning torchlight, down the stairs to the empty bar. Raising dust and grit under her slippers, she grabs the giant wooden pepper mill from its home with the serviettes and brand-new cutlery. Just in case.

'Hang on,' she calls through the frigid air. 'Just coming.'

She takes a deep breath before sliding the bolts and opening the heavy door. Rainwater spills along the guttering and Melanie stretches out, torch in one hand, brandishing the pepper mill in the other.

'Hello?' she calls, mindful of the dog trembling against her pyjama bottoms. 'Who's there?' A gust of wind drives hard, dappled rain over her feet. 'Is anyone there?'

The torch finally gives up the ghost. She can't see a thing, and is about to close up again when lightning charges the sky.

A face.

Clarified by the flare of light. Deathly pale and framed in wet hair hanging down like black rats' tails.

Delyth.

'Jesus!' Melanie yelps her surprise. 'You scared the shit out of me hammering the door like that. I thought you were the bloody police.' She steps back, but only enough to allow Delyth as far as the welcome mat. 'How the hell did you get here?' The telltale whiff of a recent cigarette. 'I thought the roads were all flooded.'

Delyth, dripping rainwater, switches on the torch she's

carrying and pokes its yellow beam beyond Melanie and into the darkened bar. 'I guessed the power would be down.' She shakes her wet hair off her face. The movement flicks cold water over Melanie and the dog. 'The houses from the school to here are out too.'

'How did you make it? Gareth's stuck out on the coast road. He can't get home. It's a bloody nightmare.'

'Please don't swear, Melanie.' Delyth's small voice competes with the downpour going on over her shoulders. 'I don't like to hear you swear. It doesn't suit you.'

Ticked off like a naughty child, Melanie is indignant. She should be the one calling the shots, setting the rules, not this woman who thinks it's perfectly acceptable to turn up here late at night and scare her half to death.

'I came to see if you were all right.'

'Why would we be a concern of yours?' She knows this is ungracious, but she can't hide her irritation at the way she's been so swiftly brought into line.

'Because we're friends?'

Delyth's way of moulding what ought to be a statement of fact into a question is clever. It shames Melanie into an apology. 'But it's ever so late.' She leans her redundant torch against a skirting board. 'I was going to bed.' Rainwater from Delyth's sopping coat drips to the floor. Melanie isn't going to get an answer. 'Well—' She moves to close the door, hoping the woman gets the message without the need to spell it out. 'Thanks for coming over, but you can see we're all right.'

'Oh dear, you've cut yourself?' Delyth points at the plaster on Melanie's foot. 'Are you all right?'

'That was ages ago.' She flaps away the unwanted concern.

'This place is a death trap.' Delyth tuts as she bends to retrieve something from the doorstep. 'I brought you this. Been promising Georgie a casserole for ages.' She passes Melanie a lidded Pyrex dish.

'What? Oh, no, you shouldn't have bothered... The stove's been fitted now.' Melanie's sputtered protest as she takes what's being offered to her. Its wet sides, still warm, are slippery in her hands. 'It's very kind of you, but did you need to bring it over now?' She can't believe it. What this woman must have risked to get it here. There's no way Melanie would have ventured out in this weather. 'They said on the news the roads were all flooded. How did you manage to get through?'

'I drive a Defender, Melanie,' Delyth says as if this explains everything.

'You'd better come in.' She steps aside then forces the door shut against the storm. 'Take that wet thing off, peg it up there.' Delyth does as she's told, and takes off her coat. 'Go on through, I'll find you a towel.' She turns, but without her own torch, she needs Delyth to lead the way. 'Not that I've anything much to offer you,' she mutters, following along behind with the casserole, the pepper mill tucked under an arm. 'I can't even boil a kettle.'

With Delyth's torch, Melanie locates the box of candles from under the sink.

'Matches? Where did we put them?'

'Here.' Delyth pulls a box from her trouser pocket.

Candle lit, Melanie places it on a saucer in the centre of the table. The spent match evokes the smell of Christmas as their shadows grow tall as giants against the walls.

'This is so kind of you,' she says again and lifts the lid of the Pyrex dish. 'Smells delicious, what's in it?'

'Beef and carrots and onions mostly.'

'Lovely. We'll have it tomorrow. Gareth should be home by then.'

'I didn't think he'd be able to get through in that silly car of his.' Delyth gives her opinion. 'That Porsche of his might be okay in the city, but it's hopeless round here.'

'I won't put it in the fridge.' Melanie talks to herself. 'They say to keep the doors closed in a power cut, don't they?'

'Not that your Mazda's much better.'

Melanie ignores the comment and retrieves what she hopes isn't one of her best tea towels.

'To dry your hair.' She passes it to Delyth who stands within arm's reach. 'Sit down,' she urges. 'Try not to trip up over him.' The dog's dark shape sneaks between them, before parking himself on the toes of Melanie's slippers. 'He's terrified. He's been stuck to me all night.'

Another blaze of lightning is followed by a distant rumble of thunder. The storm is finally moving away. The woman gives her head a vigorous rub, then jiggles her mane of hair back into place.

'Scary for you too. Here on your own.' Delyth tips forwards in her chair: a dark-winged moth drawn to the candle flame.

'I was fine until the electricity went.' She encourages Slinky onto his bed, shakes out some of his biscuits.

'How's things up at the farm? You're really remote out there.'

'Doesn't bother us. We've our own generator. You might want to think about getting one yourself. You don't want this happening when you've guests staying.'

'I'll have a word with Bryn.' Dog settled, Melanie looks about for a bottle of wine and finds two of the long-stemmed glasses they use on special occasions. *Is this a special occasion?* Hardly. '*Brrr.*' Melanie shivers and pours out the wine. 'It's cold in here.'

She retrieves her parka from behind the door and zips herself inside it. She sits down and notices Delyth hasn't touched her wine. At first, she assumes it's because she's driving and then she remembers her saying she loathed alcohol because of her mother's addiction. If anyone should be anti-drinking, it's Melanie – her own mother's ruinous dependency destroyed her childhood.

Hail against the window: a deafening round of applause. With it comes a cold draught of air that makes the candle flame duck and dance. Throwing liquid, shadowy shapes against the walls. They talk small talk to cover the boredom and Melanie yawns. She just wants her bed and the cool, white linen. She wants Gareth. He should be the one here with her, not Delyth.

She peers through the gloom at the dog. Sees he's asleep on his blanket. Such a darling, she loves that he appreciates his home comforts. John said that she had saved him. Melanie, lost in private thought, forgets herself and smiles. *Dear John...* she hopes he's keeping warm and dry in the vestry's back room.

'Mummy? Mummy?' Georgie calls to her from upstairs. 'Where are you?'

Melanie springs to her feet and grabs the saucer with its candle. 'I'm here, sweetheart.' She rushes into the bar. 'Don't worry, the electricity's gone down for a minute.'

'I'm frightened. Where's Slinky?' Georgie's voice filters through the guttering candlelight. 'I can't find him.'

'It's okay. He's with me. He was scared of the thunder.' A few purposeful strides and Melanie is at the foot of the stairs. 'You stay where you are, I'm coming up.' She calls to the dog, and together, with Delyth in tow, they head up to the flat.

'Do you mind waiting here? I won't be a minute,' she says to Delyth who hovers at her back. 'She had another of those tummy aches earlier. I hope it's not come back.'

'Poor Georgie. I should've brought some of that peppermint.' Delyth's face floats pale as a moon in the dimness. 'I'll bring some next time.'

'You got your torch?' Melanie's concern is for her daughter – she's only half listening to what this woman says.

Delyth answers by switching it on.

'Good, okay. I won't be long.' She leaves her at the top of the stairs. Walks away through the dark, haloed by candle flame: a pyjama and parka-clad Florence Nightingale.

After a quick rendition of Peter Rabbit, mostly from memory because there is little more than a flickering flame to read by, Georgie settles down. Happy the storm is easing, Slinky, now curled at the foot of her bed, is fast asleep. When Melanie emerges from Georgie's room, Delyth isn't where she left her. The landing is empty. But there's a muted light leaking from the living room and she carries the stubby candle towards it, pushes open the door to find her standing in a hoop of torchlight.

'Do you mind if we call it a night?' Melanie yawns and hopes her unwanted visitor gets the hint.

There is no resistance and Melanie escorts Delyth out into the rain. Waits on the step until the Defender reverses between the pillars and the red tail-lights disappear into the road. She learnt her lesson and won't risk a repeat of what happened the last time she thought Delyth had gone home. As she closes the pub door, Melanie thinks how Delyth's visits don't end. That like the vague waft of unhappiness she leaves behind with her cigarette smell, they hang in the air and eventually evaporate.

What was she doing in here? Melanie, upstairs in the living room again, extends her candle-holding arm out through the dark. The gambolling flame illuminates the contents of the last of the crates left to unpack and it has been rummaged through. Her books have been taken out and not put back properly. Blaming Georgie, or Gareth, but she knows this isn't true.

Georgie wouldn't be interested and Gareth hasn't been home for a week.

'Ouch!'

The sting of hot wax has her pull back her hand. This is a waste of time, she can't see enough anyway. But hang on, a thought nudging forwards – wasn't this the box Gareth's old school photo was in? And hadn't Delyth been especially interested in looking at it the first time she invited her inside the pub?

The electricity clicks back into life. Lights. Sudden, and stinging her eyes. Yes, she realises, adapting to the brightness – Gareth's photograph has gone.

CHAPTER TWENTY-EIGHT

The following afternoon, Melanie stands looking out through the tall glass patio doors. What a view. It never fails to amaze. She shifts her gaze beyond the beer garden to the white-tipped breakers. And higher, to slow, fat clouds, pink as corn cockles. Calmer now, the thunderstorm that raged all night has blown away inland.

Gareth has spent most of the time he's been home erecting a swing, and now that it's finished, he's lifting Georgie onto the blue plastic seat and pushing her higher and higher. Sounds of excited laughter find her through the glass. They have no idea she's here. Guilty pleasures. Watching them play together is one of her favourite pastimes. This is what fathers are. They are for the small things in life, the practicalities, such as tying shoelaces and stringing kites. A pang for her own father, and wherever he might be in the world, if indeed he is still in the world. Because Melanie has never met him. Her mother has always claimed she was too drunk to remember who he was, so he doesn't even have a name. It used to make her sad, imagining him looking up at the same moon she was and knowing nothing of her existence. But not anymore. Since meeting Gareth, she rarely thinks of her father at all. Her heart surges with love for her little family, and tears fill her eyes. Happy tears, grateful tears. Wiping them with a thumb, she backs away to go and prepare an early dinner. Which, thanks to Delyth, means there is very little to do.

'Mm, that smells good.' Gareth, fresh from the shower, nuzzles into Melanie's neck.

She puts down her paring knife and the cooking apple she's peeling, breathes in his aftershave.

'What are we having? I'm starved.' He peers through the glass doors of their newly installed kitchen range.

Melanie puts on oven gloves and lifts Delyth's Pyrex dish out onto the iron trivet.

'Delicious.' Gareth grins when she lifts the lid for him to see. 'What's in it?'

'Beef, I think.' Melanie, instantly realising her mistake, returns the casserole to the oven. 'I mean, beef,' she asserts. 'Yes, it's beef.'

'You don't sound sure.' He eyes her quizzically.

'Yes, I am. It's beef.' She resumes her peeling. 'And there's apple pie for pudding.'

'You spoil me.' Gareth kisses her. 'D'you want me to fetch Georgie?'

'Please.'

'I don't like it.' Georgie sucks on the end of her plait and turns her nose up at the serving Melanie ladles on her plate. 'What sort of meat is it?' She pushes the cubes of pork-like protein around with a spoon. 'Beef, darling. It's beef.' It's what Delyth told her, so she's sticking to it. 'What d'you think, Gareth? Is it okay?'

'I'm sorry, Mel, I'm with Georgie.' He pushes his plate away.

'I'm not eating anymore.' Georgie spits out what's in her mouth and makes a face in the upside of her spoon.

'Have you got a tummy ache again?'

Georgie shakes her head.

'Okay. Good girl.' Melanie puts her fork down. She has to agree with her family, the casserole is inedible. 'Well, who's for pudding?'

'Better not tell Delyth we didn't like her dinner,' Georgie says sweetly. 'Because we love her cakes and stuff, don't we, Mummy?'

'Delyth... what's that about Delyth?'

'No, sweetheart.' Melanie ducks her husband's question and replies to her daughter. 'There's no need to say anything because that would be rude.'

'You're not telling me Delyth cooked that?' Gareth's expression is darkening.

'I don't think savoury is her forte.' Melanie's stomach clenches. Stupid of her to think he wouldn't find out, and stupid to think he'd let it go if he did. 'But not to worry. I've made us a nice pudding, and Slinky will do the casserole justice, won't you, boy?' She rallies the dog. 'Dustbin that you are... Here you go.' And she slides the uneaten meals into his bowl.

'Do I have to have custard?' Georgie whines. 'I don't like custard.'

'Are you going to answer me?' Gareth isn't going to let this drop.

'How about ice cream?'

Georgie responds with whoops and cheers.

'Melanie!' Gareth secures her attention. 'Tell me.'

'Yes, yes, okay. Delyth made the casserole. She brought it over last night. I didn't tell you because I knew you'd go off on one.'

'Go off on one? I don't go off on one.'

'You do when that woman's name comes up in conversation.'

'So what? She brought it round. You didn't have to cook it.'

'I didn't want to waste it, it smelt perfectly lovely, you said so yourself.' Hands on hips, determined not to argue in front of their child. 'Would you like some pudding?'

He nods grimly. 'But only because you made it. I told you before, I don't want—'

'I know, Gareth, but please.' A sidelong glance at Georgie. 'I didn't ask her. She just turned up with it.'

'All right. I don't want to argue about it either. But honestly, Mel...' Whatever he was going to say, he keeps to himself.

Melanie lifts the apple pie out onto a plate. Hot and glossy from the oven, she cuts three slices. 'I don't want anything to spoil our time together. I honestly didn't think you were going to make it home at all this weekend.'

'Me neither.' His voice is gravelly. 'Hardly slept a wink all night.'

'Me neither.'

'Make up for it tonight?' He winks. 'Have an early one?'

Dinner over, Melanie rinses the plates and casserole dish and loads the dishwasher that was only plumbed in a day or so ago. She listens to her chattering daughter. A sound that should be coming from two little girls. Was what happened to Sophie punishment for what she and Gareth did to Elizabeth? Is that how it works? The unanswerable question is accompanied by a memory of those distressing phone calls early on in their marriage. Brandy-fuelled tirades in the night. Then the solicitor's letters, fake and threatening, that Elizabeth would type out and push through their letter box. Threatening what? Melanie can't remember, but she remembers feeling sorry for her. Although not sorry enough to let her inside the time she turned up while Gareth was at work, shortly after the twins were born. A wreck of a woman, flabby and wrung out. There was nothing of the girl in the photograph Bronwyn keeps of her. But Elizabeth would look wrung out, wouldn't she? She had lost the man she loved, along with any chance of having a family with him. It was why Melanie paid for her taxi home. Why she took two twenty-pound notes from her purse and pushed them into her husband's ex-wife's hand, telling her she was sorry and that she hadn't set out to hurt her. Elizabeth stopped hounding them after that, and according to Bronwyn, she immersed herself in her academic world and has been there ever since. Not that Melanie can relax, the fear that there is yet more trouble to come – whether from Elizabeth or elsewhere – has never gone away. And she suspects she will spend the rest of her life holding her breath for it.

'Mummy... Daddy!' Georgie shrieks. 'It's Slinky, look! He won't get up. His mouth's gone all bubbly.'

'What?' Melanie, snapping back to the present, rapidly dries her hands and spins to find the dog slumped against the legs of Gareth's chair. 'What's going on? What have you done?' she shouts at her husband and child, dropping to her knees to cradle Slinky's head in her hands.

'It's not me,' Georgie shouts back.

'No, we've not done anything.' Gareth is beside her on the floor. 'It's that horrible stuff Delyth gave you. I told you something was wrong with it.'

CHAPTER TWENTY-NINE

Melanie, Gareth and Georgie, tacking their way across the darkening car park, still in their slippers, push through the swing doors. The waiting room at the veterinary surgery is crowded with every conceivable pet. Melanie's shoulders ache under the weight of the dog who lies like a colossal baby in her arms. Refusing all offers to carry him, she babbles nervous nonsense to the woman at the desk.

'If you could hang on for me, just a minute.' The receptionist sees the situation. 'I'll get someone to look at him right away.'

Within seconds they are guided into a consulting room.

'You best wait here with Georgie. Just in case,' Melanie says before she and Slinky disappear beyond a rubber-coated door.

She lowers the dog, frothy-mouthed and shaking, onto the examination table. A tall, bearded man in a white coat snaps on a pair of latex gloves and sets about examining him. Melanie shifts from foot to foot in the silence. Her anxiety intensifying amid the antiseptic smells and posters warning of lungworm and ticks.

'It looks to me, Mrs Sayer,' the senior partner lifts his sombre gaze to hers, 'like he's been poisoned.'

'Poisoned?' She shouts her alarm.

'I believe so.' His tone is heavy. 'Can you tell me what it is he's eaten, where he's been?'

'He's not been anywhere. Only the usual. A walk on the beach, or was it up on the headland?' The fierce lights are making her eyes hurt. 'Hang on, I remember now.' She strokes Slinky's side. His violent convulsions are frightening her. 'We had to stay on the beach today, didn't we, boy?' she says to the dog. 'It was too windy, really windy. After the storm, I suppose.' She knows she's rambling, that this is useless information. 'But that was hours ago, and I watched him all the time. I threw his ball for him, that was all.'

'Which beach was this?'

'Pencarew. We live in Pencarew. Me and my husband. We've bought the Monkstone Arms... we're in the process of—' She closes her mouth, realises this too is unnecessary information. 'Yes, the beach at Pencarew.' She focuses on the top of the vet's head as he takes Slinky's temperature; sees his dark hair is threaded with grey.

'Now, tell me. What's he eaten?' The vet rootles the cupboards behind him, returns with a syringe of something in his hand.

'He had his food. Burns food.'

'Good. Nothing wrong with that.' The vet strokes Slinky's juddering body, then administers the injection of clear liquid into his neck without explaining what it is. 'What else?'

'Erm,' fingers against her mouth, then remembering, 'Oh, yes, some casserole. Nothing wrong with that either, is there?'

'There could be. What was in it?' The vet, calm and steady, strokes the dog.

'I don't bloody well know,' she snaps: panicky, forgetting

herself. 'I'm sorry. I didn't mean to shout. But can't you do something? Stop him shaking?'

'The casserole? Mrs Sayer,' he pushes.

'I don't know what was in it. A friend made it.' Babbling again. 'But me and my family didn't much like it. And Slinky, well, you know what dogs are like? We gave it to him. Oh, please, do something. You've got to help him.'

'We'll do all we can. We'll keep him in overnight. See how he responds.' The vet has finished injecting whatever it was, and her dog goes limp in her hands.

'He's going to be all right, though, isn't he?' It is Melanie's turn to shake. 'Y-you see, m-my husband, our little girl...' She begins to cry. 'We've grown ever so fond of him, and-and we've-we've only... Sophie... Not long ago. We can't lose Slinky too.'

'We'll do our best, Mrs Sayer. But you must prepare yourself for the worst. The prognosis is not looking good.'

'Oh, please... *please*. You can't let him die. You can't let him die.' She wails, grabbing the sleeve of his white coat.

The vet takes her hands in a way you might a hysterical child, squeezes them gently and returns them to her.

'What would be good,' he says, 'is if you could bring us a sample of what he's eaten... a sample of the casserole. It would greatly help his chances if we could analyse it. We'd know what we're dealing with then.'

'Right,' she agrees, grateful to have something constructive to do. 'We'll nip home. Be back as soon as we can.'

She rushes out into the waiting room, to a sombre Gareth and a teary-eyed Georgie. Forgetting – as her husband presses his foot to the floor of the Mazda, skipping at least one red light – that any remnants of Delyth's casserole have either been eaten by the dog or washed away.

CHAPTER THIRTY

November. A time of rotting windfalls and the swallows long gone. Melanie identifies autumn's melancholy breath when she drops her passenger window to look out on the town netted in a fine sea mist. The Co-op car park, with its stunning sea views, is enveloped by low cloud and is surprisingly full for a Sunday morning. Gareth, already in a foul temper after the shock of the evening before, must do a double lap before he finds a parking place.

'We could drive to Pwllglas and make a day of it?' Melanie suggests, in the hope of lifting the mood.

'I'm too knackered to do much more than this.' He yawns.

'Might have been better than moping around waiting for the vet to ring. And you won't like it in here,' she warns, quickly doing up her window before he cuts the engine. 'There's never much left on Sundays.'

'It'll have to do. We only need a few bits.' Gareth secures the handbrake. 'I can hardly keep my eyes open.'

'Terrible night.' She checks her mobile for any news.

'I hardly slept a wink.'

'That's two nights on the trot.' Melanie's turn to yawn. 'Are you going to be okay for work tomorrow? For the drive back, I mean.'

'Going to have to be.' Gareth sighs and undoes his seatbelt, but he still doesn't move.

'It's been one thing after another.' Melanie swivels in her seat to check on Georgie, her parka rustling in the tight metal void of the car. 'You're looking better, sweetheart.' And she is, her dimpled cheeks are swirled with pink. 'How are you feeling?'

'I'm okay,' Georgie says, her eyes like two wet pools. 'I just want Slinky home.'

'I know you do. So do I.' Melanie reaches behind her, rubs her daughter's legs to jolly her along. 'We should hear something soon.'

'D'you think it was the casserole that made him sick, Daddy?'

'Course it was.' Gareth rubs an irritable hand over his dark stubble. 'What else could it be?'

'We don't know that.' Melanie frowns at him. 'Not for sure.'

'Don't we?' His fierceness makes her jump. 'What other explanation is there? One minute he's right as rain, the next, wallop.'

'But if it was the casserole, it doesn't mean Delyth did it deliberately.'

'Course it was sodding deliberate.'

'That's one hell of an accusation.'

'I keep telling you that she's dangerous, that she's a nutter. But you won't listen.'

'For goodness' sake.' Melanie's conscious that Georgie's listening and wishes they could have this conversation out of her earshot. 'Have you heard yourself? That woman couldn't hurt a fly.'

'You just can't see it, can you? You're so gullible. Always

seeing the good in people. It's a-a,' he bites his lip, and she can tell it takes everything he's got not to swear again, 'it's a flaming annoying habit. Cos you're forgetting something crucial here—'

'And what's that?'

'That casserole was meant for us.'

Melanie considers this cold, bald fact for a moment. Pretends it doesn't bother her. 'Oh, she wouldn't.' A vehement shake of her head. 'She wouldn't.'

'Yes, Daddy, Delyth's our friend,' Georgie pipes up. 'She wouldn't want to hurt us.'

'I'm not so sure.' Gareth slides his gaze to Melanie. 'How much more proof d'you need?'

'Gareth, please?' She really doesn't want to have this discussion in front of their child. 'We need to wait, hear what the vet has to say. Georgie's right, Delyth's our friend. Let's not get carried away, yeah?'

'The vet said poisoned, didn't he? Well, that casserole was poisoned.'

Gareth is right, the vet did say poisoned, Melanie thinks, but fearful of stoking his fire, says nothing.

'I know she's trying to poison us.' His eyes are hard. 'Why else has Georgie been having these tummy problems all of a sudden? You thought about that?'

'What?' Melanie stares at him – has he finally lost the plot? 'I've taken her to see Dr Cassidy. Twice. I'll make another appointment next week. He's talking about running some allergy tests, he's as flummoxed as we are, but he doesn't think it's anything serious.'

'Blasted doctors. What do they know? I'll tell you what's wrong with her, shall I?' Gareth smacks his palms against the steering wheel. 'It's those cakes that woman brings round.'

'Oh, come on. I eat them too, and I'm okay,' Melanie tries to reason. 'Look, Gareth, I'm not having this conversation now.' A glance at their daughter. 'Please, we need to wait. We need the facts.'

'And we'd have had them by now if you hadn't washed the evidence away.'

'Oh, I wondered how long it would take you.' She unclips her seatbelt, tips herself out of the car. 'That's it, put the blame on me.' She talks to the back of his head while she opens the rear door to help Georgie from her car seat. Gareth reaches behind him for his sweater, tugs it on over his head. Whatever else he says is lost to the muffle of mouth on material.

'Right then, let's get this over with,' he says, locking the car and jogging away through the hiss of the supermarket's automatic doors. Pausing to collect a basket on the way.

'Don't worry, Slinky's going to be fine.' Melanie fastens Georgie into her silver puffer jacket. 'I don't know why Daddy's got such a problem with Delyth. She's a nice person, isn't she? She's been very kind to us.'

'I like her.' Georgie squeezes out a smile.

'There we go then. We're not going to listen to any more of your daddy's nonsense.'

Georgie holds out her hand for her mother to take, and they look up at the unexpected rhythmic flap of a heron as it passes low overhead. A bird so huge, it momentarily blocks out the light.

Melanie grips Georgie's hand and jigs it up and down. 'Let's go and get something for dinner. Something nice and easy.' At the entrance, Melanie puts a ten-pound note into the poppy appeal box, takes three poppies. 'What d'you fancy?' she asks, pinning one to Georgie's lapel and one to her own.

'Pizza. Can we have pizza?'

'Let's go and have a look.'

———

They find Gareth halfway down the bread aisle, flapping his list. Melanie pockets the third poppy, deciding now isn't the time. The store is still dressed for Halloween and Melanie trails the strings of skulls and plastic spiders journeying the polystyrene ceiling tiles that nobody's taken down. The usual piped medley of eighties music is more irritating than usual, although it won't be long before it will be wall-to-wall Christmas jingles, she thinks gloomily, unable to decide what's worse.

'Would you credit it?' Gareth, too loud, rubs a hand over his hair. 'They haven't even got a wholemeal loaf. It's totally useless in here.'

'I did warn you. They always run out of stuff on Sundays.' Melanie surrenders Georgie's hand and squats to check the lower shelves. 'They've got a sliced Hovis. Thick cut. That'll do, won't it?' Upright, she shakes it under his nose before dropping it into the basket.

They turn their heads to the sound of clanking and see a huge trolley roll towards them.

'Can I be of any help?' the tiny voice from behind it asks. 'What are you looking for?'

Gareth spins on his heels. 'You? What are you doing here?'

'I work here.' Delyth, swamped by her Co-op uniform, is filling shelves from the large metal trolley that is an obvious struggle to manoeuvre.

'Hi, Delyth.' Melanie smiles at the woman who looks as vulnerable as a child on her first day of school.

'Useless shop.' Gareth sulks, picking up a tin of something, inspecting the label, then slamming it back down.

'If you tell me what you're looking for, maybe I could help.' Flicking her long black hair over her shoulders, Delyth returns Melanie's smile.

'I think you've done enough, don't you?' Gareth growls at her.

'Things are a bit fraught at the moment, Delyth.' Melanie steps between them, keen to explain.

'Too right.' He drops his face dangerously close to Delyth's. 'Since you poisoned our dog.'

'Poisoned your dog?' Delyth looks blank. 'That's horrible, what are you saying?' She lifts her eyes to Melanie: helpless, pleading.

'That casserole you made us.' Gareth swings the shopping basket at the end of his arm: a pendulum in the dangling moments it takes Delyth to answer.

'Casserole?'

'Yes. It was so disgusting, we fed it to the dog. And now, thanks to you, he's on a drip at the vets and is probably going to die.'

At the word *die*, Georgie's face crumples and she bursts into tears.

'Now look what you've done.' Melanie bends to comfort her. 'Daddy didn't mean it, sweetheart. Slinky's going to be just fine, you'll see.'

'We don't know that,' he says, then returns his attention to Delyth who cowers and backs away.

'I'm sorry about this,' Melanie says to her. 'Gareth's convinced—'

'Stay out of this,' he warns her before refocusing his anger on Delyth: 'You meant for us to eat that stuff. It's us you want dead.'

'I don't know what you're talking about?' Delyth scans the aisle, nervously fretting the hem of her grey tunic.

'Liar!' Gareth shouts. 'Try telling that to the police.'

'The police?' Her voice is small and pleading. 'What are you talking about the police for?'

'Don't come the innocent with me. You know what you did.' Gareth is oblivious to the small crowd of shoppers that have gathered to watch. But Melanie isn't and, abandoning her daughter, steps up beside him.

'Stop it. Stop it. We don't know this is what happened, not yet.' She tugs his arm, but he throws her off, determined to have his say.

'You can't stand it, can you?' Gareth to Delyth. 'You can't stand to see other people happy. You were a miserable cow at school and you're even more of a miserable cow now.'

'Gareth!' Melanie, consoling Georgie, who is visibly distressed by her father's behaviour, shouts at him from the sidelines. 'Why are you being like this?' His aggression frightens her. 'Delyth's done nothing wrong. Not deliberately. For goodness' sake, stop it. Leave her alone.'

Melanie watches Delyth. Wonders why she doesn't kick back and defend herself. There's no way she would let someone speak to her like this. But not Delyth. It seems her nature won't permit her to be bold. Not about this. With him. Because she's certainly been bold enough with Melanie on occasion. Perhaps Delyth thinks she can win him round. That this show of self-effacing goodness will ultimately disarm him. But why would she want to win him round? It's obvious Gareth despises her – he makes no attempt to disguise it. And now, with whatever might have happened to the dog, he feels he's got a legitimate excuse to treat her badly. *What does she want?* Melanie's silent question. Is she as besotted with him as an adult as she was as a teenager?

Delyth grips her gold crucifix, her large, dark eyes welling with tears.

'Look at her.' Gareth challenges the shoppers who've gathered to see what the fuss is about. 'Playing the sympathy card. It's pathetic.' A breath. 'Convincing though, isn't she?

She's always been good at playing the poor-little-me. But it's all a bloody act.'

Someone must have fetched the manager, because he is suddenly amongst them, threatening to remove Gareth from the premises. Not that Melanie thinks he is equipped to carry out his threat. He only looks about sixteen, with his spots and bum fluff; he's certainly no match for her burly husband when he's as pumped-up as this.

Delyth is sobbing openly now. Melanie reaches out to Gareth but again he shoves her away. Delyth sees it, the crowd of shoppers see it too. And they whisper about him behind their hands.

'I'm sorry, sir, but we're going to have to ask you to leave if you don't calm down.'

'Calm down!' Gareth jabs an angry finger. 'I'd like to see how any of you lot would react if she'd tried to poison your family.'

The store manager gives Delyth a questioning look. She returns it with a shrug, her mouth wobbling through her tears.

'Sir, I do have to warn you,' the young man tries again, 'if you don't do as I ask, then I will have to call the police.'

'Good,' Gareth, forceful, 'it'll save me from having to.'

'I don't think you're listening, sir. The abuse of staff is something we take very seriously.' The store manager briefly closes his eyes and Melanie can tell he knows he's out of his depth but perseveres anyway. 'So, if you would please—'

'It's okay.' Melanie does what he can't, and grabs hold of her husband. Feels the tautness of his bicep, the power of his body beneath his pullover. And perhaps for the first time, understands his potential for violence. 'We're going.'

Holding Georgie's hand and steering Gareth, she marches them out of the store. Dumping the basket with the sliced loaf they will need for breakfast at the exit, they stride out into the blustery car park.

'Have you completely lost your mind?'

'No. I'm just saying what needs to be said.' Gareth stomps away, forcing Melanie and Georgie to run to catch him. 'She riles me up.' He clenches his jaw. 'Standing there, all-all... she makes me sick.'

'What you did, it was horrible. Horrible,' she shouts. 'Gareth, stop. Listen to me. Listen to me. You can't go hurling accusations around. You made her cry. You're nothing but a bully.' Melanie clutches Georgie's hand and feels like crying herself.

'Ouch, Mummy.' Georgie grizzles. 'You're hurting me.'

'Am I? Oh, dear, I'm sorry.' She loosens her hold and looks behind her at the store's entrance. Sees Delyth hovering by the buckets of flowers. 'She's there. Look. She's followed us out. Go back and apologise to her.'

'*Apologise?*' Gareth turns when he reaches the car, his expression indignant.

'Yes.'

'No way. She's probably enjoying this – *us*, arguing.'

Melanie drags an exasperated hand through her hair.

The mist they woke to has blown away to reveal a sparkling blue day and something, probably the dark undercarriage of a seabird, has her looking up to the vast bow of the cliff. She sees John, alone on one of the benches, staring out to sea. When he turns his head, she forgets herself and lifts an arm to wave in his direction. Not that he signals back and, feeling an idiot, she tells herself he was too far away to see her.

'Who are you waving at?' Her husband's question is automatic.

'No one.'

Gareth gives a cursory nod before starting up again. 'She's

jealous of us, that's her problem. She wants you to leave me, so she can have me all to herself.'

Melanie searches his face for the irony that isn't there.

'Why the hell would she want you? You're awful to her.'

'Well, all right then.' Gareth rejigs his argument. 'She wants to split us up. She wants to destroy our marriage.'

'Is that right?' Melanie laughs; brittle, derisive. 'I don't think you need anyone else's help in that department, I think you're managing perfectly well on your own.'

'She is.' He insists, wringing his hands. 'She wants to split us up.'

Melanie glances around, is grateful no one from the town is close enough to hear the contents of their argument.

'Why can't you see her for what she is?' Gareth again.

'I don't know who you are anymore. You're frightening me.'

'And you're frightening me.' His look is more pitiful than angry now. 'You're so gullible. You're everyone's bloody friend.'

'Why are you being so horrible? I've not done anything wrong.' Melanie fights back tears. 'What is it with you and that woman? Did you two have something going once?'

'With that?' he spits. 'Don't be ridiculous.'

'Ridiculous now, am I? Why? Because I refuse to buy the drivel you keep feeding me? I'm not stupid, Gareth, I know something's gone on.'

He says nothing. He simply turns and walks to the rear of the car park. Hands in his pockets, eyes fixed on the sea.

'If you don't tell me, I'm sure Delyth will,' Melanie threatens, following on behind with Georgie. 'I could tell she wanted to talk.' A burst of the blood on the kitchen floor, the cold feel of the steel blade. She winces at the memory. 'Delyth was going on about some bloke who'd ruined her life. That was you, wasn't it?' Melanie accuses, trying to remember if this is what the woman said. 'Yes, I get it now,' she states, even though she plainly doesn't. 'She was on about you, and that's what all this is about.'

'Don't be so bloody stupid.' He turns and marches back to the car. 'D'you honestly think someone like me would've been interested in her?'

'You don't half think a lot of yourself.' She cradles Georgie's head in her hands. She's given up trying to curb his bad language, but she worries for their daughter and wishes again that they could have had this argument away from her.

Gareth unlocks the Mazda, bounces the keys in his hand: dice he is about to cast. 'Look, I don't know what it is, I just can't stand her.'

'You want to get a grip. You're not in the playground anymore.' She senses the weight of his gaze but refuses to receive it. 'We're going to be opening up for business in a month. Do you think people are going to want to patronise us after that performance? Half the town was in there today; in case you didn't notice. And you were vicious, Gareth. Vicious.' The accusation is heavy, too heavy for the wind shuffling up from the shore to disperse. 'This is a small place, word gets about.' She echoes the warning Bethan gave her about her friendship with John. 'You can't go behaving like that. What sort of example are you setting our child?' She bends to guide Georgie into the back of the car and fastens her seatbelt. 'Are you even listening to me?'

From her position in the front passenger seat, Melanie looks sideways at her husband: a man she is struggling to recognise. Gareth drums his fingers on the steering wheel and she comes to realise he is a person of empty gestures. His habit of jangling loose change in his pocket, the way he clears his throat. Who is he? – this man she married and fell in love with. The father of her child.

'You can't blame me for being suspicious,' she says finally.

'Suspicious of what?'

'Of the two of you.' Melanie follows his gaze as it travels the horizon. 'Because something's gone on, you've definitely got history.'

'She tried to poison us, Mel.' His tone is reasonable. 'Isn't that enough?'

'No, it isn't. Not when we don't know that for sure.' She squints through a sudden shaft of sunlight spearing the windscreen. 'There's something more going on here, I know it.'

'You know it, do you?' The look is nasty.

'Okay,' she says, relenting a little, wanting to give him the chance to redeem himself. 'I know she can seem odd sometimes.' Another flash of the blood against the floor tiles, the raw cuts on the tender insides of Delyth's arms. 'But she's got a good heart, she's been—'

'I want you to stay away from her.' Gareth cuts her off: a boulder thrown into a stream. 'I mean it, Mel. You've got to stay away.'

She turns her head, stares out at the last of summer's leaves being blown around the car park. Thinks again how they shouldn't be having this discussion in front of their child.

'You telling me to stay away from Delyth's not going to work. Being like you were just now, it's only making me more suspicious. Why won't you just tell me? What are you hiding?'

Her questions go unanswered and, wary of pushing him anymore, the three of them sit in frostbitten dumbness.

Then Melanie's mobile rings. The violence of it splinters the silence.

She looks at Gareth, then at Georgie, and pulls it from her coat pocket. Stares at the illuminated screen in alarm.

'It's the vets.'

She closes her eyes and takes a deep breath before answering the call.

CHAPTER THIRTY-ONE

'Mrs Sayer?' The voice, a young woman's, competes with canine whimpering and yelps. 'It's Sara, from Bishop Lane Vets.'

'Hi, Sara.' Melanie tries to keep the trepidation that's hammering in her chest out of her voice. 'Have you got news for us?'

'Slinky's fine, Mrs Sayer.'

'Sorry, you what?' Melanie's unsure if she heard correctly and activates the loudspeaker for them all to listen.

'Slinky's finally out of the woods. He's off his drip and doing fine.'

'Oh, that's wonderful news.' She whips her head to Georgie who is squealing and clapping her hands. 'Thank you so much.'

'Yes, he's breathing normally, and he's comfortable.'

'Oh, thank goodness.' She exhales, looks down at Gareth's hand that has found its way onto her thigh. She squeezes it and grins at him.

'Yes, Mrs Sayer,' the voice is solemn, 'your dog was lucky to survive.'

'W-was it... poison?' Melanie is frightened to ask.

'Of a sort, yes.'

'From the casserole?'

'No, nothing you fed him.'

'Right,' she says, and sees Gareth smack his skull back against the headrest.

'Test results show he ingested some algae. A blue-green algae that's found in stagnant water. It can be lethal.'

'But how? How's that possible?'

'It's been traced to a pond at the north end of Pencarew Bay.'

'A pond?' Melanie struggles for breath. 'I didn't know about any pond.'

'It wouldn't usually be a problem, but with it being milder than normal for the time of year, the algae, well, it contaminated the water. There've been other dogs showing similar symptoms. We've been inundated.'

'How dreadful.' Melanie frowns.

'It is. We've had problems like this before. Stagnant water isn't a hazard many people appreciate. And as a dog owner, you do need to be aware.'

'Right, okay, I've never heard of that before.' Melanie removes her hand from Gareth's and presses it to her chest. 'So, just to make sure, it wasn't anything he ate, nothing we gave him?' She lifts her eyes to Gareth's, wanting him to hear, to understand. 'The thing is you see, we rather jumped the gun. Blamed the friend who made us the casserole.' She is enjoying this – rubbing it in.

'No, it was definitely the algae,' Sara confirms. 'Cyanobacteria. That's the proper name for it.'

'Okay, good. I'm just glad we didn't call the police because as you say, no one's to blame.' This is for Gareth's benefit. 'It's easy to jump to the wrong conclusion in the panic of it all.'

'I suppose so,' the veterinary nurse agrees.

'When can we come and fetch him?'

'Ooh, let me see, I think we'll want to observe him for a little longer... Shall we say midday tomorrow?'

'That's great. Thank you so much for calling and for everything you've done for him.'

'It's a pleasure. We'll see you tomorrow.'

Melanie hangs up. Returns the phone to her pocket.

'Right,' she says to Gareth. 'You're going to have to go and apologise to Delyth. Go on,' she pushes, sensing his reluctance. 'She's still standing outside.'

Gareth unclips his seatbelt and gets out of the car.

Melanie watches him in the wing mirror. She might not be able to hear what is said, but going by his frantic hand gestures, she's certain he's raising his voice. She admires Delyth – her composure, the dignified way she holds her ground – while Gareth undoubtedly dishonours himself yet again.

'What did you say to her?' she asks when he's back in the driving seat.

Not that he answers. His mouth set in a thin, grim line as he reverses out of the parking space. Thinking how this demonstrates how little she knows him, Melanie is too scared to demand that he tell her.

CHAPTER THIRTY-TWO

Over a fortnight later, on a day when winter has well and truly blown in, Melanie, home from taking Georgie to school and a walk with the dog who has fully recovered, sets about tidying the kitchen. A small smile curves her lips as she appreciates the gleaming walls and marble-topped units. Bryn's team have worked magic turning this from a bomb site into the luxurious space it now is. With only the extractor fan to fit and the electric fly-zapper to secure to the wall, everything is finished in here. She counts the weeks until Christmas, lists the jobs still left to do in readiness for opening and realises she is well on track. There is nothing to fret about.

Tantalising smells of warm chocolate and sweet amaretto remind her of the second batch of biscuits. The ones she's made for John. With Delyth conspicuously absent since that unpleasantness at the Co-op, Melanie's been putting in some practice of her own. And she's been busy. Pleased with this morning's creations, she hopes these sugared offerings will lift John's heart. Such a kind and gentle man, she likes spending time with him. Qualities she loved in Gareth that, since moving here, seem to have evaporated.

John's room is smaller than Melanie remembers and the whitewashed stone walls look wet to the touch. With all that winter still has to bring, she worries what effect the damp might be having on him. She heard him coughing the last time she was here and it doesn't sound much better today.

'D'you want to take your coat off?' John fills the metal kettle from the only tap while Slinky lies down on the frayed rug.

'No, it's okay.' She removes her gloves, rubs her cold thighs through her jeans to generate some warmth. 'How d'you manage? You don't seem to have any kind of heating in here.' Bolder today, she crosses from one side of the room to the other, counting it takes less than five paces before butting up against his wretched little camp bed.

'I like the cold. It makes me feel alive. After the suffocating heat of that godforsaken desert.' He gives her a look. 'I'd rather put on extra layers.'

The air is cold enough to see her breath as she drags her fingers over the tatty spines of paperbacks crammed into the bookcase. 'You've read all these?'

'Yep. Some more than once. Most of them are falling to bits, but I couldn't part with them. They're like old friends.'

'I'm the same, I love reading.' She watches John ignite the flame on his camping stove. She can tell it's a struggle with his one good hand, but he is a proud man who's survived conditions she can't possibly imagine, and she stops herself from offering to help. 'I drive Gareth up the wall with my books.'

John coughs. A dry miserable sound that leaves him hoarse. 'Doesn't he read?'

'Not novels. He'll read the sports pages and biographies if they're about some rugby legend.'

'You and me could do swaps?' John suggests and Melanie

says she'd like that. 'I used to have a mate in the army I'd swap books with. Not that I've seen him for years. He moved to France to open a second-hand bookshop.' He gestures to the armchair, while he perches on a wooden chair he's far too big for.

They listen as the water rises to the boil. It competes with the rain hammering the roof and John's occasional coughing. Melanie wonders about asking if he's seen a doctor, but remembers his complaint about his sister's interfering and changes her mind.

'Do you know how to cut hair?' John shoots his question across the room.

Melanie, surprised by it, needs a second to arrange her answer. 'I'm not professional but I cut Georgie's.'

'Could you cut mine?'

'If you like,' she agrees, thinking again how sweet he is, how gentle. A gentle giant.

'I meant to ask you last time.'

It's clear to Melanie why she's drawn to John. She's responding to the qualities her husband once had. Qualities she fell in love with, that for some reason have been replaced with anger and a desire to control. 'If you've a decent pair of scissors?'

The kettle whistles and fills the room with its steaming breath. John rises to his feet and shuffles forwards; the movement makes him cough again.

'Thanks for bringing coffee.' The clink of a spoon and he hands her an enamel mug, reaching over the dog who is up on his haunches, nosing the carrier bag Melanie pulls onto her lap.

'Would you like one of these to go with it?' She unwraps the greaseproof parcel, holds it out to him. 'I made them specially.'

'This is delicious.' John lifts his biscuit as if saluting her. 'You're a wonderful cook.'

'Make you some more, if you like?' she offers, bathing in the glow of his approval. 'I've loads of recipes I want to try before we open.'

'You seem down today.' John lets the dog nuzzle into his hand. 'Is everything all right?'

She makes a face. Her biscuit finished. 'I wouldn't know where to start.'

'From the beginning?'

An automatic smile as her thoughts slide to Sophie's anniversary... Georgie's worrying tummy aches... Her husband's aggressive treatment of Delyth... The knock-on effect that means the two of them are at constant loggerheads. 'You said something once, about Gareth being a jammy bugger. What did you mean?'

'Just that he's always been lucky. Gareth Sayer could do no wrong in certain quarters.'

'Why don't you like him?'

John laughs. 'You're perceptive.'

'I'm right then. Can I ask why?'

He returns his attention to the dog.

'Come on,' she urges. 'Tell me.'

Still nothing.

'Is that why you didn't wave when I saw you at the Co-op a few weeks back? Because I was with Gareth?' Met with a stubborn silence, Melanie wonders if John would be more inclined to talk if she wasn't looking directly at him. 'Shall I cut your hair now?' She places her mug on the floor and gets up.

'You don't mind?'

'Not at all.'

She takes the scissors he finds for her. 'Do you have a towel and a bowl? To catch the hair,' she explains. 'Oh, and a comb?' John passes her a shallow plastic basin and a towel. He locates a comb from somewhere in his jacket. 'You sit there and hold the bowl.' She motions him back to the chair and puts the towel around his shoulders, tucks it into his collar.

It isn't warm enough to remove her coat, so she folds back the cuffs instead. Concentrating on the back of his head, she works methodically, carefully, combing his hair that, unlike his beard – toughened by a life spent outdoors in the salt sea spray – is easily as soft as Georgie's.

'It's in great condition,' she says as it falls through her fingers. 'How much d'you want me to take off?'

'Enough to make me look respectable.'

'Respectable?' She laughs. 'Who wants to look respectable?'

'I do.' His voice is serious. 'I'd like to look respectable for you.'

John's declaration makes her blush, and she's glad he can't see her. When she makes a start on his beard, she notices, up close, how it's threaded with silver. Then that same smell of carbolic soap again, and she is hurled back to the horrors of the care home that is never far away.

Like a prison camp, the only way to describe her years in institutionalised care. The routine, rules and noise. What she needed was love and protection, but the place she was sent to was no safer than the home she had been removed from. It was a brutal, abusive regime. Not that she discusses it with anyone. Even Gareth's only been given the bare bones of her perceived incarceration. Perceived, because as a grown-up, there are moments when she will grill her younger self as to why she didn't run away. Life on the streets, her only alternative at the time, was surely preferable to the endless drudge and lack of privacy.

'Were they really dreadful?' she asks, preferring John's story to her own. 'Your experiences in Afghanistan?'

'I still have nightmares.'

'Do you want to talk about them? I'm a good listener.' Melanie cuts his hair slowly, fearful of making a mistake.

'It's the nightmares. Same ones. Most nights.' He leans sideways for his mug, drinks some of his coffee. 'They said I was suffering from PTSD, but they didn't help me with it. I think the counselling was only so they could work out what to pension me off with, it didn't prepare me for civvy street. It didn't help me to undo what they turned me into. What I've become through that stinking war.'

'Tell me how you got your injuries. It might help stop the nightmares if you can get it off your chest.'

'You sound as if you have them yourself.'

'We're talking about you.' Reluctant to share her sorrows, she fears they will sound paltry in comparison.

'It was a bomb. Strapped to a young mother. She had a baby in her arms.' He pauses, and she hears him heave down air, fighting back tears. 'It was a split-second decision: it was all I had. My lot were shouting orders to shoot, but I couldn't, all I could see was that baby. Such huge black eyes, innocent, you know? I see them every time I close my eyes. I can see them now.' John sniffs, wipes his nose with the back of his hand. 'I didn't think the mother would do it, but she did. She detonated the bomb that was strapped round her middle. They kept shouting "shoot, shoot", and she was babbling stuff I couldn't understand. But how could I shoot? She had a baby in her arms. I'm not a monster.'

'No, you're not.' She combs his hair, cutting a little more each time.

'But people died. Some of my battalion was killed when the bomb went off. I was one of the lucky ones.' *Hardly lucky,* Melanie thinks, but doesn't say. 'And the woman and her baby died anyway. They thought I was cowardly.' He rubs his eyes, sniffs again.

'I think you were in an impossible situation. No one had the right to call you a coward. How could you have lived with yourself if you'd shot that mother, killed her child?'

'I don't know. But I'm struggling to live now.'

'Why did you join up?'

John takes a breath before answering. 'Because of your husband.'

'Gareth?' Melanie stops what she's doing, holds the scissors aloft. An unexplained chill, colder than the room, tracks through her. 'Why – what did he do?'

'I'm not sure I should say.'

'You can't say something like that and not tell me.' She squeezes his shoulder through the thick wool of his jacket to push him on.

'Well, you must know Gareth's got a real issue with any kind of weakness. Any physical weakness.'

'Has he?' Melanie sifts through what she knows of her husband. 'I'm sure he hasn't.'

'If he hasn't got a problem with it now, he certainly used to.'

'Not with you though, surely?'

'Believe it or not, I was puny as a kid. And Gareth hated puny. If you weren't one of the gang. If you weren't like him.' He pauses, rubs his chin through what remains of his beard. 'I'm sorry to have to say it, but he was a bully. If he took against you, he made your life hell.'

Bully.

Melanie unfurls the word. A bully is what she accused him of being after his abysmal treatment of Delyth.

'Is that what he did? He made your life hell?'

'Put it this way, I signed up to get him off my back. To prove to people round here that the rumours he was spreading about me were wrong.'

'What rumours?'

'That I was gay. That I wasn't a proper man.' John coughs into his hand. 'I know it doesn't sound much now, but back then it was a big deal. I used to get beaten up regularly for it.'

What John says lodges inside her like a shard of ice. She could pretend he was talking about someone else, had she not witnessed Gareth's cruelty with Delyth. John isn't telling her anything new. Recent events have opened her eyes to what her husband is capable of and it frightens her. Could she have been hoodwinked by him all these years? It's possible. Although they only have weekends together here, it's a solid chunk of time and far more than either of them is used to. Their Bromley life was hectic, most of it spent apart and, aside from a few snatched hours on weekday evenings, weekends were for socialising with friends or him off playing golf. Until Sophie was killed and they were consumed in other ways.

'I'm sorry. That's a horrible way to behave.' It occurs to her she's been doing rather a lot of apologising on her husband's behalf since arriving in Wales.

'Thank you, but it's not for you to be sorry.' John inadvertently echoes what Delyth said. 'You don't sound surprised by what I'm telling you.'

Melanie drops her scissor-holding hand to her side. 'I would have been, a few months ago. But recently, I've sort of seen him in action for myself.'

'He bullies you?' John twists in his chair, his eyes brimming with concern.

'No, not me.' She repositions his head to continue her trimming. 'It's Delyth he's got the problem with.'

'Oh, I see. Well, she was another one he was cruel to at school. I used to think it was because she wasn't pretty, and because of that, of no use to him. Yeah, Delyth Powell...' John appears to be momentarily lost to whatever his memories dredge to the surface. 'Gareth used to be especially vicious to her.'

'It seems as if he still is.' Melanie ruffles John's hair into place, pleased with how neatly the shortened layers follow the contours of his head.

'But why, what trouble could she be to anyone?'

'That's what I say.'

'She's had a tough life.'

'I know, poor thing. I told Gareth about her struggles but he doesn't care, he's so unfeeling.' She sighs. 'I hate to admit it, but I've seen a side of my husband lately that I don't like.'

John doesn't respond.

'Gareth says everyone hated Delyth at school.'

'That's not true.' John sets her straight. 'She was shy, that's all. Kept herself to herself. From what I remember, it was only Gareth who had the problem with her.'

'Do you know why? I don't mean about how they were at school, I sort of understand that, I mean why would he still have a problem with her now? Because for some reason she brings out the worst in him.'

'That's his shame, that is.' John replies, thoughtful. 'His shame and guilt. Seeing her again after all these years. She probably just reminds him of what a shit he used to be.'

'You might be onto something there because I'm struggling to come up with any logical explanation for his irrational and unprovoked attack of the woman.'

John finishes his coffee. 'Your Gareth drives a black Porsche, doesn't he?'

'Yes.' Melanie brushes stray hairs from his collar.

'I saw him. Monday morning. Out on the coast road. He turned off at the entrance to the Powells' farm.'

'Do you remember what time?' Doing her best to sound casual, she offers him another biscuit.

'First thing. I was on the bus.' John feeds a chunk to Slinky who is salivating against his knees.

Melanie's thoughts, chasing themselves like snapping dogs...
*What was he doing there? – he was supposed to be on his way
back to London.*

'Are you sure it was him?' She tucks a strand of her own hair
behind an ear.

'It was a black Porsche. Latest model. I'm pretty good with
motors, it's a sort of hobby.' John rubs the dog's head, whispers
sweet nothings against his silky ears. 'And I can't think of
anyone else round here with one like it.'

'No, they're impractical for these parts. It's a company car.
He doesn't own it,' Melanie is quick to add. Sensitive to what a
vehicle like that costs and how little John has. 'Whereabouts is
Delyth's farm?'

'Remote. Way out on the coast road, towards St David's.'

'That's going in the complete opposite direction to Pwllglas.'
And London, she thinks.

'You didn't know, did you?'

'No, I didn't.'

'Delyth had a hell of a crush on your husband when they
were at school.'

'So I keep hearing,' she says, more sourly than she intends.

'You can't be jealous?' He smiles. 'A woman as attractive as
you. Because me saying Gareth thought she was a nightmare
would be the understatement of the year.' John swallows the last
of his biscuit, his breath an almondy sweetness. 'Delyth was a
bit of a sad case. I don't mean to be unkind or anything, but she
wouldn't accept that he wanted nothing to do with her. It was
humiliating, to be honest.'

'There,' Melanie announces, pleased with the job she's
done. 'I think you'll do. You got a mirror?'

'No. Mirrors aren't allowed.' He grins.

'Hang on.' She dives into her handbag, retrieves her vanity

mirror. 'There.' She passes it to him. 'Have a look at the new you.'

He holds the mirror up and moves his head from side to side. 'Look at that. Am I going to lose all my strength now, Delilah?' They laugh. 'Grand job. You should go into business.'

'I am, remember.' She laughs, and returns the mirror to her bag.

'Thanks. I feel almost human again.' He uses his good hand to feel her handiwork.

'Not too short?'

'Perfect.' John gives way to more laughing, this time showing a row of surprisingly neat white teeth. 'God, Melanie, I can't tell you the last time I laughed. I honestly thought I'd forgotten how to. See how good you are for me?'

She returns to the armchair, sits opposite him. 'She cut herself in our sink.' Melanie says with no preamble.

'Cut herself?' John gasps. 'Who did?'

'Delyth.'

'I don't understand – are you telling me she tried to kill herself?'

A sombre nod. 'But I don't think she meant to do it.'

'Didn't mean to do it? I should think she did.' John is resolute. 'I've come close myself, more times than I care to remember. I nearly managed it once. But my sister found me in the nick of time.' He slumps back in his wooden chair.

'Oh, John.' Melanie presses her fingers to her lips. 'I'm so sorry you were driven to that. You must have been in a bad way.'

'Like Delyth must be.' He sidesteps her observation. 'Where was Gareth when this was going on?'

'In London. It was just me and Georgie.'

'Good God. Your daughter saw it?' He looks aghast.

'No, thank goodness. She was in the flat upstairs.'

'And she... Delyth. She did it in your kitchen... in your sink?'

'Bad, isn't it? But I could tell she didn't want to do it. Kill herself, I mean—' She breaks off. 'The cuts were deep, yes, but if she wanted to do it, if that had been her true intention, she'd have done it where there was no chance of being found.'

John coughs into his hand. 'What was she thinking?'

'I don't suppose she can have been thinking. It seemed like a desperate cry for help.'

He grimaces. Coughs again.

'Has she done anything like this before?' Melanie asks.

John's look is thoughtful. 'I don't know. She was an unhappy kid, and then with everything that happened – you've probably heard that her father was killed just after she finished her A Levels.' John waits for her to nod. 'The mother hit the bottle, big time, or so they say... well, Delyth says, actually. I don't think anyone's seen Norah for years. Rumours are she's not left the farm since Erin died and she retired. What did Gareth say, when you told him what Delyth did?'

'I haven't told him. She swore me to secrecy.'

'But you're telling me?'

'I am, yes. I knew you wouldn't dismiss it as being an attention-seeking stunt like Gareth would. Because I'm sure he would,' she adds to justify her decision. 'Going by what he already calls her. I'm telling you because I know you'll be sympathetic, that you might help me to understand.'

'Have you talked to Delyth about it since?'

'Once. Yes. I asked if she'd ever thought about getting help, talking to a therapist, that kind of thing. But it fell on stony ground. She just kept telling me how sorry she was.'

'You know what happened to Delyth's sister, don't you?'

'Erin? Yes, she fell from an upstairs window. Such a terrible thing... A terrible accident.'

John nodded. Slow and thoughtful. 'If it was an accident.'

'What d'you mean? What else could it have been?'

'Oh, take no notice of me.'

'You can't just say that and leave it. Tell me what you mean.'

'Nothing. Honestly. It's nothing.' He held up a hand. 'The police... The coroner. They all concluded she died from the fall and foul play wasn't suspected.'

'But you don't sound sure.'

'I'm sorry, Melanie, I shouldn't have said anything. I mean, what would I know?' John cleared his throat. 'All I know is that Erin was so young and pretty. She had her whole life ahead of her. It's hardly any wonder why Delyth's so sad.'

Saturday morning has somehow come around again. Melanie opens her eyes to find Gareth standing at the bedroom window, peering out through the parted curtains at what promises to be a sunny day.

'What's up?' She turns on her side.

'Can't sleep.'

'What's the matter?'

'Stuff on my mind.'

'Want to tell me?' He doesn't answer. 'No, okay. What time is it?'

'Half seven.'

'Early for a Saturday.' She lifts the duvet, pats his side of the bed. 'Little lie-in?'

Gareth drops the curtains and the room goes dark again. She feels the mattress shift when he gets in beside her.

'That's better.' She cuddles him. 'Let's try and have another half hour.'

It is their daughter who finally wakes them. Not to complain of stomach cramps for a change, but to present them with a milk tooth on the cushion of her outstretched palm.

Gareth sits up and rubs his eyes. 'Put it under your pillow and the Tooth Fairy will come and give you something.'

'Hang on a minute. Show me, please.' Melanie yawns, not quite with it. 'You tricked me last time, using the same one.'

Georgie giggles and uses a finger to peel back her lip to show the new gap in her teeth.

'Go on, quick.' Melanie yawns again. 'She might come for it before breakfast if you're lucky.'

Georgie goes, and Melanie snuggles into Gareth. His arms are tight around her, not letting go. She smiles, happily imagining his red Welsh dragon tattoo pressed against her back. Things have been good between them since he arrived home yesterday evening, and she prays it will stay that way.

Later, with breakfast almost over, Melanie and Gareth drink what's left of their tea and finish their toast standing up.

'Your hair's getting long.' He kisses her. 'It suits you.'

'Good, because I fancy a change.'

Georgie skips into the kitchen with the post and Slinky trotting alongside.

'She's looking loads better than last weekend.' Gareth lifts the teapot, directs the spout at Melanie's mug.

It's a bad habit of his, talking about their child in the third person as if Georgie wasn't there. But for the sake of a weekend free of disagreements, she lets it go.

'How long before we get her test results?' He drains what's left of his tea.

Georgie is divvying out the mail. 'One for Daddy.' She reads the name on a brown envelope and passes it to her father. 'Looks like a bill.' She grins, showing off the asymmetric spaces between her teeth.

'Electricity.' A groan, and he slides a finger under the flap.

'Tuesday.' Toast and tea finished, Melanie places her crockery in the dishwasher. 'I'm to ring the surgery.'

'That long?' Perplexed, but not by her, with the bill he's reading. 'What tests did they do?'

'Bloods. Loads for different allergies. They were very thorough, weren't they, Georgie?' Melanie strokes her child's hair that, still to be brushed and braided into plaits, fans over her narrow shoulders. 'And you were such a brave girl?'

'Yes, I was.' Georgie frowns in concentration. She is taking her role as postmistress very seriously. 'One more for Mummy. One more for Daddy.' Job done, she steps back to admire the two tidy piles of envelopes on the work surface.

'Thank you, sweetheart.' Melanie smiles, proud of her daughter's efficiency, her ability to read so well. 'Have you checked under your pillow? Maybe the Tooth Fairy's visited you.'

Georgie sucks on her bottom lip.

'Best go and look then. We'll have to get going in a minute. I booked your riding lesson for eleven.'

She watches her daughter bound away.

'I hope you booked yourself one too?' Gareth looks up.

Melanie nods. 'If that was okay?'

'Definitely. I think it's fantastic you're getting into it again.' He sounds genuinely enthusiastic about the idea. 'I know how much you loved horses as a kid.'

'I'm really hoping the doctors get to the bottom of whatever it is.' She pulls their conversation back to their child. 'Great thing is, she's been feeling loads better this week. I don't think she's complained about a tummy ache for a while.'

'Bit of a coincidence, isn't it? Georgie's tummy aches stopping when Delyth finally gets the message and stays away.'

'Oh, not this again.' She slumps against the counter.

'I'm serious, Mel. Georgie's been feeling well because she's not eating the stuff that woman cooks. I told you she was bad news.'

Melanie sighs into the sourness that always accompanies any mention of Delyth Powell. But she refuses to respond. If she doesn't respond, they might be able to get through to Monday morning without falling out. She picks up an envelope from the top of her pile. Something from the bank. She rips it open and scans November's payments, the standing orders, the direct debits...

'Oh no. Sorry, Gareth.' She realises her mistake. 'This isn't mine, it's yours,' and is about to hand it over when she notices a three-thousand-pound cash withdrawal halfway down the first sheet. 'What's this? What the hell did you need to take all that out for?'

Gareth tries to snatch the statement from her grasp but, quicker than him, she whips it behind her back.

'Give it to me.'

'Not until you tell me what you needed all that cash for?'

'It's none of your business.' His hand opens and closes with impatience.

'I think it is my business.' She flaps the statement at him.

'I just needed it, okay? I needed it for London. Something I had to do.'

'Oh, right. London, was it?' She refers to the printout again. 'So why does it say the cash was withdrawn from the NatWest branch here in Pencarew?'

'You what?'

'On the statement. It says Pencarew,' she repeats, the blood rushing to her face. 'On the thirteenth,' She looks up. 'That was a Monday, wasn't it?'

'So what if it was?'

'You always leave at the crack of dawn, Mondays. To be back at your desk, you say. What were you still doing in town?'

His expression clouds and he moves away. She follows him. Thinks that less than an hour ago they were making love, and now they are on the brink of yet another vicious argument.

'Answer me. I want to know. Jesus, Gareth, you'd want to know if I'd withdrawn that much. Three grand's a lot of money.'

'Give it to me.' He snaps his fingers.

'What were you still doing in Pencarew?' She gives him the statement. 'The bank doesn't open until nine?'

He refolds the sheets back into their torn envelope, pushes it into the back pocket of his jeans. Melanie remembers something John said, decides to approach things from another angle.

'Your car was seen up at Delyth's farm. Has this mysterious need for a walloping load of cash got something to do with her?'

'What d'you mean my car was seen? Who says?'

'Does it matter? You were seen at the turn-off to the farm.'

'Rubbish.' He butters himself a cold triangle of toast, bites it in half.

'You've got a very distinctive car,' she challenges.

'But it's not the only one in the world.' Gareth chews through his words.

'Around here it is.' Firm. She wants an answer. 'What were you going to the farm for, if you hate her so much?'

'I told you it wasn't me. Whoever said they saw me; they must've been mistaken.'

'I don't believe you. You told me you were heading back to London. Why didn't you say you were going up there?'

'Because I didn't.' He takes another bite of toast, then gives the last of the crust to the dog.

'Stop lying to me. I'm not an idiot.'

'What is this? Twenty bloody questions?' He licks butter from his fingers.

'You've drawn out a huge amount of money and I want to know what it's for. We can't afford to be spending like that.'

'I can't tell you.' He stops munching and swallows. 'Because it's a surprise. Okay?'

'A surprise? Oh, no, Gareth, I'm sorry, but that's not good enough.'

'Well, it's all you're getting.' He smiles, irritatingly reasonable; it makes her want to thump him.

'Tell me.'

'*Doh!*' He makes a face. 'It wouldn't be a surprise then, would it?'

'A bit of a theme this.' Hands on hips.

'What is?' He wipes his hands on a tea towel and turns away.

Melanie wants to reach out to him. For their marriage to go back to what it was before ever meeting Delyth Powell.

'This brick wall you put up whenever her name gets mentioned.' She dives in front of him to stop him walking off. 'And you wonder why I'm suspicious? What is it with you and her?'

'What is it with you and your bloody questions?' He pushes her aside. A flash of the aggression she saw him display that day in the Co-op with Delyth.

'Excuse me? I don't think I'm being the unreasonable one here. I'm not the one withdrawing thousands of pounds from our account.'

'*My* account. And you weren't supposed to see it.'

'Obviously.'

'Oh, just leave it, can't you?' He moves past her and into the bar.

'I don't know you at all.' Melanie follows on behind. 'What did you do to Delyth when you were kids?'

'I said leave it.' A muscle twitches in his jaw. 'You'll find out soon enough what the money was for.'

'God, Gareth. This isn't you. Or is it – and you've just kept it from me all this time? Because I don't like what I'm seeing.'

'Tough.' He turns and lifts an arm. She ducks instinctively, believing he is about to strike her. He smacks the wall instead. 'You can keep on all you like, but I'm not telling.'

Something communicated in his eyes makes Melanie recoil. The mask slips, and again she sees his potential. Her insides go cold and for the first time in their lives together she is afraid of him.

Georgie is suddenly there. The pound coin her father left under her pillow held high above her head.

'Are you all right, Mummy?' Her little face drains of colour. 'What's the matter?'

'Nothing, darling. Everything's fine.' Melanie puts a protective arm around her child and guides her out of harm's way – throwing Gareth a look she hopes communicates her disgust, rather than the fear that is knocking against her ribcage.

CHAPTER THIRTY-FOUR

Less than a week later, disaster strikes. A severed water main in the downstairs cloakroom means the pub is under a foot of water. It also means Melanie is late collecting Georgie from school. The clock on the Mazda's dashboard blinks accusingly on the drive through town.

'It's okay,' she tells it, swinging into the near-deserted car park. 'It's Wednesday, they'll have let Georgie join the after-school club.' Admittedly, she didn't book a place in advance, but they're not going to mind.

What a day. She grabs her handbag and locks the car. It's been non-stop since she woke that morning, with problem after problem, culminating at three o'clock this afternoon when one of Bryn's men sawed through a pipe they shouldn't have. She had to leave them to it in the end. Pray it didn't flood the kitchen. Thankfully, the parquet flooring in the bar, unlike the restaurant and guest lounge, has yet to go down, because that would have been catastrophic.

Handbag banging, she runs to the entrance of St Ishmael's Primary School. The metal doors are stiff on their hinges and screech when she pushes them wide: a sound that settles into an unnerving silence. There is nothing of the children's laughter she was anticipating, only an emptiness made bleaker by the fluorescent strip lights above.

'Hello?' she calls and, serenaded by the heels of her boots, moves deeper into the building. Dipping in and out of the vacated classrooms, she is alarmed by the rapidly descending fog that is rubbing itself against the wide school windows. 'Hello?' she tries again, her despair intensifying when she peers into the main hall and finds it deserted, save for its rubber and polish smells.

She is met by a set of large double doors at the end of the corridor and tests their handles. Locked. Squinting through the safety glass into the unlit canteen and abandoned rooms beyond, there seems to be no sign of life.

'Where the hell is everyone? Where's Georgie?'

Panic – a butterfly caught in a jar – flaps inside her.

'Stay calm. Stay calm. She has to be somewhere,' she gabbles. 'Please? There must be someone around. Why else are the main doors still open? Is anyone here?' She holds her breath for the answer that doesn't come.

With little choice other than to turn back the way she came, she dashes out under the lowering sky to circle the empty playground. Hunting the shadows, the darkened spaces between the dormant spread of the magnolia tree and the boundary wall.

'Georgie! Georgie!' she wails. The markings for hopscotch and number mazes, a muddle of colour through her mounting desperation. 'Where are you?'

Melanie veers off sideways, in the direction of the car park. Sees a vehicle, the only one apart from hers. It means someone is still here. A surge of hope has her sprinting towards a yellowy light leaking from deep inside the building. Scrabbling through a thatch of nettles, she must slide between a steep bank of grass and grip a series of flaking windowsills to haul herself along the rear school wall. Panting, out of breath, she is about halfway along when she identifies where the light is coming from. Makes out what she assumes is the back of a cleaner dragging a mop from side to side.

She shouts and raps on the glass, believing her daughter is with them. The woman looks up, turns momentarily in Melanie's direction, but with a frown of annoyance returns to her mopping again. She bangs the glass a second time. Harder. Keeping on until her knuckles hurt. It works. The woman drops her mop in the bucket and sways towards her. Another bulb is flicked on and Melanie waves her arms. Shines the torch on her phone at the glass. The window is thrown open, toppling her against the bank.

'Oh, thank goodness,' she gushes, fumbling upright. 'I'm Georgie's Mum. Melanie... Melanie Sayer?'

The woman gives her a bemused smile. 'Goodness, what are you doing? The main door's open, you know.'

'I tried that. I came in, but I couldn't find anyone. I was getting worried. But it's okay, it's after-school club this evening. Sorry, I'm so late collecting Georgie, we had an emergency at home.'

'You've got the wrong day. After-school club's Tuesdays and Thursdays. It's Wednesday today.'

'It can't be. I'm sure I was told Tuesdays and Wednesdays.'

A shrug. 'Then you were given duff information.'

'Are there any teachers around?' Mind racing, Melanie could swear those were the days Delyth told her, but accepts she must have misheard. 'Is Mrs Jenkins here? Can I speak to her?'

'She's gone home. All the teachers have gone home. I'm the only one here.'

'Where is she then? Where's Georgie?' Panic bubbles in her throat.

'I'm sorry, I'm just the cleaner.'

'Is Delyth here?'

A stiff shake of the head. 'Gone home for the day, I'm afraid.'

'But someone must know. Georgie has to be somewhere.' Melanie is shouting now. She can't help it. 'Where's my daughter? I thought this school had a strict safeguarding policy. Her class teacher said she wouldn't let her go with anyone unless I'd given her verbal or written confirmation.'

'Oh, dear, please don't upset yourself.' The cleaner's hand flutters between them. 'Your daughter can't have gone far.'

'Can you give me Mrs Jenkins' number? I've got to ring her... Find out where Georgie is.'

'I'm sorry, the office is locked for the night. I haven't access to that kind of thing.'

Melanie isn't listening. Her mind is racing ahead to the places Georgie might be. And without another word, she struggles back between bank and wall to the car park. Stinging her hand on a nettle along the way. A glance at the sky, to where a thin moon claims its space in what remains of the dun-coloured day. Colder now, a fine drizzle through the fog settles on her hair, on the sleeves of her parka. She must find her child and get her into the warm, it's going to be totally dark soon. She drives around the town, keeping close to the kerb, not accelerating above second gear. The engine growls in protest when she speeds up to pass alongside the string of benches lining the seafront.

'Georgie!'

She slams the brakes and lurches forwards in her seat. Luckily there's no one behind her. But this isn't Georgie, this is another child with honey-coloured plaits and a Smiggle backpack walking hand in hand with what she supposes is an older sibling. She gulps down her spiralling anxiety and freewheels as far down as the harbour wall, before circling back up to the playing field with its empty swings and vacated climbing frame on the fringes of town. A burst of that happy, sunny afternoon, when she, Georgie and Gareth played in there. Taking photos on their phones to share with the friends they'd left behind. Her face crumples, preparing itself to cry. But she won't cry, there isn't time. She must find Georgie.

Melanie stops the car whenever she sees someone. Strangers mostly, black-clad, androgynous figures fastened into winter coats. She doesn't care, wild with worry, she buttonholes anyone and everyone, asking her desperate question: 'Have you seen her? Please, you must've seen her.'

She catches sight of herself in the Mazda's side mirror: frantic, feverish, leaning over the passenger seat to appeal through the open car window.

'Excuse me, excuse me?' she tries not to shriek. 'Have you seen Georgie? My little girl. She's seven, nearly eight. She's got light-brown plaits and she's wearing a silver puffer coat... No? Are you sure?'

Met with little more than a series of befuddled faces, it terrifies her. Do they even know who her child is?

She drives past bright shop interiors with windows already dressed for Christmas. Searches down street after street. Until she reaches the terraced houses on Castle Row. Nia. Could Georgie have gone to her house after school? She sometimes does. Melanie scratches her hand, her fingers tracing the loop of raised bumps from the nettle sting. Did Georgie say she was doing that this evening and Melanie, increasingly distracted by the countdown to opening night, wasn't listening? She parks outside the Wilsons' house, ratchets up the handbrake and slips out from behind the wheel. A spark of optimism as she sprints up the garden path to slam the knocker against the door. But any rosiness she has when she thinks she has finally located her child is snuffed out when she presses the tip of her nose to the cold windowpane. Nothing. The rooms beyond the Wilsons' white nets fall away into black.

'Where the bloody hell is everybody? The place is deserted. Where's Georgie?' A hand to her mouth, her muffled entreaty as she backs away.

The pub, she thinks, letting number seven's gate snap shut on her heels. It is possible Georgie went home, that she missed her by minutes and her daughter is there. Where she usually is at this time of day: in front of CBeebies with Bumble and Slinky. She might be.

'Oh, please, please have gone home, Georgie, please...' Tyres skid on gravel, she leaves the motor running in the pub car park, unlocks the door and rushes inside to check.

A smudge of a gibbous moon hangs mellow and low beyond the pub's darkened windows. Its pale face filtering through the thickening fog is mirrored in what remains of the flooded bar. She tiptoes inside, dark except for a single light spilling out from the kitchen. At least the electricity's not out. She tiptoes over what has dried to shallow pools of water, pleads with the perpetual gloaming of the stairwell and the flat above.

'Georgie? Are you up there, darling?'

But Georgie isn't here. She isn't anywhere. And when Melanie reaches the kitchen, apart from the dog, she finds it is empty too.

'Have you seen her?' she asks Slinky who just wags his tail. 'Bloody hell,' she says, sprinting back outside.

'Georgie, please? Where are you?' she wails through the dripping dusk, then it occurs to her. 'Of course you're not here, you don't have a key, you're too young. You're not a latchkey kid like I was. I've got a bloody cheek criticising my mother when I'm such a shit one myself.'

Her mobile rings from inside her coat pocket, it severs her self-recriminations. She tugs it free, along with the British Legion poppy she never did manage to fix to Gareth's coat.

'Oh, please, please—'

It's Gareth.

The chink of brightness dims. She can't speak to him, not now, not until Georgie's been found safe and sound. *Safe and sound.* She churns the words until they become a sickening sludge and stares at her phone. She can't, she can't. Tears sprout and she wipes them away. She can't tell him Georgie's missing. Not when it's her fault their other daughter died.

In the pub car park, the late-afternoon dark of a day that never grew properly light enfolds her like a wing. Not that it provides any comfort. Quite the contrary. With dusk threatening, the town, shrouded in thin grey cloud, is eerily quiet. There isn't even the snuffle of the wind. Filmed in a layer of drizzle that has now extinguished the moon, Melanie doesn't move. Can't move. She has run out of places to try and is going to have to ring the police... Who will notify Gareth... Bethan... Bronwyn. These terrible thoughts spear the cotton-wool feel inside her head until an idea jostles forwards. Could Georgie be with Bethan? And if so, should she drive there or phone? Quicker to phone. But her fingers won't work. Clumsy and wet, sliding over the screen of her handset, she eventually activates the number.

It rings and it rings. At last Bethan picks up.

'Thank God you're there.'

'What's up?' her sister-in-law asks.

'Is Georgie with you?' Melanie rubs the nettle sting on her hand.

'No.'

'No?' Her legs give way and she topples backwards. 'You were my last hope.' Her body sags against the wet car.

'What are you on about, Mel? What's the matter?'

'Shit, Bethan. She's missing. Georgie's missing. I was late collecting her from school... The pub was flooded, didn't Bryn say? Georgie wasn't there. She isn't anywhere. Oh, God, Bethan, I don't know what to do.'

'Calm down, Mel. Georgie can't have gone far.' Bethan tries to reason. 'This is Pencarew, not Bromley.'

'But she's nowhere.' She grips a handful of her hair in a frantic fist. 'I've tried the school. I've driven all round town.'

'D'you want me to call the police?' Bethan offers.

'I don't know, I don't want Gareth finding out... because they'll need to tell him, won't they?'

'And what's wrong with that?'

'Oh, Bethan, he'll bloody kill me.' She grips her hair harder, hurting her scalp.

'Could Georgie have gone home with someone from school?'

'I've tried Nia's, but no one's home. I've tried everywhere. Oh, God, Bethan.' Melanie is in danger of losing it completely. 'This is all my fault. I was forty minutes late... forty minutes. We were up to our calves in water. Bryn's lot hit a water main.' She paces the darkened car park, the Mazda's engine still running. 'I can't believe I forgot about her. My *own* daughter. I thought Wednesdays was after-school club.' Melanie is shaking and scrubs a frantic hand over her face. Tries to get a hold on her escalating emotions.

'Melanie... Mel?' Bethan again. 'Calm down. You sound weird, your breathing's all funny.'

'My chest hurts.' She squeezes the sudden shooting pain in her shoulder.

'You've got to try and stay calm. You'll give yourself a heart attack.'

'How can I stay calm!' she shrieks. 'I've lost her... How can I have forgotten my own daughter? What kind of a mother am I?'

'Come on. Everything's going to be fine.'

'You don't know that.' Melanie, pacing around, helpless and agitated. 'Georgie could be dead in a ditch for all I know. And it's all my fault.'

'D'you want me to come over? Where are you?'

'At the pub. I thought she might be here, but she's not.'

'She's got to be somewhere. Mel, listen to me, she can't have gone far. Think – where could she have gone?'

'I don't know.' A dreadful pause and into it drops a dreadful thought. 'I'm going to have to call the police. I haven't got a choice,' Melanie bawls. 'The likes of me don't deserve to have children.'

'Don't be ridiculous.' Bethan's quick to set her straight.

'This is punishment for Elizabeth, for Sophie.' Melanie doesn't give Bethan the chance to interrupt. 'Don't tell me it's not, because it's punishment for something,' she rambles. 'Gareth's been ringing, but I can't talk to him. You won't tell him, will you? Not yet.'

'Mel, listen to me. I'm coming over—'

'No, Bethan, don't. What if Georgie turns up at yours? Oh, God!' A fresh cold wave of panic sloshes through her. 'It's happening all over again. We're going to lose Georgie too.'

'What happened to Sophie was an accident, Mel. It wasn't your fault.'

'I don't know how you can even say that, after what I did.'

'You've got to stop beating yourself up. The fault lies with that speeding motorist, not you. You're an amazing mother. Georgie's evidence of that.'

'I'll tell you just how amazing I am as a mother, shall I?' Melanie listens to the bitterness in her voice, hears the self-loathing. Knows her sister-in-law hears it too. 'I was late collecting Georgie before. We'd only been here a week.' She blinks through wet lashes. 'It was lucky Delyth was there to look after her. She's a good woman. She's been so kind to me,' she reminds herself as she continues to pace around the car park. 'So,' she gulps down a lungful of damp sea air, her chest feeling desperately tight, 'that's how I know I'm not responsible enough. That I can't be trusted. After everything that happened with Sophie, I still haven't learnt my lesson. I still screw up.'

'Georgie was with Delyth that day, you say?'

'Yes. She loves Georgie, they get on really well.'

'Could she be with Delyth now, d'you think?'

Bethan's suggestion: a lifeline through the thickening sea fret.

'What? Where?'

'At the farm, maybe?'

'But why?' Melanie isn't totally dismissing the idea. 'If she'd seen I hadn't collected her, wouldn't she just have brought her back here?'

'Maybe she tried, and you'd already left.'

'Yeah, but...' Mind whirling. 'She'd have told me. Phoned the pub. She wouldn't just take her.'

'She might've been trying to, for all you know.'

'Do you think?' The nettle sting is still smarting. She gives it a vigorous rub.

'Have you got her number?' Bethan asks. 'I don't think I have.'

'I'm not sure.' Then Melanie remembers. 'Yes. We swapped them ages ago. Yeah, bloody hell, you might be onto something there.'

'What's that?'

'Georgie came home from school the other day, all excited because Delyth told her they had kittens up at the farm. Oh, I think that's where she is.' The pain in her chest easing a little. 'I've not seen Delyth for ages. Not since the Co-op when Gareth had a go at her in front of everybody... I think she's been avoiding me.'

'What was that about?' Bethan is keen to know.

'I'll tell you another time. Let me ring her... I've got to ring her.'

'Yes, yes. Go on, quick. I'll hang up. Let me know what's happening, okay?'

CHAPTER THIRTY-SIX

'It keeps going through to bloody voicemail. I've left two messages.' Melanie, back behind the wheel of the Mazda. 'Can you give me directions to the farm?'

'What – you're not driving there?' Bethan sounds alarmed. 'You're in no fit state to drive.'

'I've not got a choice.' She straps herself in and starts to reverse out of the pub car park.

'You could ring the police?'

'Let me try the farm first. It's not far, is it?'

'I still think we should notify the police, Mel.'

'All right, but you do it, will you? I need to get there. Give me the directions.' She doesn't tell Bethan that in between dialling Delyth's number, Gareth called again and she didn't pick up. Not so long ago, Melanie could tell him anything, no matter how bad. She recognises a change in herself, a change in the dynamics of their marriage and takes it as a clear indication of the distance that's growing between them.

Melanie is frightened of him. There, she's admitted it. And telling Bethan he would kill her if he found out about Georgie may only be a figure of speech, but remembering his recent hot-faced aggression, his volatile temper, the threat of violence, it has a menacing ring.

Melanie abides by Bethan's directions and heads along the coast. Up high, with Pencarew far behind, the main A road follows the jagged bow of the cliff. In her driving mirror, lights from the town throw a tangerine belt across the sky and ahead, a sliver of orange, as the sun goes down red beyond the sea. Other than this, the world beyond the Mazda's windows is leached of colour, and into this realisation, an unwelcome thought unfurls. This is winter. This colourless existence will be her life if something has happened to her child. If she doesn't bring Georgie home safe. This is how things will be from now on. Nothing will ever bloom again. Everything will be trapped in this grey, barren drabness.

Delyth's number is on redial, but there is still no answer and with the mobile signal intermittent, then disappearing completely, she is forced to give up. Why won't the woman answer? If Georgie is with her, then surely she would appreciate Melanie's need for reassurance. The road dips sharply. Flanked by ravaged hedgerows and wind-licked trees, their black and crippled limbs stamped against the dusk. Melanie bites her lip. Realises just how hard when she tastes blood. She drops the window an inch, and the sound of tyres on wet road fills the car. Darker now, she switches on the headlamps. With nothing more than patches of cloud showing lighter on the horizon, she doubts there is more than ten minutes of daylight left. Her expression grim, she's too anxious for the company of the radio and, closing the window, she plugs the silence by chanting the directions she's been given to Gweld Y Môr. Listening to her voice bounce around her, she's terrified she will forget, with no way of calling

Bethan back to clarify. She chucks the redundant mobile down onto the empty passenger seat, not daring to think beyond the journey to Delyth's farm. The possibility that her daughter isn't there is unimaginable.

The road soars up into the rain again. Thoughts of Georgie, cold and alone and out in it somewhere, butt up against the thump, thump of windscreen wipers. More doubts crowd in. Supposing Melanie doesn't find her? A sense of dread has her tighten her grip on the steering wheel, the whites of her knuckles showing through the skin. She glances at her wedding ring, wonders if Bethan's telephoned the police yet, if Gareth knows the terrible thing she's done. This is madness, she shivers despite the car's cosy interior, Georgie isn't going to be with Delyth. This is a wild goose chase, and one she is going to come to regret. She shudders and clamps her jaw shut to trap the billowing trepidation in her mouth.

At last, the way ahead opens out. She makes the most of it and, foot to the floor, she pushes the car up into fifth, then sixth, for the first time. But not for long. Red tail-lights snaking ahead, the spray from other vehicles drenching the windscreen. Forced to squeeze to a stop, she joins a queue around the next bend. Roadworks. The usual assortment of signs. The Welsh must be read first, and an English translation given beneath.

'Just my bloody luck.' She bangs the dashboard, desperation rising. 'Come on. Come on.' Her pulse thumps in her neck as she inches forwards in first gear, only to jerk to a standstill moments later.

Everything is wet and dank and heavy. She drops the window a fraction, wanting the little air there is. Stares out on the disappearing world, breathing into the flaccid moments of eerie calm. What was that? She's sure she saw something scurry up the bank, but too quick and far away to be certain. She locks her doors as a precaution and swallows, hears the Jurassic creep of the tide in her ears and waits for confirmation. For whatever it was to show itself again. But nothing does. The high-pitched keening of a buzzard has her looking up to a floating shape above the filigreed branches. Mimicking the cry of a baby, the bird sounds as distressed as she is. She watches it land on top of a nearby telegraph pole and settle inside its feathers.

The red traffic light turns green and she is finally on the move again. The rain eases to a drizzle and she cuts the windscreen wipers, swaps their squeaking for the spooky stillness going on beyond the car. The blackened boughs of deciduous trees sprinkle the way ahead with what remains of their yellow leaves. They spiral down like gold sovereigns through the gloom. At last, she picks up speed, the tail-lights thinning as she passes a series of triangular road signs warning of hairpin bends and blind spots. Slowing to thirty for a smattering of low-slung cottages, their stone faces turned to the road. She wonders fleetingly who lives in these places. There's nothing here. No shops, no pub, only swathes of conifers dissolving up into the cloud. Wide timber gates leading off into dark, lonely woodland, littered with "land for sale" signs. There are other notices too, advertising "eggs for sale"... "hay for sale"... "Shetland ponies for sale". Would Georgie like a pony? The idea stabs her tightly-knotted concern for her daughter's safety.

'When I find you and bring you home,' she whispers, sending something of herself out to wherever Georgie is, 'that's what we'll do. We'll buy you a pony. Would you like that? A pony to love.' The painful prickle of tears has her biting her lip again, wanting them to stop, but they fall regardless. 'We will, we'll get you one.' She wipes the tears away, continues to talk to her missing child. 'Must be easy enough to rent a field nearby, there must be loads of grazing.' She tries not to think of the unwelcoming hills squatting under the mist, and that Georgie could be out there somewhere, lost and frightened, cold and wet. 'Don't worry, sweetheart,' she says, pressing a hand to her abdomen in a way she would when she was pregnant. 'Mummy won't let anything bad happen to you.'

As she says this, a powerful memory of Sophie heaves into view. Her sweet face, vivid as ever, shines lantern-bright above the bonnet. Enough to make her gasp. To have known the colour of her eyes, to have touched her skin... What a brutal end. Black thoughts rise and fall with the contours of the road. To have let go of her little hand like that... She may as well have pushed her into the path of that car herself. Melanie picks over her dream, the one she has most nights, when she gives birth to twins. Sees again how they fit into her palms. One perfect, the other disfigured. Until someone comes and takes them away. Bethan pushing her to have more children, she should tell her this. Give her the images that haunt her night after night.

The sight of a white Luton van hurtling towards her at breakneck speed ruptures her dismal contemplations and snaps her into the present with a jolt. Blinded by the sudden headlights, Melanie swerves. The danger of the water-logged verge bouncing beneath her wheels. She pulls her mouth wide in a silent scream as shrubbery scrapes the metal sides of the car. A blare of her horn and she follows the van's momentum in her driving mirror, only looking back at the way ahead in the nick of time.

Cows.

Blocking the road.

Nothing more than shifting shapes through the mist. Until she is almost upon them.

She slams the brakes and skids to a stop. In seconds, the Mazda's surrounded. High walls of muscle jostle the car and their bovine breath steams into the air.

'This is a main road, and it's nearly bloody dark,' she yells, pushing her fingers to her collarbone to feel the heightened force of her heartbeat. 'Who in their right mind moves livestock in these conditions?' She sees the mud the cows trail from field to tarmac. Smacks the steering wheel over and over, until her hands hurt. 'Bloody selfish idiots,' she screams, borderline hysterical. Not that she can be heard above the herdsmen's shouts, the mooing protest. Farmer and son, she guesses, unfurling a memory of her grandmother... the grandfather and the dairy herd she never knew. She tells herself to calm down, to have a little sympathy. Sharing ruddy complexions and identical blue overalls, these two, positioned on opposite verges, are unperturbed.

'I've got to find my child... I've got to find my child,' she pleads to no one. These men are as indifferent to her distress as they are to the weather.

The placid, liquid-eyed creatures mosey ever closer to the car. Trapped and tense behind her seatbelt, Melanie's dismal thoughts are accompanied by that pain in her left arm again. Is this what extreme stress does to her now? She rubs what remains of her nettle sting and checks her phone again.

'Oh!' She pounces on it when she sees a single bar of mobile signal. Uses it to dial Delyth and listens to it ring and ring. *Breathe*, she reminds herself, there is nothing she can do. She lets it ring out, looks past the illuminated handset to her frightened face reflected in the side window. Half-mad and helpless. The woman she sees is almost unrecognisable.

The older farmer brandishes a stick, threatening. He barks orders to the sheepdogs that, slinking and weaving, run the gauntlet between the muddy hocks. The cows are the colours of those pebble sweets in clear glass jars she would now and again win at the funfair in Hunstanton. Black, brown, fawn. Their rope tails swinging, their rubbery muzzles smearing the Mazda's bonnet. Nothing she can do. She cuts the engine. A car pulls up behind her. Headlamps blinding. Another waiting beyond the cows. Sharp green smells from their dung waft in through the partially open window. Dung that splatters the insides of their hind legs. Warm again, she drops the window further, feels the chilly clamminess slap her cheeks. How uncannily still the surrounding countryside is. Without a breath of wind, the fog has draped itself over the land like a damp, grey blanket.

The cows saunter on into the farmyard, udders swaying. Then she is on the move again. But only to part-exchange the dairy herd for a Land Rover tugging a rusted trailer.

'Bastard!' she says when it pulls out in front of her at the next junction. 'You could have waited. There's sod all behind me.'

Crawling along, the trailer rattling and bumping, its red tail-lights blinking on and off as the driver repeatedly slows then accelerates for no apparent reason. This is purgatory. She repeatedly smacks the dashboard. She just wants to get there... She just wants this agony to be over and to find her child.

'Drive to the road.' She bawls her exasperation. 'Go on, you moron, some of us have places to be.'

Slowing again, she uses the opportunity to recheck her mobile. But there is no signal. Emergency calls only. But this is an emergency. She should have telephoned the police herself, not left it to Bethan. She could be making the biggest mistake in her life. Supposing this is a waste of time – then what? The same unanswerable questions turn like a relentless carousel in her head.

'Finally.' She exhales when the person in front turns off down some mud track. 'A clear road.'

The world beyond the Mazda's windows has darkened to an impenetrable indigo-blue and she presses her foot to the floor, accelerates. She knows she is driving too fast, but the urgency of finding Georgie outweighs any fear she'll end up in a hedge. Then, veering around the next bend, she is met by a wall of pulsating ice-blue lights. They puncture the dark, mimicking her racing heart.

An ambulance.

'Oh, God, no! It's Georgie, I know it is!' she screams. 'Oh, please... Please, don't let it be Georgie.'

CHAPTER THIRTY-SEVEN

Melanie abandons the Mazda in the middle of the road. Engine running. Deaf to the blare of horns, her boots skidding on the wet tarmac as she hurtles towards the ambulance.

'I can't lose her too,' she shouts through the rain she doesn't notice. 'Please, don't let me lose her too.'

She jumps at shadows carved out by car headlamps. At the sharp shapes thrown up and over the blackened hedgerows.

'Georgie. Is it Georgie?' her desperate cries as she leaps over puddles.

Up close, a sweaty-faced paramedic. His mouth a wide, black hole as he steers her away.

'Please return to your car.' He grabs her by the forearm. 'There's nothing to see here.'

But there is. And wrenching free, she twists backwards, nearly losing her footing again. A red motorbike is buried in the briar and thorn-choked undergrowth. Smoking. Its rear wheel spinning in the mud. With it, a flash of the boys who come to ride along the beach at night. The sounds of their engines she listens to when she can't sleep. A memory too, of her motorbike-mad boyfriend, Dave, from years ago. Then it's a stretcher she sees. Transported by the paramedic who told her to get in her car and his female colleague. It grazes past her, catching the hem of her parka. She shouldn't be here. She's no rubbernecker. But Melanie can't avert her eyes and it means she inadvertently sees the injured biker. Leather-clad and bleeding, an oxygen mask fixed to the battered face. This is a man. Someone's husband, brother, son. Not Georgie.

On her return to the car, under the blaze of headlights, she eavesdrops on the conversations of drivers leaning out through their open windows.

'Took the bend too fast. Didn't stand a chance.'

'Death trap for motorbikes.'

'Emergency services probably got here too late.'

A squeal of sirens and the ambulance disappears down the tunnel of trees. When the traffic eventually picks up speed, she swings the car from left to right. The centre road markings have faded to a chalky scuff and there are no cat's eyes to lead the way. Fields of sheep, partly engulfed by fog, whizz by. Shrunken trees straddle the road, their parasitic ivy and artificially bright moss are picked out by the Mazda's headlights, before fading into obscurity again. A fox tucked into the verge, his red eyes unblinking.

'Stay there,' she breathes. 'Don't step out.'

Melanie passes side roads and crossroads, but with Bethan's warning, 'Don't turn off anywhere... The sign for the farm will be clear from the road,' she does as she was told.

'Keep going, keep going,' she chants into her escalating distress. 'You've not come far enough yet.'

Stone-fronted farmsteads, stern as Welsh chapels, rear up beyond high metal gates. Their wet yards lit by searing security lights show corrugated barns crammed with haylage bales in readiness of snow. Farm names... Tan-Y-Waen... Bal Mawr... Caer Eithin... hurtle by. None of them Gweld Y Môr. A long-abandoned tea shop, its windows boarded against the seasons. A sign for a stud farm boasting Dutch Warmbloods she remembers Bethan telling her to watch out for. It means she must be close.

Heavy raindrops strike the windscreen like a shower of bullets. She jumps, flicks the wipers on again. Then she sees it. A large wrought-iron gateway just as Bethan described. Wide enough for a car, but so enveloped in ivy, she could easily have missed it. A quick check in her driving mirror before indicating and pulling into a lay-by. Lurching to a standstill, she identifies the mouth of the entrance: a tunnel made darkest green by rhododendron leaves. She gets out to investigate, uncovers a metal plate nailed to a gatepost, reads: Gweld Y Môr, as the rain slaps her face.

Back behind the wheel, she turns onto the dirt track. Focuses on the central spine of grass and weeds growing between the tyre tracks. Ghostly. The murky sulphur tubes of the car headlamps lurch with each pothole. Mind-numbing in its endlessness, the trail is overarched by the buckled boughs of trees, and scales what she supposes to be a death-defying cliff. Eyes peeled, a momentary lapse in concentration could be fatal. She is imagining what sliding down the sheer drop that is alarmingly close to where the hardcore ends and fields begin would mean, when the rattle of a cattle grid under the Mazda's tyres has her jerking the wheel. The car veers suddenly to the left. She screams into the hammering panic and manages, just, to right the car in time.

'Please,' she prays to the dark, with a fierce determination, 'let Georgie be here.'

The track snakes on, rising higher and higher. This is steep, impossibly steep, she responds to the strain of the engine, unable to push up into second gear. Another fear she has is that the Mazda won't make it to the top. She'd be better off on a horse and wonders what vehicle could manage this day in, day out. Not many. She thinks of Delyth's Defender. A boneshaker like that could manage it, she decides, or a tractor. She remembers what John said about seeing Gareth's Porsche heading off up here. Really? She can't see him risking his gorgeous motor along a track like this.

On and on, nudging past a series of large, corrugated iron sheds with heavy bolted doors and sagging barbed wire. Her body jolts at the sight of an owl. It lifts her from the wandering dread of her thoughts. The wonderment of its white, angel spread of wings as it follows the updraft of the car, floodlit by headlamps. Then, a final push over the withers in the track and a row of lofty Scots pines loom into view. Bent to the wind and working as gateposts, they mark the entrance to the surprisingly palatial and high-sided farmstead up ahead.

'At last.'

Melanie steers in through a double set of grand metal gates and skids to a halt, scattering chickens which flap and wheel away. Free of her seatbelt, she leaps from the car and charges out across the muddied twilight of the yard. Head down through the downpour, smelling wood smoke from a nearby fire, she is drawn like a moth to a thin light from the porch, its guiding beam rendered almost useless in the leaden blackness.

CHAPTER THIRTY-EIGHT

The door of the farmhouse opens and there stands Delyth. All smiles and backlit by the hall light.

'Is Georgie here? Is Georgie with you?' Melanie shrieks.

'What?' Delyth is evidently surprised by her question. 'Course she's here, I texted to tell you.'

'Georgie's here? She's definitely with you?' At the end of her reserves she wobbles, unsteady in the dripping porch.

'I told you. In a text message.' The woman stares at her as if she's stupid.

'But I didn't get it.' She bursts into tears. 'And I've been ringing and ringing.'

'Oh, dear, don't upset yourself.' Delyth takes her hand and pulls her in out of the rain. 'Georgie's here. She's fine.'

Melanie stumbles over the threshold and into a fug of perfume. *Delyth's wearing perfume?*

'I've left you loads of messages. Didn't you get them?' She sobs, too relieved to be properly angry. 'Look.' She holds up her phone with its miraculous full five bars of signal for Delyth to see. 'I've had messages from Gareth, one from Bethan, but nothing from you. I've been frantic with worry. Bethan's rung the police.'

'Well, I did send it. And I didn't think for a minute you'd be worried,' Delyth replies mildly. 'The school must've told you she was with me. Where did you think she was?'

'I didn't know.' Melanie blows her nose on a tissue and glances sideways at a serene plaster figurine of the Madonna and Child. It is an image she's always found unsettling. 'I thought... I thought...' But she can't formulate her thoughts, bleak as they are, into any kind of order.

'Oh, well, never mind. You're here now.'

'And you're sure Georgie's safe?' Still disbelieving, Melanie wipes away tears that have mixed with rainwater. 'She's really here? She's really safe, with you?' She keeps on, automatically scraping her boots clean on the doormat.

'Yes, silly.' Delyth continues with her smile. 'Your daughter's through here.' And she leads the way along the hall. 'I'd have brought her straight back to the pub, but she was so insistent, she wanted to see the kittens. And you weren't around to ask.' She turns and gives Melanie a look. 'So, I brought her back with me.'

When the kitchen door is eased open, they are greeted by a blast of warm air, along with the smell of rising bread dough.

'*Georgieeee!*' Melanie runs forwards, scoops her child in her arms. 'Oh, thank heavens, you're all right.'

'Ow, Mummy, you're hurting me. And you're all wet.' Georgie laughs, not the least perturbed as to where her mother has been.

'Sorry, darling. Mummy's so sorry.' Melanie, still holding her tight, is not letting go.

'Delyth's got kittens.' Georgie wriggles free and, round-eyed, her legs swinging, is oblivious to her mother's distress. 'Can we have one? Please, can we have one?' She jumps down from the scrubbed wooden table and leads Melanie over.

'Aw, they're adorable.' Still weeping with joy that her daughter is safe, she crouches for a closer look. 'Is it okay to touch them?'

'Perfectly fine,' Delyth assures. 'Georgie's been playing with them. Their mammy doesn't mind, I think she's had enough of them.'

A plastic crate lined with a blanket has been pushed up against the warm side of the Aga. Inside, there is a bundle of fluff-balls and an attentive tabby with green eyes. Melanie counts two greys and three gingers but can tell her daughter's heart's been lost to the most affectionate of the bunch – the prettiest black kitten with a puff of white on his chest.

'Please can I have him?' Georgie jigs around. 'Delyth says we can take one home today, if we want.'

'Aren't they too small?'

'They're fine.' Delyth steps between them. 'Been on solids a fortnight.'

'I don't know, sweetheart. I think we should ask Slinky what he thinks first.'

'He'd love a kitten. He told me he wants a little friend. Can we, Mummy? Can we?'

'Maybe.' Melanie hugs Georgie. The trauma of the drive and the dread she was never going to see her child again is at last ebbing away. 'Do you think he'd be any good at keeping mice down?'

'It's why we have them on the farm.'

'I should check with Gareth.' Melanie dithers, letting go of Georgie and straightening up. 'Mm, I love that smell.'

'D'you want some?' Behind her, Delyth is close enough for Melanie to smell her perfume again.

'Um.' Fingers combing her wet hair, she looks directly at Delyth, tries to work out what's different about her.

'It's delicious, Mummy.' Georgie, seated up at the table again, is about to take another bite of the buttered slice she's been given.

'I'm sure it is, sweetheart. But I hope you're not spoiling your dinner?'

'Let her have it.' Delyth overrides her concern. 'She could do with feeding up. She looks thinner to me. Is she eating properly?'

'She's like me, burns it off in a second.'

'If you say so. I wondered if it might have something to do with those tummy aches you said she was having?'

'We've been back to see the doctor.'

'Dr Cassidy?'

Melanie nods. 'Test results came back negative.'

'That's good. Maybe it was just a phase she was going through.'

'Let's hope.' A stiff smile. She's feeling a bad enough mother as it is and Delyth's comments make her feel worse. 'Because you've not had one of those bad tummies for a while, have you, Georgie?'

'No,' her daughter says, licking butter from her wrist. 'Not for ages.'

Remembering Bethan and her need to ring her, to let her know everything is all right, Melanie pulls out her mobile and scrolls through her contacts. Perhaps it would be enough to just send a text for now, tell her Georgie's safe and well and ask her to let the police know. Gareth too. Say she hasn't had a clear signal and that she will phone as soon as she's home. And with more than enough mobile signal, she dashes off two quick messages.

'Thanks for looking after Georgie.' Melanie twists to

Delyth. 'I'm sorry if I was short with you when I got here. None of it was your fault. I was the one who was late collecting her.'

'Bread?' The woman isn't interested in her apology. 'Fresh from the oven. Go on, you look like you could do with something.' She saws open the crusty-topped loaf with a serrated knife. 'There's jam. Home-made.' Delyth points to a jar that is waiting, ready with spoon and hands Melanie the plate. 'Go on. Help yourself.'

The bread knife is dropped into the sink with a clatter and the sharp sound of metal against ceramic sparks an image of Delyth slicing into her arms in the pub kitchen. And fighting through what remains of that traumatic afternoon, is when Melanie realises what is different about the woman today.

'You've cut your hair.'

'Pardon?' Delyth screws up her face. A face – Melanie is seeing, now she's looking properly – that's been sensitively enhanced with a silvery smear of eyeshadow, a blush of lipstick.

'Wow! Only now I'm noticing.' She lifts an admiring hand to the chic, black bob that's as shiny as tar. 'You look lovely.'

'Oh, this?' Delyth touches the tantalising bounce of her newly styled hair. 'I got it done this afternoon.'

'And your make-up?' Melanie appreciates. 'Did you have that done professionally too?'

Delyth nods.

'Well, you look lovely. The best I've ever seen you.'

'Thanks.' The woman responds as if she's been complimented on one of her pastries.

'Did you get your outfit today too?' Melanie clocks the designer jeans, the gauzy material of the shirt – nothing off the jumble sale here.

'Thought I'd treat myself.'

'Good for you. Are you off somewhere special?'

'A works Christmas do at the golf club. D'you want to be my plus one?'

'Best not.' Melanie's eyes slide to Georgie.

'Oh, now I'm seeing it. Your coat's wet through. Give it to me, I'll dry it on the Aga.' Delyth's request is more of a demand.

'Best not tip it up.' She removes her parka and hands it over. 'I've got seashells in the pockets.'

Melanie wanders the kitchen, eating her bread and jam. This is the hub of the house, with its laundry drying on a rack and the kettle on perpetual boil. It reminds her of her grandmother's farm. Chewing on the last of the crust, she spots a crop of framed photographs balancing on a shelf. Interested in Delyth's life, her family, she peers at a young couple on their wedding day.

'Are they your parents?' She sets the empty plate aside. The bride is as petite as Delyth and she has a headful of flame-red hair. The man beside her is tall with dark eyes.

'Yes, that's them.' A mug of milky tea is pushed into Melanie's hand.

'Your mum's very beautiful.' She looks at the fawn-coloured liquid, unsure if she can drink it. Already queasy after her angst-ridden drive. She hates milky tea.

'It was taken a long time ago.' The voice is dry. 'You can meet Mam, if you like?'

Melanie consults her watch. 'Maybe another time, we ought to be getting back.'

'A few minutes won't hurt. She's been looking forward to meeting you.'

'Has she?' Melanie isn't all that keen to meet a woman with a drink problem like the mother she grew up with.

'Very much so.'

'All right. I don't suppose another half hour will matter.'

'That's the spirit.' Delyth bends to retrieve a set of loaves from the oven. 'Just give me a minute to finish up here.'

Melanie's gaze returns to the photographs and she focuses on a family portrait in which a young Delyth is sitting beside another little girl.

Is this Erin? She assumes it must be. Sandwiching their offspring, a noticeably older Mr and Mrs Powell wear weathered complexions made ruddier under the stark studio lights. How gawky they look in their Sunday best. Delyth's mother in a cattle-red dress with pearls about her neck. The father in suit and tie.

'Little Miss Nosy, aren't you?' Delyth swoops up behind her.

'You take after your father.' Melanie shares her observation. 'It's the eyes. Very attractive,' she adds to soften it. Appreciating, even though she's never known her own, daughters don't necessarily want to hear they resemble their fathers. Then she spots something else. 'Hey!' she yelps, reaching to the back of the shelf. 'That's Gareth's school photograph. You didn't have to take it. I'd have got you a copy if you'd asked.'

'I was going to give it back.' Delyth is sheepish beneath her elegant haircut. 'It's just that I haven't got many photos of my—' Hearing her voice crack, Melanie fills in the gaps and knows she means Erin.

'Oh, don't worry. Gareth won't notice. You can give it back at some point.'

She tries her tea again. She must drink it, if only to be polite. Doing so, her eyes land on another framed photograph of the younger girl from the family portrait. Her glorious red hair as bright as her smile in the high summer sunshine. She is wearing a light cotton sundress and is standing barefoot on a patch of grass. The man Melanie recognises as Delyth's father stands beside her, his hands around her waist. Both are laughing into the camera.

'She's pretty. Who is she?' Melanie has already guessed this is Erin, but she wants the excuse it gives to ask questions.

'Sorry?' Delyth stands at the sink, the cuffs of her top folded back to the elbows.

'The girl here.' Melanie points to the photograph. 'She looks just like your mother in her wedding photo. Who is she?'

Delyth turns off the taps and dries her hands. 'Ready?' The look is enigmatic as she twiddles the crucifix gleaming at her neckline. 'Let's take you to see Mam.'

CHAPTER THIRTY-NINE

'Mammy. Mam?' Delyth snaps at the elderly woman asleep in an armchair in the adjacent room. Melanie is about to say, *Don't wake her, let her sleep*, when Delyth shakes her mother's bony shoulder. 'This is Melanie, Mam. Gareth's wife.'

The woman judders awake and blinks like a rodent might in unaccustomed light. She looks like a rodent. Something that sleeps a lot during daylight hours. A dormouse, perhaps. Her eyes are dark and huge enough; their lustre and size exaggerated in the face of such a small person. And the way her long white hair, worn in a single plait, swishes around, it could be a tail.

'What did you say?'

'I said this is Melanie.'

The face, unclouded by thought, stares out at them blankly.

'You remember me telling you about her?' Delyth prompts.

'Oh, Del, you do look nice. You off somewhere?'

'Yes.' An impatient sigh. 'I told you. Christmas bash at the golf club. Oh, I give up.' Delyth tosses Melanie a hopeless look. 'I won't be long.' A hand on her arm. 'I've just got to lock my hens up for the night. Are you happy to stay with Mam?'

'No probs.' She plonks down opposite Mrs Powell, whose

flickering eyelids suggest she might have drifted off to sleep again.

'Shall I take Georgie with me?' Delyth asks. 'She said she wanted to see the chickens.'

'If you like.'

'Be back in a minute.' Delyth puts on the padded jacket she carried from the kitchen, and zips her smart new clothes away inside. 'I'll call Andrew down. I'd like him to meet you.'

The room is large, falling away into shadow. Heavy oak furniture stoops in its unlit perimeters. The glow from a handsome log fire is cosy, as is the pink blush of a single tasselled lamp and, when an outer door slams, she wonders just how keen Georgie is to be tottering out with Delyth into the rain she can hear thrashing the windows. Watching the flames in the hearth fling crumpled shapes across the floorboards, Melanie could fall asleep herself and, tilting her head to yawn, she sees a framed print on the wall above the TV. It is the kind of landscape depicting impossible skies and cliffs and yellow sand, along with the usual fishing boats on an absurdly blue sea. Yet something about it is oddly familiar. Hunstanton. She recognises the layered cliffs she used to think looked like the Battenberg cake her gran used to make at Easter – vanilla and strawberry sponge, sandwiched together with apricot jam. Staring into the imagined scene, she lets the fist of her memories push her back to a time when her Uncle Pete would take her and Cassie fishing on that very beach. The three of them, clanking down to the shore when the tide was right, for what he termed, 'A spot of sea fishing.' Cassie landed a sea bass once. They cooked over an open fire. Stood around the flames eating with their fingers, picking out the bones.

Her mobile beeps. It's a text from Bethan. There's a smiley face emoji and seven kisses. Melanie smiles herself and, lifting her gaze, finds Mrs Powell, eyes open, smiling back at her.

'Hello, I'm Melanie.' She extends a hand in greeting.

'I'm Norah,' the woman croaks, her lips ungluing themselves. Norah holds her hand and stares into her eyes. 'Sorry to fall asleep on you.'

'Don't be silly. Soporific, aren't they?'

'You what?' Norah fiddles with the tartan rug spread over her knees.

'They make you sleepy.' She points at the flames.

'Oh, I'm terrible. Fall asleep on a drawing pin, my Wally used to say.'

'Lucky you.'

'You have trouble then?'

'You could say that.' Reluctant to elaborate, Melanie steers the conversation elsewhere by asking, 'Is that Hunstanton?'

Norah looks up through glassy eyes. 'How clever of you. Wally and me had our honeymoon there. Lovely it was.'

'I used to think it was the best beach in the world.' Withered memories of her and Cassie splashing in the shallows fall like petals. 'Until I came here.'

'Oh, yes. Home is best.' Norah tilts sideways and tugs the little brass handle on a rickety sideboard. 'You'll have a drink?'

'Oh, no, I'm fine. Delyth made me tea earlier.'

'I mean a proper drink.' Norah twinkles.

'Better not, I'm driving.' Melanie scratches her nettle sting which is still smarting.

Norah notices. 'I'll give you something for that. I swear by sage and comfrey.'

'Oh, no. It's fine.' She tucks her hand away.

'But you'll have a small sherry?' A swish of the tail of hair.

'Go on, keep me company. Delyth's such a stick-in-the-mud, she never touches the stuff.'

'No, I'd better not.'

'Help get you down the track. You need nerves of steel to do that in the dark.'

They laugh.

'All right.' Melanie uncrosses her legs. 'But only a tiny one.'

'There's no need to be frightened.'

'Sorry, what?'

'Yes, just push them away.' Norah wags a thin wrist.

'Sorry, push who away?' She takes the dainty glass that is handed to her.

'The dogs. If they're a bother.'

Melanie twists in her seat, peers into the darkened corners of the room. There aren't any dogs.

'We've always had sheepdogs. Lovely breed. My Wally loved them.' A sad sigh. 'Such dear, faithful dogs. And such energy, they keep me on my toes, I can tell you.'

'They're a popular breed.' Melanie, while being a little concerned, doesn't want to insult her host by pointing out the obvious.

'Now.' Up on her feet and surprisingly agile, Norah bends to stroke her imaginary companions. 'Now, boys... Boys,' she warns, wagging a finger. 'That's enough. On your beds.' She claps and points to a pair of beanbags beside a dark Welsh dresser. 'On your beds.' She repeats the order, lowering her voice to a growl. And seemingly satisfied the phantom dogs have done as they're told, she returns to her chair. 'They do take liberties. You've got to keep on at them. All the time.'

'I'm sure you do.' Melanie plays along, half-believing there are a pair of boisterous sheepdogs in the room.

Norah sips her sherry and Melanie does the same; feels the welcoming warmth of it spread through her. 'Brothers they are.'

Norah stares fondly into the darkness at whatever it is she sees. 'Great company for me, stuck here on my own.' She speaks with her hands. 'Since I retired, well, I don't get out no more.'

'That's a shame.' She remembers what John told her. No wonder the woman's inventing dogs for company, it sounds a grim existence. 'Couldn't Delyth take you somewhere now and again?'

'Too busy working, the girl don't go nowhere socially.'

'She's going out tonight.'

'Hah!' Norah splutters, licks her lips. 'Is there a blue moon behind them rain clouds?'

Melanie watches Norah and finds nothing of the woman Delyth made her out to be. So what? She enjoys a drop of sherry; there's no harm in that. Familiar with how miserable life is with a drunk, she decides to have a word with Delyth when she gets the chance. Engulfed by the big leather armchair she sits in, Norah, like Delyth, is doll-like, and with elbows as sharp as the corners of her furniture, she guesses the woman can't weigh more than six stone.

The sound of logs collapsing in the grate has Norah motioning to the hearth. 'Be a love and shove a log on.'

Melanie, putting her glass down on a dinky table, is pleased to have something to do.

'As a girl, my Del used to have a map of the world on her bedroom wall and dream of all the places she was going to go.' Norah chuckles while Melanie jabs the flames into life with the poker. 'But shame of it is,' the chuckling stops, 'she never gets to go nowhere. All the poor dab does is cook and clean. Keep house. Play mother.'

Satisfied with the fire, Melanie returns to the couch. She wonders what Norah would say if she knew how Delyth goes about painting her to the wider community.

'I wanted her to get married and have her own babies.'

Norah's voice is sad. 'She never goes nowhere,' she repeats herself. 'And what kind of life is that for a young woman? She should have seen something of life. Not slaving away at three jobs for bugger-all money. I want her to find a nice man, someone to take care of her. It's not natural being on your own.'

Did Norah just swear? There isn't the time for private thought.

'Talking of nice men.' Norah winks. 'How's your lovely Gareth?'

'He's fine.' She picks up her glass, considers the amber-coloured liquid. Going by the photographs in the kitchen, the woman sitting opposite her had hair as glorious as this once upon a time.

'Bit of a catch, if you don't mind me saying. He was such a star at school, everybody loved him.'

Melanie forces a smile. 'Yes, I know.'

'My Delyth would make someone a lovely wife.' Norah fiddles with her plait of long white hair and Melanie's grateful that Gareth seems to have been forgotten. 'I suppose, if things had turned out different... If Wally hadn't died... If Erin hadn't got herself pregnant.'

Melanie doesn't move. This is the first time Erin has been mentioned and she doesn't want to do anything to distract Norah. She wants to know what went on.

'But at least Erin got to spread her wings and experience a few things. I know she fell in with the wrong crowd and that, but it was loads better than living a nothing kind of life like Del. Yes, she could be selfish and irresponsible, but it took guts to run away like that. I didn't mind her leaving her boy with me. She was too young to have a babby. I told Delyth, I said for her to go too. Using me as an excuse, I can look after myself, thank you very much. I could've looked after Andrew too. But Del wouldn't have it. Besotted with him from the moment he was born, she was. More besotted with him than Erin ever was.'

'How long was Erin gone for?'

'About two years.'

'Long time to leave your child.'

'Nah, the boy was always more Delyth's than hers. Erin knew that. I think it's why she ran away.'

'Andrew's going to be doing his own thing soon. Delyth will be free then.'

'Not how she sees it.' Norah snorts. 'She says she's missed the boat. That no one will want her now.'

'That's rubbish.'

'Try telling her that.'

'I have.'

'Then you're wasting your breath, love.' Norah gives an eye roll. 'My Delyth don't want no help. Give her a solution, she'll ignore it. You can't fix her. She's *un-bloody-fixable*.'

Norah has no idea but she has echoed Gareth's complaint: about Delyth, and about Melanie. It makes her wonder if this is what she does? With Delyth, with John, with people in her life before now. Does she try to fix people's lives because it makes her feel better about the wrongs she's done? Like stealing Gareth from Elizabeth. Sophie's death. The fact she can't do anything to help her own mother who is rotting away in a horrid little flat on the other side of the country.

'How did you two meet?' Norah's question slices between her deliberations.

'Me and Delyth?'

'No. You and Gareth.' Norah tugs on her plait then drops it over her shoulder with a satisfying thump.

Melanie spends the next few minutes glossing over their affair, talks of Gareth already being married. 'I'm not proud of hurting Elizabeth like that, it wasn't fair.'

'There's nothing fair in love. It's got everything to do with luck. I was very lucky with my Wally. We were very happy. But I was still relatively young when he died... I had needs.' Norah lifts her watery eyes, lets Melanie fill in the gaps. Which she can't quite do. 'It's why Delyth had such a problem with what happened to Erin. A strictly no-sex-before-marriage girl, is our Del. Me?' Norah winks. 'I'm a woman of the world.'

Melanie's gaze wanders beyond the comforting crackle of the fire, to the beamed ceiling that is flaking and cobwebby at the corners. Sees where damp patches have stained the wallpaper brown like the liver spots on the backs of Norah's hands.

'How d'you manage it all here? It's a big place to maintain.'

'I don't think we do.' A weak smile.

'Have you thought about selling up? She remembers the conversation with Bethan and Sian.

'Oh, no. All my memories are here. Delyth's always on at me. Saying we should sell up, move to town, but I can't. She's a good girl, Del, but I think her wanting to move has more to do with the bad memories she has of her da. He never bothered with her. Erin was his favourite. It was Erin this, Erin that. Soft as butter, my Wally, he wouldn't let the wind blow on her.' Norah drains her sherry while Melanie's remains relatively untouched. 'That's why I'm glad my Wally weren't around to see what became of her. Erin, I mean. It would have broken his heart. Spoilt her rotten, he did. And there was Delyth, doing for him more than me when I was flat out with my job.' She pauses. 'You know I used to work for Gareth's father?'

'Delyth said. What was he like? I never met him.'

'Rhodri?' Norah is aghast. 'Didn't you know Rhodri?'

'No, he didn't approve of me. Blamed me for splitting Gareth and Elizabeth up. Him and Bronwyn.' A tight laugh. 'They didn't even come to our wedding.'

'Well, I never.' Norah's eyebrows shoot up. 'Was he really like that? I thought he was broad-minded about matters of the heart.' She floats away on her memories for a moment. 'He took me up in his plane once. Ah, we used to have some laughs, me and Rhod. Anyway, where was I?'

'You were saying how busy you were at work.'

'That's right. Wally and Del. Oh, my memory's going terrible. Don't be telling her, she worries about me enough as it is.' A click of her false teeth. 'Poor Del, cooking for him, pouring his tea, ironing his best shirt for chapel every Sunday. But he barely noticed her.'

'That must've been hard.'

'To tell you the truth, it was. And I'd like to say Erin was deserving of her father's doting, but she weren't.' Norah is surprisingly candid from her armchair. 'I have to say, I couldn't cope with Erin. Not after my Wally died.' Pulling no punches, she pours herself another sherry. 'I loved her, course I did, but she was always trouble.' She takes a sip. 'I tried to bring her up right, like I brought Delyth up right, but Erin was so rebellious, with her make-up and short skirts. Her drinking. Oh, you're not to mind me. Silly old woman going on about stuff.' The expression borders on apologetic. 'You don't mind, do you?'

'Not at all,' Melanie assures. 'It's lovely listening to you.'

'Thing is, see, I couldn't do no more, I washed my hands of her. I'm not proud of it, but my Wally, he was the only one who could get her to see sense, to do her homework, to leave the boys alone. But after he died, *ugh*,' Norah squeezes the stem of her glass, 'she went completely off the rails. Staying out all hours. I never knew where she was half the time.'

'What happened to her?' Melanie asks gently.

'She fell out of her bedroom window. She was drunk,' Norah says bluntly. Her thin arm pointing upwards through the firelight. 'Top of the house it was. This place has got a third floor and an attic room above. It's a big space. Nice and roomy for Erin and shut off from the rest of us. Delyth thought it'd be good for her to have her own space when the babby came along. Some privacy. You know?'

The words *shut off* have a sinister ring. Especially as it echoes the suggestion Sian made when Erin came up in conversation at Plas Newydd that morning. But there isn't the time to ask Norah to elaborate. The rasp of carpet when it snags against the door interrupts them.

'Andrew! There you are.' Norah greets the teenager loitering on the threshold, his face lit by the ten-inch screen he holds in his hands. 'Come and meet Melanie.'

'Hi-ya,' he mumbles, without raising his eyes.

Melanie looks at him. How tall he is. Tall and leggy in his ripped jeans and grey hoodie. When at last he lifts his face, she hunts it, wanting the man he almost is. She finds him for a moment and tries to hold him there, but he slips away again. How handsome he is, she thinks, judging him to be at least as tall as Delyth's father in the photographs Melanie saw of him, but with the same auburn hair as Erin, and Norah before her.

'Can't you put that thing down for a minute?' Norah sighs. 'Come and be sociable. Melanie's been dying to meet you, haven't you, Melanie?'

'I have, yes.'

'Sorry. Only had it today. It's new.' Andrew grins his excuse, dazzling them with his smile. 'Del bought me it.'

'Lucky you.' Melanie returns his smile. 'Is it an early Christmas present?'

'Something like that.' A shy glance up through his conker-shiny fringe.

'I got myself a new smartphone not so long ago. I love it, couldn't do without it now. I'm not sure how I'd get on with those.' She gestures to his portable PC with its LCD touchscreen.

'I've got a smartphone too,' he says, blowing air up through his flap of hair. 'But this is *awesome*.' Eyes down, he stretches the adjective like a piece of bubble gum.

'Andrew!' Norah is sharp from her chair. 'Put it away. I won't tell you again.'

He does and, moving into the room, takes the seat beside Melanie on the couch.

'I think I need to change my network provider.' She winks when she catches his eye. 'I had next to no mobile signal all the way here.' Then adding, to keep the conversation going, 'How are you liking the sixth form?'

'Not much. Waste of time. I don't even need A levels to join the army. There's tests and stuff you've gotta pass, but I reckon I'd do them easy.'

'You're going to join the army?'

A spirited nod. 'I'll go off my head if I have to stay here.' He sneaks a look over at his grandmother who gives him a knowing smile.

'I suppose it's a great way to see the world.' A brief thought of John and the damage his years in the armed forces caused him. But she can't mention any of this to Andrew – it isn't her place.

'Too right.' Andrew, drawn to his tablet, is, within seconds, scrolling through the glossy lives of others on his Instagram page again.

The door behind them wheezes open a little wider and Delyth, trailing Georgie, steps into the room.

'Ah, there you are,' she addresses Andrew, a brand-new mobile phone held close to her chin. 'Melanie must've been wondering if I'd made you up.'

'Andrew's been telling me about his plans to join the army.'

'Over my dead body,' Delyth snaps, dropping the smartphone to her side. 'He's going to university. And not too far away from home, either.' She focuses briefly on Melanie, then back to her mobile. 'He's such a whizz with technology, I don't know how he keeps up with all the latest gizmos.'

'Come by the fire, love.' Norah, tapping her thin knees, beckons Georgie closer. 'You must be freezing. Fancy Delyth making you go out in that horrible weather.'

'But I wanted to,' Georgie informs her. 'I wanted to see the chickens.'

'Chickens?' Norah scoffs. 'Mangy buggers, the lot of them.'

'Mam!' Delyth barks from her standing position by the door.

'Well, they are.' Norah takes Georgie's hands and rubs them between her own. 'Oh, dear, they're like two blocks of ice. That's it, you sit there. Close to the fire. Delyth used to sit on that when she was little.' Norah uses a foot to shift a small tapestried stool in Georgie's direction. 'And never mind the dogs. It's only because they like you.'

'What dogs?' Georgie sits down. 'There aren't any—'

A hand on her child's arm, Melanie stops her from saying what everyone, apart from Norah is aware of.

'I've tried to teach them since they were puppies,' Norah babbles.

Georgie giggles, but plays along with what she supposes is a game.

'Beautiful. Just beautiful. The pair of you.' Norah smiles, turning her head from Georgie to Melanie. 'Oh, they're such naughty dogs. Just push them away, love.' Her attention swivelling again. 'I've told them not to lick faces, but they won't listen.'

Delyth points at a photograph of two black-and-white Border collies on the mantelpiece then drags a finger across her throat.

'What pretty hair you have, little one.' Norah compliments Georgie. The dogs forgotten. 'Does Mammy brush it into those plaits for you?' Georgie nods, curiously coy under this woman's kindly interest. 'I do my own. It's been a long time since I had a mammy.'

'You don't do so bad.' Delyth sounds hurt.

'No, you look after me, lovely.' Norah angles her head at Georgie. 'She does, mind.' She drops back into the mound of cushions. 'Delyth and Erin both had long hair when they were little. I used to love brushing it for them too. How old are you again? I know you told me already, but my memory's going terrible.'

'I'm going to be eight soon.' Georgie pushes her tongue through the gaps in her teeth. 'Delyth had long hair until today, didn't you, Delyth? Long hair like you.' She points at Norah's.

Norah picks up her long white plait, pretends to be surprised by it; it makes Georgie giggle again. 'Indeed, she did. And now she's had it all cut off. What a clever little one you are.'

'What are you trying to do?' Andrew gets up off the sofa to give Delyth whatever instructions she seems to need with her newfangled phone.

'Oh, look, Melanie. Here's that text I sent you. It's still in my outbox,' Delyth announces. Casual and breezy, she leans forwards, her crucifix swinging, to show her the screen. 'I'm having real trouble working out how to use this thing.'

'She is hopeless,' Andrew concurs, pulling faces behind her back.

'Oi, less of it, you. I can't help if I liked it better when you had buttons to press.'

'You're still hopeless.' Andrew laughs. Everyone except Melanie joins in.

'Give me a chance, I only got it today.'

'Came into a nice little windfall, didn't you, Del?' Norah tells her. 'Got lucky on the scratch cards.'

'Really?' Melanie raises her eyebrows. She doesn't believe that's where Delyth had the money from – she is thinking about Gareth's three-thousand-pound cash withdrawal.

'Delyth fetched me new slippers today too.' Norah wriggles her toes, shows off a pair of expensive sheepskin ankle boots. 'We need them here. Place is so draughty.'

'You decided if you're having a kitten?' Delyth puts Melanie on the spot. 'Because I think a certain little someone's set her heart on it.'

'Oh, please, Mummy. Please,' Georgie chimes in.

'Talk about being pushed into a corner.' Melanie exhales heavily. 'But okay, you can have a kitten.'

'Yes, yes, yes.' Georgie, squealing, is up on her feet.

'Have you decided which one you'd like?' Delyth asks Melanie.

'I'll let Georgie choose.'

'Go on then. You as well, Andrew.' Delyth ushers Georgie and her nephew out into the hall. 'Help sort a box for them to take it home in, would you?' She pats him on the arm. 'Oh, and check the loaves. Take them out if they're done. There's a good boy. Your gran and I have some important things to discuss with Melanie.'

'Right,' Delyth says, as soon as Andrew and Georgie have gone. 'You've told Melanie then, have you, Mam?'

'Told her what?' Norah blinks.

'What we agreed.' After a final look along the hall, Delyth closes the door.

'Oh, for God's sake, we don't want to go raking all that up again, Del. Leave it alone.' Norah floats a hand through the flickering firelight.

'No, I'm sorry, Mam. We agreed, she has to know.'

'Has to know what?' Melanie is bewildered by the sudden frostiness between mother and daughter.

'Just what kind of a man you're married to.' Delyth throws her a look.

'Erin. It was Erin. She was besotted with him,' Norah starts to explain. 'None of it was Gareth's fault. The girl played him like a fiddle.'

'Gareth's fault?' Melanie is alarmed. 'What wasn't Gareth's fault?'

'I wanted to go to the police, but Mam wouldn't have it.' Delyth's face is flushed and angry. 'Quick enough to call them when Erin fell out of the window, though, weren't you?' She directs her complaint to her mother. 'Happy to have them crawling all over our lives... All over the farm, then. Gareth forced himself on Erin, Mam. Why won't you listen? He as good as raped her.'

The appalling accusation hangs in the air.

Melanie is winded by it. And with two sets of eyes watching her, poised for her reaction, she gulps it down. Feels it splinter her precious life apart.

'Forced himself on her? Bah, don't give me that.' It's Norah who speaks, saving Melanie the need to respond, which she can't. 'Your sister knew exactly what she was doing, especially where boys were concerned.'

'Mam!' Delyth wrings her hands. 'She was barely fourteen. She was a little girl.'

'Going on thirty.'

'None of that excuses him. Not when he was eighteen.'

Norah laughs: a dry, empty sound that spirals around the room.

'I saw what he did. I saw it, Mam. Plying her with drink at our end-of-school party. Erin wasn't even supposed to be there, but he fixed it so she was. He engineered the whole damn thing.' Delyth is the boldest and most assertive Melanie has ever seen her. 'But we all know why you didn't do anything about it, don't we? We all know where your loyalties lay. They were with his father.'

'Don't talk rubbish. My relationship with Rhodri Sayer had nothing to do with my decision about not going to the police about his son.'

'Now who's talking rubbish? He was always more important than the family you had left. If it was anyone's fault Erin went off the rails, then it was yours. You were always at work, or sneaking off to be with him. It was Rhodri this, Rhodri that.'

Norah stares across the room at Delyth who, in turn, keeps her spine pressed to the door. Fearful, perhaps, of Andrew or Georgie bursting in on them. 'Delyth, love, you saw what you wanted to see that night at the party.' Her voice is calm. 'And you can go on kidding yourself if you like, but I know different. That sister of yours was out of control. Yes, Gareth was naughty to take advantage of her, what with her being so young, but she gave herself willingly, I'm sure of it.' A glance at Melanie who is still too dumbfounded to speak.

'You weren't there. I was the one who witnessed it, not you.' Delyth, her cheeks flushed in the pinkish lamplight, refuses to back down.

'You saw what you wanted to see.' Norah dismisses her. 'And I'll tell you why, shall I? Because you was jealous. It screwed you up to see Gareth with Erin, knowing you'd never have a chance with him.'

'My feelings for him had nothing to do with any of it. *Okay*,' Delyth stresses, 'he forced himself on Erin that night. And if you'd been any kind of mother and taken me seriously... If you'd gone to the police...' Her voice breaks under the weight of her grief. 'Then Erin might still be here now.'

Melanie doesn't move. She can't move. The shock of what she's heard has rendered her speechless. Watching the flames in the hearth throw disorganised patterns on the opposite wall, she tries to keep pace with their argument.

'For God's sake, Delyth. Stop being so silly, it was years ago, you've got to let it go.' Norah frowns. 'You've got to forgive, it's not healthy carrying all that bitterness around.'

'Forgive him? He destroyed Erin's life. Getting her pregnant, then disappearing off to university. None of it impacted him.' Delyth is vehement. 'So, no, I can't forgive him.'

'Not very Christian of you,' Norah bats back, deliberately provocative. Then whispers to Melanie: 'Got the heart of a lion, that one. Fiercely protective of her little sister, even now. That's why she can't forgive your Gareth.'

Sickened by the first revelation of Gareth forcing himself on a fourteen-year-old girl, when she hears he got her pregnant, Melanie is incredulous. 'What?' she gasps, slapping a hand to her throat. 'Are you saying Andrew is Gareth's son?'

'That's right.'

Melanie flops back into the sofa. Too shocked to speak. Discovering that the man she has built her life with is Andrew's father is too much for her to get her head around.

'Your Gareth's not a bad person.' Norah shuffles forwards in her chair and takes Melanie's hand in hers. 'I'd hate for any of this to cause trouble between you both.'

'Oh, that's right.' Delyth, strident from the sidelines. 'The Golden Boy must be allowed to get away with it scot-free. Yet again.'

'B-but, d-does he know?' Melanie stammers to Norah. 'Does Gareth know about Andrew?'

'No, love. He doesn't have the first idea. You know what boys are like when they're that age? Gareth was just your typical teenage boy. Erin made herself available to him and he went along with it. End of. Delyth's problem is that she can't bear the idea that her sister was a bit slutty.' Norah speaks as if Delyth isn't there. 'I've tried, but I'll never make her see otherwise. It's easier for her to blame it all on Gareth.'

'What he did, it really doesn't trouble you, does it?' Melanie can't believe what she's hearing.

'Oh, it troubles me, but you can't keep living in the past. What's done is done, none of us can change it. You just have to make the best of things, which is what we did. Because by the time any of us knew, Gareth was long gone. He wouldn't have had the first idea Erin was expecting, or that Andrew was his.'

'You reckon, do you?' Delyth plays with her new hair. 'I wouldn't bet on that.'

'How could he know?' Norah shouts at her daughter then turns to Melanie. 'Erin swore us to secrecy. She wouldn't even let us tell Gareth's parents. I don't know why. But the girl wouldn't even let us fetch a midwife when the babby came. Andrew was born here. Me and Del delivered him.'

'Of course Erin told him.' Delyth is adamant. 'She must've been in touch with him all along. It's not a coincidence. Her having that *accident* the same week Gareth was back here for his father's funeral.'

'What are you saying it like that for? Course it was an accident. Honestly, what rubbish you talk, you silly girl,' Norah argues. 'You never let her go nowhere. After the police brought her back from that squat, you never let her out of your sight.'

'You make it sound like I kept her prisoner. I was only looking out for her, keeping her safe. Keeping her safe for Andrew's sake. She never wanted for nothing.'

'If you mean booze and fags.' Norah drops her voice a notch. 'No, she weren't never short of them.'

'I did my best by her, Mam. You know I did. Not my fault she got a taste for it. And anyway, I'm telling you, Erin must've seen Gareth. He could have come to the farm that week he was home for his father's funeral. How would you know? You were never here.'

'Don't be too hard on your Gareth, love,' Norah says to Melanie. 'Take no notice of Del. He weren't in touch with Erin. I bet he clean forgot about her as soon as he left Pencarew.'

Norah's fervent defence of Gareth bothers Melanie. As a mother, she should be on Erin's side, no matter how troublesome or provocative her daughter might or might not have been. There's no way she could imagine showing this kind of disloyalty to Georgie, no matter what she'd done. Because whatever blame Norah thinks she can put on Erin, Delyth's right – she was only a child and blameless because of it.

'Don't you think about her then?' Delyth speaks to her mother from the shadows. 'Does Erin never cross your mind when you're in here watching *Coronation Street* and *EastEnders?*' Melanie listens to the anger tighten in her voice. 'I don't know how you do it, living here, in this house. This house!' She is almost shrieking. 'If I had my way, I'd burn this place to the ground.' She stares up at the ceiling and raises her arms to whatever went on in those rooms under the eaves. 'So, I'm sorry if it affects your sensitivities, that it makes me silly.'

'Don't you judge me, Delyth. Don't you dare judge me. I wanted Erin to have an abortion.'

'How can you even say that?' A touch of the crucifix around her neck. 'Shame on you, Mam.'

'It was you what talked her out of it. I didn't want her getting tied down with a babby at her age. It was so... unnecessary.'

'*Unnecessary!* That's my Andrew you're talking about.'

The log in the hearth splits open with a firework of sparks. Delyth pitches from the room, leaving Norah behind in the bloated aftermath of their argument.

Melanie doesn't move. Frantically filtering through all she's been told and struggling to believe it, she leans over her knees and fears she might be about to be sick.

CHAPTER FORTY-ONE

Friday, five o'clock. A glass of what will be the Monkstone Arm's house red in her hand, Melanie wanders where the late-afternoon shadows fall into the vacant downstairs rooms. She is celebrating. Alone. It was the workmen's last day today. The refurbishments are complete and aside from a few last-minute touches and a final trip to the cash-and-carry, they are set to open for business in a week.

Flicking on the main switch in the bar, her heart soars with pride at the chrome pendant lighting, the glamour of the high leather stools, the bur oak counter with its polished beer pumps and glasses. The huge inglenook fireplace, restored to its former glory and cleared of rubble, has been installed with a wood burner that looks the part. Especially with the leather fender she sourced on eBay for next to nothing.

She thinks how pleased Gareth is going to be until she remembers the shock of what Delyth and Norah revealed, and her insides cartwheel with dread. She ambles into the restaurant, moseys around the wooden tables prettified with potted ferns and glass cruets, the soles of her slippers sliding over the beautiful parquet floor. Looking up, her eyes travel the reconditioned beams, the Victorian red-papered walls dressed with shabby-chic menu boards and ornate mirrors. Onto the wide picture windows with the disappearing view. She walks the length of the room, fingers trailing the framed sepia prints of the horse-drawn town and local rugby sides dating back to before the Great War. All that remains of the pub from before they came.

Her mobile beeps in her jeans pocket. It's a text from Gareth telling her he's about two hours away. She doesn't reply, she's been avoiding his messages since Wednesday's trip to Gweld Y Môr. How much has changed in a few short months. When they first bought this place, she used to count the days, desperate for the week to pass quickly so she could have him home. Now she spends the weekends willing Monday mornings to come around and for him to be gone again. She is dreading his homecoming tonight more than usual. Knowing full well, with the bombshell she is about to drop, there will be a fight. He's got a lot of explaining to do, she thinks, draining her wine and returning to the kitchen for a refill.

Minutes later, seated at the kitchen table, she pours herself another wine and works through her list. Ticking things off, clearing the way. Even though she's not looking forward to seeing Gareth, he still needs feeding, as does Georgie, who, because she's finally feeling better after another nasty bout of tummy aches that kept her off school for the last two days, Melanie thought she'd try out one of Nigella's chicken tray bakes as it might be an option for the restaurant menu. Amid the tantalising smells of vermouth and dill, she finds it difficult to concentrate on her list, so pushes it aside. Her eyes close and imagined images of her husband cavorting with the pretty, red-haired girl... a child... in those photographs in Delyth's kitchen, flicker behind her eyelids.

When she opens them next, it is onto Gareth throwing a dark shadow over her.

'You're home.' Melanie, disoriented, has no idea how long she's been asleep. All she's sure of is the cold and empty sensation in the pit of her stomach. She used to think, when she and Gareth first got together, that he was a man who could do anything: climb a tree, jump a gate. Her saviour. Her knight in shining armour. She thought she knew him inside out. But looking at him now, with the awfulness of what she learnt two evenings ago, it is as if to gaze upon a stranger.

He leans down for a kiss. His inky-black stubble close to her face, the tang of tube trains still clinging to the fibres of his suit.

She twists her head in time. She can't bear to have him touch her. She had hoped they would be able to find a way through this mess together, that he would explain and help her to understand why he did what he did to a fourteen-year-old girl, and everything would be right with them again. But now he's here, standing in their kitchen, the reality is that she can hardly bring herself to look at him.

'Some dream you were having,' he says.

'Yeah.' She yawns and rubs her eyes. It's been a while since she bothered applying make-up in readiness of his homecoming. 'I was on my way to Manderley again.'

'You what?'

'Nothing,' she says, up on her feet, avoiding eye contact. 'Good journey?'

'Not bad.'

'Much traffic?' Sidestepping him, she opens the oven door and checks on dinner. Small talk is about all she can manage, until she can find a way to ask him to explain. But appalled, outraged and disgusted with what she discovered less than forty-eight hours ago, it's a struggle to maintain even this bland civility. The unpleasantness of what she is trapped into rears its head again: they are married; they have Georgie; they have risked everything by selling their house and piling their savings into this business. The worry of it has been keeping her awake at night because, as she reminds herself, they must make this work. There is no alternative.

'Reasonable.' Gareth removes his tie, undoes his top button. 'Where's Georgie?' Apparently not the least bothered by Melanie ducking his advances.

'Upstairs, playing.'

'Has she been feeling all right this week?'

'Great until Wednesday night. I had to keep her home yesterday and today.'

'And now? Is she better now?' She listens to the alarm in his voice. 'Because you haven't exactly been keeping in touch with me the last couple of days.'

'She's fine now.' Melanie ignores his complaint – she has bigger ones of her own.

'You're going to have to take her back to the doctors. Start demanding answers. This has been going on for too long.'

'I called the surgery. She's seeing Dr Cassidy on Monday. He says he'll run more tests.'

'More tests? Why didn't they just do all the tests in one go?' Gareth looks tired, the skin around his eyes looks purple under the halogen lights. 'I'm going up to get changed. Will dinner be long?'

'Not long.' She moves to follow him. 'Gareth? Can you hang on a minute, there's something we need to talk about.'

He yawns. 'Can't it wait? I'll be down in a minute.'

'No, it can't.'

'Get on with it then. Going all cryptic on me. What's the matter?'

She steps back, hands reaching for the work surface,

needing its support. 'I was up at Gweld Y Môr on Wednesday evening.'

A shift of his feet informs her he's familiar with the name of the farm. 'Where?' he asks, with a tiny flick of his head.

'You heard me.' She chucks the oven gloves down. 'And now, I want you to tell me about Erin. I want to hear your side of things.'

'Erin?' An uneasy laugh. 'Am I supposed to know who that is?'

'Erin Powell.'

'Sorry, Mel, you're going to have to give me more of a clue than that.'

'Delyth's sister.'

He looks at her, his expression vacant.

'Come off it, Gareth, I'm not an idiot. Erin's why you've got a problem with Delyth. It's why you didn't want me spending time with her. Admit it. I can see why. You were afraid she'd spill the beans. Well, the beans have been spilt now, so you might as well come clean.'

'I'm sorry, Mel.' He rubs his eyes. 'But I haven't the first idea what you're on about.'

'Tell me what happened the night of your end-of-school party. You know, the one you had to celebrate A level results.'

'But that was years ago.'

'Tell me what happened.'

'What d'you mean, tell you about it?' He yawns again, his eyes watering from the effort. 'It was a lifetime ago. How am I supposed to remember?'

'Tell me.'

'All right.' He lifts a hand; some kind of surrender. 'I was pretty wasted.' Another laugh she can tell is false.

'You're going to have to do better than that.' She folds her arms and leans back against the counter. 'I'm giving you a chance here, can't you see? I already know what you did, Gareth. Delyth told me.'

'I'm sorry, what?' He scowls. 'Whatever I'm supposed to have done that night, I don't remember. As I already said, I'd had a skinful.'

'But you remember Erin, right? You remember Delyth's younger sister.'

'I don't think I do, no.'

'Come on, Gareth, we both know that's a lie.'

'I don't remember any sister. *Okay?*'

'Delyth saw you, don't you understand? She saw what you did.'

'Spying on me, was she?' The tone is both hostile and belligerent, and again, Melanie is more than a little frightened of him. 'If she didn't like whatever it was she says she saw, then why didn't she stop me?' His countenance, unyielding as usual, gives nothing away. 'Look, Mel, I don't know what Delyth's told you, but she probably just made it up because I wasn't interested in her.'

'If you're so sure she made it up, then tell me why you've been adamant I stay away from her?'

'Because she's a moany old cow. I was frightened she'd drag you down again, just when you'd started to feel better about things.'

'I don't believe you. It's way more than that, and you know it. What did she see, Gareth? What did Delyth see you do to her little sister that night? Did you make sure Erin got wasted too – as you so eloquently put it? Plied her with booze so you could force yourself on her? Please tell me, because honestly, I've had enough of you pissing me about.'

Gareth drags out a chair and sits down at the table, head in hands. 'All right.' His declaration is muffled by his fingers. 'I remember her. I remember Erin.'

'And?'

'And nothing.'

'Gareth – tell me.'

He closes his eyes, and she listens to him breathing. He remains silent for so long she isn't sure she is going to get an answer.

'It was a one-night stand,' he admits, at last. 'Me and Erin. We'd both drunk too much. It was nothing. It meant nothing. God knows why Delyth's still going on about it, the saddo.'

'Recovered your memory all of a sudden?' Melanie is as acerbic as she can be. 'Delyth's still going on about it because Erin was her little sister. She was a child. A fourteen-year-old child. She's saying you raped her. That you raped her little sister.'

'Raped her!' Gareth holds his hands up: the innocent. 'For fuck's sake, Mel.' His look is desperate. 'This is me you're talking to. I didn't rape her. She came onto me.' He gets up, reaches out for her arm, but she pulls away. 'You've got to believe me, Mel... Mel?' he pleads, but seeing he gets nowhere, gives up and sits back down again. 'You didn't know what she was like, you never knew her. Please?' He holds his hands out to her, but again she recoils. 'She handed it to me on a plate. Show me an eighteen-year-old boy who'd refuse that?'

'You disgust me. She was just a child!' Melanie flies at him.

'Who went about looking like a grown-up woman.'

'And, what? Because you were so used to getting your own way, getting everything you wanted, you took it, is that it? You took her?'

He exhales, braces himself. 'Look, I can see how bad it looks now. But not then. You can't judge me for what I did then. I was only a kid myself.'

'You were eighteen. And you should've known better. What do you think it was like for me, having to sit there, listening to that? It shouldn't have been Delyth and Norah telling me what you did, what you caused, it should have been you. I'm your wife.'

'I didn't tell you because I'd forgotten all about it. Jesus, Mel.' He slams his palms against the tabletop violently, enough to knock her glass of wine over. 'D'you seriously think if I'd remembered doing that, then I'd have wanted to come back here?' Aggressive, volatile, everything she hates in a person. Everything she hoped she'd left behind in her childhood.

Who is he? she asks herself again, staring at him, barely recognising him.

She grabs a dishcloth and mops up the spilt wine. 'At least now I understand why you didn't want me spending time with Delyth. Why you've been so hostile with her from the moment we arrived. You didn't want me finding out your dirty little secret.' She rinses out the cloth. 'Is that why you went to the farm?' She dries her hands. 'I told you someone saw your car. You've given her money, haven't you?' An image of the new Delyth: chic bobbed hair, designer clothes and smartphone. 'Hush money. You were trying to shut her up. She's telling everyone she won it on the scratch cards, but I know different.' Anger curls its fist behind her ribcage. 'Well—' Her turn to laugh; jagged and brittle. A sound that separates them further. 'Let me tell you, it didn't work.'

Gareth doesn't respond and doesn't shift from his position at the table.

'You're pathetic, do you know that? Pathetic.' She backs away from him, alarmed by the menacing gleam in his eye. 'Because you're not telling me if that happened to Georgie when she was only fourteen, that you'd dismiss it as easily. I think you'd insist she was still a child, just as I'm insisting Erin was a child. Double standards, if you ask me. I know you. If a bloke did that at the age you were, you'd string him up. If he defiled your daughter. And let's not forget one major fact here, shall we?' She is shouting now. 'It's against the bloody law for a reason.'

Melanie studies him, unsure if they are ever going to be able to get past this. If only he would say he was sorry, it would be something. But he won't be made to see what he did was wrong. She knows she has got to make their marriage work – for Georgie, for the business they're about to launch. But how? When their marriage is little more than a charade and so easily dissolved, with her unable to bear the idea of him anywhere near her. All it would take is the stroke of a pen. But is a future without him even possible? If she wants out, how will she do it? She hasn't the finances to support her and Georgie alone, and where would they go?

'Delyth wanted to report you to the police.'

Gareth gawps at her, open-mouthed.

'You've got Norah to thank that she didn't. She's the one who stopped her. I don't know why, but Norah never blamed you. You're like Teflon Man in her eyes. Wipe clean, apparently.'

'But not in Delyth's?'

'No. And I'm sorry, Gareth, but I'm with her on this.'

'If it's such a big deal, why's she waited until now to tell you?' He scratches his stubbly chin.

'How do I know?'

'It's because she wants to split us up,' he says darkly.

'What – so she can take my place?' Melanie splutters. 'You seriously think she's still got a crush on you?'

'Of course she has. And she's spiteful and vindictive. She always was.'

'You're deluded, d'you know that? Deluded.' Melanie, fists

on hips. 'Delyth hates you, don't you understand that yet? She hates you for destroying her sister's life... For destroying her own life.'

'Destroying her life? Anyone would think I'm a monster.'

'Well, aren't you?'

'I can't believe you're even asking that. Why are you siding with her? You're my wife, you're supposed to be on my side. I was a kid, for crying out loud. Come on, Mel. What I did, was it really so very wrong?'

'Yes! It was wrong. Very wrong. On every count. And what you did, it had far-reaching consequences. You knew how young Erin was, and yet you still did it.' She takes a breath, feels her blood slow. 'Don't you take any responsibility? What kind of a person are you?'

'But I didn't do anything. Not deliberately.'

'So, you accidentally shagged her? A fourteen-year-old girl? Of course it was deliberate, and it had consequences. Everything's got consequences, Gareth. Don't you understand that yet? Erin was too young... she couldn't cope. She was so depressed she drank. Drank herself to death, pretty much... She died falling out of a top-floor window because she'd been drinking.'

'What?' Gareth is up on his feet and heading her way. 'What did you say?'

'Didn't you know?'

'Of course I didn't fucking know.'

'Didn't your mother fill you in? Or Bethan?'

'Why would they?' He looks baffled. 'When did this happen?'

'Not right away, poor kid. She struggled on for nine years. Norah said Erin tried to make the best of it but... What makes it worse is that I don't reckon Delyth believes it was an accident.'

And neither does John Hughes, she thinks but doesn't say. 'I get the feeling she thinks her sister killed herself. That in the end, she just couldn't see a way to go on.'

'A way to go on? What the hell does that mean? I'm not taking the bloody blame for that.'

'I don't see why not. What you did, it tore that family apart. Thank God for dear, dutiful Delyth.' Melanie takes a second to think of her. Perhaps understanding, with particular clarity, what drove her to slice into herself in their kitchen sink. 'Picking up the pieces after you'd cleared off. Because she was the one who brought that boy up. And he's a lovely kid. All credit to her. You owe her, big time.'

'Boy? What boy?'

'Aw, pull the other one.'

Gareth seizes her by the shoulders. His grip makes her wince in pain.

'What boy? What bloody boy?' He shakes her.

'Andrew.' Defiant, despite her trembling. 'He's yours. That time with Erin, you got her pregnant. But you already knew that. Delyth reckons you and Erin never lost touch. She seems to think you went to see her during that week we were here for your father's funeral. You did disappear for quite a while. We weren't together all the time.'

Gareth shoves her away. Angry. The movement is awkward and Melanie isn't ready for it. She staggers forwards and cracks the side of her head against the sharp-edged work surface as she falls to the floor. The world spins and slows in the quivering aftershock. Melanie puts a tentative hand to where it hurts. Brings her fingers away and sees blood. Gareth sees it too.

'Mel... Mel! Oh, my God. I'm sorry.' Contrite and pleading, he sinks to his knees beside her.

'Get off me!' she screams, blood trickling into her eye.

'You're a bloody bully.' And as she scrambles to her feet, she thinks of what John told her about Gareth's treatment of him at school; indignities that had floated in the abstract until now.

'Mel, please?' Gareth sobs from the floor, his arms spread wide; desperate, begging. 'Are you all right? Let me... I-I didn't mean to hurt you. P-please... *please.* I'll do it. I'll make amends with Delyth and her mother. I'll make it up with the boy. I can try and put things right.'

'It's too late.' Melanie turns away. Reaches for the dishcloth to stem the flow, the purple stain of wine mixing with her blood. 'The damage is done.' She means her and Gareth. She means Erin Powell and the family she left behind. 'I never knew you, did I? But I sure as hell know you now.'

She sees herself reflected in the blackened glass of the windowpane. The skin around the cut above her eye is already blackening to a bruise. Then, over her shoulder, it's her daughter she's seeing. Drifting into the kitchen, the thin light of the bar, pale as a lemon, in her hair.

'Daddy, Daddy. Look what I've got,' Georgie squeals excitedly, the fluffy black kitten she refuses to let out of her sight, in her arms. 'I've called him Bingo.'

Melanie follows her daughter's gaze as it leaps from Gareth then up to her. Then the tick-tick-tick of claws and Slinky is there, following Georgie downstairs. He makes a beeline to Gareth and licks his hand.

'What's happened to Mummy's face?' The enthusiasm about her father being home for the weekend, along with a week's worth of things she's been waiting to share with him, crackle with uncertainty. 'Why's Daddy sitting on the floor?'

Then Melanie smells their burning dinner.

'Shit!' She leaps forwards, remembering the oven gloves just in time.

The kitchen fills with acrid black smoke that stings the back of her throat. She lifts the blind to the accompaniment of Gareth and Georgie's coughing, opens a window and listens to the rain patter on what remains of the leaves.

She heaves down a lungful of salty air, sensing somewhere, out beyond the night and her burgeoning despair, the constant sway of the dark, silver sea, and gives way to hopeless tears.

CHAPTER FORTY-TWO

An early dawn light licks the edges of the curtains but doesn't penetrate the bedroom. Melanie turns her bruised head to the side and makes out Gareth's silhouette stretching out like a mountain range. Flanked by darkness and daybreak, she rolls over, away from him. Senses the gulf between their backs grow wider than the universe.

She knows he's awake; she can tell from his breathing. Neither of them slept much last night. Keeping to their own sides of the bed, lying stiffly along the edges of the mattress, because no matter how uncomfortable, it is easier than if the two of them should accidentally touch. Because then what?

Her body stiffens at the sound of rustling sheets. The bed creaks as Gareth sits up. He's cold, she thinks, resisting the desire to reach out to him. The sudden feeling of helplessness this brings makes her gasp.

'Are you asleep?' His whispered accusation rasps against the bedlinen. She can smell the remnants of his aftershave.

'No.' Her fingers curl themselves into agitated fists.

'Shit night.'

'Me too.'

'I hope you're not going to blame me for that too. If it's all right by you, I think I've taken the blame for enough.'

'No, I'm not blaming you,' she says but only because there's no way they can have a row with Georgie asleep in the adjacent room.

'I've been going over and over it in my mind all night.' She can tell he wants to shout, that it's the hardest thing to stop himself. 'And I just want to know why you took that woman's side before even talking to me?'

Melanie turns her aching head. Sees the curve of his spine as he bends low over the side of the bed. 'Because whenever I asked you about her, you said it was nothing. Because you lied to me.' A tentative hand to the injury on her brow and she winces.

'How many more times? I didn't lie to you.' Gareth speaks as if he is quite literally stuffing his fists into his mouth. 'I couldn't remember. I still don't. Not fully.'

'Okay.'

She has learnt there's no point pursuing things when he's in this mood. How is it possible they've been reduced to this? She and Gareth used to be so close; their deep connection was the envy of all their friends. She sobs into her pillow. It was awful to hear Delyth say those things about him, and the way he reacted when she tried to make him explain. But what did she expect? For them to be able to patch things up, for things to go back to the way they were? *Get real, girl.* This is how it's going to be from now on, and when the pub opens and he's here full time, things are going to get a whole lot worse. Better to keep her mouth shut from now on. Put up and shut up. It was a favourite saying of her mother's, and, because Melanie hasn't exactly got a choice, that they have come too far to go back, she had better buckle down and make the best of it.

Up and dressed, with the pretence of breakfast no one can eat, a lid of silence has closed over the Sayer family. It seems now so much has been said, there is nothing left to say. Gareth looks as if he's about to speak, but then gives up, no longer seeing the point in whatever it was. Melanie avoids his bloodshot eyes and doesn't bother making him toast, doesn't bother pouring his tea, and it doesn't seem as if Gareth cares. All talk of the pub's opening night, what still needs to be done and when Gareth intends to hand in his notice. Forgotten.

Someone is knocking at the main door. Three heads dart to the sound. But only Melanie gets to her feet. The wooden legs of the chair screeching against the floor.

'Dear me.' Delyth gasps on the doorstep, a tin decorated with blue peacocks in her hands. 'You've been in the wars.'

'It's fine.' Melanie is unsure whether to let her inside, she doesn't think she has the strength if Gareth kicks off again.

'It doesn't look fine.' The woman fiddles with her shiny cap of hair that is obviously still a novelty.

Melanie lifts a cautious hand to touch the cut with its purple bruise that's already hardened to a rind of congealed blood.

'Looks nasty. How did you do that?' Delyth keeps on with her enquiry.

'Daddy pushed her.' Georgie has squeezed between them. 'He didn't mean to do it. It was an accident.'

'Was it now?' She passes Georgie the pretty blue tin. 'These are for you.' A friendly wink. 'A little birdie told me you had another bad tummy ache last week.' She glances up at Melanie. 'The same little birdie who told me my cakes are the only things you like to eat when you're feeling poorly. And you've got to keep your strength up.'

'Look how pretty they are, Mummy.' Georgie admires the twelve fairy cakes with runny pink icing.

'What do we say?' Melanie prompts, smiling with difficulty; the muscles in her face are sore.

'Thank you. Very, very much.' And with a little bow, Georgie skips away.

'Thanks so much.' Melanie echoes her daughter's gratitude. 'It's kind of you to think of her.'

'My pleasure. Although,' Delyth's expression clouding, 'she's still looking peaky. Are you sure she's okay? I was concerned to hear she was off school again last week. I thought you'd got to the bottom of all that.'

'So did I,' Melanie groans. 'She was doing great. But that night we came home from you with the kitten.' She screws up her face. 'Not so good. I'm taking her back to the doctor first thing Monday. She's feeling better today, but still a little off her food, so the cakes are lovely. She'll eat them.'

'Let's hope they help get her appetite back.' Delyth keeps playing with her hair. 'How's the kitten settling in?'

'Bingo? Oh, he's gorgeous.' Briefly forgetting her troubles, she laughs. 'Georgie's utterly besotted with him. Keeps pestering me to let her take him to school.'

Delyth turns away from her for a moment, her gaze wandering the gravelled car park, to the glassy sea beyond. 'Do you want me to call the police?' she says, when she refocuses on Melanie. A hand fluttering at her temple.

'What I want, is for you to clear the hell off.' Gareth, swooping out of nowhere, shoves himself between his wife and the outside world. His body spread across the entrance. 'Happy now, are you?' he snarls at Delyth, and Melanie hears his breathing change the angrier he gets. 'Happy we're now as miserable as you? The damage you've done, you evil bitch.' His temper is in danger of bubbling over. 'I thought I made it clear when we arrived here that you're not welcome.'

Delyth gawps at him.

'Are you deaf?' he shouts. 'I said, clear off. Go on, get outta here.'

So much for him wanting to put things right, to make it up to Delyth and her family. Melanie watches him, appalled. What a fake he is. Contrite in the shock of the moment, fearing she was seriously hurt, but she can tell from the way he's behaving now he didn't mean it, that nothing will change.

'Gareth. D'you mind?' Melanie squares up to him. 'Since when do you get to tell me who I can or cannot spend time with?' And clasping Delyth's coat sleeve, she says, 'Come on, let's get out of here.' And swaps her slippers for wellingtons, and lifts her parka from the peg. Hurriedly checking its pockets for her purse, keys and mobile. Happy she has everything she needs, she calls for the dog. 'You can look after Georgie for an hour or two. I won't be long.'

She doesn't wait for his agreement. Once Slinky has joined them, she walks off without bothering to close the door.

Recent rain means the steep track from the pub to the beach is too slippery to negotiate safely, so Melanie and Delyth saunter side by side, barely speaking, down through the windy town to the seafront. Slinky tugging them along like a sail.

'Are the two of you going to be all right?' Delyth asks when they reach the dunes.

Melanie doesn't immediately answer. Head down, over the braided river channels now the tide has gone out, their boots crunch the pleat of seashells left behind by the high watermark.

'I honestly don't know,' she says eventually. Inhaling the smell of wet sand and seaweed. 'Because it's not just what you told me he did to Erin, it's the way he's behaved with you since we got here. I don't even know if I like him anymore.' They stop for her to shake a stray stone from her boot. 'You and me,' she starts up again. 'I know we've not talked about it since, but the way he spoke to you at the Co-op, in front of all those people, it was terrible. Shameful. I'm so sorry.'

'I know you are, and it's not your fault. But you and Gareth...' Delyth's nose is pink with cold. 'You are going to get through this all right?'

They listen to the cold, rippling call of a curlew. Melanie doesn't have the words to express the weight of despair she's been carrying around inside, and dabs away tears with the cuff of her coat.

'Oh, don't cry.' Delyth slips an arm around Melanie's middle. The sudden contact, although meant to be a comfort, is awkward. 'Please don't cry.'

'I don't think I can trust him. I'm not sure I know who he is.' She pulls away from Delyth. 'He's not the person I thought he was. He's not the man I married.'

'I'm worried you're going to split up over this. You're not, are you?'

'I don't know,' Melanie repeats.

'I should never have told you.' Delyth sounds distressed. 'This is all my fault.'

'No, Delyth, it's Gareth's fault. He should have told me. Letting me find out like that, it was awful. But how can we split up? We've too much at stake. The pub's set to open any day. We've got to start clawing back some of the money we've spent on the place.'

'But if he hit you?'

'It's not what it looks like, Delyth, really it isn't.' They walk to the lip of the shore. 'Things got out of hand. A bit heated.' Her skin tightens when she thinks how quickly their argument had unravelled. 'It wasn't the easiest thing for us to talk about, as you can imagine. I fell, that's all. He didn't mean for it to happen.'

'Isn't that what all women say when their husband's abuse them?' Her little voice is almost lost to the wind bucking in off the sea.

Melanie watches clouds being blown sideways over the horizon. The word "abuse", anchor-heavy and dangerous, swings above their heads. More than accustomed to abuse, she touches the small scar above her other eye that is luckily hidden under her eyebrow. Not from Gareth – until moving to Wales, they had barely exchanged a cross word – this is an injury from her mother. A time during one of her binges when she lashed out, only to claim later how she had no knowledge of the harm she'd done. An easy get-out clause, she was happy to go along with, as to admit the alternative was too dreadful. 'Just an accident,' she would say to anyone who bothered to enquire about her injuries. 'I walked into a door... I tripped over the cat. No, it's nothing. It was my fault, really, it was. Everything's fine at home.' As fiercely loyal to her mother as she is now being about Gareth. It's what you do, isn't it?

'Gareth finally confessed to knowing Erin,' Melanie confides. 'But I couldn't get him to admit that he forced her into anything.'

'And Andrew? Did he know about him?'

'He says not.'

'And you believe him?'

'I want to.' She looks up at a sky punctuated by seabirds. 'But either way, it's hardly fair that Gareth paid no child maintenance for Andrew. You shouldn't have had to cope with the financial burden on your own. Especially when he wasn't actually your son.'

'As good as.' Delyth sounds hurt. 'And Andrew could never be a burden to me. I love that boy with all my heart.'

'You do, and you've been a wonderful mother to him,' Melanie, backpedalling. 'I know you said Erin swore you to secrecy, but after she died, why didn't you just contact Gareth yourself? Insist he pay something towards Andrew's keep. Be some kind of father to him. I would have done.'

'I'm sorry, Melanie, but I didn't want that husband of yours involved. After what he did to my sister, he didn't deserve to have anything to do with Andrew.'

'I understand.' She hopes Delyth might say something about the three-thousand pounds Gareth gave her recently, but she doesn't, and Melanie can't think of a way to ask. 'He says he wants to make it up to you and your mum. That he wants to make it up to Andrew.'

'Funny way of showing it.' Delyth picks up a seashell and passes it to Melanie to admire.

'It's made you very sad, hasn't it? All that with Erin.' She rolls the shell over in her gloved hand. 'What Gareth did, it ruined your life too. I can see that now. It's what drove you to do what you did in our kitchen, you poor thing.'

Melanie doesn't expect an answer, which is good because she doesn't get one. And as they walk through the frilled surf, she unpacks what remains of her marriage and realises how little there is.

'I miss him. I miss how we used to be. But even if we could be put back together, how can I trust him?' She closes her mouth. Grateful Delyth gives no indication she's heard what she can barely bring herself to admit. The idea that she was seduced by Gareth's offer of protection, by his power, his money, is not a comfortable one. Blinded, where others with more self-belief would have seen straight through him, he had been a piece of driftwood at the time. Something to cling to. Needing him, and only him, to keep her afloat after the messy break-up with her first boyfriend and the misery of a childhood spent in and out of care. It was easy to buy into his promise. To exchange an unhappy life for one with him. She can't blame her younger self if she was duped. But since moving here, and witnessing his appalling treatment of Delyth (and Melanie, when she dares to question him), whoever she thought Gareth was is a fantasy. A fantasy that's taken the likes of Delyth Powell to show her the truth.

'Oh, is that the time? I should really get going.' Delyth tips her out of her gloomy introspection.

'Right, yes.' Melanie puts the pretty shell into a pocket. 'I'll walk you to your car,' she says and calls to the dog.

A crunch of gravel as the Defender inches out between the pillars and onto the road. Darker now that rain has begun to fall, Melanie pulls up her hood and looks at the half-timbered sides of the pub. At the newly commissioned sign with its squatting Friar Tuck. And despite the cold that's nibbling her ears, she can't go inside just yet. So, with Slinky fully extended on his leash, Melanie turns her back on the Monkstone Arms and Gareth, and heads for the church. For the little stone room tacked onto the back of the vestry, and the friendship she is sure she will find there.

CHAPTER FORTY-THREE

John stands with his broad back to her, busy with whatever it was she interrupted. 'I don't know how you could hit the face of someone you love.'

'He didn't hit me, John. Gareth pushed me and I fell, that's all.'

'That's all?' He pulls up a chair and sits down opposite. His dark eyes hunting her expression, wanting the truth.

She trembles with emotion, her hand absent-mindedly stroking Slinky who is slumped between them on the rug. 'It was just a horrible argument that got out of hand.'

'Can I ask what the argument was about?'

It is some time before she is able to answer. Seated in the only armchair, Melanie stares at the untidy bundle of her hands in her lap. Focuses on her wedding ring; the plain band of gold she doesn't think she believes in anymore. Then she opens up to John, tells him everything she learnt about Erin and what Gareth did or didn't do. Feeling closer than ever to this big, gentle man, she must remind herself she is a mother, a married woman – even if it is only to someone who bullies and frightens and was capable of exploiting a fourteen-year-old child.

'And that's about the long and short of it,' she concludes.

'You seem to have taken Delyth's side in all this,' John says.

'Are you saying you don't think I should?'

'No, it's not that. It's just, well.' He pauses to cough, a hand covering his mouth.

'That sounds nasty. Do you think you should go and see about it?'

'It's nothing,' he sidesteps. 'This is Gareth we're talking about, and I can't imagine he's happy that you're siding with her.'

'I'm siding with Delyth because what he did was despicable. And look at the damage it went on to cause. No, he can come up with as many excuses as he likes, and believe me, he has. Blaming it on being drunk and some nonsense about Erin coming onto him. But nothing excuses what he did.'

'What did Norah have to say about it?'

'Oh, she's a lovely woman. I like her very much but I'm not sure how reliable she is. She seemed confused to me.' Melanie is thinking about the phantom sheepdogs.

'Because she was sozzled?'

'No. Norah's not a drinker. I don't know why Delyth says she is. But anyway, she doesn't seem to blame Gareth at all.'

'Doesn't she?' John frowns.

'Delyth said she wanted to go to the police at the time, but Norah stopped her. And I might just have a theory as to why that is.'

'You do?'

Melanie nods. 'It involves Gareth's father.'

'Rhodri Sayer?'

'Delyth said, well, Norah said some things too. She implied, and I don't think I got it wrong, that Norah and Rhodri got pretty close during the years she worked for him.'

'That's interesting.'

'From the way she spoke about Rhodri, it was plain she had a soft spot for the man. Perhaps it was enough for her not to rock the boat so far as Gareth was concerned.'

'I remember some rumours doing the rounds. But like all the other rumours in this town, I didn't pay much attention.' He gets up to light the only lamp. It washes the tiny space in a warm yellow. 'She was quite a looker, Norah. In her day.'

'I saw photos of her up at the farm. Erin looked just like her, didn't she?'

John coughs his answer. 'D'you think that all this has got something to do with why I saw Gareth's car up by the farm that morning?'

'Yes, I think Gareth gave Delyth money to keep her mouth shut.'

'Are you sure?'

'He withdrew a substantial sum from our account and wouldn't tell me what he needed it for. And when I went to the farm it was pretty obvious Delyth had been spending big time. She said she won it on the scratch cards, but I didn't believe her.'

'Well, she could've done. People do. Did you ask her?'

Melanie shakes her head.

'Well, if Gareth did give her the money, he must be gutted because it didn't stop her telling you.' John sighs and leans back in his chair. 'So, Andrew's Gareth's kid then?'

Melanie nods.

'How d'you feel about that?'

'I don't know.'

'But why are we only hearing about this now? Pencarew's a small place, it never usually takes long for news to do the rounds.'

'Not if they kept shtum. And it sounds as if they did. All of them. People obviously got to hear that Erin had given birth, but not who the father was. They said Erin swore Norah and Delyth to secrecy. Even Gareth's sister, Bethan, didn't know.'

'And that one knows everyone else's business.' John smiles.

'She means well.'

'If you say so.'

Melanie considers what she believes to be her washed-out reflection in the only window. Devastated after discovering her husband's dreadful secret, she feels better after talking it through with her friend. John Hughes: the ex-squaddie who opened his heart, let her cut his hair; a man who hasn't a vain or deceitful bone in his body. She wishes she could do something to help ease his torment. Her thoughts as she watches the day darken to night beyond the small square of glass.

Her phone beeps from her pocket. She takes it out and looks at the screen. 'I should get back.' She rises to her feet.

'So soon?'

'Best had.'

She senses something shift and a moment passes between them. John stares at the floor as if to measure whatever it is that he wants to say. Melanie thinks she knows what it is but doesn't want it. She watches Slinky sprawled between them and feels the cold dampness of the room cling to her clothes. Why does everything need to be so complicated? Because she can't do whatever this is. Whatever it is that John wants. She can't. She may be unhappy about Gareth but John isn't the answer.

And as if reading her mind, he says: 'It's okay, Melanie. I understand.'

'You do?'

'Yes.' He holds out his hand for her to take. Big and broad, she reaches to claim it. Then lets it go again.

'I'm sorry,' she says even though she isn't entirely sure what she's apologising for.

'Don't be.'

'Thank you, John. Our friendship's very important to me.'

'For me too.'

'Take care of yourself, won't you.' She bends to kiss his cheek then leaves.

CHAPTER FORTY-FOUR

Two days to go until opening night. Melanie, Georgie and Slinky are on their way home from Pwllglas. The Mazda's boot is chock-a-block with last-minute supplies.

With big wet trees looming on either side and telephone cables sagging dangerously low to the verges, Melanie drives through what looks like sleet, taking care to keep to her side of the road. Up ahead, a row of larches, their feathered tops touching the low-hanging clouds as they whizz past open gateways leading to lonely footpaths strangled with bramble. She loves driving, the feeling of freedom it gives. The only downside was seeing roadkill. It upset her. It upset Georgie more. And there was so much of it on these rural roads. Not that its frequency lessens the impact, her body jolting at the horror of seeing each fresh mound of bloodied fur or feathers. Noting, with the passing of days and flattened by tyres, how they become desiccated discs embedded into the tarmac. All she can do to console herself is hope that whatever was hit by a vehicle travelling at speed, equalled a swift and painless death. That the dozens of hedgehogs, foxes, pheasants and squirrels didn't suffer.

Dark enough for sidelights, she switches them on. Then, catching sight of her face in the driving mirror – the fading bruise and the semicircular cut that has almost healed over – her eyes drift from the road.

'Mummy!' Georgie shrieks from the back seat. 'Stop!'

A badger. Its saffron eye reflected in the Mazda's headlamps. Too slow, she applies the brake, but without enough conviction. Believing, as she half-heartedly presses her foot to the floor, that the animal has time to cross. She hits it. A sickening thump. Then nothing. A hush beyond the ticking down of her engine and the cry of a faraway owl.

'Stay there, sweetheart,' she instructs Georgie and parks up in an adjacent lay-by. With hazard lights flashing, she slips from the driver's seat and goes to investigate.

She sees the sheen of fresh blood streaked on tarmac. A trail that leads her eye up the bank and into the undergrowth. It's nowhere. There's nothing. Only the badger's sour smell, trapped in the space that hangs between the parallel channels of light radiating from her car. She calls out for it through the steadily falling sleet. Her voice sounding feeble, stupid, ringing in her ears. The animal was hardly going to respond, it wasn't a dog. If – and it was a big if – the creature was still alive, it would be badly injured and only the pain of a protracted death awaited it.

Melanie takes this awful thought back to the car. Sits with the bleakness of it, cold between her and the wet material of her parka. She sees herself as she was only moments before, pacing the road, the white puff of her repeated regret: inadequate and dissolving into the icy evening air.

'I'm so sorry,' she says to Georgie, to the dog, blinking back tears.

She twists in her seat to kiss her daughter, then buries her nose in the denseness of Slinky's neck. The dog, in turn, enjoying the attention, licks her face, cleansing it of guilt. *Don't worry* – his black eyes shining – *he wasn't a relative of mine.*

Her thoughts turn again to Gareth's anger. Cradling Slinky's skull in her hands, she understands its fragility with stark clarity, and an unwelcome thought elbows its way into her head.

It would be easy for Gareth to kill her. All it would take is one blow, correctly placed, to despatch her. She shivers and touches the crust of black blood above her eye. Realising just how dangerously close she came and that next time she might not be so lucky.

CHAPTER FORTY-FIVE

The bar at the Monkstone Arms is filled with the penetrating heat of those who have been invited to celebrate its opening. Smartly dressed friends from London are mixing with Pencarew dignitaries and local businesspeople. The spill of guests even includes the town's mayor, her well-upholstered figure more heavily decorated than the Christmas tree. Bethan and Bryn, along with Sian and Tom, are huddled with unknown others by the bar. Where Gareth – excelling in his role as *bon viveur* by keeping them entertained and keeping up the pretence – is ladling mulled wine from a huge crystal bowl he unearthed in the cellar.

Melanie stops carving the thin slices of cold roast beef and glances over at her husband. Still reeling after his announcement that he's not giving up his city job as promised, and the horrendous row that ensued, it took some doing for her to put on a brave face and carry on with this evening's event. Gareth cited her friendship with Delyth as his reason for not wanting to be in Pencarew full time. And after the string of awful things they said to one another in the heat of the moment, they have barely exchanged a word since. But look at him. How convincing he is, in his dark-blue shirt and crisply ironed chinos. Who would guess the trouble their marriage is in? She is grateful to him for playing along, for the sake of the business, for the sake of whatever their future might be here. This is a small town and, as John said, bad news travels fast. The last thing she wants is people – potential customers – knowing their life has capsized and they have no clear idea how to set it right again. But how long can they keep it a secret? Even if Gareth's expression, as usual, gives nothing away, it's only a matter of time before the hawk-eyed Bethan sniffs them out. She's already been asking questions. The fact that Melanie has been steering clear and wearing concealer to disguise what's left of the cut above her eye isn't fooling her.

An explosive laugh: firework-loud from somewhere in the crowd. It's Bronwyn. Her head flung back, mouth open to the beamed ceiling. She is sporting a new hairdo for the occasion, and is, as usual, surrounded by her coffee morning tribe. Women, hot inside cashmere knitwear and snug tweed skirts, who seem to flush bright red whenever Melanie talks to them. She listens to their chatter rise above the music she carefully selected and set to play on the sound system.

'Do help yourselves to cutlery and plates,' she invites those who have formed an orderly queue. Melanie looks down at the blade of the carving knife and her thoughts wander to Delyth. She was invited along tonight, but she hasn't come. Not that this is any great surprise. Dropping by with a beautifully iced chocolate cake she decorated with Smarties. 'For Georgie,' she said. 'For her not to feel left out of the celebrations.'

Melanie never ceases to be amazed by Delyth's generosity. Especially when she thinks how abysmally Gareth has behaved towards her. But whispering her good luck for this evening's event, saying she would drop by on Monday when Gareth was safely back in London, Delyth wouldn't be persuaded inside.

Even though Gareth had taken himself off for a game of golf with Bryn.

Poor Delyth, she thinks, lifting her head to the Chinese lanterns that float like pretend moons at the windows. She probably hates parties as much as Melanie. Looking around the bar, at the Christmas tree and the fairy lights she pinned up along the beams, the amazing feast she's spent the last week preparing, she can't help but be pleased with how well everything's come together. That her hard work has paid off and their party guests appear to be enjoying themselves is a great relief.

'Delicious spread you've done us.' A silver-haired man in a maroon jacket, works his way along the buffet table. 'Done us proud.' He takes a sausage roll, bites it in half.

'I'm glad you're enjoying it.' She smiles.

'Make it all yourself, did you?' As he chews, flakes of pastry drift like dandruff to his jacket lapels.

'I did, yes.' Another smile.

'Me and the wife, we love what you've done with the place.'

'Thanks.' Melanie, awkward under his compliment, fiddles with the clip she needs to wear to keep her lengthening hair off her face. 'Although, Bryn's the mastermind behind the refurbishments. Him and his crew did a super job.'

'Well, I never.' The man takes an exaggerated look around. 'And you're to do Sian and Tom's wedding, I heard.'

'That's right.'

'Lucky me, I'd say.' He grins. 'Because I'm invited to that too.'

'A lot to manage on your own though, isn't it, love?' A woman Melanie presumes is his wife, steps up behind him. 'You're doing bed and breakfast too?'

'That's right. We've been awarded four stars from the Welsh

tourist board.' Melanie reels off her condensed sales pitch. 'Got bookings in the diary already.'

'Aye, but all on your own? She won't be able to manage, will she, Aled?' The woman prods her husband.

'Bit ambitious.' Aled, a splayed hand floating over a salver of mini quiches, chimes in.

'I'm not on my own, I've got Gareth.'

'But not in the week. He told us he's still going to be away in London. That it's best if he keeps going with his job in the meantime. How will you cope?'

'I'll be fine. I can always hire some help if things get really busy.' A forced laugh. What she feels like doing is crying. How dare Gareth share their private business. Does it mean the whole town knows?

'We thought it would be too much for him to give up.'

'Why?' Melanie snaps, she can't help it.

'Well, London. Compared to here?' The woman gawps at her as if she's stupid. 'I know what I'd choose.'

Melanie puts the carving knife down and picks up her empty glass. 'Do excuse me. I've things to fetch from the oven.'

She thought the couple of mulled wines she drank had bolstered her, but en route to the kitchen, pausing at the bar for a refill, she needs a couple more sips to loosen her tongue.

'Gareth?' Melanie smiles hello to Bethan and the others. 'Can I have a word?'

'What, now?' Gareth, midway through some hilarious anecdote, his audience in raptures, is seated on one of the high bar stools. Flushed in the face, a tumbler in his hand, it appears he has moved on to the whisky and if she's going to get any sense out of him, she needs to act soon.

She sips her mulled wine and loops an arm around him. So much of her wants to forgive him, wants their old lives back. In many ways she still loves him. 'Yes, Gareth, now. If that's all right?' she coaxes, smiling, keeping up the charade, aware of eyes. 'In private, yeah?'

He stiffens under her touch. 'Oh, so you want to talk now, do you?' he hisses into her ear, still smiling, still keeping up the act as she is. 'No. You've made your choice. Siding with that woman over me. I've got nothing to say to you.' He swivels on his stool, back to his audience, and lets his body communicate what he can't be bothered to articulate.

Melanie shrinks from him, despising herself for relenting. He's the one in the wrong, not her. Hiding her humiliation, she strides away to the safety of the kitchen. Glass in hand and her head held high for the benefit of the eyes she knows are watching. A glance back at the bar, at the gathering of people who've already closed over the gap she left behind, keen to hear whatever else Gareth has to say. Such a small thing yet glaring in what it communicates. She is the outsider here, and if push came to shove and she and Gareth did split up, she knows where loyalties would fall. And this sad realisation leaves her the loneliest she's felt in her life.

***

Mulled wine finished, she transfers the final trays of savoury pastries, hot from the oven, onto a platter. Is wondering whether to take a couple up to Georgie, when Bethan leans around the doorway, motioning for her to come back into the bar.

Gareth is on his feet, a slight wobble. A crash as his bar stool topples over. He drains the whisky in his glass, then gropes the bar top for something. Finds a teaspoon, taps his glass. He is going to make a speech.

'Quiet, everyone.'

Someone turns the music off. A thickening silence swells through the room.

'I'd like to start—' Gareth breaks off, drags his fist across his mouth and stares down at his shiny brown brogues for a second. 'I'd like to start by thanking you all for coming here tonight to celebrate the opening of—' He breaks off again. This time because of a disturbance at the rear of the pub.

'Help!' a shout goes up. 'Someone, help. Quick! She's collapsed.'

Melanie, propelled into action, pushes through the ballooning commotion.

'Give her some air.' Another shout. 'Step back, get back. All of you, give her some space.'

Melanie wades through her party guests who stand around squawking and squabbling like the gulls down on the shore and eventually reaches the foot of the stairs leading up to the flat.

'Georgie!' She kneels to hold her daughter's sticky little hand. 'Someone, call an ambulance!' She strokes the soft skin of Georgie's forearm, speaking gibberish in hushed, reassuring tones. 'What happened, sweetheart?'

'I've been sick again, Mummy.' A single fat tear rolls down Georgie's flushed little cheek.

'Oh, darling.' Melanie, crying too, tests her daughter's clammy brow with the back of her hand. 'You're baking... Oh, Georgie, I'm so sorry, I meant to come and check on you, I'm sorry. I'm so sorry.'

'My hands and feet have gone all funny,' Georgie mumbles, her eyes strangely bright. 'They've got pins and needles.'

There is a dollop of chocolate icing on Georgie's jumper, the giveaway rainbow stain of Smarties on her baby fist. Melanie feels a hand on her shoulder and looks up, expecting Gareth, but it's her mother-in-law who comforts her.

'Hang on in there.' Bronwyn, kinder than Melanie's ever known. The pallor beneath her powder and paint, washed to grey. 'The ambulance is on its way.'

'I t-tried to c-come to tell you,' Georgie slurs and, running out of puff, her eyelids flutter and close.

'No, no, no. Don't close your eyes.' Melanie, watching it on some hospital TV drama, shakes her daughter awake. 'You mustn't sleep. Stay with Mummy.'

'Get out of my way... Out of my way.'

Melanie hears her husband before she sees him.

'Georgie.' A swaying Gareth towers over them. 'What the hell's wrong with her? What's she lying there for?' He gives Melanie a desperate look.

'She's had another funny turn. Says she's been sick.'

'We saw her come down the stairs, then she just dropped down there. Right there in front of us.' Someone, on the edge of the circle that's formed around them, tries to be helpful.

'We can't lose her too, Mel. We can't.' Gareth wrings his hands: the gesture shrieks of despair.

'Try to stay calm, boy.' Bronwyn talks to her son. 'The ambulance is coming.'

'What's that stuff round her mouth?' He jabs a finger. 'That's chocolate. Chocolate icing off that cake that bloody woman brought round. Look at her fingers.' He shouts and guests scatter, nervous as birds. 'That's it. I'm going over there... I'm going to sort her out. Right now.'

'Gareth, please.' Melanie appeals to him from the floor. 'This has nothing to do with Delyth.' Her eyes skim the crowd before refocusing on her daughter, fearful she could slip into unconsciousness. 'Remember what happened when you jumped the gun about the dog?'

'This isn't about the dog!' he screeches. 'This is our child.'

'I know, Gareth, but please.' Up on her feet, reluctant to leave her child for a second. 'This has got nothing to do with Delyth.' She grapples with him, trying to get him to see sense. 'Let's just get Georgie to hospital. Okay?'

'Yes, Gareth. Calm down.' Bronwyn slips an arm through his.

'Get off me.' He pushes his mother away. 'It's that woman's fault, Mel, I'm telling you. I've been telling you since we got here. But you won't listen.' The ring of spectators flinches in unison. 'I'm going over there. I'm going to put a stop to that fucking woman once and for all.'

'Gareth, stop it. You're frightening Georgie... You're frightening me.' Melanie – admitting this to half the town, to her in-laws – ducks down to her child, then up again. 'You're not helping, please calm down.' She reaches out to him a second time.

Gareth, eyes wild and staring, shoves her away: violent, brutish; slamming her against the wall to the gasp of partygoers.

'You've sided with that woman over me from the off. I've been telling you; she wants to damage us. I told you she's evil. She's done this to Georgie. I can't believe it's taken this to prove to you exactly how evil she is. I'll never forgive you, not if our child dies. Never. Not this time.'

'Gareth! Calm down, boy.' Bronwyn, appalled, steps between him and Melanie, but whatever she sees in her son's eyes makes her shrink away again.

'Oh, let him go.' Melanie, exasperated. 'He's no use to anyone in that state. He's just making things worse.' And kneeling beside her daughter again, she picks up Georgie's clammy hand. 'Shush, shush, now, little one,' she whispers. 'Don't worry about Daddy, it's you we've got to take care of. Come on, little one, don't fall asleep.'

From her kneeling position, Melanie watches Gareth go. She sees the way the crowd parts to let him through, their eyes accusing. A man, she can't see who, steps forwards to dissuade him, insisting he's way over the limit, that it would be madness to drive. But he throws him off too, determined as a freight train in his quest to damage.

All goes quiet. Quiet enough to hear the outer door slam and what must be the Mazda's engine starting up. Melanie fears for Delyth and wonders, in the tightening seconds, whether she should ring and warn her of what's coming. But unlike Gareth, she can't abandon their daughter. It speaks volumes that his primary concern, through anger, is Delyth Powell, rather than their child.

'It'll be all right, I promise.' She is still clasping Georgie's hand when the cool blue lights of the ambulance splinter the dark beyond the pub's windows. 'Everything will be all right, sweetheart.' She murmurs platitudes she doesn't believe. About the seriousness of her daughter's health or her marriage. But her marriage is going to have to take care of itself for the time being, her priority has to be Georgie, not Gareth. She thanks the paramedics, energetic and efficient in their green uniforms, as she oversees her daughter's safe transference from stretcher to ambulance.

'Can you look after things for me here? I've got to stay with Georgie,' she says to Bronwyn, who has been stuck to her side. 'I'll ring as soon as I know anything.'

'Yes, yes, Mel. Go... *Go!*' Her mother-in-law gives her an affectionate kiss on the cheek, then waves her away. 'Don't worry, I'll take care of things here.'

CHAPTER FORTY-SIX

In the days that follow, making the daily return drive between the hospital and pub, Melanie sees the same dead badger again and again. Its black-and-white stripes stiffening on the verge along the route she took with Georgie returning home from the cash-and-carry the previous week. Is it the one she hit? Was she to blame? She doesn't want to think about it. Except there it is, on each round trip, working like a burning reminder of the crime she committed against the animal kingdom. Nothing eats it. Nothing of the wild goes near it. It just lies there. Its black snout pointing accusingly dry and hard into the road.

Although Bryn's been kindly nipping over to let Slinky out morning and evenings, Melanie's gone back each lunchtime to give the dog his quick once-around-the-block and bowl of food, before racing back to the hospital to be with Georgie again. Taking the third exit off the roundabout on the outskirts of Pwllglas, it is clogged with traffic lights and road works all along the dual carriageway. When she finally reaches the turn-off for the Princess Diana Hospital, she is forced to join an already lengthy queue for the car park. The car park costs money, and she's never organised enough to have the correct change. So, along with the stress and worry over Georgie, she has the added concern of being clamped.

Jotting down a note to leave on the dashboard, explaining why she hasn't purchased a ticket, Melanie scrambles around for the bag of her daughter's things. Then her mobile beeps. It's a text from Gareth.

HOPE GEORGIE & YOU ARE OK.

GIVE ME A RING WHEN YOU GET THE CHANCE X

She thinks about replying but can't bring herself to do it. He should be here, at Georgie's bedside, not swanning off back to London. Let him wait. Leaving her with their sick child before the ambulance even arrived. Yes, she told him to go, but that isn't the point. Besides, there isn't time to call him now. The consultant paediatrician phoned just before she left the pub, saying she needed to speak to them as soon as possible. She will text him later. When she has something specific to tell. After all, they aren't exactly exchanging niceties at the moment.

It is raining. A cold mean rain that slides down inside her collar. It promises the winter still to be lived through before spring comes around again. By the time she's walked the length of the car park and in through the automatic doors, her parka is soaking. The children's unit is on the fourth floor, so she takes the lift. Shares it with a nurse wheeling an elderly gentleman in striped pyjamas. Leaving them behind, she pushes through a stiff set of fire doors decorated with stars and walks the length of corridor embellished with rainbows and giant butterflies. The reception desk looks empty and, conscious of her dishevelled appearance, she uses the seconds available to tidy her hair in the reflective sides of a medicine trolley.

'Can I help you?' A nurse she hadn't seen, prises her eyes from the computer screen.

'Hi, yes. I'm Mrs Sayer, Georgie's mum. Mrs Brookes asked me to let her know when I got back. She said she needed to talk to me?'

'She should be on the ward somewhere.' The nurse smiles. 'I'll bleep her for you.'

'Thank you.' Melanie taps the desk with fidgety fingers. 'Do you want me to wait here?'

'If you like.' The nurse lifts the receiver of a telephone, presses in a series of numbers. 'But I've no idea how long she'll be.'

'Would you be able to tell her I'm with Georgie? That I'll see her when she's ready?'

'No problem.'

Melanie takes the first right into Georgie's unexpectedly noisy room, stopping briefly at the hand sanitiser for a squirt of foam. She rubs her palms together and sidesteps a huge, red octopus transfer stamped to the linoleum, its tentacles groping into the ward. Bypassing rows of little children rigged up to monitors and tubes, their pale-green hospital beds huddled with relatives, Melanie reaches the window end and pulls back the screen that isn't usually drawn.

Georgie's bed is empty.

Stripped back to the plastic undersheet. The cards and sweets on the bedside table have been cleared away.

Her hand flies to her mouth. She can't breathe.

'Georgie?' she asks the eyes that have turned to her. 'Where's my daughter?'

Then she runs, handbag swinging, back to the reception desk. Slaps the counter loudly, startling the brigade of nurses now gathered there.

'Where's Georgie?' She chokes on desperate tears. 'What's happened to her?'

'Mrs Sayer.' A voice at her shoulder. Mrs Brookes: wire-haired and bespectacled; pressing a clipboard to her chest. 'Georgie's fine.'

'Where is she then?' she shrieks. 'It's her father. He's taken her, hasn't he? He's taken my baby away from me.'

'No, no. She's fine. We moved Georgie to another room, that's all.' A hand on Melanie's arm, the weight of it ominous. 'I'm sorry if we gave you a fright.'

'Oh, thank God. So, she's okay?'

'Yes, don't worry.'

Melanie takes the tissue a nurse passes her, and wipes her eyes. 'Can I see her?'

'Of course, but shall we go and have a little chat first?'

'Y-yes.' Melanie follows the white-coated woman into a small room.

'Do have a seat.' The consultant paediatrician points with a biro to a long, low sofa.

'Is Georgie getting worse, is that it?' Melanie, her heart pounding, is anxious for reassurance.

'Georgie's doing well, Mrs Sayer.' The pressure of that hand again; scrubbed and pale and ringless, before it's released.

'If that's the case then why was she still connected to a drip this morning? I was told she was coming off that today.' This is the first opportunity Melanie's had to talk to the consultant, and she has a string of questions.

'It's just a precaution. Your daughter was very dehydrated when she was admitted Saturday night. We'll be able to take her off it soon, especially now she's started eating again. You know she managed a little of her lunch today. Which is a good sign. And she's been generally more comfortable this afternoon, and even managed to sit up for a little while.'

'But there was something you wanted to talk to me about?'

'Yes, Mrs Sayer. Ideally, I'd have liked to chat to you and your husband, but I understand he had to return to London?'

'That's right, he drove back late last night. He's not due home till Friday.' Melanie has seen him since Georgie was admitted but, aside from the odd text message, she and Gareth haven't spoken directly. Taking it in turns to sit by their daughter's bedside, deliberately avoiding one another.

'The test results have come back.'

'And?' Panicking again, she grips her knees to steady herself.

'They're showing us that Georgie has coeliac disease.'

'*Coeliac disease?*' Melanie parrots, not understanding. 'That sounds serious. Is it serious?'

'If it goes undetected, yes, extremely.' Mrs Brookes is blunt. 'I understand Georgie's been feeling quite unwell for some time?'

'On and off, yes. Complaining of tummy aches, bloated, occasionally vomiting. I noticed a rash on her neck, too, the day before she collapsed and was brought in here. I thought it was a reaction to a new washing powder I was using,' Melanie explains.

'All symptoms of this condition, I'm afraid.'

'But why wasn't it diagnosed before now? We've been to our doctor at the Pencarew surgery loads of times. He ran tests, but they didn't reveal anything.'

The consultant looks at the printouts on her clipboard. 'Your daughter is rather underweight for her age. Did you notice she was losing weight?'

'Yes, I told the doctor about that too. I told him she'd been wheezy as well. I've been noticing it on our walks to school together,' Melanie adds. 'Our doctor told me it was probably just a cold, but could that be connected too?'

'This condition can often go undetected for a long time,' the paediatrician sidesteps, 'but Georgie's been lucky, there's been no obvious damage done to her small intestine, which sometimes, if this goes undiagnosed for too long, can be a problem, especially in children.'

'Is she going to get better?' Melanie is imagining all sorts.

'She's going to be fine, so long as she avoids gluten from now on.'

'So, this is, what? An allergy to gluten?'

'To wheat, rye and barley,' Mrs Brookes confirms.

'But how did she get it? Was it something I did?'

'No, nothing you did. It's something the body can develop. We've no idea why. But, please, don't be alarmed, we can help you with diet sheets, what not to eat, that kind of thing. All the supermarkets sell gluten-free products now.'

'Yes, I'm familiar with that. I've got friends who are intolerant to wheat.'

'This condition is rather more serious than an intolerance, Mrs Sayer. Your daughter cannot eat any gluten at all. If she does, she will very quickly become ill again.' The tone is firm, and Melanie listens to it carefully.

'So, we're talking no cakes or bread or biscuits, that kind of thing?' She is thinking of Delyth, of the countless treats she's brought round and how much Georgie's loved them. In a way, Gareth was right, wasn't he? They were making her ill. But this isn't Delyth's fault, no one knew Georgie had a problem.

'That's right. But you can bake with alternatives, buy alternatives. So long as everything's gluten-free, she'll be safe.' Mrs Brookes eyes her through her pebble glasses. 'You'll be sure to pass this news on to your husband?'

'Yes, I will,' Melanie says, unsure why she's being asked this.

'It's just that he's been ringing the hospital non-stop, wanting to know how Georgie is and what's happening. You are happy to explain things to him? Because from what he said, it sounded as if the two of you weren't in touch. And with him not being here...' The consultant pauses. 'Things are okay at home, are they, Mrs Sayer?'

Out in the corridor, a leaflet on coeliac disease in her hand, Melanie goes off in the direction she's been given to find Georgie.

'Melanie... Melanie Sayer?'

Someone calls her name and she turns to a stout woman fastened into a winter coat.

'Are you Melanie?' the woman asks, fiddling with her cuffs.

'I am.' She stares, thinking there is something oddly familiar about her.

'How's your daughter? We heard she was poorly.'

Melanie flutters the leaflet between them and smiles. 'She's doing okay, thank you. Gave us quite a fright, but, yes,' she hesitates, thinks about how different things could have been, 'yes, she's going to be okay.'

'That is good. We've been so worried. The two of us.'

'*The two of us?*' Melanie repeats. 'I'm sorry, have we met?'

'Oh, sorry. I didn't say, did I? I'm John's sister. Nerys. John's been telling me how kind you've been by looking after his dog and bringing him food.'

'I see.' They have the same lopsided smile; Melanie sees the resemblance clearly now.

'Blasted thing, he brought it to live with me before. Couldn't stand it, I'm not a dog person, so good on you.'

'*Erm,*' Melanie hesitates, 'how did you know about Georgie?'

'The whole town knows.' Nerys gives Melanie a look that says the state of her daughter's health isn't the only detail of their opening night that's doing the rounds. 'It's not gossiping.' Nerys knits her brows together. 'People are worried about Georgie, and about you.'

'About me? I'm not sure I like being the talk of the town.' Melanie scratches her nose. 'So, did you come to the hospital to see me?'

'Oh, no.' A nervous laugh that withers before it's properly formed. 'I'm here to see my neighbour. As John's babysitting the kids, I thought I'd take—'

'John's babysitting?' Melanie smiles, the idea amuses her. 'How come?'

'He's living with us again. Just for a bit. Until his cough gets better. Sleeping in that cold, damp room. The daft sod.' Nerys shifts sideways for a nurse pushing a child in a wheelchair to pass. 'I don't know why he likes it so much. I've said he can have a room at mine anytime... Especially as you've got his dog living with you.'

Melanie looks at the floor. 'I thought his cough sounded bad the last time I saw him. I should've made him go and see about it. But he doesn't like people fussing, does he?'

'No, he doesn't.' The sister's eyes tell a story. 'But it's all right, the doctor's given him antibiotics.'

'Tell him I'll come and see him... I mean, if it's okay with you?'

'Won't your Gareth mind?' Eyes glinting with mischief.

'Gareth? Of course not. And anyway, he's not here to mind, he's in London.'

'With your little kiddie in hospital?'

'He had to go back to work.'

'If you say so.' Nerys wrinkles her nose. 'Give you that, did he?'

Melanie's hand flies to her brow, to the residue of bruise and the inch of scar tissue that she's forgotten to touch-up with concealer. 'Yes, but...' Her excuse fizzles out.

'There's always a but, my love.'

'It's not what it looks like.'

'It never is.' A knowing look. 'I had a bloke like that once. Used to beat me black and blue. Always sorry afterwards.'

Melanie doesn't answer, her fingers sifting the sand and shells in her coat pocket.

'You should go to the police if he hits you. He shouldn't be allowed to get away with it. Your Gareth always was a nasty sort. Used to bully my John something terrible. He hasn't hit your daughter, has he?'

'Georgie? God, no.' Melanie is resolute.

'I'm just saying to watch him. I wouldn't trust him, not that one.' Nerys holds her gaze. 'A lovely-looking woman like you doesn't deserve that.'

But a less lovely-looking woman would deserve it, would she? Melanie thinks, but doesn't say; she supposes the woman means well.

'I really should get going, but it was lovely to meet you. Do give John my best,' Melanie says, before making her excuses.

CHAPTER FORTY-SEVEN

Melanie drifts off to sleep in the armchair beside Georgie's hospital bed. When she eventually opens her eyes, it's a shock to find someone standing over her.

'Delyth.' She jerks upright. Half of her wondering if she could still be dreaming. 'My God!' She rubs her eyes to clear the way. But, no, she's not mistaken. 'What the hell happened to you?'

Delyth looks as if she's been involved in a motor accident. Her left arm is in a sling, and the discoloured bruising around her eye looks so tender and raw, it makes Melanie grimace. As does the nasty-looking cut on the bridge of her nose that someone's tried to cover with a plaster.

A flashback to the opening night at the Monkstone Arms. Gareth, drunk and wild with rage, threatening to *put a stop to that fucking woman once and for all.*

'Please don't tell me Gareth did that to you?' The horror of Melanie's question oscillates between them.

Delyth doesn't reply. She hangs her head. Her newly-styled hair knotted and dull-looking, her eyes wet with tears. And when she unzips her coat a fraction, Melanie notices what looks like dried blood on her top.

'Please, tell me.' Her voice is a whisper, fearful of waking Georgie.

Melanie hears the click of Delyth's tongue, a dry sound in the over-warm room. 'Yes, it was Gareth,' she admits at last. 'He came up to the farm Saturday night. He just lost it with me.'

A nurse comes and busies herself around the sleeping Georgie. Inspecting her monitor, the IV drip, tucking Bumble in on the other side of the bed. It's a frustrating few minutes waiting for her to go, but when she does, Melanie pulls the screen around them, wanting the privacy.

'He did that? To you?' She gulps down her revulsion as she waves a feeble hand over Delyth's injuries. 'I can't believe it, I can't.' Her voice trembling. 'It's terrible. How could he?'

'Easy. He hates me. He always has.'

Melanie makes an involuntary noise and twists to check on Georgie. The disgust for her husband is trapped in her throat. 'No, I think his abominable behaviour towards you is...' she swallows, recalling John's theory about Gareth's problem with this woman, 'because he hates himself. You remind him of what a shit he used to be at school.'

'But he did it to you too, and he's supposed to love you.' Delyth ignores the expletive and adjusts her damaged arm inside its sling, emitting a groan of pain.

'I married a monster.' Melanie looks up at a woeful Delyth. 'I can't believe anyone would do such a thing to another person. I'm appalled, but I don't know what to say to make it better... There's no way for me to make this right. I'm so ashamed. It's terrible. Does your arm hurt dreadfully?' She takes a breath, leans out to offer comfort, but Delyth pulls away, screws up her face in agony. 'Is it broken? Have you had someone take a look at it?'

The things John's sister said find Melanie again, as she turns to the sleeping Georgie for a moment. What's to stop him from hurting her? Her daughter is as defenceless as Delyth. Why has she never seen this side of him before? And more importantly, why has it taken this timid, submissive woman to show her what her husband is capable of? Were there really no clues in all the years they've been together?

'I tried to stop him. I did.' Up on her feet, Melanie wants to console her friend, but again Delyth ducks away. Obviously in too much pain to be touched. 'Christ.' She plonks back down in the armchair, raises a hand of apology for swearing, then echoes herself. 'I did. I married a monster.'

'None of this is your fault, Melanie. Please don't get upset, you're not to blame. You've been a good friend to me.' Delyth, as compliant as ever, displays no hint of animosity. 'Anyway, more to the point, how's this little one doing?' She moves to stand at the bottom of Georgie's bed.

'She's going to be okay.' Melanie swings her attention back to her child again. Looks at the wires, the IV, the beeping monitor, then returns to Delyth. 'But what about you, what are you going to do? Have you reported him?'

'No.'

'Are you going to?'

Delyth shrugs and clutches her bad arm.

Melanie, troubled by the small, childlike quality of this woman, tries not to stare at her damaged face. She is as vulnerable as an orphan. The way that old wax coat drowns her narrow frame, it's pitiful. How could anyone, let alone the man she's shared such intimacies with, the father of her child, raise a hand of violence against her? The idea is so distressing, it makes her stomach heave.

It is a loathsome act.

An unforgivable act.

It is the final straw.

'I hope your decision not to go to the police isn't out of some loyalty to me? Because Gareth shouldn't be allowed to get away with what he's done.'

Delyth lifts her dark irises but declines to speak. It seems things have gone way too far for words. Melanie touches what remains of the cut on her own temple, traces the inch-long snake of proud flesh she fears may leave a scar.

'We're over. Me and Gareth,' Melanie announces suddenly, her voice low. 'There's no way back for us now.' Turning to her sleeping daughter to hide her hot and painful tears. 'He's not even sorry.' She sobs. 'He's not sorry about any of it. He couldn't care less that his actions destroyed your family, that you needed to sacrifice your life to bring up his son. No, I'm sorry to say, but there's no way back for us, we're over. Finished. I can only take so much, I'm not a mug. I'm sorry, Delyth, but I can't be like you and turn the other cheek. I've got to protect Georgie.'

Delyth passes her a tissue from the box on the bedside cabinet then, unzipping her smart new leather bag, she takes out the school photo she took without asking. 'You can have this back now,' she says, passing it over.

'No. You keep it, I insist.' Melanie raises the flat of her hand.

'So, you and Gareth are definitely over?' Delyth puts the photograph away.

'Yes.' Melanie bites her lip, determined not to give way to further tears.

'Have you told him?'

'Not yet.'

'Don't you think you should?'

'I will, when I next see him.' Melanie wipes her eyes. She wants to say it's the damage he's done to Delyth that has ultimately made her decide. But would hate for her to feel responsible for the breakdown of her marriage.

'What about the pub? You had such plans.'

'I honestly don't know.' Melanie sighs into the torpid air. 'I haven't thought that far ahead.'

'But you'll keep in touch with me, won't you? Let me know what you decide.' Delyth reaches out for Melanie with her damaged arm. Then, appearing to change her mind, she pulls it back into position. 'I'll ring you some time.' She pushes aside the curtain and makes to leave. 'You've been a true friend to me, Melanie.' She turns briefly before stepping away. 'Thank you for that. And for what it's worth, I'm sorry it's come to this between you and Gareth.'

'Don't be. This was all his doing.' Melanie gives her a weak smile. 'It had nothing whatever to do with you.'

CHAPTER FORTY-EIGHT

Delyth hobbles out through the children's ward and along the corridor. She takes the lift to the ground floor and crosses the bristled threshold through the automatic doors. It has stopped raining, and she steps out into the surprisingly bright endorsement of the mid-afternoon sunshine, relieved to finally be free of the clouded eye of the CCTV that always makes her nervous.

She follows a paved pathway that leads away from the hospital entrance and car park to a patch of wet grass under a row of leafless winter trees. Finds an empty bench that, once she's swept it free of rainwater, she sits down on. Cold enough to see her breath, she looks around at patients in wheelchairs, others rigged up to IV drips, in dressing gowns and slippers. People who, like her, have wandered outside for a smoke now the sun's come out. Delyth shoves a cigarette from a bashed-up packet of Marlboro into her mouth and lights up. Smokes it leisurely, while her mind returns to the conversation she just had with Melanie. She chuckles to herself.

The squealing siren of an ambulance. Delyth watches it wheeze to a halt at the entrance to A&E. She sees a troop of competent paramedics and porters transferring a patient from stretcher to gurney and wheeling it inside. She looks away and yawns. It's been a hectic few days, what with one thing and another. Yawning again, she forgets for a moment that she mustn't touch her face and rubs her eye by mistake. Sees some of the make-up that was pretending to be bruises has come off on her fingers.

'Fuck!' She fishes around in her bag for the vanity mirror that had once belonged to her sister, Erin. 'Oh, good...' she mutters to herself. 'I haven't smudged anything.'

Safe from prying eyes, Delyth scrutinises her face and admires her injuries. *Convincing, or what?* A sly smile creeps over her mouth. Her idea to fix a plaster on the bridge of her nose, so the pretend cut beneath was still visible, was genius. The wound is realistic enough even to make her cringe. Not surprising Melanie reacted the way she did. It took several goes to get it right, but it was worth the effort. The stupid bitch might not have been persuaded to leave her shit of a husband if she hadn't gone the extra mile.

You really can find anything on Google, and it's especially easy with her new smartphone. Delyth was amazed by the amount of YouTube videos giving step-by-step guides on how to apply the right colour make-up to give yourself pretend black eyes and facial injuries to shock at Halloween. Luckily, she kept hold of Erin's old make-up. She knew the brassy rainbow colours her whore of a sister liked to plaster on herself would come in handy one day. Those tips on how to act that you were in agony were especially useful as well; to accidentally touch your fake bruises and, in Delyth's case, her left arm, and make out they hurt.

It only began as a germ of an idea, not for a minute did Delyth think it would be possible to dupe people this easily. But, as it turned out, it's been a breeze from start to finish. And the great thing is that Gareth brought it all on himself; she hasn't so much as needed to raise her voice. Apart from showing up now and again to rattle his cage, all she's had to do is keep up the pretence and persist with her timid, hard-done-by act. Quite brilliant to achieve what she set out to do, quietly, without violence or committing any sort of crime – not this time, anyway. Delyth thinks she's more brilliant than Google in many ways, as she doubts there are websites giving instructions on how to destroy a marriage and walk away scot-free, as she has done.

Still peering at her reflection, she presses her fingers firmly against the plaster on her nose to satisfy herself it's stuck fast. The bruising around her eye was so positively inspired, she admired it again. She had them all fooled. It's good that people are always eager to hear the worst of others, and men who hit women are the worst kinds of scumbags. She must've looked totally convincing because even those nurses at the desk kept gawping at her, all concerned. She wishes they'd asked her who had beaten her up, because she had prepared her story in advance. Delyth, more than most, knows how important it is for lies to be consistent. She would never have got away with the bad things she's done in her past if she hadn't been a good liar.

Delyth sets the mirror aside and finishes her smoke. Drops the spent butt on the grass. She reaches inside her collar and fumbles for the chain with its crucifix. Rips it clean off. Nasty and cheap, she can see how the metal has already tarnished, and throws it into the litter bin beside the bench. Like the cuts and bruises she painted on herself, the crucifix was also a prop. Making out that she was good and holy. What a joke that is.

Warm in the unexpected sunshine, she pulls the sling off over her head and removes her coat. Folds back both sets of sleeves to the elbows to examine the thin red scores that have healed into scars. She will probably always have these, which is a shame, as they're pretty unsightly. But who has she got that's going to notice? *A bit excessive?* she asks herself. *No.* The other voice in her head is vehement. How else was she going to get that dopey wife of his on her side? Delyth had to make Melanie feel properly sorry for her. She pulls down her sleeves, loops the sling back over head and repositions her left arm inside it, then grins at her reflection for the final time before returning the vanity mirror to her bag. Best she stops fiddling with her fake injuries. If this trick is going to work, she's going to need to keep up the pretence for a while longer. Although, with a few weeks off work, as planned, it's going to be a doddle to hide away at the farm. She got away with hiding Erin for all those years, didn't she? Aside from the time she escaped and ran away to that squat in Swansea, it was easy to keep her sister prisoner in that attic room. Erin never got to learn to drive, and with their mother either working or too loved-up with her fancy man to notice what was going on under her own roof, Delyth was free to do what she wanted. No one, not even the post van, comes up to the house. The track to the farm, treacherous as it is, has served her well over the years.

Hey, look who it is.

Talk of the devil and the devil appears. Careful to stay out of his eyeline, she watches Gareth get out of a taxi and straighten himself inside his suit, put a hand to tidy his hair. Recent events are obviously taking a toll. She smiles. He looks totally washed-out and is sporting a nasty set of hammocks under his eyes. But he's still a good-looking bastard, and he knows it.

Oh, shit!

There's a heart-stopping moment when Delyth fears he's spotted her. She turns away; the last thing she wants is him seeing her. It's okay, he disappears inside the hospital entrance.

'Ooh, I wouldn't want to be in your shoes, boyo. You're in

for one hell of a shock.' Delyth chuckles again. 'Your wife's had it with you, thanks to me. She's pulling the plug on your marriage.'

The sight of Gareth reminds her of the old school photograph she stole from the pub, and she takes it out of her new leather bag to shred it into strips. Taking special care to rip Erin's face clean in half, before dumping the lot in the litter bin.

Delyth couldn't believe it when Gareth moved back to Pencarew with his beautiful wife, his lovely child: a big, fat success story. Yes, she was jealous. Show her someone who wouldn't have been. But in the end, it was better for her because it meant he had so much more to lose. No one would say she hasn't had to wait to get revenge. Seventeen years is a long time. But, in the end, she couldn't have planned it better. Even down to their kid getting sick. Talk about playing into her hands. Then Gareth, overreacting like he did – he was more of an idiot than she ever gave him credit for. Her grin widens further when she thinks about him turning up at the farm pissed out of his skull that night. She can't remember the last time she needed to wield her father's old Purdey. And what a hoot that was. Putting the shits up him, the arrogant fuck. She's always been a cracking shot and could have easily blasted him away if she'd wanted to. And in many ways, she wishes she had. Because if you've killed once, it's always easier the second time. Or so they say.

CHAPTER FORTY-NINE

'Oh, it's you.' Melanie isn't pleased to see him. She hasn't seen him since the night of the opening. Since Georgie was first admitted they have been managing to avoid one another.

'How is she?' Gareth gazes at their sleeping child. His eyes roaming over the tubes and monitors. He looks worn out. 'What did the consultant have to say?'

'I wasn't expecting to see you. I thought you were in London.'

'I was, but I caught the train back. Got a taxi from the station.'

'Delyth's just been in to see Georgie. You must've just missed her.'

'Yeah?'

Melanie watches him closely, but not a glimmer betrays him. 'She looks as if she's been in a road-traffic accident.'

'Oh dear.' His voice is devoid of feeling.

'Black and blue, she is. What did you do to her, Gareth? I know it was you. I got her to admit it too, eventually. She didn't want to land you in it, but I made her tell me. She says you went up to the farm that night and from the state she was in, you must've knocked ten bells out of her.'

'Been telling lies again, has she? God, Mel, this is me you're talking to. *Me*. You don't seriously believe I could do such a thing? Yes, I went up there. I'm not denying that. But, come on...' He whispers, reluctant to wake Georgie. 'You can't seriously think I could hurt her?' He pulls up a chair. Sits close to Georgie's bed. 'I never laid a finger on her. I swear to you.'

'Stop lying to me, Gareth. Of course you hurt Delyth. Who else was it?'

'I've no idea. But it wasn't me.'

Melanie touches what remains of the cut above her eye. She wants him to see. He does, but says nothing.

'I'm sick of us arguing. Arguing about that bloody woman.'

'Keep your voice down,' Melanie hisses.

'Look.' He sighs. 'D'you want to go and get a coffee or something? Go somewhere we can talk?'

'No, I don't.' She doesn't bother to hide her disgust. Seeing the state Delyth was in, it's a struggle to share any space with him. How could he do such a terrible thing to a defenceless woman? It makes her sick to her stomach. What a fool she's been to let him dupe her all these years. But no more. She's not letting him do it to her anymore.

'Can you please tell me what the consultant said?'

'Not until you tell me what went on with you and Delyth.'

'Is Georgie all right? Is she going to be all right?' He looks on the verge of tears.

'Why did you go up there?'

'I told you. To tell her once and for all to back off. To leave us alone. But I'm not lying, Mel. I didn't lay a finger on her. I thought I could but I couldn't. Not when it came down to it. I don't hit women.'

'Really?' She touched what remained of her injury again.

'That's not fair. You know that was an accident.'

'Do I?'

'For God's sake, Mel. You know I could never hurt you.'

He looks terrible. As if he hasn't slept for a week. A nurse passes by. The soles of her safety shoes squeak against the vinyl floor tiles. Walking the length of the ward, she turns to them but says nothing. Melanie listens to Gareth's breathing change when she comes over to check on Georgie.

'Ah, is she sleeping? I won't wake her. Just call me if you need anything,' the nurse says in her soft Welsh accent. 'I'm only a second away.'

Melanie thanks her and watches the nurse move away to administer to another patient.

'Delyth told me she's not going to the police.'

'Not surprised.'

'How d'you work that out?'

'Because she pulled a bloody shotgun on me.' He rubbed a hand over his face. The rasp of his five o'clock shadow sets her on edge.

'Serves you right. You must've scared the poor thing half to death, turning up there in the dead of night like that.' Melanie has no sympathy for him. 'And anyway, if that's true, why didn't you report her to the police?' She crosses her arms over her chest. Watches him squirm.

'I was worried she'd make something up. That she'd say I assaulted her, in the way she's claimed I did to you. And I'd been drinking and driving. Don't forget that.'

'No, I don't.' She tuts.

The hospital ward is as warm as a bakery. The air sluggish. Gareth yawns into his fist. He really looks exhausted and it takes a lot for Melanie to steel her heart against him. But seeing Delyth in that state...

Sitting beside the bed, she watches him cautiously stroke

the exposed skin on Georgie's arm between the taped-on tubing. Behind them, the clamour of a hectic hospital ward, and the rise and fall of unknown voices.

'I don't want to be married to you anymore, Gareth. I want a divorce.'

'You what?'

'You heard me.' She watches his hands grip the arms of the chair. His knuckles like a snow-capped mountain range through his skin.

'We can't have this conversation here.' He flicks a look at Georgie. 'Can't we go and get a coffee? Please, Mel. We need to talk about this properly.'

'No. I've made my mind up, Gareth. Nothing you can say will make a difference. What you did to Delyth, it's the last straw. How can I be married to a man who could do such a terrible thing? You're not even sorry... You're not sorry for any of it.'

'That's because I haven't done anything. Oh, Mel, you can't be serious? You can't be.'

'I am. You've given me no choice.'

'Of course you've got a choice. You can choose to believe me. I didn't touch her, Mel. I didn't lay a finger on her.'

'I just want you to go. I want you to leave.'

'You don't mean that. After everything we've been through.' He looks panicky. She can see the whites of his eyes. 'What about Georgie?'

Melanie shrugs. With tears threatening, she turns to the window and looks out at the day. Watches clouds glide over the hospital car park.

'I can't believe you're taking her side over mine. That you believe her over me. Right, I tell you what we'll do—' An idea forming, taking shape behind his eyes. 'Come with me to the farm. We'll go and see her together. Confront her together.'

'Why would I want to do that?'

'Because whatever those injuries she's claiming I gave her, they aren't real.'

'I'm telling you, Gareth. I saw her. She stood right there and she was covered in cuts and bruises. Had her arm in a sling and everything.'

'She's lying, Mel. I don't know how she's done it but she's lying. And you've fallen for her games hook, line and sinker. If she's got injuries, then she did them to herself. They've got nothing to do with me.'

'I want you to leave. Go back to London. Just go. I need some time on my own. I've got to sort my head out. Georgie's my priority now, not you.'

'But what about the pub?'

'You're the one who won't give your job up. You tell me?'

'I'm only keeping on with work so we've got money coming in, Mel. I thought we agreed?'

'We didn't agree anything. You decided and then went about telling half the town. You broke your promise.'

'I know, and I'm sorry about that. But I'm just trying to be sensible. Surely you can understand? It's so we've got a cushion, if things don't work out. The refurbishments cost a fortune; it's nearly cleaned us out. I just want to make sure we're back in the black, that's all. I don't like it any more than you do.' He leans forwards over his knees and reaches for her hand. But Melanie recoils from him. 'What do you want to do? Do you want to stay here? Can we still be business partners? I can't see how you'd be able to buy me out.'

'Business partners might work.' She bites her lip. Half of her couldn't believe she was talking this way, but she told herself to be firm. That this was the only way forward for her and Georgie. 'To be honest, it was feeling like that kind of arrangement to me anyway. It wouldn't be so different. What with you staying in London for your job all week. It's not such a big deal if you don't come home weekends.'

'And how long d'you think we can keep going like that?'

'Until I get things up and running. As soon as I'm able to buy you out.'

'So, what, are you saying you want a trial separation?' There is a flare of hope in his eyes now.

'No. It's not a trial. I don't want to be with you anymore. I can't trust you.' She watches his hope gutter out like an expended candle flame.

'Christ, you're serious, aren't you?' He rubs an agitated hand over his face again. 'Well, the lovely Delyth certainly got what she wanted. She wanted to split us up and now she has.'

'Oh, shut up, Gareth. I'm sick of hearing it. You split us up. *You*. Nothing to do with anyone else, you did it all on your own. Now, if you'd kindly leave. I don't want you here when this little one wakes up.' She checks on Georgie, who by some miracle is still asleep.

'But I want to see her. It's what I came back for. You can't stop me from seeing her.'

'I'd never do that, Gareth. But not like this, okay? And I suggest you call the consultant to ask her directly about the test results and what they mean. She can explain it better than me.'

'Mummy?' Georgie's eyes snap open. They look unnervingly bright in the fluorescent lighting of the ward.

'Hello, sleepyhead.' Melanie places a hand on Georgie's forehead and is totally absorbed with her sick child. When she does eventually look to where Gareth was sitting, she finds he has gone.

CHAPTER FIFTY

A weak wind blows flakes of snow against the patio doors. Melanie hopes it settles; she has a childish fascination with snow. Staring out over the desolate beer garden, at the flutter of house sparrows she has tamed in from the wild to feed from her bird tables, a memory of her, Gareth and the twins finds her. That bright, crisp morning when they woke to a silent world of white and built a snowman on the front lawn of their Bromley home is so sharp it could have been yesterday. And yet it was a lifetime ago, she thinks sadly, the image gradually furling backwards into her memory. They used to be happy, didn't they? They used to laugh and dance and love one another. Melanie's problem is that so much of her still loves Gareth and life as a single parent is proving difficult to adjust to. Come the weekend, half of her hopes it could all have been a horrible dream and he's going to walk back through the door and be the man he always was.

But here she is, in the last few days of December, after a Christmas that, aside from Sian and Tom's wedding, came and went with little celebration. It's good she has plenty to occupy her. Running this place and looking after Georgie means there's little time to dwell on things. If truth be told, Melanie's finding it a strain on her own the busier it gets, but she's determined to succeed. She needs to think about employing staff and getting them trained up before the holiday season opens out. John's been kind, and helps when he can. He's looking after Slinky this afternoon, and she's to drop by and pick him up on her way back from collecting Georgie from Nia's. Not that she's going to have John around for much longer. He told her yesterday that he's decided to leave Pencarew. That he's moving to France to join forces with his ex-squaddie friend who's opened a second-hand bookshop. He says the warmer climate will be good for his chest, and that he can't stand living with his sister anymore. Melanie's going to miss him, but since their strange exchange that day, things between them have been awkward. And although they haven't discussed it, she knows John's decision to move abroad has more to do with her.

Weird to have seen nothing of Delyth though. Melanie's sent a couple of texts, telling her there's a job here if she wants one, but she hasn't replied. She can hardly blame her. After what Gareth did, Melanie's probably the last person she wants to see. But it's only a matter of time before they bump into one another in town, or at Georgie's school. Melanie, as well as wondering if Andrew got his wish and joined the army, has been toying with the idea of driving up to the farm with the Christmas presents she never got to give them.

Cold, she tugs her chunky cardigan around her and buttons it to her throat. She's debating whether to light the wood burner early, when the call of the telephone slices between her indecisions.

'Good morning, Monkstone Arms,' she says into the receiver. Bingo, handsome and well on the way to being the fully-grown cat he's going to be, circles her ankles.

'Erm, hello... could I speak to Gareth Sayer, please?' The

Welsh accent is strong and doesn't belong to a voice she recognises.

'I'm sorry, but he isn't here,' she answers. 'What I mean is,' she clears her throat, 'he doesn't live here anymore.' She swaps the receiver to her other ear, pushes it under her hair which is now almost shoulder-length. 'But...' she dithers, then decides it can't do any harm. 'I can take a message for him.'

'Well, yes... it's Dai Williams. It's about this horse of his, see. I've been keeping hold of it as a favour, like. I've sold it to him, I have, but the thing is, I can't be keeping it on my land no more. Lovely gelding. Dutch Warmblood. Got all his papers. Bloody brilliant horse. Oh, hang on... I shouldn't be giving too much away... better check with you.' The speaker pauses. 'You're not his wife, are you? You're not Gareth's wife?'

Melanie looks at her hand. No wedding ring. As if she needed the reminder. This man can't be all that local otherwise he'd know. News that she and Gareth split up did the rounds almost before she brought Georgie home from hospital. 'No,' she replies eventually. 'I run the pub. He's my-my... business partner.'

'Good. Because this is meant to be a secret, see?' the voice rumbles on. 'Gareth, such a generous boy, he went and bought the horse for his wife. Surprise present, he said, for Christmas. But I've heard nothing from him for weeks. Bloody smart horse. He had a good buy there... and he was good enough to give me cash because I can't be messing with cheques and stuff.' The man's accent thickens to a glue inside her ear. 'Anyway, I've been ringing his mobile, but not getting no answer. And the problem is I'm needing the grazing and he promised he'd find new pasture soon as.' The speaker takes a breather. 'I don't mean to bother you, but the problem is, see, I've been happy holding on to the horse till now, but it's getting difficult with new foals coming.'

Melanie knits the words together, grasping at *horse... surprise present...* and bites down on her bottom lip. Hard. 'Yes,' she says, barely a whisper. 'Yes, I see.'

'So, there you are.' The man coughs loudly into the handset. 'If you get to speak to him, could you tell him? Tell him to ring Dai Williams as soon as possible. I can't be keeping the horse for much longer. But, Gareth... lovely boy he is. Gave me the full asking price. A full three grand. Aye, he's a really lovely boy is Gareth...'

CHAPTER FIFTY-ONE

Bumping over potholes, the indicator ticking, Melanie, giddy with excitement after meeting her gorgeous chestnut gelding for the first time, wonders if she should text Gareth. Thank him and send him one of the many photos she took of Maximus – that's his name, and it suits him. Then she told herself to wait. That she needed to think. Even though she now knew he hadn't lied about the money and didn't give it to Delyth, was it enough to redeem him? What about all the other things he's done? Their marriage was over, wasn't it? She needed to be consistent. The fact that he didn't lie about the three thousand pounds didn't change the fact that he beat up a small, defenceless woman. No, that is just unforgivable. It still frightens her to think he was capable of inflicting such violence, and was sorry, but no surprise gift of a beautiful horse was going to change that.

Thinking of Delyth brings with it an idea and, instead of taking a right in the direction of home when she reaches the main coast road, she heads north towards St David's. Sees the sign for Gweld Y Môr up ahead. Should she phone in advance? No, just call in. She can say she was in the area, which is true. Melanie has given up messaging her; she doesn't reply. She can't really blame her; she probably wouldn't reply either if she were her. But she wants to try to put things right between them, and it would be easier to do face to face. Delyth called her a true friend that day she came to see Georgie in the hospital, and seemed to have in no way blamed Melanie for Gareth's actions. She has to bite the bullet. If she wants to have some kind of friendship with Delyth, if she wants her to come and work for her at the pub, and she thinks she does, there is no way to avoid it.

Her journey up the steep track to the farmhouse is nothing as fraught as the night she came looking for Georgie. Better in the daylight too. She pushes the gearstick into second and before too long is steering the Mazda over the withers at the top of the track. The familiar row of lofty Scots pines loom into view. Bent to the wind and working as gateposts, they mark the entrance to the farmyard and she turns into it and parks up. But there is no sign of Delyth's muddy blue Defender.

Melanie unclips her seatbelt and steps out of the car. The yard is deserted; there aren't even any chickens today. She feels the first spots of rain and pulls up the hood of her coat. Then turns her back to the farmhouse to take in the view, that is every bit as spectacular as she was told.

'Wow. What a spot this is. It's like being on top of the world.'

Melanie can understand why Norah's reluctant to sell up, but looking around, she can see they aren't exactly managing things well. Apart from the substantial farmhouse, the rest is nothing more than a ramshackle of tilting byers pinned together by sheets of corrugated iron. How they survive the barrage of weather they must get all the way up here, she doesn't know. Heart-breaking, with its sagging barbed wire and rotting fence posts. Nothing like the stud centre she's just come from. That's a paradise of shaded paddocks with a magnificent stable block with indoor and outdoor manège.

She feels the same pinch of pity she often feels when she thinks of Delyth. But scanning around, she gets to thinking about Maximus again. Since first speaking to Dai Williams, she has taken action by ringing around all the livery yards in the area. Put her name down on waiting lists, in the hope a space will become available soon. But meeting Mr Williams today, he stressed again the lack of room and his inability to hold on to the horse for much longer. Might bringing him here be a possibility, just for the short term? She could ask Delyth if she can rent a paddock and an outhouse to use as a stable until she sorts something more permanent. It's not ideal keeping a horse on its own, but it wouldn't be for long and she might be able to borrow another as a companion, to keep Maximus company. It's a big favour and, casting a quick look inside the Mazda, at her handbag and the collection of Christmas presents in their jolly wrappings on the passenger seat, she hopes Delyth will be receptive to it. That the money might also be helpful to her.

Unsure what to do. Whether it's best to wait or not. No car means Delyth isn't home. But Norah will be. The poor thing said she never went anywhere. It really is too cold to hang around out here and she's sure Delyth's mother won't mind if she waits in the warm of their kitchen until her daughter comes home. She will go and knock on the door. Explain why she was there. It would be nice to see Norah. She likes her.

'Melanie! Melanie!'

Sudden shouts spike the air. Slightly alarmed, she can't immediately trace the source and she wonders if she's imagined it.

'Melanie! Please! Help me! I'm up here... She's locked me in. Help me, *please!*'

High and shrill and panicky. It's the cry of a woman. She

follows the arc of sound and looks upwards to an open window right at the top of the house. Sees a bedraggled figure leaning dangerously far out of an open attic window. Shouting and waving frantically. Her long white hair flapping in the wind that's coming in off the sea.

It's Norah.

What the hell?

Melanie breaks into a run, and charges towards the farmhouse.

'Quick! Quick! Oh please.' Norah sounds desperate, her cries full of terror. 'Help me! Get me out of here. For God's sake, get me out!'

'I'm coming, I'm coming. Just hang on!' Melanie reaches the door and scrabbles with the handle, but it doesn't budge. She tries it again with both hands but it won't open. She calls up to Norah, 'It's locked. What do I do? I can't get in.'

'Try round the back,' Norah shouts down. 'If it's locked, just break in. Smash a window.'

'God, I can't do that... perhaps we should wait for Delyth. You're not hurt, are you?' Melanie, flustered and red in the face.

'Wait for Delyth? It's her who locked me in here, and I will be bloody hurt if she comes back and finds you here! Just hurry, for God's sake, Melanie. Get me out! Hurry!'

With Norah's frantic pleas ringing in her ears, Melanie rounds the corner of the farmhouse, hunting for the back door and a way inside. Careering through a graveyard of old tractor tyres, dustbins and mouldy hay bales, she follows a path plundered by weeds. Eventually pushing through a little wrought-iron gate and then around to the rear of the house. When she finds the back door, she tries the handle. It opens onto the kitchen. She runs inside, trying one door after another. A walk-in larder, a utility room, until finally a door that leads out into the hallway she remembers from the time she came before. The stairs must be along here somewhere. Gloomy and choked in shadows, Melanie moves over the lumpy carpet. Finds the bottom of the stairs and runs up to the first landing. Then up and up again. Panting for breath, she reaches what she supposes to be the top landing and the very top of the house. The floor is only bare wooden boards and the air is icy. She can see the white puff of her breath.

'Norah! Where the hell are you?' Melanie shouts as she sprints along the narrow passageway, trying door after door. All of them are locked. She reaches a door at the end and when she opens it, she hears Norah calling to her from somewhere above. Directly in front of her is a tight curve of rickety staircase with a wobbly banister dusty with woodworm. She climbs it, and at its summit she reaches yet another flight of rickety stairs which takes her right up under the eaves of the house. Thick with cobwebs, she must be directly under the roof now and needs to stoop under the severe angling of the ceiling to avoid banging her head against the dark wood beams.

Finally emerging at the very top, she stands on the small square of landing to catch her breath. Peers down on the steep double set of stairs she's just climbed and identifies the familiar dry rot and mouldy plaster smell that was the Monkstone Arms before Bryn and his team got to work. The parts of the floorboards that aren't rotten, are worn smooth and tilt alarmingly to the left. They must be hundreds of years old and they creak and groan under her weight as she steps up to the heavy oak door in front of her.

'Norah? Are you in there?' She rattles the handle, but it's locked. 'Norah?' she shouts again.

'I'm here.' The voice from within is weaker now. Breathy. 'I think she keeps the key on the ledge above the door.'

Melanie, her heart thumping, lifts a hand and gropes the ledge. Finds the key. Fumbles. Drops it. It clatters to the floor.

More frantic now, she gropes around on her hands and knees. Eventually teases the key out from between a gap in the boards.

'Hurry. For God's sake, hurry,' Norah pleads from the other side of the door. 'She'll be back any minute. She's only gone to check on the sheep. You have to get me out. You got to get me away from her!'

Melanie eventually opens up. Swings the door wide onto Norah, and is immediately struck dumb by the pathetic figure in front of her. A terrified Norah, so frail and old with her matted hair and dirty, inadequate clothing, locked in this cold, stark cell like some mad pariah. The room falls away into shadow behind her. It's a sparsely-furnished room. Bare floors, bare walls. The old dressing table and mirror. The single bed with its filthy covers. Dismal and gloomy, cloaked in dust and cobwebs. She shivers.

'My God. What the hell's been going on?'

Norah falls forwards and clings desperately to Melanie. 'We've got to get out of here. She'll be back soon. Del's mad, she's gone totally mad!' Norah now slumps back against the wall. Her skin looks blue from the cold. 'She's been keeping me prisoner.'

Melanie removes her parka and drapes it around Norah's shoulders. The coat drowns her and while she is quickly smoothing down her long white hair, she clocks the nasty bruise on the woman's cheek.

'Delyth did it.' Norah sees what she's looking at and lifts a hand to her face. 'Please, Melanie, please. Get me out of here before she comes back.'

'Right, yes. Yes.' Melanie, shocked, confused, takes the old woman's arm. So small and frail, she can't believe her own daughter would lock her away up here. Like this. 'I don't understand any of it... Where's Andrew?'

'He's cleared out. Gone.'

'Gone where?' Melanie wonders if she should carry Norah. She probably isn't much heavier than Georgie. But those stairs. She can't carry her down them. She can barely negotiate them herself.

'He's joined the army. I signed the papers for him. Del wouldn't do it, so I did.' Norah moves slowly. Shuffles forwards, unsteady inside her sheepskin slippers. 'It's why I've been locked up. Punishment, you see. For going against Del's wishes. She was going to keep Andrew prisoner too.'

'Hold on to me. I'll steady you.'

Norah does and her grip is surprisingly strong. 'You don't know what she's capable of. She's mad, I tell you. She's going to kill me too!'

'Kill you too? What are you saying?'

But Norah, not answering Melanie's question, just keeps repeating the words. 'She'll kill me too, she will, she'll kill me too... Just like she did before!'

As they edge down the first steep set of stairs, Melanie stops and turns to Norah. 'What are you saying – what did Delyth do before?'

Norah, her words coming in breathy bursts. 'She told me. She pushed her out of the window. In that attic room where she's been keeping me.'

'Pushed who? You're not making any sense.'

'Delyth killed her sister. She murdered Erin!'

A coldness greater than that of the air on the stairwell settles over Melanie. But before she can fully assimilate Norah's words, she hears the heavy crunch of tyres on the gravel in the yard outside.

Delyth is back.

CHAPTER FIFTY-TWO

'Oh no! That's her. Delyth's back. Now we're bloody for it. What are we going to do? I'm so scared of her, Mel. She's gone crazy. There's no talking to her.' A sob has now invaded Norah's voice. 'If she finds you here, she'll kill you too!'

'But she will know I'm here. My car's out the front.'

'Oh, God. I forgot... I forgot.'

Melanie and Norah are just about to make it back up to the threshold of the attic room, when the creak of floorboards makes them turn. Delyth is suddenly there. Shotgun in hand and blocking their only escape.

'What the bloody hell are you doing?' she pants, out of breath. 'Has my stupid bitch of a mother told you what she's gone and done?' Delyth wipes her perspiring brow with a fist. 'Told you what she's done with my Andrew?'

'Just put the gun down, Del. Come on, love.' Norah is quaking with fear. It shudders through Melanie, who is keeping a protective arm firmly around her. 'Let's be sensible about this.'

'Fuck off, Mam. I've had it with you. He was my boy; you had no right to interfere.'

Trapped in the terror of the moment, it takes Melanie

longer than it usually might to realise that Delyth is completely free of her injuries. No bruises. No cuts. No arm in a sling.

'You've healed up quickly,' she challenges, when her mind is screaming at her not to provoke the woman. 'What's going on? You were covered in cuts and bruises at the hospital less than a fortnight ago.'

'Yeah, well.' Delyth curls her lip, her eyes livid and staring. 'I'm a quick healer.'

'Liar!' Melanie spits. She can see it clearly now. 'To think I was concerned for you. Believed you over my own husband. Gareth never laid a finger on you! You let me believe he'd done that to you, that he'd beaten you half to death.'

'Not the only thing I let you believe.' A sickly grin. 'Gareth didn't rape Erin. I made that up and, because you're so stupid, you fell for it. You never deserved him. Same as Erin didn't, the druggy little slut. It should've been me with Gareth. Me with him that night of our end-of-school party. *ME!*'

'My God!' Melanie can't believe what she's hearing. 'What kind of person are you?'

'The kind who's got her dad's old Purdey pointed right at you.' Delyth takes a step closer, quietly determined and focused. The muzzle of the shotgun only inches away. 'So shut your fucking mouth, or I'll blow you in half!'

Although frightened, Melanie is suddenly incensed and raging at the realisation of what Delyth's done. Everything she's ruined. 'You've cost me my marriage. You and your scheming and lies. You're the bloody monster, not Gareth!'

'Tell someone who gives a shit.' Delyth laughs.

'I've called the police. They're on their way.' Melanie has done no such thing – her phone is in her bag and her bag is in the car. But Delyth doesn't know that.

'Come on, Del. Let's just forget all this nonsense. We can

work this out, love.' Norah tries to talk her daughter round. 'I know you're upset about Andrew but...'

'You're not even sorry, are you, Mam? What you did. And *you*—' Delyth shifts her position, the gun pointing directly at Melanie again. 'You deserve all you get.' Another ugly laugh. 'Remember that night when someone broke into the pub and smashed that vase of roses on the floor? Well, that was me. And when I say, "broke in", I didn't actually need to – I still had a key from when I worked there before. I used to come and go whenever I liked, until you went and spoilt my fun by changing the locks.' Delyth responds to Melanie's incredulity; eyes gleaming with hate and menace. 'Yeah. It felt good to frighten you, you dopey bitch. Just like I'm frightening you now.'

'Del. Listen to what Melanie's saying. The police are on their way. Put the gun down, there's a good girl. This is just silly.'

'Shut your mouth, Mam. Unless you want me to blast you away too. You've ruined everything, and I can't let you get away with that, can I?'

Melanie steps in front of Norah. Shields her with her body. She is bursting with anger about what Delyth has done and if she could get a hold of her, she swears she would strangle her with her own hands.

'Please put the gun down, love,' Norah tries again. 'You don't want to do this.'

Delyth waves the barrel of the shotgun around. Increasingly dangerous and mad-eyed with rage. 'You haven't got a clue what I want to do?'

'I know you don't want to kill us. Not really. You won't get away with it this time. They'll lock you up forever.'

'Shut your mouth or I'll shoot you. I will. I'll shoot the bloody pair of you.'

Delyth adjusts herself and repositions her hands on the gun.

Lifts the muzzle and aims it at Melanie's head. Melanie steps forwards again. Brave or stupid? She doesn't know, but she holds her palms up in some kind of mute surrender.

'Get back. I'll pull the trigger... Don't think I won't.'

Melanie takes yet another step forwards, still shielding Norah. Although unclear what she's doing, she's driven on by an increasing fury and hatred for this woman and the devastation she's caused.

Delyth must see this in her face and starts to back away. 'I'll do it. I will, I'll fucking kill the pair of you. I don't give a shit about the police – it'll be worth it.'

But adjusting her hold on the shotgun yet again, Delyth leans too heavily on the rickety banister. The crack of the worm-riddled wood is as loud as gunshot in the confined space.

Melanie watches, as if in slow motion, when Delyth slips sideways, fumbling for the curve of the broken banister. And before there is time to understand what's happening, she sees Delyth suddenly let go of the gun and flail around helplessly, trying to break her fall. But she falls anyway. Crashing down through the lower stairwell and landing two floors below with a sickening thump.

Melanie, with Norah, shaky and unsteady beside her, peers down on Delyth's broken and lifeless body. Her legs and arms splayed. Her neck at an impossible angle. The blood oozing from her mouth.

CHAPTER FIFTY-THREE

TEN DAYS LATER

Melanie and Bethan stroll out across the dappled dampness of the town. Aside from the usual squabbling seabirds, Pencarew, worn out after the busy festive period, is quiet. The women head in the direction of the sea, over the paved square and uphill towards the old market house with its grand Tuscan columns and shops selling everything from fudge to Welsh love spoons. The sun is shining. The crisp January air is full of promise.

'I should've just worn jeans.' Melanie tugged at the throat of her dress. 'Do I look too dressed up?'

'No, Mel. You look lovely. You always do.'

She squeezes Bethan's hand, and passing one of the bus shelters, they see an elderly man strike a match and light his pipe. It alerts Melanie to a boy and a girl cramped in the corner. Cuddling close. They make her smile and remind her of when she and Gareth were first together. Snatching secret moments whenever and wherever they could.

'I think it's best if I leave you here.' Bethan plucks her from her introspection.

'Okay.' Melanie looks ahead to the café's glass frontage at

the top of the street, to take in the view of the collection of tables set up outside.

'Right then.' Bethan reaches for a strand of Melanie's hair and loops it behind her ear. 'All set?'

'You think I'm doing the right thing, don't you?' Her insides heave with butterflies.

'Absolutely. Ah, don't look so worried.' Bethan chuckles. 'It's going to be fine.'

'I hope you're right.'

'You worry too much, that's your trouble.'

'What are you going to do?'

'I'm going to make the most of my freedom as Mam's looking after Ffion.'

'There's a nice new toy shop opened up on the main street. Great New Year sale on. I bought some lovely things for Georgie.'

Their eyes leave each other's for a moment to stare beyond the promenade to the sandy beach and out to sea, and they watch a girl on a milk-white horse, cantering along the surf's edge as if in a film.

'You'll let me know how it goes, won't you?' Bethan tightens her scarf.

'I'll message as soon as I can... God, I know it's silly, but I'm really nervous.' Melanie hops from foot to foot.

'It's going to be great. You'll see.'

'I hope so.'

'Off you go then. You don't want to be late.' Bethan swivels her around by her shoulders and gives her a little shove. 'Good luck... Not that you're going to need it.'

Melanie walks to the corner and turns to wave, but Bethan has already gone. Then on she strides, past cobbled ginnels sloping seawards and giving glimpses of the low tide and bristle-backed dunes. In no time at all, she reaches the Peppermint Post Espresso Bar. Its sign flapping in the wind as she grips the handrail and climbs the steps to peek inside.

'There you are.' Her breath mists the wide glass entrance doors.

Sitting alone at a table at the rear, gazing out at the view through enormous windows and sipping a latte, Melanie quickly identifies the person she's arranged to meet among the smattering of other customers. With a quick hand to her hair and a moment to adjust the strap of her handbag, she steps inside. The place is virtually empty. Quiet enough to hear the tide scuff the beach below.

'Please let us be okay,' she mutters under her breath, her nerves trembling at the base of her throat. 'Just let us be okay.'

She edges forwards, into the seating area. Her heels click, click, against the bare wood floor. Too loud, they announce her arrival before she's ready. The head of short dark curls lifts and turns in her direction. Their gazes collide. Bold then timid: flickering shutters on a camera lens.

'Hello.' Melanie gives him her best smile and takes another tentative step closer.

'You came?' His blue eyes are wet with tears.

'Of course I did.'

'Oh, Mel, I can't tell you how good it is to see you.' Gareth leaps to his feet. Banging the table and nearly spilling his coffee. 'God, I've missed you. I've missed you so much.'

'And I've missed you too.' Melanie swallows, close to tears herself.

Then Gareth is beside her. Holding out his arms. Melanie falls into them and, scooped against him, her love for this man crackles like static into his hair, the weave of his sweater. And the smell of his aftershave opens the door onto the life they had before ever hearing about the Monkstone Arms and moving to Pencarew and meeting that woman who blighted their lives.

But Delyth Powell is dead, Melanie reminds herself. She can never trouble either of them again. And free of her and her evil manipulations, Melanie knows now she's here, held in Gareth's embrace, that she and Gareth and Georgie are going to be able to work things out. That things are going to be fine. That they are going to be more than fine.

ACKNOWLEDGMENTS

Special thanks must go to Hannah Baxter-Deuce and Lexi Curtis, and all the wonderful team at Bloodhound Books. Especially Tara Lyons for her kindness, commitment and efficiency. Patricia Dixon for her invaluable editing advice, and Ian Skewis for his enthusiasm and expertise. But most of all my thanks must go again to my husband Steven, for his indomitable belief, love and creative inspiration.

ABOUT THE AUTHOR

Rebecca Griffiths grew up in mid-Wales and went on to gain a first-class honours degree in English literature. After a successful business career in London, Dublin and Scotland she returned to rural Wales where she lives with her husband, a prolific artist, their giant black cat called Mouse, and writes full time. *No Place to Hide* is her ninth novel.

A NOTE FROM THE PUBLISHER

Thank you for reading this book. If you enjoyed it please do consider leaving a review on Amazon to help others find it too.

We hate typos. All of our books have been rigorously edited and proofread, but sometimes mistakes do slip through. If you have spotted a typo, please do let us know and we can get it amended within hours.

info@bloodhoundbooks.com